D1077735

The Funny Thing about Norman Foreman

www.penguin.co.uk

The Funny Thing about Norman Foreman

Julietta Henderson

BANTAM PRESS

TRANSWORLD PUBLISHERS
Penguin Random House, One Embassy Gardens,
8 Viaduct Gardens, London SW11 7BW
www.penguin.co.uk

Transworld is part of the Penguin Random House group of companies
whose addresses can be found at global.penguinrandomhouse.com

Penguin
Random House
UK

First published in Great Britain in 2020 by
Bantam Press an imprint of Transworld Publishers

ISBNs 9781787633506 (hb)
9781787633513 (tpb)

Typeset in 11.25/15.25pt Sabon LT Std by Jouve (UK), Milton Keynes.
Printed and bound in Great Britain by Clays Ltd, Elcograf S.p.A.

The authorized representative in the EEA is Penguin Random House Ireland,
Morrison Chambers, 32 Nassau Street, Dublin D02 YH68

Penguin Random House is committed to a sustainable
future for our business, our readers and our planet. This book
is made from Forest Stewardship Council® certified paper.

For the original Big Al

1

Sadie

When I was born my insides lay outside my body for twenty-one days. Which is unexpected, but not nearly as unusual as you might think. For every 3,999 babies that come out with everything tucked in neatly and sealed away exactly where it should be, there's one like me. Nobody really knows why. Luck of the draw, my father used to say.

For those three weeks, while I lay spreadeagled in an incubator like a Nando's special, a crowd of doctors gathered every morning to discuss their cleverness and, as my organs shrank to their correct size, bit by bit they gently posted a little more of the me-parts that had made a break for it back inside.

Well, that's the way my mother told it anyway. The way my father told it, the doctors gathered around the incubator every morning to discuss whether they'd be having my large intestine or my liver for their lunch, and whether it'd be with chips or salad. And that right there might tell you almost everything you need to know about my parents.

On my insides' final day of freedom the head surgeon pushed the last bit through the slit in my stomach and stitched it closed, presumably with everything in its rightful place. I was declared whole and sent home to begin life almost like nothing had ever happened.

Except that even when the regular hospital check-ups stopped and the scar on my stomach that I'd never lived without faded to a thin silver seam, I can always remember still feeling the tugging behind it. Something I could never quite name, nudging at the fleshy edges whenever things were going badly, or too well. Or just for fun. To remind me how easily those parts of me that never quite fitted could come sliding out. *Any time we like, Sadie. Any time we like.*

It wasn't until I held my own son for the first time that the constant, dull pressure of keeping the scar together receded. When a nurse placed that slippery, crumpled-up bundle of boy on my chest, I tightened my grip on a handful of hospital sheet as my world creaked on its axis, bumped into a comfy spot and was finally facing the right way.

I didn't feel the tug on the scar again until a different boy died, and to say I wasn't ready for it isn't even the most important thing. Because by then there was a whole lot more at stake than just my own stupid insides spilling out into the world. I was as scared as hell and I had no idea how to fix any of it. And that right there might tell you almost everything you need to know about me.

2

NORMAN

First rule of comedy: Timing is everything.

Timing is everything. First rule of comedy, Jax says. Because when push comes to shove, if you can get the timing right, you can get a laugh. He says. Well I don't really know how to tell when push is coming to shove, but I'll tell you something I do know. That rule works the other way too. Because when the you-know-what starts to hit the fan, if your timing's wrong there's pretty much zilcho you can do to stop it from splattering all over the place.

Stare straight ahead and think about nothing. That's a world-famous Jax Fenton tactic for what to do when you get yourself into a bit of a mess. Works every time he reckons, and he should know. Only maybe it doesn't. Because when I stare straight ahead all I can see is that big, shiny wooden box and instead of nothing I'm thinking about everything. And loads of it. Like does any light get in through the joins and did they let Jax wear his Frankie Boyle Tramadol Nights tour T-shirt. And does whoever put him in there know he only likes to sleep on his side.

The massive scab on my chest feels so tight that I'm scared to breathe too deep in case it splits down the middle and bleeds all over my new shirt. *Stare straight ahead.* I move just a bit so I almost can't see the box behind a couple of heads, and my arm touches Mum's. When I feel her, straight away the mess on my chest relaxes and lets me take half an almost good in-breath. Nearly a whole one. Right before it stabs me all the way through to my back and kazams like a rocket down to my toes. I'm pretty sure I can hear it laughing. *Timing is everything, sucker.*

And by the way, that's another thing I know. That you can't trust your timing, no matter how good it's been in the past. Not even for people as excellently funny as Ronnie Barker or Dave Allen or Bob Mortimer. Or Jax.

Because even if you nick a little bit of money for sweets every weekday morning from your mum's purse, even if you accidentally-on-purpose leave your stepfather's car door open so the cats get in and wee on the seats, and even if you're the naughtiest kid in the whole school by a long shot, when you're eleven years, 297 days and from what the paramedics can tell anything between twelve and sixteen hours old, it's definitely not a good time to die.

Stare straight ahead and think about nothing.

3

Sadie

Squashed into the end of the pew with my body leaning into the shape of the space that Norman's made, I could feel the tense and release of his arms as his small-boy hands curled in and out of fists. The buttoned-down cuffs of his sleeves rode up ever so slightly with every movement to reveal the trail of psoriasis that spread triumphantly down to the second knuckles. His face was blank as a brick. Dry eyes staring straight ahead.

'Just hold on. Hold on, son. You'll get through this,' I murmured reassuringly. Telepathically. But Norman's hands kept on curling and flexing and then I noticed his chest was keeping time, rising and collapsing with the movement of his hands. I knew what was lying in wait underneath the thin fabric of his shirt, so then I had another thing to worry about.

I had to admit, it looked like he wasn't getting my message, possibly because my best telepathic motherly voice was being all but drowned out by the other, very much louder one that lived in luxury inside my head. *Fuck you, Sadie. You can't even get this right.* As usual, it wasn't pulling any punches.

The priest who had never met him declared the end to Jax's life and people began shuffling out of the pews as fast as they could, as if death might still be hanging around, looking for company. They knocked our knees, murmured apologies and spilled their overflow of sadness all over us. Like we needed it. The moving huddle in the aisle parted from the back as Jax's parents set off on their million-mile walk, and without turning my head I felt more than saw Josie Fenton hesitate ever so slightly as they passed us. But then they were gone. And my son's eyes remained fixed on some invisible point that I could only hope lay somewhere far, far beyond the awfulness of the moment.

A good forty minutes after the last person had left I reached for Norman's nearest hand and closed it gently between mine. The chill of the empty church had sidled deep into my bones and I was shocked at the heat of his raw knuckles on my palms. The voice in my head began stage-whispering nonsense louder and louder and Norman's hand stayed rigid in its fist. But I didn't need that voice to tell me what I'd already figured out about thirty-eight minutes before. I wasn't going to be nearly enough for this.

4

There's a good chance Norman's father is one of four people. Now I know how that makes me sound, but it's a fairly reasonable alternative to the other scenario, which is that he would quite possibly have been one of several more if circumstances had allowed.

But anyhow, who provided the champion Y chromosome that coasted up a lager-and-lemonade river to victory in my ovaries never really came up in Norman's first twelve years of life. Mainly because I'd pretty much convinced myself that I was all the parent he needed. I was enough. And, to be fair, Norman had never given me any reason to question my conviction, no matter how many mistakes I made on the job. And there's been a lot, believe me. Which you probably do, based on first impressions.

I never knew a thing about boys until I became the mother of one, even though, in theory, a boy is just a smaller version of a man and clearly I thought I knew quite a lot about them at one point. As a general rule, I've found men don't really require any complicated directions, so you're pretty much guaranteed to get exactly what's on the tin when you bring one home. And serves you right, most of the time. But it turns out a boy is nothing like a man at all, because they could definitely do with coming with some directions. And when you bring one of them home, before you even get him through the front door he's already got your heart scrunched up in his fat baby fist like a bad betting slip. And he's starting to squeeze.

I named my son Norman because there was nobody to tell me not to. And because I liked it. That could have been my first mistake and, who knows, maybe I would have listened if someone had told me that Charlie or Harry or Freddie might be a lighter load for a kid to swing on to his back and carry around for an entire lifetime. That other children, and even adults who should bloody well know better, might find a thousand cruel ways to use a name chosen with love to try to bring your boy down. That maybe, just maybe, naming a post-millennial baby after a 1950s comedian was not the best idea I'd ever had. Although you should know that it also wasn't the worst.

The fact that his name had to attach itself to the caboose of our surname was probably my second mistake. And although I've always thought that Norman Foreman has a certain resonance to it, I've yet to find someone that wholeheartedly agrees. Except Jax, of course.

'Coolest name ever, Normie boy!' Coolest kid ever.

Norman never had a best friend before Jax. In fact, if I'm honest, he never really had a proper friend at all. But when Jax showed up at Alverton Community Primary wielding a truncheon of six-year-old East London bravado over his shell-shocked Cornish classmates, for Norman it was love at first sight. Just like he always does, though, even when he wants something really, really badly, he sat back politely and waited his turn.

It took Jax less than a week to alienate every kid in his class, and most of the teachers as well, before noticing Norman and deciding that he could well be his last chance in the best-friend saloon. That was six years ago, and from the moment the deal was sealed over a shared two-week detention for switching around the contents of the entire Year 3's school bags (verdict: Jax guilty as hell; Norman guilty of being an inexperienced and therefore ultimately unsuccessful lookout), you couldn't separate those two with a scalpel. I'd lay money that there weren't two more different boys on the planet and yet, somehow, they just clicked. They were 'The bloody Rolls-bloody-Royce of bloody best friends,' as Jax so eloquently put it.

But Jax died. And so it came to be that on the kind of day sons should be out in a park kicking a football, or chasing dogs down on the beach with their mates, I sat next to my good boy in a church full of damp cheeks. Trying hard not to think about that other rude, grubby, magnificent bad boy lying just a few metres away. And even though there was no chance in hell of it coming true, I'd still half expected to hear a kicking at the lid of that coffin at any moment, and a wild-haired, laughing kid to splinter through and shout, '*Gotcha, suckers!*'

Because that was Jax's approach to life, the universe and everything, really. Feet first, break the door down and damn the consequences. He'd arrive at our house nearly every day like that, body lengths ahead of Norman, bullying our front-door handle nearly off its thread and following up with a totally unnecessary karate kick to make sure the job was done. Then he'd charge straight down the hallway on a direct route to the biscuit tin, leaving Norman to catch hold of the twanging door and close it softly as he brought up the rear.

It used to drive me crazy every time I'd catch sight of the

mortally injured wall where the front door handle bounced, day after day. But in the weeks after Jax died I saw the way Norman glanced over at that crumbling hole in the plaster as he passed, and it made me give silent thanks for lying, no-good, unreliable tradesmen that don't know their four o'clocks from their fourth of Junes.

That hole is all that's left of Jax in our house now, and it's eating away at the wall like it's got teeth.

5

NORMAN

First rule of comedy:
Always know where the joke is going.

Jax says that if you don't know where you're going you're never going to know when you get there and you can't argue with that, Normie boy. Not that I'd want to, because it makes pretty good sense when you think about it. I mean, imagine if you just walked out the door every morning without having any idea of where you're on your way to. How would you know to stop walking when you got to the bus stop and not just keep going to the beach? Or even further? Or if you didn't know you were supposed to get off at school, how would you know not to just sit on the bus all day doing loops around Penzance and Newlyn?

Jax reckons it's the same with a joke. Because you've got to know where the punchline is before you set off, otherwise you're just going to end up going round and round in circles, looking for a way out. And there's nothing too funny about someone wandering round and round in circles, although there are probably some exceptions to that and I think maybe Dave Allen is one of them.

Mum says there isn't anyone else on the planet whose brain works the way that Jaxy's does, and I'm pretty sure she's right. I reckon it's because he's the coolest guy on this or any other planet, but he says it's because the inside of his head is just like a big old ideas factory and he wouldn't be able to stop them coming out even if he tried. Which luckily he never has, or else we wouldn't have had some of the most excellent fun ever.

Like when I suggested we should have a comedy DVD marathon so we could work out once and for all who our favourites were. Jax said that if we were going to do it, then we had to make a plan and do it right, and that's how he invented DVD Dynamite Saturday Night. We made a proper folded-up paper programme with a list of the DVDs we were going to watch and in what exact order we'd play them, and even the times for when it was intermission so we could go for a wee and make cheese on toast and hot chocolates and stuff. Then we got dressed up in our comedy outfits, because Jax said that was called getting into character, and we even made a ticket with 'Admit One: DVD Dynamite Saturday Night' on it so we could invite Mum to come as well. And she did, and it was the best Saturday night ever, even though we had so much fun we totally forgot to decide who we liked the best and now I'm never going to know who would have got Jaxy's vote.

Another time we were just sitting in my room talking about what cheese we reckoned was the best for melting and *kapow!* Jax came up with the Ultimate Cheese-Off Experiment plan. We made a banner out of an old pillowcase with U.C.O.E 2017 on it because the whole name didn't fit, and Mum took us to Tesco's and we bought loads of different kinds of cheese. Even the expensive ones. Then Jax made a list with the names of them and five columns labelled gooey, gooier, gooiest, rubbish and totally rubbish to put our ticks or crosses. It turned out he needn't have bothered with the last two, because they stayed totally empty, but then we ended up writing a really cool joke about never meeting a cheese we didn't like. So that was like two ideas out of the factory for the price of one.

A lot of Jax's best ideas pop into his head when he's supposed to be doing other things, like homework or sleeping or taking out the bins for his mum. Or watching the *One Show* Children in Need special, which is when out of nowhere he goes, Norman, I reckon we need to make a mega-genius-super-supreme comedy plan so we know where we're going. And all I knew was that if Jax was going somewhere, I wanted to be with him when he got there.

When we finished Jax and Norman's Five Year Plan, Jax goes, Norman Foreman you are the bee's knees and I am the dog's bollocks and there's nothing in the world that can stop us now. And I knew straight away that he was right, because not only did we know for absolute sure where we were going, we also knew exactly when we were going to get there. Which was 7.15 p.m. on the first Friday in August after two changes on National Rail.

6

Sadie

Norman's been different right from the start. It's like he was born already knowing everything he needed to know and anything else is just going to be gravy. He's also got more guts than anyone I've ever met, and I'm not just saying that because I'm his mum. I mean, who's braver than a shorter than average kid who's spent the better part of his life covered in a solid scale of psoriasis that hurts like hell, looks like shit and who still keeps smiling? A kid who stands up beside his naughty best mate and tries to get people to see the good in him, and keeps on trying, even when it's pretty hard to see. A kid whose only parent can barely rustle up the enthusiasm to walk out into the world every day, even when the world's just a half-pint town at the bum's end of Britain. And he still manages to love her. You tell me who's braver than that guy.

I spend a lot of my time wishing I were better. Better at cooking, better at cleaning, better at making conversation with strangers. And people I know. But mostly, when I've got some hours to idle away, I like to spend them wishing I was better at being Norman's mother. That's the one that snores away in the background and regularly wakes up to jab me with a pointy elbow when I don't show up for parent–teacher meetings, or forget to buy ham for school lunches, or when he has to wear yesterday's underwear because I watched six back-to-back episodes of *Come Dine with Me* when I got home from work instead of doing the washing. And still couldn't cook a decent dinner.

If you could take all the thousands of random moments of poor mothering, dry dinners and crusty undies and knit them into a lovely warm blanket of denial to pull over your head for about a decade, you'd get a pretty accurate picture of where all my wishing has got me. Nowhere. And definitely not better.

But Norman's always been OK, in spite of me. He's polite, he's kind to old people and animals, he's got good hygiene (despite his poor, tortured skin and the occasional two-day-old underpants, neither of which is his fault) and he's smart. He can usually figure people out a lot quicker than they figure him out, which is a pretty handy talent that he definitely didn't get from me.

Being shorter, cleverer and a hell of a lot scalier than everyone else isn't exactly a recipe for winning friends and influencing people in the school playground, but since Jax came along Norman's never needed anyone else. And as Jax always said, one really and truly best friend is a hundred times better than having a whole bunch that aren't quite sure.

So, apart from his chronic, bastarding psoriasis, the only other thing I've ever really had to worry about with Norman is the almost certainly unhealthy amount of cheese on toast he eats (see problem number one), and his most definitely unhealthy habit of worrying about other people. And by other people, I mean me.

When the boys came up with Jax and Norman's Five Year Plan to perform at the Edinburgh Fringe Festival when they turned fifteen, they were ten. Which shows you how serious they were about comedy. I mean, how many ten-year-olds do you know with a five-year plan? I'm thirty-two, and the closest I've ever come to a five-year plan is signing up for a sofa on Tesco no-interest store credit. Come to think of it, apart from Norman, that sofa is the biggest commitment I've ever made.

Their plan was so outlandish I actually believed they just might do it. Because the thing is, despite their age and lack of credentials, as a comedy double act those boys were funny. Honest, proper, not-just-because-you're-the-mother kind of funny. Jax had a presence, timing and quickness of wit way more developed than a kid his age had any business with, and Norman, well, Norman's got gravitas. He loves it when I tell him that, like it's the biggest compliment you could ever get. And maybe it is. I'm no expert. Sometimes I say it just to make him laugh, because that's the best sound in the world.

'Norman, may I be so bold as to say that your astonishing gravitas is only exceeded by your devastating good looks.' Or something like that. He's always delighted to hear it, even if it's out of the blue and it's clear I'm just filling in a gap until the queue at the bank moves, or waiting around trying to get a couple of soft-boiled eggs over the line.

Ever since he was old enough to talk I'd forever be finding Norman out in the back garden rattling off a corny comedy routine in a very serious voice, or re-enacting some sketch or another verbatim that he'd memorized from the telly or one of my dad's old BBC classic-comedy DVDs. It might go something like this.

'Ladies and gentlemen,' with a deep bow to the hedges and hose reel. 'May I present to you . . . me, Norman Foreman! In my exclusive new show, for one night only, Sausages and Gravitas! And now for a few questions, ladies and gentlemen. I ask you, what is a tree's least favourite month? Seppptimberrr! What do you call a fake noodle? An immmpasta! What do you call an alligator in a vest? An investiiigator! Thank you. Thank you. Thank you very much!'

The thing was, though, that even with all that astounding gravitas and notwithstanding his devastating good looks, no matter how much he practised and how closely he tried to emulate his old-school comedy heroes, Norman could never quite master the art of comic timing. The jokes were there, every punchline was delivered word perfect, but they always pulled into the station a little too late, or too early, or ended up on the completely wrong platform with a commuter under the wheels.

It wasn't until he joined forces with Jax that he was able to wrangle his earnestness to perfection to play the straight man, serving up the spotlight for his fearless mate's outrageous showmanship. They had the makings of a young Abbott and Costello, the Two Ronnies, or their favourite comparison, Reeves and Mortimer. The perfect comedy duo. At least to their appreciative audience of me and the hedges.

Teachers, classmates and even Jax's parents never understood what Jax and Norman saw in each other and said as much at every opportunity. Presumably in an effort to steer Norman away from a potential life of petty crime, the direction in which everyone was convinced Jax was headed. But I understood. Because by introducing Jax to his comedy heroes, Norman opened that kid up to a way all that energy, bravado and even the little bit of genuine badness inside him could be funnelled into a different kind of outlet.

Norman gave Jax comedy and Jax gave Norman the best friend he'd never had. And oh how I loved him for it. It was a good deal all round.

*

I know everything there is to know about Norman. From every scab and scale that's ever tormented his poor, defeated skin to the crease that appears in his forehead when he smiles and the other one that forms when he frowns. When his psoriasis is particularly vicious that one moves in for an extended stay. I know his left eyebrow is hairier than his right, and that his ears move up and down far more than other people's when he chews. Although I've never told him that last one, because, let's face it, the kid has enough to deal with.

But after Jax died I found myself having to do a double take when I caught sight of the stranger sitting on the sofa staring into a blank TV screen. Or standing in the bathroom brushing his teeth. Or glancing sideways at a hole in the wall. Nothing about Norman looked the same as it had for the past nearly twelve years. He was also more measured than he'd been before, like he was carefully acting his part in every scene according to how he thought I wanted it to play out. Doing just enough to fool me into thinking he was still with the rest of us in the land of the living, and not maybe wishing he was somewhere else with his best friend in the land of the not-so-living.

But no matter how many times he said he was all right, I knew Norman was so far from all right you'd have needed a three-day hike to catch sight of the tail end of it disappearing around the corner. He even slept differently. He'd always had a habit of winding his top sheet around his legs as he read in bed, as if he was trying to dig in his heels and get as deep into the story world as possible. Every night after he fell asleep I'd creep into his room to turn off his light, retrieve whatever book he'd been reading and untangle the knot of bed linen. When he was younger he could never believe I was able to do it without disturbing him and was convinced some kind of nocturnal sheet-straightening aliens were at work.

To prove it was me, I'd get one of my lipsticks and, every night, I gently drew a small red kiss 'X' on his forehead as he slept. In the morning Norman would rush to the bathroom mirror to check for the mark and squeal in a five-, seven- or eight-year-old muddle of delight and frustration.

'I didn't feel a thing, Mum!' he'd say. 'Nothing, *nada, niente, nyet*! How'd you do it?' Even when he got older and I eventually stopped doing the kiss (and, come to think of it, wearing lipstick), he was still fascinated by how deeply he could sleep. He asked me once if I thought it was how being dead felt.

'Like you go off to sleep and one day you just don't feel anything ever again, Mum? You reckon?'

In the bad-parenting manual I'm thinking of writing I'd have to say I've never been able to give Norman a definitive answer on death, because, frankly, I still haven't worked out where I stand on it myself. You'd think after both my parents dying by the time I was twenty I would have formulated some kind of theory to pass on to my son, just in case. But after hauling up a few stuttering 'maybe's, a very lame 'quite possibly' and the grand finale of 'I don't really know', I had nothing. *Nada. Niente. Nyet.*

Whenever I came into Norman's room after Jax died, I'd find him just lying there, sheets and blankets spread smoothly over the mini-dune of his body. Not reading, not writing down a joke that had suddenly popped into his head; just staring at the wall where my father's shabby old mulberry-coloured velvet suit jacket hung. All gussied up in that jacket, with his polished shoes and a rainbow Lurex cravat, Norman had been the perfect complement to Jax in his performance outfit of baggy trousers, T-shirt and braces.

Now the mulberry jacket hung in a semi-open-armed stance, straining its wire hanger shoulders, slowly sagging into a depressing shrug and, if I wasn't mistaken, taking Norman with it. And those sheets stayed smooth all night.

The other thing that happened was that Norman stopped telling me his nightly joke. Every night, for as long as I could remember, bedtime was when he'd try out his new material on me.

'Mum! Hey, Mum!' he'd call out as I passed by on my way to the bathroom. 'Why did the scarecrow get promoted?' I'd stop and pretend to have a think, but he'd never give me any time before shouting out the answer. 'Because he was outstanding in his field, Mum!' Or whatever the punchline was, before whacking the bed with a flourish. 'I reckon Jax'll love that one!'

And while it might seem pretty par for the course for a boy who's lost his best friend to stop making jokes, when it went from Norman, you should understand it was a lot to lose. Two weeks after his twelfth birthday, which made it four weeks after Jax died, as I passed Norman's room I slowed down, giving him time and hoping for even the faintest 'Hey, Mum!' to stop me in my tracks. It didn't come, like I knew it wouldn't come, like it hadn't come for the past month. His bedside lamp was dimmed down as low as it could go and he looked like a sad little bat blinking in the bed.

'Hey, Norman,' I whispered into the doorway. 'You still awake?'

'Still awake, Mum.'

I took the deepest breath I could and prepared to launch the joke I'd been silently deliberating on for ten minutes at the top of the stairs. *Go, Sadie, go.*

'I . . . I was just wondering. What do porcupines say when they kiss?' I thought I saw the corner of the bat's mouth curl up a little in the half-dark. But I couldn't be sure.

'I dunno, Mum. What *do* porcupines say when they kiss?' I

could imagine the cogs and wheels moving beneath his flattened fringe and I wished I could see them grinding. Anything to show he was still there.

'Ouch!' I saw a flash of teeth as Norman's lips opened slightly, mouthing the punchline, miraculously getting there at almost the same time I did. I'd said it too loudly, though, and the word was left hanging out on an uncomfortable limb in the silence. But he managed a snuffle into his chest in a pretend laugh anyhow.

'That's a good one, Mum.' The hanging ouch breathed a sigh of relief, but my heart ached at the distance in Norman's voice. It was like someone throwing it back over his shoulder as he walked away down a long hallway with a heavy suitcase, not like someone who'd just been treated to a reasonably funny joke. I was about to concede defeat and continue my trek to the bathroom when he spoke again.

'Hey, Mum?' His voice was very soft and it sounded like he'd reached the end of the hallway but not turned back around. I held my breath. Hoping for anything. 'Do you think Jaxy's in heaven?'

My heart leapt and dropped at the same time and I had to put my hand up against the doorframe to stop myself from doubling over with its hijinks. Whatever was coming didn't feel like it could possibly go well, bearing in mind my lack of answers on death and, consequently, beyond.

It didn't help that I hadn't believed in God since I was about eight, coinciding with the death of my mother and the ensuing six months of constant prayers down on my knees, joined by Camper Van Barbie and a posse of three adoring Kens, begging him to bring her back. I think I can speak for all of us when I say that we knew it was a big ask, but prior to that I always had faith that the God sold to me by my teachers, the local priest and my mother herself was actually up to the job.

So when after those six months my mother hadn't returned and there hadn't been so much as a stink of rotting evidence that she was 'with you every day watching over you from heaven', as promised by my father and everyone else I encountered, I decided God was free to dwell in his own house in the Anglican church down the road but he wasn't coming anywhere near mine. Not unless he showed up accompanied by my mother and a damn good reason for keeping me, Barbie and the Kens waiting so long.

Even so, there was no way I wanted to be responsible for taking anything that could masquerade as comfort away from Norman. He'd lost enough. I sidled into the bedroom, delving into the depths of my sadly lacking motherlode in search of a gem and came up with a tin can.

'Of . . . of course he is, Norman. I'm sure of it.'

'But Mum?' I knew what was coming. Sometimes Norman's cleverness is not in my own best interests. 'You don't believe in God, though. So how . . . how can you be sure of it?'

I'd have renounced my atheism on a sky-high stack of Bibles right then and there if I'd thought it would help, but I knew Norman would never buy it. I sat down on his bed and he budged his little body over to make room. In the semi-darkness the lumps and craters of his psoriasis looked like a beautiful miniature landscape on his face. I stroked his forehead gently, playing for time and fooling nobody.

Oh, Jax, where are you now, you lovely little bugger, with your smart mouth and your theories on everything? I knew exactly what he'd do in this situation, though. He'd put his hands on his hips, poke out his chin and stare right down the barrel. He could have you believing anything within seconds, that kid,

even as he was disposing of the evidence against it right in front
of you. So, in honour of Jax, I gave it my best shot.

'Well, I . . . I never said I didn't believe in heaven, Norman. It's
just God I've got a problem with. But you know, there's got to . . .
I mean, I'm sure there's definitely some kind of better place we go
when . . . when we die. Where people don't get sick and everybody gets on with each other and there aren't any wars or traffic
jams or gas bills. And you can eat all the chocolate and fried food
you like and not get fat.'

I was on a roll. This was way easier than I'd imagined it would
be. It was almost invigorating, and if this was how Jax felt, the
kid might have been even smarter than I'd thought.

'And so . . . well, if there is a place like that, which there is, do
you really think our Jax would even dream of missing out on it?'
I was quite proud of my deft quickstep followed by a sidestep.
Until Norman hit me with his doublestep.

'So then, Mum, if there *is* a heaven, that . . . that means Granny
and Grandad are there too, right?' I realized I was just being
blown off course by one shitstorm into another.

'Mmmm.'

'So then, do you reckon they would . . . that they might be
keeping an eye out for Jax? Do you reckon it matters if they don't
know what he looks like? And do . . . do you think they know
he's my best friend?'

I knew my limitations. 'Norman, have you brushed your teeth
tonight? I smell cheese.' I reached over to pat his leg, and it felt
like stroking a ruler. His already tiny frame was becoming even
thinner, and it scared me how small the pile of Norman under
those sheets and blankets was.

'Hey, Mum?' His voice was so soft I had to lean right in to
catch it. 'I reckon you're right, though.' My heart did an extra

pirouette then stubbed its toe on the way round just to show me who was in charge. *There he goes, still trying to make you feel better, Sadie.*

Seconds ticked by like omnibuses and, when it became clear to both of us there would be no more reassuring motherly advice forthcoming, Norman unfurled out of the bed. He still had his school uniform on underneath his pyjamas. I stood up and wrapped both my arms around him as tight and close as I dared without knocking the top off a scab or hurting him and wondered if it were possible to hug the sadness out of someone. Squeeze and squeeze so hard that it just pops out the top of their head like a pimple, and then all that's left is for time to do its work and heal it over. I felt Norman's hip bone press against mine as he squeezed me tighter, too, and I wondered what he was trying to pop out of me. Answers, probably. Chance'd be a fine thing.

When I heard the tap running in the bathroom sink and the hollow sound of Norman's methodical teeth-brushing, I sank back on to his bed and rolled into the shallow imprint he'd left behind. I lay there, in his musty, boy-smelling dent and tried to imagine what it felt like to be a kid who'd lost his best and only friend in the world. Bad. It felt bad. I had to stop after just a few seconds when my chest threatened to cave in on itself.

From the bed, I could see the poster Norman and Jax had made a couple of years before hanging above his bookshelf. I knew everything on it by heart and after seeing it up on the wall for so long I barely had to look at it to know what it said.

JAX AND NORMAN'S FIVE YEAR PLAN
Edinburgh Fringe 2023: For One Night Only.
Norman and Jax – Teenage Comedy Geniuses!!!

Steps:
1. Get to the Edinburgh Fringe, baby!
2. Get famous
3. Get rich

The yellow cardboard was way oversized for the sparse letter-
ing of their five-year intentions, but the lack of literary substance
was made up for by the abundance of carefully stuck-on photos.
Jax and Norman had worked on that poster for a whole weekend, debating the position of every picture, the colour of the
writing, the best adjectives to describe themselves. 'Teenage
Super Fucking Comedy Geniuses' had been one of Jax's suggestions. It had been grudgingly vetoed, due to the risk of alienating
an older audience and a younger audience not actually being
allowed to come. A fairly astute decision, in my opinion.

Photos of Jax and Norman in various poses were interspersed
with cut-out pictures of Eric Morecambe, Ernie Wise, Jack Dee,
the Two Ronnies, Dave Allen, Frankie Boyle, Vic Reeves, Bob
Mortimer and Norman Wisdom, all radiating around a handsome, smiling man in a dapper mulberry suit. A faded Polaroid
that could still make my heart creak, no matter how many times
I saw it. Robert Foreman. Norman's grandfather. My father.
Would-be comedy superstar. Actual alcoholic, gambler, benefit
fraudster and, if we're being honest, comedy absolutely bloody
nobody. Although if you were a kid at a Butlin's in the late 1980s
you might have a faint memory of him trying to chat up your
mother after his show.

As my eyes adjusted to a low-light focus I realized something
looked different about the poster. There seemed to be a lot of
crossing out, some words had been outlined more thickly than
others and there was some new writing on it that was a lot fainter

25

than the original. I tried squinting to get a better look, but in the end I had to drag myself out of Norman's warm hollow and go over to the wall to make it out properly.

When the extent of the changes to Jax and Norman's Five Year Plan became clear, my heart was just too smart for its own good and attempted a double reverse spin before crashing to the floor.

JAX AND NORMAN'S FIVE YEAR PLAN

Edinburgh Fringe 2023: For One Night Only. –
Norman and Jax – Teenage Comedy Geniuses!!!
Edinburgh Fringe Festival – Norman Foreman,
For One Night Only
Sausages and Gravitas, the Jax Fenton Tribute Show

Steps:
1. Get to the Edinburgh Fringe, baby!
2. Get famous
3. Get rich
1. Look after Mum
2. Find Dad
3. Get to the Edinburgh Fringe

7

NORMAN

First rule of comedy: It's only funny if someone laughs.

Twelve's a helluvan age. Or else it should be, according to Mum. It's kind of a joke between us now, because when I was five she told me that five was a helluvan age and when I turned six that was also a helluvan age. When seven came around and she reckoned that was a helluvan age too I started thinking well, this looks like it's here to stay.

I only twigged something might be up with that when we were in Tilley's Bakery getting my second eighth-birthday cake. We had to get another one because the first one that Mum made somehow missed out having the butter in it. She could have sworn she put it in, she said, but she sometimes muddles stuff up when she's cooking. Not that I care, because a lot of the time it ends up even cooler than how it's supposed to be. Like once we had paprika-flavoured chocolate-and-supposedly-cinnamon biscuits, which Jax reckoned were doubly delicious because first they gave you a sweet, sugary kiss then they turned around and *kapow!* gave you a paprika punch in the mouth just for fun.

But it doesn't always turn out that good because without the butter my first eighth-birthday cake tasted a bit like an omelette-flavoured dishcloth, or maybe it could have been a dishcloth-flavoured omelette. Anyway, I'm pretty sure neither of those are any good in case you're thinking of trying them. So Mum chucked it in the bin and said that there was something to be said for letting the experts do their jobs.

When we got to the bakery and Mum said what we were looking for Mr Tilley leaned over the counter and stuck his face right into mine and goes, a birthday cake is it, eh? So how old are we today then young man? I always try to make Mr Tilley talk as much as possible, because when he does all these little puffs of flour explode off the sides of his cheeks and out of his ears and hair from all the baking he does. Even when I don't actually have anything to say except like maybe two finger buns please Mr Tilley, I try really hard to think of a question as well so he has to talk.

Like I might say, two finger buns please Mr Tilley, and do your buns have a secret ingredient, because me and Jax reckon they're the best in Penzance. Then Mr Tilley can't help but start talking about how he uses this special Italian flour and that's why his buns are the best and why thank you very much young man. And all those bits of flour go crazy, puffing out and floating all around his head, and it always makes me and Jax laugh really hard. But on the inside mostly, if we can.

When Mr Tilley asked how old I was that time, before I could think of a question to go along with my very short answer, which was just going to be eight, Mum piped up and goes, he's eight today, aren't you Norman? So then I said, yes, and I think it's probably a helluvan age.

Well, it didn't matter that I hadn't thought up a question to make Mr Tilley talk more because when I said that he laughed so hard the puffs of flour that came out of his ears nearly blew me sideways. But it was a nice laugh. The kind that means I'm laughing with you, not at you because your skin is gross and I'm trying to impress my mates by being mean. I reckon there should be a different word for that kind of nasty laughing. Naughing, maybe.

When he stopped laughing and the air around him cleared Mr Tilley gave us what he reckoned was his best banana and walnut cake and goes, eight eh? Well, good luck to you son, and I hope you have a helluva year. Which made him start laughing all over again.

Later on, when Mum was rubbing stinking tar cream on my stinking psoriasis, which by the way had given me a present of getting just a bit worse for my birthday, I asked her why Mr T had cracked up so much at what I said because I hadn't actually been trying to be funny. Well, when Mum found out that for all those other birthdays I thought that the Helluvan Age was something like the Ice Age or the Neolithic Age she thought it was so hilarious that she nearly peed. That's her words, not mine.

She explained that what she'd meant was that every year was a great time in a boy's life and that sometimes adults used inappropriate words to describe something when they felt quite strongly about it. When I asked her if that was why she sometimes called Dennis her boss at the car yard where she worked xeno-fucking-phobic I thought she might nearly pee again. Exactly, Norman. Exactly fucking like that, is what she said.

My mum reckons that just because she sets a bad example doesn't mean I'm going to follow it, because I'm way smarter than her. And by the way, that's her words again, not mine. Because actually me and Jax reckon that my mum is probably one of the smartest people in the world. She was the first Foreman to go to university and everything, even though she didn't stay that long because of me coming along. But that wasn't her fault.

Anyhow, Mum says she knows that even if I hear her use bad language it's not going to make me do it. And she's right. I never say the F word, except for repeating if someone else says it, which I don't think counts. I didn't even say it when Archie Lowry reefed the collar of my jacket up over my head and pulled so hard the scabs on my underarms bled right through. Not even when I lost a whole pocket full of new jokes when I accidentally went swimming in my school uniform because Jax reckoned surf was up and the last one in was a manky toe. Not even when Mum told me Jax was dead.

Even after Mr Tilley ruined the joke of the Helluvan Age, my mum kept carrying it on, just for fun. And I went along with it because I've noticed that she sometimes gets a bit sad over weird things that don't even matter. Like when she burns the dinner or forgets to do the washing or she's the only parent that forgot to go to the parent–teacher meeting.

When my twelfth birthday came along, which was two weeks and one day after Jax died, Mum woke me up with two bits of melted cheese on toast with candles stuck in them and a huge card made out of an inside-out cereal box with a drawing of a dog saying *Happy Barkday, Norman*. Because that's the Foreman birthday rule. Home-made cards and jokes only. When she asked me how it felt to be twelve, even though it was two weeks and one day after Jax died and what I really wanted to say was that more than anything I wished I could make time go backwards to when I was eleven and eleven months so I could change everything, that the last part of my own body had dirty-double-crossed me again for my birthday and my psoriasis had spread down to my willy, that being twelve and having to go back to school without Jax felt like the scariest, loneliest age I've ever been so far, I didn't. I just blew out the candles, picked the pink and blue wax off my cheesy toast, stuffed a whole piece into my mouth in one go and said I reckon twelve is going to be a helluvan age, Mum.

She hugged me really hard and looked so happy I felt guilty that I'd ever wanted to drop that dumb joke and that I was nearly being sick at the thought of having to swallow that big old mouthful of cheese on toast. And by the way, no matter how much you put in your mouth at one time, the actual amount you have to swallow in the end doesn't get any smaller. That's just physics. Also, me and Jax have tested it out.

All I could think about while Mum was hugging me and the toast got to halfway down my throat and stopped there in a globby lump was the weekend that Jax and I ate cheese on toast for breakfast, lunch and dinner both days, even though I knew it was probably going to make my psoriasis worse. And how we didn't even get sick of it after twelve pieces each, plus a couple of crusts that didn't count. And how that was never going to happen again. I mean, I suppose the cheese-on-toastathon could if I want to risk it, but not the Jax part.

So anyway, it looks like that joke's still going to be with me for a helluva long time. Jax reckoned I was probably going to get a note from the Queen or Charles and Camilla or whoever telling me to have a Helluva Fun Time on my hundredth. That's if I make it that far. And Jax dying like that two weeks and a day before my birthday all on his own on the floor of his bedroom with a brand-new inhaler downstairs in his backpack and his mum and stepdad snoring away just through the wall goes to show that, really and truly, one never knows.

Me and Jax decided ages ago that's actually the best and

cleverest sentence in the world. One. Never. Knows. It's actually so good that a whole bunch of people even made it into a motto. Which Jax found out when he was googling cockney comedians, which led him to the history of the East End, which led him to the story of the Pearly Kings and Queens of London and their cool outfits and super-genius motto. Which shows you how cool Google is, because you end up finding out stuff you didn't even know you were looking for and sometimes it's even more useful than what you were looking for in the first place. A bit like Mum's cooking. Jax says that's called synchronicity, and I don't even have to google that because unless he's telling proper on purpose lies for a good reason, Jax is always right.

Anyhow, one never knows means that no matter how much you *think* you know, even if you go to university and get honours in astrophysics and make a moped that can get you to Venus, which by the way was one of Jax's actual ideas minus the honours degree, the one thing you'll never be able to know is the future. Not even what's going to happen in the very next second. No matter how many guesses or phone-a-friends you had.

I know gazillions of people probably would have said one never knows before the Pearly Kings and Queens, but they helped loads and loads of poor people by turning it into their Pearly Motto. They believe you should always try to help those that aren't as lucky as you and maybe don't have stuff, like food, or their own room, or even a mum. Because you just never know what could happen tomorrow or next week or next year, and maybe one day it could be you that needs the help.

Jax reckons he might start the Pearly Kings of Penzance one day and that if you keep those three words in the back of your head that's pretty much all you'll ever need to be a good person. And I reckon he's right. Except I don't think most people have those words in the back of their head when they think of Jax. Because most people only see the side that gets him into trouble, and even though I know he does actually do a fair bit of naughty stuff, it's a pretty big shame nobody ever really notices the good stuff.

Like here's a for instance. Instead of eating the mini Crunchie bar his mum puts in his lunch box every day, he walks for an extra ten minutes in the morning to give it to this old lady who sits at the bus stop out the front of her bedsit on Bay Terrace and talks to herself. And every day, even though he's been doing it for absolute ages, when he hands her the mini Crunchie bar she always looks at it like he's just handed her an alien light saber and goes, what's this? It cracks him up.

One day when Jax was home sick with a bad asthma attack he made me do a Crunchie Run after school because he said the old lady would have been waiting for her treat all day. When I got to the bus stop she was still sitting there just like he said she would be, and when I handed her the mini Crunchie she looked at it and then looked at me and goes, what's this? Geez, it cracked me up.

Mum notices the good stuff about Jax though, and she reckons he's the equal best kid in the world. I know she means it too, because she lets him come over every day whenever he likes and never sends him home until he wants to go. And I know I'm talking about Jax like he's still here but I'm probably going to stop doing that one day.

8

First rule of comedy: Always have a plan.

When me and Jax made our Five Year Plan we figured that by the time we were fifteen we'd have hopefully saved enough money for a hotel and the train from Penzance to Edinburgh. Which takes eleven hours and costs ninety-five pounds on a cheap ticket. Even if the prices went up we reckoned with another few years of birthday and Christmas money it was doable.

The plan was to stay in the Premier Inn in Edinburgh, because that's where Lenny Henry said he stays all over Britain, although Mum reckons it's possible he doesn't actually stay there and he's just getting paid to say he does. I really hope Lenny's not a liar though, even if most people say he must be because of when he did the dirty on Dawn.

Mum promised she'd come with us too, which was good because a couple of kids probably shouldn't be going all the way from Penzance to Scotland on their own even when they're fifteen. Also, Edinburgh is where she used to go to university before I was born so she thought maybe she'd like to see it again by then.

Also, I don't think I'd want to go a whole few days without seeing my mum. Not even when I'm fifteen.

Me and Jax know everything about the Edinburgh Fringe. Well, all the important stuff anyhow, like who's been the headline acts ever since it started in 1947 and who was the comedy dark horse for each year and who the *Guardian* said came up with the best joke of the festival.

Mum says the Fringe is almost as big an event in our house as the actual festival, which is pretty funny and also probably true, I reckon. She lets me stay up really late to watch as many of the comedy shows as possible on telly and Jax is allowed to sleep over even on school nights. On the Friday and Saturday we stay up all night and take loads of notes about who we liked and what they wore and what people said in the after-show interviews. So we'll be ready for when it's our turn. And then Mum lets us sleep all day and makes us cheesy toast when we wake up.

When we made the Five Year Plan we made sure we thought of everything, because Jax reckons having a plan is the first rule of comedy. He's got loads of those by the way. Last year he even made a book of all the first rules of comedy and gave it to me for my eleventh birthday. It's not really a book, it's actually five pieces of paper stapled together at the side, but it's got a cover and a contents page and it's the coolest present I ever got. It's called The First Rules of Comedy.

Anyhow, even though we made sure we thought of everything we were actually wrong, because there was one thing we didn't think of. Which was what would happen if the other person in your comedy duo died. Because you don't expect that, do you? Although considering one never knows and Ronnie Barker, maybe we should have.

*

I think I'm OK about dying, just as long as it's not people I know. Like when Marnie Cunningham's father was killed fighting the Taliban in Afghanistan when I was eight and we had a special assembly at school, I couldn't really feel too sad because I didn't know him. But I did do what the Head said, which was take a moment to think about him in silence and consider the ultimate sacrifice he'd made for our country. Even though Jax said that it was all BS and Mr Cunningham had actually made the ultimate sacrifice for a whole lot of stuff that had nothing to do with any of us.

It's funny how your brain works, and I mean my brain really, because I don't know how anyone else's works. But I say that because when Mum woke me up to tell me about Jax the first thing that popped into my head was that I wished I'd gone up and patted Marnie Cunningham on the shoulder, or made her a card or given her a mini Crunchie bar. Anything apart from what I actually did, which was nothing except what the Head told us to.

I just lay there in my bed with Mum holding my hand telling me the worst thing I'd ever heard and I wished I'd said something to Marnie that might have stopped her from feeling like a massive hairy yin was trying to eat its way out of her insides with a rusty knife and fork, which was how I felt when Mum told me about Jax. That was *actually* my first thought, so you can see why I say my brain works in a funny way.

I can't remember when my granny and grandad died because I wasn't even born, so I can't really feel sad when I think about them either. It's kind of like thinking about Tommy Cooper, like you knew he was great and you wished he wasn't dead and all, but there are no hairy yins chewing up your tummy from the inside when you think about him.

I know Mum gets sad when she thinks about them though. Granny and Grandad I mean, not Tommy Cooper. Grandad mainly. That's her dad. Even though he never got as famous as all those other guys like Morecambe and Wise and Dave Allen and Norman Wisdom, I reckon Grandad must have been a really ace comedian, because he got to do absolutely loads of shows.

Apart from the photos of him and Granny getting married and having Mum and stuff, all the pictures of him are when he's dressed up in his best suit standing in front of places like The Slip Inn, The Rose & Crown or the Suffolk YHA, with a big smile on his face and pointing to the name signs like he was about to have the most fun of his life. Which I reckon would have been true.

Mum says I look just like him when I put on his old velvet jacket, and sometimes I hold one of those photos right up next to my face in the mirror to check. I can't really see what Mum sees but I just hope one day I can get as good at comedy as him anyway.

Even though Grandad would definitely have been a cool guy to know in person, he was pretty old when he died, so it's different to being a kid like Jax and dying when you're not even twelve yet. Plus Jax was my best friend in real life not just someone I've only seen in a bunch of old photos so it's not even on the same planet really.

I know it's selfish to worry about myself when Mum has to look after me and go to work and cook dinners and wash our clothes and pay the leccy bill and all that other stuff. But with Jax gone it's just so hard for me to stop thinking about how I don't have a best mate any more. And how much I miss him every single second of every single hour of every single day.

The worst thing is how it feels like there's always so much

room around me now, because I'm used to all the space being taken up by Jax. Now it's just me. And I'll tell you something, I think I might be half gone too because when I look in the mirror all I can see is a big red scab with none of the good parts left. I think maybe all the parts of me that were good were actually made of Jax. And I think about that a lot because I'm pretty sure it's true.

Even though I didn't take the Five Year Plan off the wall I decided to stop looking at it, because every time I did it just made me think of Jax. And not in a good way. It was kind of hard not to look at it though, because of it being so big, and it may as well have had flashing lights around it. Actually Jax did want to put flashing lights around it when we first made it but then we thought about Mum's leccy bill and decided maybe that wasn't such a good idea.

You know what it's like when you try not to look at something so hard that it just makes you want to look at it more? Well, the Five Year Plan kept on trying to make me to look at it for the whole week after Jax died. But I held out because if I didn't look that meant I wouldn't have to think about taking it down. And if I took it down, Jax would be gone and not just for five years. For ever. Only then I did look at it when it got sneaky one morning after my alarm went off because I had to go back to school and I opened my eyes and forgot I wasn't looking over at that side of the room any more. I hit the snooze button, but then my eyes opened by themselves and straight away there I was staring at Jax and me and Grandad and all those other guys.

I lay there looking at the poster all lopsided out of one eye for ages and ages, thinking about how now me and Jaxy were never going to get to Edinburgh and how all those jokes we had on

Post-it notes would just stay in the shoebox in the second to bottom drawer in my wardrobe.

I stared at the Five Year Plan for so long Grandad started turning into Jack Dee, words started swimming around and one of the Jaxes with a pork pie hat on started doing a dance off the cardboard and on to the wall. Then the Jax head got bigger and bigger until it was like a massive lollipop on a stick body and he started jumping up and down in a huge inflatable pool of blue plastic balls and waving a sign around with his stick arms.

I yelled out to him stand still Jax, and he did. Which was really weird because Jax never ever stands still and especially not if someone tells him to. But he stood still so I could read the sign and it said One Never Knows in big red writing. And then I saw that the pool wasn't really filled with blue balls, it was actually full of about a billion asthma inhalers. Then the Jax head jumped back on to the poster and started crossing stuff out and writing new stuff and in between he kept turning around and laughing and winking at me. I swear that's how it happened, and maybe it did and maybe it didn't. But I must have gone back to sleep for a few minutes because the next thing I knew the nine minutes of snooze time were over and the alarm went off again and I had to get up for school.

After that I went back to not looking at the poster on the wall, because then I would have had to read what Jax had written about going to the Fringe without him and finding my dad and I was pretty sure I didn't want to think about that. Like I didn't want to think about getting up and going back to school on my own without Jax. Like I didn't want to think about what I was going to do every day for the rest of my life until the end of school and then even further. Like I didn't want to think about how twelve was probably going to be a Helluva Year for all the wrong reasons.

I was doing a pretty good job of not looking over at the wall the second time around too, even though I did have a permanently cricked neck. But then Mum saw the poster with the new plan and the piggin' jig, like Jax would say, was up.

9

Sadie

Finding out Norman wanted to find his father was almost as much of a shock to me as finding out I was pregnant had been. In fact, it managed to evoke pretty much the same feelings, from what I can remember. Same order, even. Bewilderment, denial, terror, followed by how the hell did this happen, and how am I going to do this without losing my mind or getting arrested. Throw in the news that it appeared Norman was aiming to get a solo gig at one of the world's most famous comedy events, and there was every possibility that both of those things would happen. And probably more.

It's not that I was scared of how the revelation would affect Norman. He's always known I honestly couldn't tell him who his father is, even if I'd ever felt inclined. Which, for the record, I definitely never have. He knows the basic concept of how he came to be, but I'm just not sure if he'd ever considered the moral aspect of how his mother could *actually* not know the identity of the father of her own child. I'm pretty sure Promiscuity for Dummies was not on the curriculum of Alverton Primary for Sex Ed in Year 6. Although, judging by the number of teen mothers that

prammed their way down our street to show off their handi-
work, they might want to consider it.

So there was that to worry about, although I have to admit that
coming across as a bit loose to my son was considerably less
worrying than how exactly I was supposed to track down the
men-most-likely from a hazy month or two in Edinburgh thirteen
years ago. Because from the moment that thin blue line appeared
and changed the shape of my family for the third time, it never
even crossed my mind that I was going to do it any other way than
alone. Ready or not.

But the worst thing by far for me was point number one on
Norman's list. Which I'd been trying very hard not to think about
since I'd seen it. The one about looking after his mum. Wouldn't
that break your heart if you were me? And even though you're
not me (but for the grace of a probably non-existent god), doesn't
it break your heart anyhow?

I probably shouldn't be surprised, though, because I get that
a fair bit. At work, I'm always getting the pat-on-the-head, don't-
you-worry-about-a-thing-little-lady treatment. Although that
could be partly because I'm the only little lady in a used-car lot
full of big men. But a counsellor I saw once not long after my dad
died, recommended by a kindly and rather observant lecturer at
university, did once tell me, almost admiringly I have to say, that
I had a 'vulnerable quality'. She pronounced each syllable very
slowly – vul-ner-ab-le – and it was a few panicky seconds before I
realized she hadn't just told me I had a serious gynaecological
condition. Which, now that I think about it, in a way was pretty
close to the mark. For a couple of months, at least. Anyhow, as
handy as coming across as a helpless female can be at my job
when it comes to getting things off the high shelves in spare parts

or the stationery cupboard, it's hardly the way you want your only child to see you, is it?

On the night I saw Norman's amendments to the Five Year Plan we lay on his bed together for a long time, just staring at it without either of us saying a word. I could feel the heat from his psoriasis seeping through his pyjamas like a third person, mixing in with the smell of toothpaste and still, faintly, cheese. Even though it always flared up when he was stressed or tired or had overdosed on dairy, so I thought I was prepared for what was coming, in the weeks after Jax died Norman's skin condition took on epic proportions. The worst it had ever been. It looked like it was positively gloating. Spreading across his arms, legs and torso and creeping up the inside of his neck to fringe his chin and cheeks like a rosy Amish beard. Claiming its best friend back. *Where ya been, buddy?*

As usual, it fell to the more mature one of us to break the deadlocked silence. And when Norman's voice finally hiked across the great divide of blankets it was high-pitched and wobbly, reminding me of the younger, lonelier, pre-Jax version of my boy that I thought had gone for ever.

'It doesn't mean anything, Mum. Honest. It doesn't matter. It's just, I dunno. I didn't even . . . I don't . . . I just thought maybe . . .'
Yes, Norman, I wanted to say. Maybe. Maybe your biological father will get over the shock of finding out he has a fully formed pre-teen son as a result of a brief encounter in a pub car park or a student bedsit with a totally forgettable girl. Maybe he and his lovely wife will be delighted at the prospect of a new addition to their family of high-achieving kids. And maybe the Edinburgh Fringe will welcome an unknown twelve-year-old boy with dubious comic timing as their headline act and the next year you'll sell

out Wembley and your father will be the proudest man alive, clapping from the front row.

Maybe all that will happen and you'll be too busy and too deliriously happy to remember about your dead best friend and having to look after your mother, when she should be looking after you. Point number one continued to hover insolently in the space between the wall and the bed, wafting its accusing breath over me. I wanted to knock its bloody block off.

I could hear the branches of the apple tree in our front garden banging up against the window downstairs. I'd been meaning to get them trimmed back for about two years. Hadn't got around to it. Just like I hadn't got around to giving Norman a father. Just like I hadn't got around to jumping back on the ride of life with the rest of the human race since my father died. Bloody serves me right now – and where did that come from?

My mouth was so thick with unspoken words I was nearly gagging. *Pick a few and just say them.* But that big, greasy word soup slurping around in my mouth was swirling so fast I couldn't quite get a tongue-hold on the right ones. The good-mother ones. *Open wide, Sadie.*

'I never knew you wanted to find your father, Norman.' Brilliant. Of all the things my son needed to hear right then, I'm pretty sure that wasn't one of them. In the silence that followed I could tell he was considering his answer carefully, so as not to hurt my feelings. And knowing that hurt more than anything he ever could have said. *Look after Mum.*

'I don't. I mean, I didn't, Mum. Not really. I just thought . . . well, with Jax gone, it's just . . . it's just me now, isn't it?' The kid's voice nearly killed me on the spot. Soft, shaky and trying so hard to be brave. And he wasn't wrong.

'I'm never going to have another friend like Jax, Mum. But

I . . . I just thought that maybe the next best thing might be a dad. You know. Like a . . . a guy.' And the thing is, it was one of the few times in my life that maybe I actually did know.

The branches were still banging against the window and the big yellow plan was still hanging on the wall. Jax was still dead and everything was just the same as it had been two minutes ago. But nothing was.

Now, I don't really know how what happened next happened, because I certainly don't recall thinking I had something useful to say. I blame point number one and wanting to knock its bloody block off, because what came out of my mouth was a total and utter surprise to me. And that's putting it mildly.

'I think maybe you're going to need some help with that new plan of yours, Norman.'

As soon as the words were out, slamming number one back against the wall in their crushing wake, I felt Norman's breathing quicken on the pillow next to me. Even the other person in the bed stirred in surprise and let off an extra puff of heat.

'Mum, I don't, I mean I didn't . . . that's not, I mean, it doesn't . . .' For one glorious moment I thought I was going to get away with it. The Bluff That Worked. Hurrah! Oh, they'd be talking about it for years.

'You . . . you mean it, Mum?' The Bluff That Worked quickly turned into the Bluff That Never Had A Chance. 'And you mean the Fringe too? This year, Mum? For Jaxy? We're going to do it? But it's only four weeks away and . . .' Yes, that's right, stupid idea. Forget I spoke. *Not likely.*

'We've – I mean, I've – got loads of material, but you know . . . I dunno how I'll go without him . . . it'd be pretty hard, but . . . but remember Jax always says that easy is for pussies? That's right, isn't it, Mum? It's true, easy is for pussies! Oh Mum, wouldn't he just love it!'

I sank deeper into the bed, scrunching the sheet tight in my hand. Savouring the sound of my son. *He's there.*

'Wouldn't he just laugh so hard to see me at the Fringe after all? And even though he wouldn't be there for real, he . . . he kind of would be. Because of his jokes. Wouldn't he? That'd really be something, wouldn't it?' Softer now. 'Wouldn't it, Mum?'

Oh, that'd be something all right. *He's still there.*

10

My boss Dennis has always insisted I get to work by 7.15 a.m. to answer the phones, which in reality never ring before nine o'clock and mostly not before eleven. It used to do my head in, because there was quite literally nothing for me to do that early except sit around and wait for the non-existent phone calls. But things have changed a bit over the last few months.

Before I go any further I should point out that the occasional male workmate putting himself out to pander to my vulnerability certainly doesn't ever include Dennis Pearl, who I'm pretty sure never spent a minute of his life looking after anyone or anything else, apart from his own gigantic quiff of hair. Although, to be fair, that does look like it needs quite a bit of maintenance.

But that's fine by me. Because if there's anything I hate more than my mind-numbing job, it's the guy who puts the Pearl into Pearl's Quality Pre-loved Cars. And if I have to hear the joke about pearls before swine as he drives his bouffant hair and rancid mouth through another doorway, knocking over anyone who happens to be heading in the same direction, one more time, I may have to consider using my vulnerability as my defence in a murder trial.

The other person who doesn't rush to help me is Leonard. Which is probably because he's finished the cleaning and gone home by the time any high reaching needs to be done, but also maybe because he's only about an inch taller than me and eighty years old if he's a day.

At first glance, Leonard Cobcroft looks like he'd be to cleaning what Prince Charles is to dubstep, and it's not just his age. I'm getting pretty used to seeing trainee OAPs on the checkout or stacking the shelves at Sainsbury's, and it always makes me a bit sad that after a life probably very decently lived, when they should be kicking back with their pipe and slippers they had to go back to work just to make ends meet. But there was something different about Leonard. He always walked with a straight back and a purpose, and he wielded a duster and a bottle of Domestos like he'd been entrusted with the upkeep of the Rosetta Stone. Like cleaning the back office and toilets of a used-car lot was exactly how he wanted to be spending the twilight years of his life.

Dennis had only taken Leonard on because he was receiving a tidy subsidy for hiring an over-seventy, and he was certainly getting way more than his money's worth. The place had never been cleaner and he'd never had such an easy or more gracious target for his bullying.

'Hey, Leonard,' he'd called out one morning as Leonard passed through the office. 'Bogs done? Kitchen done? Having a good day, are you?' Then, without waiting for a response, he'd raised himself half out of his chair and leaned over his desk to yell, 'Mind you, at your age, any day above ground's a good one, isn't it? Ha ha ha.'

A couple of the mechanics who'd just arrived for work ha ha'd along with what they no doubt hoped was the required amount of political incorrectness, even though they'd heard about a dozen variations on the theme already that week. Leonard had been there a couple of months by then and he usually acknowledged Dennis's supposed jokes with a benign smile and a gentle nod, like he'd just been complimented on his roses. But that day, as he nudged a metal bucket ahead of him with his foot, a mop resting over his shoulder and a two-litre bottle of floor cleaner in one hand, I had a perfect line of vision to see his free hand drop to his side, curl up and flip Dennis an elegant, perfectly camouflaged middle finger. As he trundled past, he tilted his head very slightly in my direction and gave me a slow, wrinkly wink.

I'd been working at that car yard for six torturous years before Leonard came along, and it's no exaggeration to say I'd been giving Dennis and his sexist, racist, misogynistic jokes the mental middle finger every single day. So when I saw Leonard do it for real, even though it was totally for my benefit and there was no chance of Dennis ever actually gaining its full, glorious effect, it felt like someone had turned a light on in my heart.

After that day I started to look forward to the early mornings at work instead of spending most of the fifteen-minute bus ride praying for an absent-minded cow to amble out on to the road and cause a pile-up just so I could run a few minutes late. Which never happened, by the way, just adding more proof, if I needed it, that my suspicions about God were true.

By the time I arrived at the car yard, the office floors would already be gleaming and Leonard would be brewing up a pot of fragrant hibiscus tea in the lunchroom. At first, I'd been doubt-ful, having never really strayed from PG Tips, except for a brief accidental dalliance with Tetley a few years ago, but once you start on Egyptian hibiscus tea it's impossible to go back. It's a taste so delectable it has the power to lift you up and transport you from a shitty used-car lot in the south-west of England to somewhere altogether more exotic.

Every morning we'd sit at the lunch table talking and drinking the crack cocaine of tea out of the silver pot Leonard had bought off a local trader under the shadow of Mount Sinai when the accompanying waft of hibiscus had reminded him of his wife's shampoo. He'd carried that pot around in his army kit for months, craving the warm, familiar comfort of its floral notes so often that it became permanently stained.

Over the perfumed steam, Leonard told me stories about his years in the army, and how it felt to kiss your wife goodbye over and over again to go off to places like Egypt and Korea and Borneo that you might never come back from, when all you really wanted were a few more days breathing in the smell of flowers in her hair.

One morning he told me how it felt when he finally came home for good, and he and Iris headed straight for the seaside, opened up a small electrical repair shop and never left. But that even to this day, when he drank hibiscus tea, if he closed his eyes, he was back there in the desert missing his beautiful young wife. Even though Iris was right there at home cooking her famous sultana biscuits and waiting for him to finish work.

Leonard also filled in a lot of spaces talking about his 1971 teal Austin Maxi, which was, by all accounts, along with Iris, the love of his life.

'I caught the train up to Birmingham to collect it two weeks after it rolled off the factory floor and we've been an item ever since,' he'd chuckled.

But now, no matter how attentive Leonard had been, after a

lifetime kept so close to the ocean, the Austin was in need of some major rust control. Leonard hadn't been sure their pensions and savings would quite stretch to the expense, he said, hence he'd been persuaded to sign up for the over-seventies return to work scheme, winning the lottery with a part-time cleaning job at Pearl's. Who knows, maybe compared to a couple of decades of active service, it didn't seem quite as bad to Leonard as it did to me.

When Leonard stopped talking, which wasn't all that often, I'd talk a little, too. Obviously, my specialist subjects of Norman and *Celebrity Come Dine with Me* weren't quite as interesting as his stories, even though, having been a fairly dedicated watcher of the latter over numerous series, I have to say I've amassed quite a few anecdotes. After a while, though, I did start to feel bad that I knew so much about Leonard and that after six months all he knew about me was that I was a bad cook, a mediocre mother and a telly addict. But I consoled myself with the fact that there really isn't that much more to know these days, and he never asked for any more than I was prepared to give.

Even when I'd disappeared from work without any notice, Leonard hadn't pushed me for an explanation. On the morning I returned, eight days after Jax was buried, he simply poured me a cup of hibiscus tea like I'd never been away. Like I hadn't just spent the past two weeks trying to hold my son's world together with my bare hands. Like I never got my grip on that all wrong from the start.

By the time a big blue Mercedes pulled into the car park every day at 9 a.m., Leonard would be back behind his cleaning trolley, his silver pot wrapped and tucked safely away into his little backpack, ready for his daily dose of Dennis. Which arrived like clockwork.

'Hey, Lenny, you old codger. What's on the agenda today? Off to get a new supply of incontinence pants? Some new hearing aids, maybe? Ha ha ha.' Every day was a delight worse than the last, but then Leonard would smile, tilt his head at me to signal it was coming and come up with some new and ingenious way to flip Dennis the bird, which got more and more daring every time. Leaving me in a desperate attempt to hide my shaking shoulders by shuffling some papers or dropping a pen, he'd glide off to finish cleaning the toilets.

At precisely eleven o'clock, Leonard would materialize at my desk with his backpack over his shoulder, wish me a very good day, then walk out the back to the car park and climb into his teal Austin Maxi to drive home to Iris and his cottage by the sea.

Those two and a half cups of hibiscus tea, the conversation and the secret flipping of the bird were the highlights of my day, and in six years of working at Pearl's, Leonard was the only friend I'd ever made there. And if you're wondering whose fault that is, all I can say is it takes more than a few high shelves to get to know me.

11

I dozed off easily the night I saw Norman's new plan. And the next. The deep, dream-free rest of a mother who'd brought her son to the brink of a smile with a promise that had come so easily she wondered why she hadn't thought of it sooner. Because wouldn't she do anything to make him happy? It wasn't until the third night, as I was hovering around the mezzanine of sleep, that things took a decidedly sharp turn in the direction of reality. *So whatcha got, Sadie?*

The hiss in my ear was so pin-sharp my head bounced off the pillow and straight into the corner of my bedside table as I was compelled almost vertical. I really should have known better than to be fooled by a couple of good nights' sleep. I half lay, half sat awkwardly, with my head pounding and one leg hanging off the side of the bed and thought about promises. Not by choice, you understand.

I've probably made about the average number in my time, including quite a few I never had any intention of following up. And no harm done, I'd say. But, hand on heart, I've never made one to Norman that I didn't absolutely mean to keep at the time. So there I was on night number three, with no hope of climbing back aboard the sleepy express and the full slap-in-the-face truth of what I'd promised my son becoming uncomfortably clear.

Because, naturally, I didn't have even the faintest clue as to how to go about getting Norman a spot to perform at the bloody Edinburgh Fringe, even if I hadn't known it was less than a month away. Which, by the way, I definitely hadn't when I opened my mouth. And as for the logistics of tracking down a month's worth of one-night-ish stands from nearly thirteen years ago, well, think about that for a minute or two then try and get yourself back to sleep. Every time I even considered trying to get horizontal again there was a tug on the strings from my invisible puppet master and I was jerked bolt upright and wide awake. After about twenty minutes of tussling I gave in, climbed out of bed and scuffed my way up the hallway to a well-worn spot.

Whenever I needed to work through some hard stuff (because, let's face it, you don't get to work for Dennis Pearl for six years without a few existential crises along the way), sitting on the floor outside Norman's bedroom had always been my favourite place to think. Even after so many years, I'd never quite got to grips with living in an actual grown-up house that I paid an actual grown-up amount of rent for, and I still always felt like the teenager who's moved back in with their parents. Except in that one spot. I feel different there. Safe. Grounded. Because behind that door is a boy who needs me.

When I leaned my head up against the cool plaster I'd sometimes fancy I could hear Norman's faint, small-boy breathing beyond the wall. I'd close my eyes and slow my own breath until it measured the same steady pace, and it didn't matter that the walls were a solid two inches thick and the sound was probably the wind. He was there and so was I.

But that night, as I pressed my back against the other side of

Norman's bedroom wall no amount of closing of eyes and counting of breaths could help me. As quickly as I played out a new possibility of how I was going to come good on my latest promise, it was swatted away. I mean, the only thing I'd really been put in charge of for the past few years was Pearl's staff Christmas party. And with the limited budget Dennis gave me to work with, there really wasn't all that much involved beyond putting a nominal sum behind the bar of the pub next door and keeping up the supply of smuggled-in packets of Tesco crisps.

But now, here I was, putting myself in charge of what felt like your classic garden-variety mission impossible. And I think you can give me that one. Norman had two weeks left of school before the summer holidays, after which I'd basically guaranteed him a spot at the world's biggest comedy festival and a delivery of a long-lost father, to boot. As you do.

I sat outside Norman's room for the longest of long times and as a sliver of first light nudged its way along the hallway I stretched out a numb leg and caught a glint of something near my foot. I reached forward to pinch the hair between my fingertips and felt a low hum of electricity travel up my arm to the back of my neck. Not one of the identical mousey browns Norman and I left behind in our communal brush in the bathroom. Blond. Golden, even. Bad-boy length.

As the sliver of light bled into the dawn of the fourth day after I made my promise to Norman, I wrapped the thread of Jax's hair around my index finger and thought about the bloody Rolls-bloody-Royce of bloody best friends. *Feet first, break the door down and damn the consequences.*

Down in the kitchen, I made tea in the red-and-white pot Norman got me from a charity shop on my last birthday. 'Keep Calm and

Drink Tea,' it advised me every morning. Although not usually this early. After rummaging through a couple of drawers I found the lined A4 notebook I'd bought to write out my favourite *Come Dine with Me* recipes. 'Keep Calm and Write Lists,' I scribbled on the front. Then I sat down at the table, took a swig of tea and brushed my hand across the paper several times, clearing away the invisible dust to prepare for the brilliance that was surely about to emerge. And, surprisingly, I did feel rather calm.

But it didn't take me long to realize this was going to be a whole different ball game to Pearl's Christmas party. Every time I was sure I'd thought of everything, I thought of something else. *Find out exact date of the Fringe* led to finding out the person in charge, finding out the rules and then eventually to simply *find out everything. Buy train tickets* led to checking off-peak prices, checking timetables and the genius *maybe check buses, too.*

The *where to stay* list filled an entire page once the plain and simple directive *book accommodation* had generated questions of where, for how long and how much we could afford. And *what to take* turned into three pages of random bulletpoints of things like buying Norman a new bag and a week's worth of new underwear, plus a separate list of the various creams and lotions to take for his skin.

It was woefully inadequate, most of it was utter drivel and I probably hadn't answered even a fraction of the most important questions I needed to, but it was a start, it was all I had and, frankly, I was exhausted. When I stood up to rinse out my teacup, the hair that was still wrapped around my finger caught on the tap and I felt it snap. I closed my eyes for longer than I could call a blink and a small blond boy darted past on the way to the biscuit tin. *Feet first and damn the consequences.* I can do this, I thought. I can do this. Because wouldn't I do anything to make Norman smile?

12

NORMAN

*First rule of comedy: When you think it
can't be done, try doing it.*

I miss him.

If I come in too early with my punchline or I'm too late and I accidentally leave Jax hanging at the end of a joke, he always goes, don't worry Norman, there's loads and loads of time until we're fifteen. But when Mum said she was going to help me make that new plan come true and I really and truly was going to go to the Fringe without Jax, all I could think was, there isn't loads of time any more. And I'm twelve and only just.

Jax says being scared is just your big old brain telling you that you can't do something and brave is when you go ahead and do it anyway. He also reckons that I'm the bravest guy he knows, which is exactly the kind of thing a best friend would say, only I'm not really sure it's true. Like even when my teacher said welcome back Norman and you're doing really well under the circumstances, I was just thinking, if you could hear what my big old brain is telling me right now I'm pretty sure you'd take that back Mrs Ferris. And I miss him.

Mum said I didn't have to go back to school until I was good and ready and that her boss Dennis could go fly a kite if he had anything to say about her taking more time off to look after me. But I'll tell you something. I knew that I probably wasn't ever going to be good and ready. Not in another week or another month or even if I stayed at home for the next couple of years and then skipped straight into Year 9. So I just went.

Mum bought me a new backpack that had aliens stole my homework written all over it, because she said she thought it might make me smile. And then she walked me all the way to the bus stop, which she hasn't done since I was ten, and goes, Norman, if it all gets too much you just get them to call me and I'll be there in a jiffy. And I said I will Mum and then because she looked so sad I said, and you can do the same and get them to call me if Dennis gets too much. Which made her laugh, but I actually meant it.

When I got off the bus at school, straight away I thought well, this backpack probably isn't going to last too long because here comes Archie Lowry and that's the first thing I have to worry about. But instead of saying, oi scabby, what's occurring and give me a look at that dumb bag you've got, Archie just goes, hello Norman and everybody's really glad you're back. Which made me think that maybe the Head did a special assembly for Jax and I should have been there, and also how weird is it that your best friend has to die before some people decide to be nice to you.

There's a lot of things you have to think about when you don't have a best friend any more. Like where you're going to sit for lunch and who you're going to talk to about last night's *Live at the Apollo*, and what you're going to say when people ask you if you're OK. And how you're going to finish your pairs biology project when the other half of your pair is gone.

Jax reckoned doing a project on the human body was going to be the easiest thing ever because we were already experts without even trying and how cool was that. We started a big red notebook and put all the weird stuff we found out from the internet in, like how it's impossible to tickle yourself and how humans can't breathe and swallow at the same time. And how every single person in the world loses about a million skin cells every day, so around 80 per cent of the dust around your house is actually made up of all that fallen-off human skin.

When Mrs Ferris gave us some quiet time to work on our projects I didn't open that red notebook for ages, because even though Archie and his mates were still being nice I didn't want to push my luck by crying in front of the whole class. When I did finally open it up, the first thing I saw was the page where Jax had written The Amazing Human Body Parts of Norman and Jax. And then underneath our names he'd put bee's knees and dog's bollocks in brackets, and drawn a picture of a bee with knobbly knees and a dog with really big you-know-whats. As soon as I saw those pictures it straight away made me think about Jax and how much me and him cracked up when he drew them. And I miss him. That's when I realized that doing a project on the human body wasn't going to be the easiest thing ever at all. It was pretty much going to be the exact opposite of that.

So when Mum said I was going to get to go to Edinburgh, even though it was pretty hard to stop listening to my brain telling me to be scared and even though it was going to be three years and maybe even more too early, I thought, well, if I can get through going back to school on my own, maybe I could do that too. And that somewhere in the 80 per cent of all the dust in our house there's maybe still a little bit of Jax.

13

Sadie

The day after my sleepless night, the bus was running twenty minutes later than usual, not down to a much-hoped-for collision with a cow but some diversionary roadworks. As we pulled up across the road from Pearl's, I could see Leonard standing at the side door of the office, looking anxiously in the direction of the bus. When he saw me get off, his face broke into a huge grin and he clapped his hands together and just held them there as I crossed the road. Like he was happy to see me or something. I had a sudden flash of guilt about those two weeks I'd been away without explanation. But if he was holding a grudge, he didn't show it.

'The best of jolly good mornings to you, my dear! Unseasonably chilly today, isn't it? Come on in. The kettle's on.' *Pop a brew on, Sadie love.*

In the lunchroom, the silver teapot and two cups were already set out and, as we were clearly behind schedule, Leonard busied himself pouring. I sat down at the table and rested my chin on my hands, allowing my eyelids to close for a few lovely, lovely seconds. Or minutes. The aroma of warm flowers brought me round and I opened my eyes to see Leonard sitting opposite me, hands folded around his cup, wearing a slightly concerned look.

'Sadie my dear, is everything . . . are you all right?' There you go.

So because it was clear he could see something was up, and because I'd been awake all night thinking about that bloody plan on Norman's bedroom wall, and because I felt guilty I'd never really given him anything about my life when I knew so much about his, he got it all.

Leonard sipped his tea while I told him how everything went wrong when my father had gone and died when I was nineteen and left me the sole survivor of our already meagre Foreman family of two. And that I'd woken up white-hot angry about that every single day for a year. So angry that I couldn't concentrate on my university course, or my procession of part-time jobs, or even on the tedious task of sucking air in and out of my lungs, which I'd not very seriously considered putting a stop to once or twice. So angry that drinking my body weight in alcohol and having it off with anyone who got in my way seemed like the best idea I'd ever had. Or OAP-appropriate words to that effect, anyhow.

'It was like . . . like maybe if I . . . oh, Leonard, I don't know. It just felt like it was the only way I could find to dilute all that anger into something almost tolerable, you know?' I was actually quite surprised by the eloquence of my explanation.

Leonard inclined his head slightly in acknowledgement, but if I'd been looking for judgement, and maybe I had, I clearly wasn't going to get it.

'Top up, my dear?'

With a full cup, I told Leonard how, all those months later when I came out the other side of my madness and brought my prize home from the hospital, I looked down at Norman's perfect baby face and swore I'd never fail him like my father had failed me.

'And the truth is, Leonard, I've probably done nothing but fail him spectacularly ever since.'

My attempt at an ironic laugh came dangerously close to being something else. Because I knew it was true. *Keep calm and drink tea.*

I told Leonard how when Norman was six he'd come home from school excited about his day for just about the first time ever. Tripping over his words to tell me about the naughty new boy from London, instead of trying to hide another bruised shin under his pulled-up socks, or clumsily sticky taping up a rip in his shirt and hoping I wouldn't notice.

Then because Leonard was still listening I told him about Jax and Norman's Five Year Plan, and how I'd really and truly believed in it because Jax was laugh-out-loud, close-one-eye, try-not-to-look-at-the-car-crash funny and Norman has gravitas. And how seeing those two boys together somehow made me better than I'd ever been.

And then, because right at that moment it didn't feel like I could stop talking even if I wanted to, I told him how Josie Fenton had called me at six o'clock on a warm summer's morning after she'd found her son cold and blue in his blue pyjamas. Wedged so hard against his bedroom door that she'd had to shove with her whole body weight to get it open, which meant that even though we'd never know for sure, maybe Jax had nearly made it. And how I sat on the floor outside my own son's bedroom door for an entire hour before I crept in to wake him with a kiss and blow his world apart. And how now all that was left of a best friend was a hole in a wall. And then, because it was eight forty-five and I was running out of time, I told Leonard about Norman's new plan.

'And I know it's only four weeks until the Edinburgh Fringe, and I'm probably going to have to read every phone book in Britain from cover to cover, and there's actually quite a bit less than a snowflake's chance in hell that I'm going to be able to deliver either of the big-ticket items on that plan, but by hell or high water, Leonard, I'm going to try.'

Now, I'm not saying my real life is anywhere near as interesting as three courses of shit food and a handful of has-beens going through each other's underwear drawers on the telly, but Leonard certainly seemed to be paying more attention than usual.

14

The thing about friends is that there are nearly always consequences to having them. Becoming friends with Leonard in
March had led to the deviation from my diversionary conversation tactics and the unexpected early-morning spilling of my guts
in July. Which led to him knowing about Norman's Plan. And
being an ex-army guy who clearly loved a plan, that led to him
wanting in on it. And I don't just mean a 'let's have a cheeky pot
of Egyptian tea when you come back and tell me all about it'
kind of thing. I mean all-the-way, hold-on-to-your-hat, I'm-
coming-with-you in on it. And the consequence of that was that,
all of a sudden, it became very real, very quickly.

Leonard's decision came the day after our slightly late early-
morning catch-up and about two minutes after he'd given Dennis
the riskiest finger yet. Right to his face, wrapped around the handle of the mop as he lifted it to swing it on to his shoulder. Dennis
was so focused on adjusting his hair in the reflection of the window and laughing at his own crack about how Leonard better
get over to Boots because they were having a two-for-one sale on
Depend he was oblivious.

I'd just about stopped chuckling and was back to rattling off some standard debtor-avoidance emails when Leonard walked past again, heading for the back door. As he nodded goodbye he dropped a folded-up piece of paper on my desk. With Dennis distracted by one of the mechanics asking how far they could get away with winding back the odometer on the Vauxhall Astra that had just come in, I unfolded the paper.

Cereal, oats, sugar, plain flour, cooking chocolate, bread, Hobnobs, madeira cake.

Aside from confirming that Leonard and Iris should probably reduce their carb intake, I wasn't quite sure what the list had to do with me. But, as with most things in life, when I turned it over and looked closer it made more sense. Underneath a phone number was a neat handwritten note.

Dear Sadie. I have given your Norman's plan a great deal of thought and I want to help, if you will allow me. I would be delighted to drive you to Edinburgh, as the Austin and I could both do with a good spin. I believe I can also help with certain other aspects of the plan. If you would be so good as to forward me your address by text to the mobile phone number above, I will call around this afternoon so that we may discuss the details.

Regards, Leonard

Just like our chats right up until the previous day, it looked like he didn't really need any input from me to have a meaningful conversation. And if it felt like his decision was all a bit sudden, for someone who could list staring down an insurgent rebellion in a jungle in Borneo on his resumé, a quick jaunt up to Edinburgh probably wasn't all that daunting.

On the other hand, for me, the more I thought about my hastily delivered promises to Norman, the more I realized that heading back to the scene of my conjugal crime with the key piece of evidence in tow had the potential to serve up the kind of consequences of which I'd never seen the like.

15

While I might have been able to kid myself with a little early-morning list-making, I'd really had next to no idea where to start on the plan. But once a certain ex-services octogenarian got involved it was more a case of where things were going to stop, because it turned out Leonard was a bit of a whizz with more than just a mop and a teapot.

He was waiting out the front of the house for me when I got home from work just after three thirty that same afternoon, as promised.

'Hello again! Twice in one day, how lovely. I've just parked there, if that's OK. Are you ready to get started?'

It was a very good question. And even though dredging up memories of some frankly inappropriate and questionable behaviour from my past was just about the last thing I wanted to do, over tea (PG Tips) and Hobnobs (sadly, always in plentiful supply since Jax died), it looked like that's exactly what Leonard had meant by 'certain other aspects'.

Judging by his eagerness, he'd clearly been more productive in a few hours than I'd been at work all day, unless you'd call getting through a six-month-old *OK! Magazine* easy sudoku in a personal best time of eight minutes a worthwhile achievement. And when he sat down at my kitchen table, pulled out a small silver laptop from his backpack and started tapping away at it like a court reporter, it was my first sign that judging a book by its cover definitely wasn't an option in Leonard's case. The second was the Excel spreadsheet labelled 'Finding Fathers' that appeared on the screen after a particularly dramatic flourish on the keyboard.

My surprise must have been obvious, and Leonard looked quite delighted about it.

'Tactical communications specialist in my army days, don't forget, my dear, so I've always been an old dog looking for new tricks. I've been part of the IT generation since 1977.' He pushed his glasses back on his nose and looked at me through the smudge of a fingerprint.

'Iris and I were selling the first Tandy TRS-80s out of our shop before most people in Penzance even knew what a personal computer was. Iris's idea, actually. Funny thing, though, she was never remotely interested herself. Pen and paper all the way it was for her, right up . . .' He trailed off and blinked rapidly a couple of times, removing his glasses and rubbing them absently on his sleeve. 'Well, I mean, why not, when you have handwriting as lovely as my Iris does? Anyhow, my dear, why don't you have a look at what I've done here?'

Which was precisely what I was afraid of doing.

I had a short-lived wave of relief when I saw that the Finding Fathers spreadsheet was actually just a lot of empty columns, before I realized the whole point was that I was supposed to be able to fill in all those missing details.

Name, phone number, location, probability, outcome. I did a double take on the last one and that initial relief took a sharp wrong turn into queasiness, which I don't think was from the six Hobnobs I'd stuffed into my mouth in quick succession. Outcomes. They were a bit like consequences. To be avoided at all costs, if you ask me.

Leonard's face remained neutral as he sat at the kitchen table nibbling on his first Hobnob, fingers poised over the keyboard, while I tried to coax information out of the murky depths of my memory into a world it was never meant to come into. I had no idea what was going through his head, but I was pretty sure that sifting through this calibre of sordid details wasn't exactly the kind of thing he was used to.

While it definitely took a while to warm to my task, after a bit, encouraged by a few more biscuits and with nowhere else to go, my mind reluctantly shuddered to a stop back at a shadowy time in Edinburgh in the months after my father's death. When, with nobody left to disappoint except myself, I'd headed boots and all down the path of self-destruction because, the way it looked to me, my father had already done the damage and I was merely tying up the loose ends. *You and me, Sadie. Us against the world, love.*

Considering the proportions of alcohol and food consumed during that brief period (lots of one and not very much of the other), with Leonard's encouragement I actually managed to dredge up more of a recollection than one might expect. And by one, I mean me, because in the end, despite more than a few stumbles around dead-end corners and several dark alleys I very hastily turned tail at before I got too far in, eventually my brain served me up some winners.

While the more names I came up with, the happier Leonard seemed to get (which was gratifying and embarrassing in equal measure), some deeper mental spadework weeded out a couple of clear non-starters. Even though the chances of Aldo the body-building steroid dealer from Latvia still being in the UK were slim anyhow, more importantly I remembered that the police had started banging on his van window before anything meaningless had actually taken place. The last time (which was very shortly after the first time) I saw him, he was running through the grounds of Edinburgh Castle with a sports bag full of illegal drugs and nary a backwards glance.

I also thought it safe to count out Taylor or Tyler, or it could even have been Jason, the beautiful brown-skinned St Lucian exchange student I'd met in a bar very late and very drunk one night after a Paul Weller concert. Because, while Paul was always going to be a hard act to follow, I think I can be fairly confident that whatever memories Taylor-Tyler-Jason might have tried his best to leave me with that evening, one of them wasn't going to be a peaches-and-cream-complexioned baby boy. So, after those couple of exemptions, that, I sincerely hoped, was that.

'Excellent work, Sadie, you've done brilliantly! That's stage one complete, I believe!'

It was all very well for Leonard to be so happy but, truth be told, I felt like I'd just gone two rough rounds with Dennis's hair in a premier kickboxing match. Here's what the first column on the spreadsheet looked like, although I should say that the descriptions were all in my head and definitely far better left there. A girl needs her pride and, no matter how non-judgemental and down with the IT crowd he was, I'm not sure Leonard was quite ready for the finer details.

Dan McLaughlin/McLachlan/McKintyre. Offensively good-looking law student who'd had a fight with his offensively good-looking girlfriend and slept with me after a party one night on the off-chance of making her jealous. A plan doomed to failure from the start. Obviously.

Tony Simmons. I sat next to him in English Lit. class for a while and accidentally slept with him after a particularly inspiring lecture involving the Brontë sisters. I'm not sure Emily and Charlotte would have approved of my behaviour, but no doubt Anne would have been cheering from the sidelines.

Adam Lindsay/Linley. Would-be professional footballer and part-time petty criminal. I'd met him through a friend of a friend and slept with him after I came home one night and found him waiting outside my halls of residence. He was looking for some pot someone had supposedly given me for safekeeping, which was possibly true and possibly not – almost anyone else's guess is better than mine. I do recall that when I woke up he was gone, and so was my toastie maker, possibly in lieu of the non-forthcoming pot. I'd be willing to bet that the probability of him being in jail now was a lot higher than that he was playing centre for-ward for Manchester United.

James Knox. Played double bass in a three-piece jazz band called Soft Knox. Corny, yes, but a very handy clue when it came to remembering the last name of a genuine stranger, charming though he had been. I slept with him after his band played a one-night gig at a pub where I worked in Edinburgh, for one night. The reasons for the second point are definitely related to the first, but I can't for the life of me remember how.

So there you had it. My conscience was cleared. Razed to the ground, in fact. Those four names or close tries, and in the correct chronological order, as it goes, were the definitive possibilities of Norman's parentage. Leonard made a few final keystrokes and turned the laptop to face me. The names on the spreadsheet came into sharp focus and I suddenly got the weirdest feeling.

Because I wasn't exaggerating when I said I never thought about who Norman's father might be. I mean, I really and truly *never* thought about it. Which I think you'll agree is a pretty impressive feat. On the other hand, it meant that seeing those names lined up neatly in their little columns, no jostling, all polite-like, was a bit of a shock, to be honest.

I was struck by the thought that now, for the first time in his life, I was going to have to face up to the fact that I had to share the credit for the miracle that is Norman. And I have to say, it wasn't a painless realization. I could feel the tentacles that had staked their claim in my stomach around the time of Jaxy's funeral begin to gather themselves in tighter. Because who the hell am I, if not Norman's entire family?

With unusually perfect timing, I heard the front door open and close softly and, seconds later, there he was. My entire family. Standing in the kitchen doorway with his school bag over one shoulder and tie askew over the other. Norman would probably be able to count on one hand the number of times he'd come home from school to find anything other than me and a hastily put-together snack waiting for him in the kitchen. Now he looked from me to Leonard and back again and, just for a nanosecond, a shadow of something other than sadness hovered nervously over his face. *It's just me now, Mum, isn't it?* I could sense them both waiting for me to say something and, somewhere deep inside, there was an almost imperceptible shift in my organs.

'Norman, this is Leonard . . . from work. Leonard, this is my

Norman. Leonard's going to . . . I told him about the plan and . . . well, he wants to help you . . . I mean . . . us . . .'

Norman stepped forward and offered his hand shyly to Leonard, who stood up from the table and took it gently in his. A couple of biscuit crumbs quivered on the old guy's chin, planning their next big move, and I felt an unexpected rush of affection.

'Well, I'm so very pleased to meet you at last, young man.' If he was shocked at the red-raw state of Norman's long-suffering little paw, he hid it well.

'Hello. I . . . you . . . I . . . I mean . . . really? You're going to help us . . . me . . . get to the Fringe? Honest? And is . . . is that your car out the front? Because that's the coolest car I've ever seen, Len . . . Leonard.' The shadow of the something else threw itself across my son's face and hung on for dear life as his tongue tried out the unfamiliar name.

I followed them out to the street and watched as Leonard gestured Norman into the driver's seat of the coolest of all cool cars. He sat there with his hands on the Austin's steering wheel and a rapt expression on his face as Leonard pointed out the polished wooden panelling and the dials on the dashboard. I looked at the top of the old man's head gently rising and ducking as he spoke, and it felt like the moment you hear the air hostess tell you to fasten your seatbelt and stow your tray table. And you know you've missed your last chance to get off the flight.

What did I think I was doing? What if this all goes completely and catastrophically wrong? What if all those guys on the spreadsheet have just disappeared off the face of the earth, or died, or moved to Australia? Or then again, what if we actually do find Norman's father and he turns out to be a heartless bastard who doesn't want anything to do with him? Could I take that kind of a risk with my already broken boy?

I felt the world slipping and I leaned into the doorway for support and felt my lids droop. As the turbulence inside me subsided, I opened my eyes. Leonard was holding the door open for Norman to step out of the Austin and, just for a split second, our eyes met over my son's head. I felt my nostrils tingle with the memory of sweet hibiscus tea and something else. *Hold on tight, Sadie. I've got you.*

16

NORMAN

First rule of comedy: Be you and nobody else but you.

It's probably for the best that I'm going to find out that Michael McIntyre and Frank Lampard aren't my dad. I mean, I never really and truly thought they were, they're just a couple of the suggestions Jax has come up with. P. Diddy is another, but I think he knew that one wasn't ever going to be true. Because Mum's never even been to America.

Jax reckons it's actually pretty cool not to know who your dad is because, when you think about it, that means it could be absolutely anyone. Like I could be walking down the street after school one day and some guy comes belting around the corner and runs right into me, and after he stops to say sorry and help me pick up my books, like in a movie, we say goodbye and never even know we're related. Which I actually think is about halfway between cool and weird.

Jax loves making up stuff about who my dad could be. Like, sometimes when we're over in Truro with Mum he'll see some guy coming towards us and without saying anything all of a sudden he'll give me the elbow and do this funny sideways look with his eyes and I know exactly what he's thinking. Or other times he'll do that thing with his hands like he's taking a photo of someone and whisper something like, just sayin', Norman. Then we crack up, because usually the guy he's pointing his hand camera at is totally no way no how ever going to be my dad. He even did it once to Mr Tilley when we were in the bakery getting sausage rolls, and that was one of the best ones ever. And if Mum ever says, what are you boys laughing about, Jax goes, we just breathed in some funny air, Sadie, you should try some.

Mum says you can look at most babies and it's hard to imagine their little faces growing up to be a teenager or a big hairy man, which she reckons is probably a good thing. But she says my face looked like me right from the start and I haven't changed at all. Except for getting lots of psoriasis. Which she didn't actually say, but it's true. I feel a bit bad that Mum doesn't know me and Jax sometimes talk about my dad, but I wouldn't want to hurt her feelings and make her think she wasn't doing a good enough job or anything. Because she is. She's totally the best at being a mum, it's just that sometimes I do wonder if there's a big hairy man walking around with a face like me.

Even when I'm not with Jax, every now and again I'll have a sneaky look around the chippie or the shop or the bus or wherever I am and play the game myself. But I always figured that unless I came across the perfect guy with wavy brown hair eating cheese on toast, watching a Dave Allen DVD and scratching his psoriasis I'd probably never even come close to knowing.

But isn't it funny about one never knows, because now there's a good chance maybe I will.

17

Sadie

Of course, Dennis refused to let Leonard take any time off. Anyone could see that coming, but especially me, because I had a ringside seat. I might even have seen Dennis's head twitch a little as Leonard walked up to my desk and asked for a leave form. I handed him one from the file and he filled it out in his lovely shaky cursive there and then. Two weeks, starting in three weeks. Then, without looking back, he walked over and knocked on the glass wall that separated my desk from Dennis's office. I'd long ago arranged a little bookshelf of catalogues and lever-arch files that was mercifully able to obscure at least two thirds of Dennis from my view, although, to be honest, nothing short of the Great Wall would be able to hide that hair. But I had to take what I could get.

Dennis took the form with no more than a fleeting glance, so whether he noticed it matched the dates of my already approved two weeks coinciding with Norman's school holidays that I'd had booked for a couple of months I don't know. I pulled out a couple of thick catalogues to create a little viewing tunnel and saw him lean back slowly in his chair and put both hands behind his immovable head of hair.

'Holidays, eh? Well, you know, Lenny, you can't just front up and expect to get holidays any time you feel like going back into retirement. I don't know how it worked back in the Dark Ages, but I'm running a business here. We can't allow you to drop everything and leave the loo walls to get splattered in shit just because you want a bit of a lie-in, can we?'

I didn't dare dismantle any more of my barrier, so Leonard was just a smudge at the edge of my vision. But his voice was clear as a bell.

'No, Dennis, of course not. I certainly understand the challenges of running a business, but it's three weeks until I require my leave and I have it on good authority that it's a simple task to get a temporary cleaner from an agency. And regarding your other point, I'm happy to say that, in all my months of employment at Pearl's, I've not yet once encountered any excrement on the walls. Your employees are to be commended for their aim.'

I had to duck my head swiftly to disguise my snort, but even without a direct eye-line I could sense Dennis bristling and his bouffant swung in my direction. I dropped my head lower and banged my forehead on the desk. I knew he could really only be bothered bullying Leonard if he thought he had an audience, and presumably he gave up on me because the dead air that was oozing out of the office would have taken a chainsaw to get through.

In fact, it was so quiet I got a little worried and risked sneaking another look. Dennis was just sitting there, not moving, and from what I could see of Leonard, which was really only a few inches of side profile, he was just standing there. He was staring so intently in Dennis's direction that for a second or two I wondered if he might have had a mini-stroke or something. It was clearly off-putting for Dennis as well, because he was the first to break.

'What the hell, Leonard? What are you gawping at? Look, I haven't got time for this. Request denied, OK? Now piss off and go and finish cleaning the bogs.'

He flicked the holiday-leave form back in Leonard's direction and it slid off the table and wafted down on to the floor. I swear, from that moment, life took its cue and everything else went into slow motion as well.

Leonard looked down at the leave form lying on the floor and Dennis looked at Leonard looking at the form. Then Leonard looked up at Dennis looking at him and Dennis turned his head and looked over at me. It was clear the jig was up so I gave up hiding and looked at Leonard. Then Leonard bent down to pick up the form, at which point Dennis appeared to lose interest and started rustling through some papers on his desk.

Then really, really slowly, even slower than the already slow motion, Leonard straightened himself up and at the same time raised his right hand. The one without the holiday-leave form in it. I swear my heart stopped and I didn't need to breathe any more as I watched him uncurl his gnarly old hand at a snail's pace and elegantly present Dennis with an actual, beautifully executed, in-the-flesh finger. Then he dropped the leave form on the desk, turned heel on his pristine white Nike trainers, gave me a wink on the way through and headed straight out the back of the building.

When I dared to look back at Dennis he was still sitting at his desk, open-mouthed. Even his hair looked shocked. It took a few more seconds before he came to and started scrambling out of his chair, papers, coffee cups and hair shooting every which way as he lunged for the door.

'You're finished, Leonard, you old buzzard! Do you hear me? You'd better not think you're coming back here. You just earned yourself a permanent holiday. Nobody gives Dennis Pearl the finger and gets away with it!'

But I could already hear the click and whirr of the Austin's starter motor turning over. By the time Dennis made it out to the car park my hero was long gone. The crowd in my heart went wild.

18

I definitely felt bad about Leonard losing his job because of us, but I cheered up when he told me that after he'd left Pearl's he'd driven straight over to the Age UK office and reported Dennis for workplace bullying. His case worker had assured him his pension wouldn't be affected, and that whenever he felt he'd sufficiently recovered from the trauma they'd find him another, more appropriate working environment.

'I've always found that, if you allow it, the universe provides you with exactly what you need at precisely the right time, don't you agree, Sadie?'

I had about as much faith in the unseen power of the universe as I did in the supposed hand of God, but I was certainly more than a little jealous of Leonard's escape from Dennis and the car yard. And by the time (under strict accountant's orders and to Dennis's unmitigated disgust) I'd bank-transferred Leonard's final wages, including, ironically, a couple of weeks' accrued holiday pay, I stopped feeling bad and started wondering if I, and possibly the universe, had actually done him quite the favour.

The other thing was that with no job to slow him down

Leonard was able to work full time on getting things happening on Norman's plan. Which was a bit of a novelty because, if I'm honest, getting things happening is not something I'm used to. Usually any big ideas I have only last just slightly longer than the realization that I may have to get off the sofa and contribute in order for them to progress. So, you know, not long.

Consequently, I was a little taken aback when Leonard arrived on our doorstep again on the Sunday morning of the week he'd left Pearl's. He'd woken me from a very deep sleep and a dream in which I was being chased along the Penzance seafront by a giant inflatable pointing finger attached to a shock of bouffant hair with a floating thought bubble above it that said *Bad Mother* in huge black letters. I'd managed to tackle the finger and was bashing away, trying to deflate it, but every time I hit it there was a noise like a doorbell being jabbed hard and insistently, and even in the dream all I could think was, *Jax is back.*

Only of course it wasn't Jax at the door, it was Leonard, and the part of me that was still a little bit asleep felt a stab of disappointment. My heart hurt, I mean *actually* physically hurt, whenever I thought about Jax, so I kept myself very busy trying hard not to let him into my head. But when he did get in it was like a sharp current that just kept on stabbing at my temples over and over. Just like Jax himself, really.

Leonard was way too polite to mention that a better mother would probably have been up before ten o'clock, even if it was a Sunday. But I did see him shoot a startled glance at my hair, which I knew from experience could give Dennis's a run for its money after a restless night.

'Oh dear, I'm terribly sorry if I woke you, Sadie. I . . . I did text when I left home to say I was on my way, as we arranged earlier in the week, or at least . . . oh dear, well, I . . . I thought I did . . .'

He started fiddling with the very new-looking iPhone he had in his hand as if to check, but while I genuinely had no memory of said text, it would be totally unsurprising to me if I'd completely forgotten. So I just made a half-hearted attempt to pat down my hair, shooed away his apology and stepped aside to let him in. I busied myself getting teabags out of the canister and when I flicked on the kettle it was still slightly warm from the cup Norman had brought me an hour or so earlier.

'Mum, Mum, I'm just going down to do the rocks. I've got my phone, I'll be back later, OK?' Even his whisper sounded like it was fading away these days.

To be honest, even though I half woke up and opened my eyes just enough to register that Norman had a warm enough jacket on and wasn't going out in his pyjamas, I wasn't sure that it truly was OK.

Whenever Jax stayed over on a Saturday night, which was almost every week, the next morning the boys would get up early and walk the hundred metres from our house down to the beach. They'd search the shingle beach for the perfect rocks among all those millions the low tide exposed every day, then, in a perfectly chosen spot just back from the water's edge, they'd spend excruciating aeons taking turns to balance them on top of each other. With boyish gruesomeness, they loved the fact that no matter how much work they put in and how high they got their little Zen stone stack, within a few hours it was doomed to obliteration by a wave anyhow.

Josie Fenton told me that one morning, when she'd gone down to collect Jax to go to a family brunch, she'd stood up on the road and watched the boys for about twenty minutes without them knowing. Seeing Jax patiently and tenderly encouraging Norman when it was his turn, and his intense concentration and considered movements as he balanced his own carefully selected rocks, it was the first time she'd dared to think there was a chance that maybe her husband, the teachers and an entire street full of angry neighbours just might be wrong about her son.

The last I'd heard, their record was eighteen high, but my only defence on Sunday mornings now when I started to think about Norman trying to balance those little piles of rocks on his own was to put the pillow over my head and go back to sleep.

Leonard sat himself down at the kitchen table and took his laptop out of his backpack. He opened it up, tapped a few keys then folded his hands in his lap and waited. I placed a cup of tea down in front of him and took a casual look over his shoulder at the screen. Despite up until then still having been vaguely daydreaming about being back in bed, suddenly I was very much awake.

A pair of familiar eyes stared back at me from the computer, brown, kind and unblinking. Only, after a closer look, I decided I was wrong and it couldn't be Norman, because I was pretty sure that last time I checked he hadn't grown a twirly handlebar moustache and sideburns. Also, this guy's skin was very smooth, without any traces of psoriasis, and he was wearing a fringed suede jacket and a top hat, both of which I could be fairly confident Norman didn't own. I shook my head and blinked hard so I could have another run at whatever it was I was looking at.

'Um, Leonard . . . what's . . . ? Is this supposed to be Norman's father? Did you . . . find one already? Because I . . . I have to say I really don't think . . . I mean, I think I'd remember this guy.'

'No, no, no, Sadie, look again!' Which was a bit hard because, as he said that, he actually zoomed the screen out so the face got smaller. 'It's Norman himself, in digital disguise!'

The computer screen was now totally filled and I realized I was looking at some kind of a promotional poster. Above the image of my twelve-year-old son masquerading as a middle-aged man I could see some words in a fancy scroll font. *Norman Foreman, Little Big Man of Comedy.* As I leaned forward over Leonard's shoulder to get a closer look, the longer I stared, the closer my jaw got to the floor.

The scene was an American Wild West-style bar and I could see now that Norman's big fake-moustachioed head was attached to a tiny cartoon body that was bursting out between two wooden saloon doors. Behind them, I could see a Calamity Jane type featuring my head leaning on the bar, and there was a horse with Leonard's face tethered out the front of the saloon. Everywhere I looked there was something else taken out of any sane context and dropped into this crazy imaginary scene. There was the Austin Maxi on top of the saloon's roof, there was Eric Morecambe sitting quietly drinking a whisky at the bar, there was my father, even, hunched over at a table, laughing into a bowl of peanuts. And just when I thought I'd seen it all, right down in the bottom-left-hand corner, waiting patiently outside the saloon, was a small white dog with Jax's smiling face balancing on its furry shoulders. My heart fell into Leonard's teacup and did a few seconds of boiling backstroke. It was completely ridiculous and I had no idea what it was supposed to be, but somehow it was also absolutely, totally, out-of-this-world wonderful.

'Leonard. This is so . . . it's amazing. Really. Where did you get . . . and how did you . . . I mean, did you do this? How do you know how to . . . ?'

Leonard put up his hand to bat away my praise, but I could see a tinge of pink rising up from underneath the collar of his shirt. He sat up a little bit straighter in the chair and I got a faint waft of clean laundry.

It turned out Leonard's mother had instilled in him an ethos that learning was a lifelong commitment. She herself had learned to speak French at the ripe old age of ninety-two, despite the fact that, crippled and confined to her bed in a studio flat, she had no hope of ever making it to Paris to put her perfectly conjugated verbs into practice. And so, even though Leonard could take apart and rebuild any television, toaster, radio or mobile phone on the face of the planet, since his retirement he'd honoured his mother by showing up for every free adult-education course the Penzance Community Centre offered, as well as quite a few others around the county as well.

So now he knew more about wedding-cake icing, woodwork, Photoshop, welding, online marketing, calligraphy, genealogy, short mat bowls, soy candle-making, screen-printing and how to cook a proper Spanish paella than his mother could ever have dreamed. And even though he knew some of the younger people on those free courses were really only there so they wouldn't get their benefits cut off, the joke was on them, because they were still learning.

'How wonderful is that, Sadie? Lifelong learning! I did this all thanks to Photoshop for Beginners, first three Wednesday evenings in March. Week two, the magnetic lasso tool! It's an extraordinary thing! Oh, and I asked Norman for some photos to use when I was here the other evening, I . . . I hope you don't mind. So . . . you like it then, my dear?'

I more than liked it. I loved it. And as for minding, I was so busy loving it I totally forgot to worry about what it was for. Anyway, Leonard wasn't waiting around for an answer.

In between proudly zooming in and out of the screen to show me some of the details, he explained that Little Big Man was a reference to a 1970s movie he and Iris loved that starred Dustin Hoffman trying to pass himself off as a half-pint Native American who was very small but also very brave.

'Your Norman put me in mind of that name as soon as I met him, Sadie. Don't you think?' Well, I did, yes, although I had no idea what it had to do with his potential comedy career. But it turned out there was at least some measure of method to Leonard's madness.

After spending a week researching the Edinburgh Fringe, Leonard had discovered that, being what's known as an open-access festival, you didn't actually need anyone's permission to perform. But the problem was finding a time slot in an appropriate participating venue in order to put on a proper show, as opposed to just setting up on a street corner. And, despite sending more than fifty emails to various places on the official festival list, as well as quite a few others that weren't, Leonard had not yet had any responses to his attempts to get Norman a performance slot. Which I didn't find the least bit surprising and is, quite frankly, the point I would have given up, if it were left to me. But not Leonard. The Fringe opened in two weeks, so with time ticking he'd decided to create Little Big Man in order to rustle up some interest.

'USP, Sadie. Unique selling point! Marketing for Small Businesses, Friday evenings in February. Or was it March? I don't suppose it matters. We need to make Norman stand out from the crowd if we're going to find him a venue at this late stage. So I thought, well now, who wouldn't be intrigued by someone called Little Big Man?'

Now, if that's not harnessing the power of free adult-education courses at its finest, I don't know what is. But I soon realized I hadn't seen anything yet. Leonard had also made a Facebook page for Little Big Man (Social Media for Beginners, last Saturday in

January) and, even though my lack of knowledge about social media is in direct correlation to my lack of enthusiasm for real-life social interaction, I took a guess that having 267 followers wasn't bad for something that was a) only a few days old, and b) a total fabrication.

'Leonard, how . . . I mean, who are all those, um . . . followers. The people?'

'Aha, well, it's very easy to make friends and influence people on Facebook, Sadie. Nothing like real life at all, is it? Nine pounds ninety-five for 250 likes! I did the research and I understand that's excellent value to make Little Big Man look like a very popular young chap!'

All I understood was that I probably owed Leonard a tenner, but beyond that, how Facebook likes worked, or why in fact they mattered, was beyond me. And I'm sure I'd had better things to do on the last Saturday in January than find out. But all of a sudden this was starting to feel a little bit like a runaway train, with Leonard adjusting the driver's hat as he chattered excitedly on.

'Tomorrow I'll start to make regular entries and . . . that is, I mean, err . . . posts, on the Facebook page, using the poster I made, some comedy videos and lots of other things concerning the festival. So very quickly it'll look like Norman has, um . . . what they call a profile. Then, when someone from one of the Fringe venues I've contacted takes a look, they'll know he's serious and no doubt offer him a slot!' *Toot toot!*

In fact, I had plenty of doubts, but for once in my life I decided to keep my mouth shut. Which turned out to be wise, because Leonard was already steaming ahead to the next level crossing.

'Right then, Sadie, I believe we're ready to start work on stage two. Take a seat next to me here.'

Honestly, the old guy was positively radiant. All I really wanted to know was when Sundays had turned into the busiest day of the week. I took a seat. And a deep breath.

When Leonard opened up the Finding Fathers spreadsheet I could see it had come along quite a bit. Where previously there'd just been empty spaces in the columns next to the names I'd prised from my memory, now each had multiple phone numbers and locations, as well as several thumbnail-sized photos lined up beside them. Except for Dan McLaughlin/McLachlan/McKintyre's line, which had about twenty photos and a whole jumble of phone numbers and place names. I saw Stockport, Alcester and Kidderminster before I needed to close my eyes. I got a good grip on the edge of the kitchen table and forced myself to open them again. Shit. Was this really happening? *Hold on tight.*

'OK. Hardest first,' said Leonard, clicking on the images beside Dan. Immediately, multiple faces filled the screen in a veritable smorgasbord of potential Dans, which Leonard lined up neatly, side by side. I was finding it hard to focus with so many choices and for a brief moment I drifted off and wondered if it was possible I'd slept with them all.

'Can you see him there? The right Dan?'

Leonard's voice brought me back to the job at hand and I pictured myself walking slowly along this virtual line-up in a real-life police station, hands behind my back, staring through the glass. I imagined stopping and examining their faces in detail, taking my time to make sure I made the right decision, then slowly raising a scrawny finger to point and say, 'That's him, he's the one!' And then the guy running forward with his arms open, shouting, 'I have a son, I have a son!'

But it wasn't like that at all, because Dan McLachlan (as it turned out) hadn't changed a bit. He still looked like the same handsome law student he'd been more than a decade ago, with just a little bit of manly wear and tear around the edges. Which got me wondering just how much wear and tear I'd accrued since my university days. As a distraction from thinking about that, I amused myself by doing the scrawny-finger-point thing at the photo of the real Dan.

'Yes? That's him?' Leonard was absolutely delighted. 'Aha! Excellent!'

I peered into Dan's slightly older, still very arrogant face (oh yes, it was all coming back to me now), searching for a sign. Because, and it's not just that he was the first on the list and looked like he'd aged well, even with my limited memory it seemed like he'd be a front-runner, if we're playing the probability game. Because he'd stayed the weekend, if you get my drift. I searched older Dan's blue eyes and perfectly shaped ears intently, but I couldn't find a thing that reminded me of Norman.

Leonard slotted the winning Dan into the spreadsheet next to his name and began dispensing with the others, which was a shame, because a couple of them looked quite nice. As their faces disappeared from the screen I thought how lovely it might be to just choose a few more of them for a set and be done with it. But Leonard was already back to the spreadsheet, deleting like a man possessed and sending the losing Dans' details into the abyss. Before I could even come to terms with the loss, he'd opened up another window on his computer.

'Google Maps, Sadie!'

He sounded so proud I wondered if he might have invented it and, frankly, at this point it wouldn't have surprised me. I only had a passing notion as to what one did with a Google Map, because I couldn't actually remember the last time I'd gone any-where I hadn't already gone a hundred times before. But all those little flags and bubbles looked impressive and I did at least recognize a map of the UK when I saw it.

Leonard's fingers were almost smoking as he copied something from the winning Dan's column, flicking from the spreadsheet to Google Maps. Next minute, a little red flag popped up on the map and even I understood what had just happened. If I wasn't mistaken, that little red flag was the very location of Dan McLachlan, the lucky man behind door number one.

I looked closer at the map and saw with a mild shock that Dan's flag was staked in Barnstaple, which was only about two and a half hours' drive away. Bloody hell, now wouldn't that be weird. Wouldn't that just take the piggin' biscuit, as Jax would say.

But while I was busy considering that if Dan was 'the one' then perhaps we could call the whole trip off with just an outing to Barnstaple and forget about the Fringe, Leonard had moved on to the next set of thumbnails.

Tony Simmons and I had sat beside each other in the same seats for a month's worth of English Lit. classes, so I was fairly confident I'd recognize him. Funny what you do remember, but we fell into the same position as those lectures after we'd fumbled our way through things that one and only afternoon in his single bed. I'm not sure if I ever actually saw him from the other side, so a profile picture would probably have made things even easier. Left, as it goes. But there were only three pictures to choose from, and even with a front view and his face half obscured by somebody else's pint, picking the correct Tony Simmons was a cinch. Once I'd confirmed his identity, Leonard went through his Google Map routine again and real Tony's possible whereabouts were duly pinpointed. Swansea. Wales. Not so close this time.

As it turned out, though, it looked like I'd chosen a pretty unadventurous bunch for my six weeks or so of mayhem and one-night stands, because if Leonard and Google were to be trusted, all four of them had ended up within a five-hundred-mile radius of Edinburgh. James Knox, the musician, looked like he might even still be there. Even though Leonard said he couldn't be quite sure, he had found a mobile phone number on a forum that the James in the photo I positively identified had been on looking to buy a second-hand Vespa in Edinburgh a year ago. Which gave me a bit of an indication as to how his musical career had panned out, because you don't see too many successful jazz musos lugging their double bass around on the back of a moped, do you?

It was mildly disappointing, because I'd kind of hoped that, if we had to do this, we'd at least end up tracking one of the possible fathers to a restored villa in Tuscany, tragically but very conveniently widowered and living with four beautiful Italian half-brothers and -sisters just dying to meet Norman. All in all, though, Leonard's work was pretty damn impressive and the absence of a Tuscan villa certainly wasn't down to a lack of effort on his part.

'Leonard, I can't believe . . . the photos, the locations and phone numbers and . . . all of it. How . . . I wouldn't even have known where to start. I mean, I know I probably should have kept up with all that sort of stuff for . . . for Norman's sake, but I just . . . and then, well . . .' I trailed off, losing interest in my own excuses, but Leonard was either too excited or tactful to care.

'Oh, well, certainly Trace Your Family History Tuesdays from back in October last year helped, but it's all out there online these days, Sadie. Extraordinary, really. LinkedIn, Facebook, forums, BT Yellow Pages – all of it. You did the hard part by remembering the names.' *Not wrong there.*

'But after that it was just a matter of patience and persistence. I didn't even have to leave the comfort of my desk, and now look what we've done! Extraordinary!' Indeed.

Leonard and I sat there staring at Google Maps with its four little perky red flags as the dregs in our teacups went cold. I've absolutely no doubt we were thinking about very different things; in fact, for a few minutes there Leonard looked like he'd drifted off to somewhere else altogether. But there it was. Barnstaple, Swansea, Bournemouth, Edinburgh. As a pilgrimage, it was hardly exotic, and even as a holiday itinerary it sounded highly unlikely.

I heard a rustle of movement at the back door, and there was Norman, hair all over the place, jacket tied around his waist and forehead red raw and blazing from his nemesis and the wind. His eyes went to straight to the laptop, taking in the spreadsheet, the photos and the Google Map with its little red flags, which, for all I knew, made perfect sense to him.

'Did we . . . did we find someone? One of the guys? My . . . the dads, Mum? Did we, Leonard?'

See what I mean? I looked over at Leonard, who all of a sudden had to tie a shoelace, then at the computer screen and back to Norman. The world ground to a halt and I knew the answer I gave here and now was going to rock both our worlds. *I've got you, Sadie.*

'We found them all, son. We fucking found them all.'

Norman sat down hard on the floor of the kitchen with a stunned look on his face. Leonard let out an embarrassed cough and his head bounced up and hit the table. I just sat there and wondered if there was any chance of me going back to bed for the rest of my life.

19

NORMAN

First rule of comedy: Easy is for pussies.

Leonard said it didn't matter that he hadn't heard back from any of the venues at the Fringe before we left, because it was just a matter of time before someone gave me a spot to do my show. Leave it to the universe, Norman, and the universe will oblige, is what he also said.

As soon as I met Leonard I knew that if anyone could get me and Mum to the Fringe it'd most likely be him. He reckons if you believe nothing is set in stone, then you can believe change is always possible. And I reckon that just really means that one never knows.

There were some things Leonard didn't leave to the universe though, and he came up with a genius plan for me to get some proper practice in before the Fringe. Not just in front of the mirror or Mum or Jax like usual, but with a real audience at real pubs where they let you get up and have a go on stage. Open mics, they're called. Leonard did a lot of googling and found one in all the places where we're going to stop and maybe meet my dad, and even though it made our trip look a bit wonky on the map so we could end up in the right place on the right night, Leonard said that was OK because the road to success is never straight. Which makes a lot of sense, and I reckon it also proves that Leonard might be the best googler in the world.

Absolutely anyone's allowed to get up at an open mic night, so I was thinking that maybe there'd be at least one or two other people that needed the practice as much as me. Although I knew I probably shouldn't really count on that.

Whenever I thought about the actual standing up there and doing jokes on my own in front of a pub-load of strangers I felt pretty scared. But Leonard reckoned that was a good thing, because if I could get as much of the scared feeling out of the way as I could, by the time I got to the Fringe there wouldn't be so much left inside me. He said that's what he used to do when he was a soldier when he had to do stuff like sneak through the jungle in the middle of the night with a bunch of enemy soldiers asleep just a few metres away. Which sounds pretty scary. And even though secretly I was thinking that there probably wasn't going to be enough open mics in the whole of England and Scotland put together to get rid of the amount of scared I had inside of me, I figured if it worked for Leonard it was worth a try.

Before Mum saw the new plan and decided we were going to make it come true I never had to think about how it would really and truly feel to have to get up and try and do comedy without Jax. But then suddenly it was only a week until we left and I had to think about it pretty much all the time. Even though I've got the best mum in the world and she sat there and listened to my jokes every single morning and every single afternoon to try and help me, even when she already knew the punchlines, how much I missed Jax got in the way quite a lot.

Sometimes when it got in the way so much that my skin started itching like it was going to turn itself inside out, I'd go down to the beach and sit there and try to guess the distance between the horizon and infinity, like me and Jax used to, which made me feel a bit better. Also, when I was sitting on the beach it felt like there was still the smallest chance that Jax might creep up behind me and hit me in the head with a massive sand ball, like he used to. And then lie there doing sand angels on the beach, cracking up laughing because he got me again. *Gotcha again, Normie-boy! You'll never learn! Woohoo, I'm the best, sand balls to the rest!*

I'll tell you something though. Most of the time I actually did know when he was coming because I could see his shadow coming out of the corner of my eye way before he got there. But I never said. Because getting hit in the head with a sand ball by Jax is about the best fun you could ever have.

Once when I was on the beach waiting for the sand ball that's never going to come and trying not to think about how much I missed Jax, I wondered how I'd feel if one of my arms got cut off and whether that'd feel worse. I decided missing Jax still hurt more and then even when I worked my way through all my major body parts it was the same for everything. So then I thought about trying to do a deal with God. Just in case. Because I thought maybe he'd consider swapping one of my eyes, or a couple of arms, or a leg or two in exchange for bringing Jax back. Or both eyes and an ear even. I got the deal right down to me being a blind, deaf, no-talking torso sitting on the beach and I still decided that would be OK if only I could have Jaxy back sitting next to me.

But it didn't look like God was in the mood for deals that day, or else Mum is right. Because when I went home I still had all my body parts and Jax was still dead. And I still had to finish the plan without him.

*

I reckon me without Jax is like Morecambe without Wise or Abbott without Costello or, worst of all, Vic without Bob. Me and Jax were perfect together because I was the one that set him up for all the good lines and he was the one who picked them up and ran with them. Sometimes he ran so fast and so far away with them I couldn't keep up, but he always made it fun to try. And trying is the only way that anyone ever gets anything done, Jax says.

'Just try, you teeny tiny flucker,' he always says. Which he reckons doesn't count as swearing because it isn't his fault if people can't listen properly. And the thing is, being with Jax always makes me want to try, even though probably more than half the time the things he makes me try aren't the best idea. But they're always the most fun. So even when I was laughing so hard at the teeny tiny flucker thing I thought I'd pee, I'd always try to do whatever it was he was trying to make me do.

If you want a for instance, it's like the time we were nine and he made me squeeze through the one broken paling gap in our back fence to pick some of Mrs Egerton's roses for Mum, with him pushing my bum with his foot to get me through and going come on you little flucker, you can do it. I made it too, but then when I had to try to squeeze back through that one paling gap without his foot to help me on the other side Jax said that the sight of half my head, one leg and one arm sticking through the fence holding a rose out in front of me was the funniest thing he'd ever seen in his life.

He also said just try, you teeny tiny flucker, when we were ten and I'd said I couldn't get up in front of a couple of the bigger kids at school and do our version of a Peter Cook and Dudley Moore 'Derek and Clive' sketch. But then I tried and even though he did all the hard work and I just fed him the lines, we did it.

And that was the only time we'd ever been able to make those kids really laugh hard and not just because Jax swore a lot.

The teachers didn't laugh though, when they heard. We got detention for a month, but boy was it worth it. Mum even said she was proud of me because it reminded her of something Grandad would have done. So every day for a month when we were sat there in detention doing extra homework I didn't even care. Because even though it was really, really hard for me, I'd tried and done it. And because who wouldn't want to be compared to an almost famous comedian like my grandad?

Anyhow, that's how I knew that no matter how much I missed Jax I had to try and make our plan come true. Because now he's not ever going to get to do it himself. I didn't know how I was going to make a double act work with just me, and I didn't know how I was going to make a proper audience laugh like a couple of Year 8s laughing at Derek and Clive, Jaxy style. And there's no way I knew how I was going to be brave enough to meet four guys who've never seen me before in their life because there's a chance they might be my dad. But I knew this teeny tiny flucker was going to try.

20

First rule of comedy: Get all your ducks in a row.

Leonard showed up on the dot of eight on the day of our trip, which is exactly when he thought he'd said he'd be there.

'Here I am, Norman! Eight I said and eight I meant. Time to get this show on the road!'

Me and Mum didn't tell him, but it was definitely the dot of nine he'd said really. But Mum ran off to get out of her pyjamas before Leonard saw her and she whispered to me that it was always better to be too early than too late and it just meant our adventure would be starting a whole hour earlier. Which was kind of nice of her to say really, because I knew she was actually pretty worried about the trip.

It was kind of a big deal that Leonard was going to drive us all the way to Edinburgh, Mum said, because he'd even got the sack so he could do it. That part made me feel a bit bad, but Leonard said not to worry because he'd just been waiting for the universe to give him a sign that he should leave Pearl's car yard anyway.

'And if you aren't that sign, Norman my boy, well, I don't know what is!'

I love the way Leonard talks. He doesn't sound like anyone else I know because his voice sort of makes you feel like you're listening to music. It goes up and down and round in circles and you're always waiting for the next word to see where it's going to land. And even though I hadn't known him long I'd already decided that he might possibly be the third coolest person in the world. After Jax and Mum.

Leonard's car is vintage, which means it was made back in the olden days in 1971 and it also means it's definitely the coolest car in the world. It's kind of small, though, and by the time we got our bags and a big box of groceries in the boot (just in case, Mum said) there wasn't much chance of Leonard seeing too much out the back window. He didn't seem to be too bothered about it, though, when I mentioned it.

'Well, you could be right, Norman,' he goes. 'But why do I need to see what's back there? We're going forward and every-thing we want is in front of us.' Isn't that cool?

He didn't even look behind him when he said back there. He just jerked his head in the direction of behind him and jiggled his eyebrows a bit. Which made me realize that I don't just like the way he talks, I also really like the way he thinks.

I also realized that it probably wasn't going to take us too long to get to Barnstaple, which was our first stop, because straight away I noticed that Leonard drives pretty fast. When we got out on the motorway it felt like we were on the dodgems or something because of the car being so small and going so fast. It was excel-lent. I did see Mum grab on to the edge of her seat, though, every time Leonard swerved in between the other cars to change lanes, and even though I could only see one side of her face, that one side didn't look very happy. But I decided right then and there that Jax would have totally loved Leonard, and especially his driving.

When I looked up ahead between Mum and Leonard I could see the M5 stretching out for forever, but when I turned around and looked behind all I could see was the top of my case with one arm of Grandad's jacket sticking out the zipper and the smallest little bit of sky through the back window. And I knew Leonard was right because it was kind of like Penzance wasn't even there any more and we were starting from zero.

Even though Leonard's driving didn't get any slower, Mum relaxed a bit when he turned on the radio and it was Oasis playing. Mum knows the words to every single one of their songs because she's got all their CDs and she reckons they were one of the best bands ever. She also says Noel Gallagher is really just a misunderstood little boy in a pop star's body and not the you-know-what-hole everybody thinks he is. Mainly because she reckons that nobody who can write lyrics like he can could be all bad and I think I agree with that.

Listening to Leonard have a go at trying to keep up while Mum and Liam and Noel sang about the wheels of their life slowly falling off was my favourite part of leaving Penzance. It was so funny that I half joined in singing too, and for nearly the whole second half of the song I forgot that soon I was going to have to get up all by myself and try to make people laugh and I forgot that we were on our way to maybe find my dad. I even forgot that Jax was gone. Mum just kept on singing every single word perfectly and me and Leonard tried to sing a few bits in between, but then suddenly out of nowhere Jax's face popped into my head, coughing and wheezing and turning a funny shade of blue. So then I had to stop singing.

Mum and Leonard stopped too, and I don't know what they

were thinking about, but while I was looking out the window at all the cows and trees and paddocks whizzing past I was thinking, well, how weird was that, that I'd actually forgotten to be sad for a few minutes. But then I started to feel really bad because I didn't want that to mean I was forgetting about Jax, so I closed my eyes and thought about being happy and being sad and how sometimes there's a million miles between them and other times there's none at all. And then Mum was shaking me awake and we were in Bude, which was a whole seventy-five miles away. Or maybe a million.

Leonard said he had to run a short errand so Mum said she'd go and get us all some sandwiches, but I decided I should start going through my jokes to get ready for the first open mic, which was at a pub not quite in Barnstaple but not too far away. Because even though I had a shoebox full up with all the loads of jokes me and Jax had written down on Post-it notes and other bits of paper, I still didn't have half a clue how to put them all together to make a show that was anything like funny.

Me and Jax called the shoebox the Comedy Pot because ideas go in and then we'd stir them around and throw in a few more things, like cool outfits and timing and strategic pauses, and then a serving of funny comes out. At least it did when Jax was around.

I'd been using the Comedy Pot as a footrest ever since we left Penzance, not just because I wanted a footrest but also so it wouldn't get lost in the boot with all our other stuff. But when I opened it up and spread all the Post-it notes and paper and crumpled-up brown sandwich bags out on the back seat of Leonard's car it just looked like someone had tipped over the bins. And then I started worrying because what if all our jokes were actually rubbish? Then the scabs on my arms and legs and forehead all started itching at the same time and just when I was thinking that I better start concentrating on not scratching, Jax popped up.

First things first, Normie boy. Get all your ducks in a row is what he said. Jax reckons that getting all your ducks in a row is the first rule of comedy because it's when you figure out the order of how you tell your jokes. The first joke is the most important one, because if you don't get people laughing from the start it's like pushing dog poo uphill from there, he says. And the last joke is the second most important one because that's probably the only one anyone will actually remember. Then you've just got to make all the ones in between fit in and be as funny as you can along the way.

I guess I kind of knew Jax wasn't really talking to me and it was probably just my brain playing a not too funny joke on me, but I did have a quick look over my shoulder anyway. Because I couldn't help it and also, one never knows. Anyhow he wasn't there so I started sorting out all the bits of paper and Post-its from the Comedy Pot so I could get all my ducks in a row. Some of them just had one word on, like *doughnut* or *chicken*, and I had to think really hard to try and remember what they meant. But some of them were so good I didn't need to try at all. Like the back of a bus ticket that said, *Land's End, asthma puffer, old guy with sausage roll, fart*. That one was easy because me and Jax had both agreed on the bus home that it had been one of the coolest and funniest days of our whole school holidays.

After a while of unfolding and sorting the notes I had piles of funny, really funny, extra funny and maybe not so funny after all and it was getting quite hard to keep them all separate. Every time there was a bit of wind a few pieces of paper blew on to another pile or on to the floor of the car and I'd have to sort them again. Which was pretty annoying, and also the itching was getting quite bad so what I really wanted to do more than anything else was just sit there and scratch my skin to smithereens.

I knew I was what Jax calls getting my Y-fronts in a tangle and I was concentrating so hard on trying not to let them that I didn't even notice that Leonard had come back. He was leaning against the side of the next car that was parked beside the Austin and he goes, what you need are some bulldog clips, young man, and then he started rummaging around in his coat pocket. He pulled out a notepad, his iPhone, heaps of pencils, some paracetamol, a few plasters, a manky packet of Mentos and then just when I thought, well, the next thing coming out of there's going to be a kitten, or a ham sandwich, would you believe it, out came six mini bulldog clips attached to each other in a little chain.

Leonard didn't even look surprised. Like he knew they were in there all the time, just waiting for the day when he finally needed them, which was today. Then he opened the car door, gave me the bulldog clips and just goes, there you are, sir, now budge over and let's get these piles sorted before we head off.

21

Sadie

From what I could remember about Dan McLachlan, Barnstaple didn't seem like the kind of place I would have expected him to end up. But then again, I think we've established I really didn't have much to base any real theories on. As we screeched into town on two wheels, or at least way too fast for my liking, I got out the printed and laminated itinerary that was exactly where it should have been in the green plastic document folder Leonard had prepared. I ran my finger down the accommodation column and cross-matched it with Barnstaple in the destination column. What a system.

'Toad Hall Bed and Breakfast, 108 Albert Walk,' I read out. 'Right, everyone, keep your eyes peeled.'

But of course, there was no way Leonard was going to leave any part of the plan to chance or human error. He fumbled around in his inside jacket pocket and pulled out his iPhone, which he passed over the back of his seat to Norman, without taking his eyes off the road.

'Norman, I've got the Google Map already prepared for Albert Walk, if you'd be so kind as to set it off and direct me.' I was slightly offended he hadn't asked me, but had to agree Norman was probably more suited to the job of navigating with an iPhone than me.

Away from the freedom of the open road, Leonard did at least seem willing to comply with the concept of traffic lights, which gave us some relief in between rally sprints. Compliments of Norman and Google, we found 108 Albert Walk with very little trouble at all and I immediately wished we hadn't.

'Is this definitely it, Norman? Are you sure? A hundred and eight?'

The place looked like it was going to live down to its name, and I was a bit worried I'd booked us into an actual residence for retired toads.

'Yes, definitely, Mum. I don't think Google's allowed to lie. And look, there's even a sign. Ta-da!'

The almost chirpy 'ta-da' made my tummy do a little jump for joy, and he was right. The ramshackle maisonette we'd pulled up in front of sported an equally depressed sign.

Toad Hall: Bed, Breakfast and Good Devon Hospitality
Your hosts, Bill and Gloria.

Attached to the bottom of the sign by a couple of rusty chains was a weather-beaten timber frame with a faded image of presumably Bill and Gloria, arm in arm and looking very Devonian and hospitable. If the sign had said, *Abandon hope all ye who enter*, it would have been far more appropriate, if you ask me.

The front garden, if you'd be so bold, looked as though nobody had inflicted a lawnmower or a pair of secateurs on it in the last decade. There was a large, unkempt bush curiously positioned right in the middle of the pathway, with an air of someone who'd showed up one day to try their luck and had hit the jackpot. The path had been worn into a deviation around it on both sides and up to the front door. It looked like bush one, path nil.

On the booking website where I'd found Toad Hall, it had been described variously as 'charming' and 'shabby chic', but at first, second and third glances, post-apocalyptic early Tuscan ruin might have been a more fitting description.

'OK, then, everybody out. If this is it, we're here!'

While my mouth was desperately having a crack at cheery, my spirits were trying to save themselves from crashing to the post-apocalyptic Tuscan tiled doorstep. This trip was already stressful enough without the prospect of having to endure our first two nights at the mercy of Bill and Gloria. Especially if, and chances were, their presentation and housekeeping were a reflection of their hospitality. I tried to remember if we'd passed any nice Best Westerns on our way into Barnstaple, but Leonard had already swung our cases out of the boot and was gently motioning Norman ahead of him up the pathway.

'Come on, Norman, the early bird gets the worm. The sooner we check in, the more time you'll have to practise for tonight. The show must go on!' Not quite yet, matey, I thought, and thank non-existent god for small mercies about that.

After I'd got back to the car in Bude, bearing ham-and-pickle toasties and apple juice, I'd sat in the front seat with the door open and listened to Norman go over some of his jokes with Leonard. My heart had sunk lower and lower with every bite and off-kilter delivery. I'd occasionally snuck a glance in the wing mirror at Norman, who was right in my line of sight, looking for all the world like he was hanging on Leonard's every word of advice. But there was no getting around it that, without Jax, there was no banter, no timing and every joke sounded lonely, stilted and way out of its depth. *Put it all back in the shoebox, Norman, and let's go home.* I shook my head a couple of times to silence the voice and, alternating on every second bite, I chimed in with what I hoped was some encouraging laughter.

Leonard had also been very enthusiastic, with a load of 'bravo's and 'hardy ha ha, young fellow's thrown in with abandon, but with his first real public airing just hours away, I couldn't help feeling Norman was far from ready.

As I listened to him fumbling through his jokes one after another, I tried telling myself that it didn't matter if he wasn't perfect, because he was just a kid, right? Even if his timing wasn't quite there, he was wonderful and brave and hopeful, and didn't he have all that astounding gravitas? Surely that would count for something. People would understand. And what did it matter if a few jokes fell flat, as long as Norman got to have a go at that plan of his for Jax? For him.

I wanted so hard to hope for the best, but the thing was, after all those years sipping warm lemonade in dark pub corners listening to my father pour his heart out on stage then watching him fall head first into a bottle of Scotch when we got home, I knew enough to know that it mattered all right. It mattered a lot. And Norman had been wearing his 'I'm OK' mask so well for so long now it was impossible to tell if he was even still in there behind it, or somewhere else altogether. As I'd searched his face in the wing mirror for clues, I'd wondered if it might even already be too late to call him back. *One two three bite. One two three laugh.*

The interior decor of Toad Hall was only slightly better than the outside had hinted at, and when Bill appeared, he, too, was the perfect match. He was about a hundred and twenty years older than his picture and slightly more unsteady on his feet than one might expect at three o'clock in the afternoon, but at least he seemed to know the way to our rooms. One for me and Norman, which smelled distinctly of mould and indistinctly of wee, and one down the hall and up a set of three stairs for Leonard, which was so small even the single bed seemed like an imposition.

There was no sign of Gloria, but Bill assured us she'd be cooking our full English breakfast whenever we wanted between seven and nine o'clock the next morning, which Norman was surprisingly excited about.

'Free breakfast, Mum! Can you believe it?' I was glad he had something to look forward to in the next twenty-four hours, because, frankly, I couldn't think of much else that was going to fit the bill.

I unpacked, which comprised taking Norman's good shirt and my good shirt out of our cases and hanging them in the musty wardrobe. Side by side, they looked remarkably similar, which made me wonder, did I dress like a twelve-year-old boy or did my son dress like a thirty-two-year-old woman? Both options were a little disturbing and I made a mental note to address the issue at some stage.

I was well aware my hanging of good shirts and mental noting were delaying tactics, but I was also well aware there was no way Leonard was going to allow us to deviate from any of the perfectly spaced bulletpoints on his laminated itinerary.

'Knock, knock.' On cue, he appeared at our slightly open door, not knocking at all but brandishing said itinerary in front of him. It could have been down to his windblown hair and cheeks, or the fact that he'd removed his tie and undone the top two buttons of his shirt, but I swear he was looking ten years younger than when we'd left Penzance just a few hours ago.

'OK, Sadie, it's four o'clock. Are you feeling brave, my dear?'

No, I bloody was not. 'Nothing ventured nothing gained, it's time to call candidate number one.'

I had to hand it to him: we were right on schedule. Right after *3 p.m., check in to Toad Hall, unpack, check oil and water in car and have slight rest*, was the thing I'd been dreading all the way from Penzance. *Sadie 4 p.m. call Dan McLachlan to set up meeting.* Just like that. Like good old Dan McLachlan was going to open his diary and move a few things around to fit an illegitimate son in between appointments with his broker and his weekly briefing with the deputy prime minister. Because if there was one thing I did remember about Dan McLachlan, it was that he was a guy who was going places. He certainly went places for a couple of nights with me, but I'm pretty sure none of them would have helped progress his career. Not unless he'd switched his law degree to gynaecology. Or drug-lordery.

I don't know how easy calling a guy you'd had a two-day dalliance with thirteen years ago out of the blue sounds to you, but if you ever have to do it I sincerely hope you handle it better than me. Leonard had already added all the potential fathers' numbers into my phone, and I'd been going over a vague script in my head for the past week, so it's not like it crept up on me or anything. But what I really wasn't prepared for was having to talk to Dan McLachlan's answering machine. And the fact that his voice sounded exactly as I hadn't even known I'd remembered it.

Hi, you've reached Dan McLachlan, arrogant bastard with good hair and a bad attitude to women. I'm way too busy and important to answer your call right now but if you leave your number I may deign to get back to you at some stage. Or, you know, something like that.

Put on the spot, I stumbled about, trying to sound light-hearted and casual, blurting out some drivel about old times and did he remember me, and just being in town for the evening and I'd love to catch up.

'And oh, hey, by the way, there's . . . there's a possibility you could be my twelve-year-old son's father. He's a really great kid. The bomb. The best kid in the world, actually. He, that is, we . . .'

At that point, Leonard began madly flapping one hand in the air and dragging the other across his neck in a desperate cut-throat sign. I didn't disagree. I'd swerved way off script, because we'd decided definitely – *definitely* – not to say anything about Norman until I'd met up with the guy and evaluated the situation. And maybe not even then. Norman also looked a bit terrified at the prospect of having to live up to my hype, but it wasn't until I hung up and dropped my mobile on the bed like a sizzling chip that I realized what that slim, insistent finger that had been tapping at my shoulder from the moment I'd heard Dan McLachlan's voice had been about. Because that wasn't the first time I'd heard him at the end of an answering machine. Oh no it wasn't.

My rusted-up brain was on furious rewind and it ground to a halt at the Tuesday after the weekend I'd slept with Dan, when he hadn't showed up where we said we'd meet. The same day I'd had a call from the solicitor to tell me that, as we'd suspected, once the bank had recouped all the money my father owed after the sale of the house, I was still almost two thousand pounds short to pay the funeral director and legal bills. And please call her back.

So it hadn't been the best of days and I remembered that, when it became clear Dan had no intention of showing up or even calling me, I'd been angry as hell. So I called him. Numerous times. More than that, actually, because numerous sounds like around six, doesn't it? I think it was more like sixty. And I hadn't spared the answering machine's sensibilities, if I remembered correctly. Unfortunately, with wonderful high-definition clarity, suddenly, I did.

112

The better my memory became, the more I realized Dan McLachlan was probably less likely to call me back than call the police. Again. But to start remembering the details of that particular early-morning haul over the coals was going to be all kinds of embarrassing, so I swerved out of there and back into the present. Which wasn't much better.

The three of us stood in a silent semicircle, staring down at my phone on the faded floral duvet. The angles of our feet reminded me of another unbreakable three that we used to be and I felt the tepid threat of tears behind my eyes. *Gotcha, suckers!*

'Don't worry, Mum, it'll be OK. That . . . that was really great for the first time. It . . . it doesn't matter that you didn't remember not to say . . . it's OK, Mum. It'll be OK, honest. You'll see.'

Norman touched my arm gently and slid his hand down into mine. His fingers curled into the shape of a well-worn spot and I held on as long as I dared.

Some time later, as Norman and Leonard settled in for some practice, I lay down on the bed, curled my knees up to my chest and got to thinking about handsome Dan McLachlan, my father and a house full of memories that sold for a song. I let my lids droop as my breath fell into step with the rise and fall of their voices, and I must have dropped off, because when I jerked awake I was suddenly and acutely aware of silence. Leonard was hunched over in the armchair, squinting at a handful of notes, glasses absently abandoned on his head. Pen in hand, Norman was sitting on the floor, using Leonard's knee as a support to cross something off a Post-it before handing it to him. I moved my arm to brush some hair out of my eyes and, when I looked back, my son was staring straight at me. And smiling.

22

The two people since 2007 that had bothered to write a Trip-Advisor review on the Noble Goat pub in Muddiford both agreed on one thing. They wouldn't be back.

'Well, that sounds perfect,' I said when I saw Norman's face as Leonard read out the comments from his laptop. 'Because neither will we.'

We were relying on the word of the online monthly North Devon gig guide Leonard had found during his research that the so-called open mic nights at the Noble Goat were even a going concern. But, as Leonard said, if you can't trust the Internet, who can you trust?

Show us what you've got! Muddiford's Best Open Mic Night, last Tuesday of the month. Sign up on the night. Registration £5.

While I was busy wondering what the possibility was of there being more than one open mic night in a place the size of a post-age stamp, a couple of other thoughts were also jostling for my attention. Firstly, maybe the lack of reviews on TripAdvisor meant that Muddiford's Best Open Mic Night wasn't all that popular, which could only be a good thing for Norman's first try. But then, secondly, what if it *was* the social event of the month and the entire town showed up every last Tuesday night to see what anyone crazy and brave enough to get up had 'got'.

As Norman heaved my father's old suit jacket over his narrow shoulders and I watched him gather up his pile of paper scraps and Post-it notes I sent out one of my silent telepathic messages. *You've got this, Norman. I'll do the crazy, you do the brave.* But I knew I was no substitute for what was missing from Norman's show and, as I searched his face, there was no sign he'd got the message.

Way down deep in my gut, I felt a sharp, sudden tug, which came and went so quickly I wasn't even sure I hadn't imagined it. But when I rested my hand on a certain place, there was no mistaking the warmth of the scar through my jeans.

While I'd spent the rest of the afternoon lying back on a pillow being asphyxiated by the smell of mould and worrying about the police showing up on the doorstep, courtesy of Dan McLachlan, I'd listened to Leonard and Norman adding to their wad of Post-it notes and chatting about Norman's psoriasis. After a handful of kindly, well-meaning questions and a curious inspection of a few scabs, Leonard leaned back in his chair with a thoughtful expression.

'You know, I know it sounds odd, Norman old chap, but my Iris always swears black and blue that a dose of cold tea can fix everything that ails a person,' I'd heard him say. 'Bites, burns, constipation, cold sores – you name it. Cold tea for everything, that woman, inside and out.'

A little later Norman asked me quietly if we could buy a big box of teabags the next day, knowing full well it would do no good, but wanting so much for Leonard to feel like he was helping. *Keep calm and drink tea.*

Naturally, Leonard had Google-Mapped our route and after a makeshift dinner of Pot Noodles and Ritz crackers in the room, at 6.15 p.m. sharp we left Toad Hall and headed off to Norman's solo comedy debut.

The Noble Goat Freehouse was literally the only sign of life in the middle of quite a lot of nowhere, and even then the signs were not particularly evident. We had our pick of the car park, simply because there wasn't a single other vehicle there, unless you count an ancient milk float jacked up on blocks. At the sound of the Austin's engine, a dozy-looking black-and-white dog poked its head out of the driver's side of the float, gave a half-hearted yip then flopped back on to the seat with the look of someone who needed to sleep off a few too many whiskies.

Out of nowhere, I had a flashback to that same feeling. You know, like when you wake up and realize you can't remember anything since dancing to Take That in the student bar at midnight with a lager top in one hand and an honours law student in the other? This time, the twang in my gut was definitely not my imagination and I reached under my shirt to rearrange the waistband of my jeans into a more comfortable position.

The North Devon gig guide had said registration for the open mic closed at seven fifteen for a seven thirty start, so Leonard had timed for us to get there by six forty-five, allowing for getting lost and there being a queue. Hooray for Google, we were early, and unless a few dozen open mic-ers had arrived cross-country on foot, it didn't look like there was going to be any problems with a queue.

Walking into the pub beside Leonard, Norman looked even smaller than usual, and it wasn't the first time I'd wondered if the effort his body had to constantly put into growing all that psoriasis was stunting the rest of his growth. Reversing it, even. The shoulders of the too-big suit jacket fell away at either side, and even though the sleeves swung along against his body as he walked, the jacket was always slightly late. Robert Foreman's comedy shoes were never going to be big ones to fill, despite what I'd somehow led Norman to believe, but his jacket was another story.

When we got to the door of the Noble Goat, Leonard stepped in front of our little procession and pushed it open with a flourish to allow Norman a grand entrance. I walked in behind him in time to see Barbara Windsor's doppelgänger raise her head listlessly from a newspaper spread across the bar. I can only imagine the grand entrance lacked some of its effect due to the fact that there wasn't another soul in the pub. Leonard was taking his role as Norman's self-appointed manager seriously and he made his way across the empty room to Barbara's bar.

'Good evening, madam. Delighted to meet you. Is the sign-up for the open mic with you?' Barbara fixed him with a cast-iron-eyelashed gaze, and a couple of decades ticked by as she tried to work out whether Leonard was taking the piss or quite serious about signing up for a stand-up performance in a pub that had no punters and, for all we knew, no open mic night. Because it was pretty clear there was also no stage, no lights and not even a rusty microphone in sight, open or otherwise.

'Well, sure, my love. Name?' The rafters sighed with relief, but Barbara didn't even have a pen in her hand so it was Leonard's turn to try and work out if she was taking the piss.

'Ahh. Not . . . not me, no. It's for the boy here,' he said. 'Norman Foreman. Little Big Man.' He raised his voice a little louder when he said the last bit and, although Norman ducked his head shyly, I saw the smudge of a smile pass his lips. I reached forward and grabbed his hand to give it a squeeze, and I felt him trembling. *Oh, you beautiful, beautiful kid.*

Barbara, who was actually Lou, according to a silver name tag pinned to her blouse, scanned us slowly, probably trying to decide who was the least insane. When she got to Norman her face seemed to soften a little. *Good choice.*

'Please yourselves. But the open mic's only open to paying customers. What'll it be?'

A round of drinks looked like it was in lieu of a registration fee so we ordered lemonades and a neat whisky for Leonard. I quickly added two packets of crisps when I saw Lou's face. To be honest, I could have done with something stronger, which would no doubt have made both Lou and I a lot happier, but while my liver was willing, my stomach was definitely not.

Despite the lack of an audience, Norman was too nervous to drink his lemonade and instead divided the time between making multiple trips to the toilet and furiously itching at his arms through the suit jacket. I knew that the heat inside the pub was probably making his psoriasis worse under that heavy fabric, but I also knew he'd never take that damn thing off. *The show must go on, Sadie.*

By seven twenty-five it looked like Lou had totally forgotten we were there and she was immersed back in the paper. Who knew there was so much hard news to be delivered in Muddiford? Then, out of nowhere, we were swept up in a gust of wind as the door of the pub swung open and somebody turned out all the lights. OK, nobody actually turned out the lights, but the man mountain standing in the doorway had the same effect. The guy was built like Hulk Hogan, although much hairier in the facial department and, thankfully, completely clothed.

'Now that was an entrance,' I whispered to Norman as I brushed his windblown fringe out of his eyes. That smudge again.

'All right, Big Al?'

Lou didn't even look up, but she'd already started pulling a pint of something black as she spoke, with one eye still on the paper. Big Al crossed the floor in three paces, took the frothing glass from Lou's hands and downed it in one. She was already pulling a second as he slammed the empty glass down on the bar and let out an almighty burp that reverberated through the rafters. The choreography was precision personified and I could only assume it had taken Lou and Big Al years of practice. With his second pint securely in hand, the mountain turned his attention to us. I could feel Norman's hot little body shrink closer into me as Big Al's eyes travelled slowly over each of us in turn.

'Well, well. I see it's a full house tonight, eh? Ha ha ha.'

When Big Al laughed, I'd lay odds the buildings shook in John o' Groats. I bounced two inches out of my seat and Leonard's head shot up like a meerkat as he let out a muttered 'Hell's bells'. Norman slid down even further into my father's jacket. Only Lou was unmoved, and she was already back to her paper. It felt like my moment and, for once, I took it.

'Hell— hello, yes. We're here for the, um . . . the open mic night. Well, I mean, Norman, my son . . . he is. But we are, too. To help.' *Brilliant, Sadie.*

'The open . . . oh, right. The open mic. Excellent! New blood, eh, Lou, well how about that!'

As Big Al spoke the tiny bubbles of froth from pint number one trembled in his beard and prepared to make a dive for it into pint number two. It was slightly mesmerizing, as was the sight of his expansive biceps, which were doing a poor job of hiding under his shirt. Thankfully, Leonard chose that moment to weigh in.

'You, too, Mr . . . err, Al? Are you . . . ?' Leonard gestured vaguely around the empty pub.

Surely not. I couldn't imagine what this guy could possibly

have to offer as a stand-up act, apart from wood-chopping maybe. The place hardly looked big enough, though, and I for one didn't want to stick around with a seven-foot giant wielding an axe in an enclosed space to confirm it. I saw Big Al send a wink in Lou's direction.

'Well, yes, yes I am, as a matter of fact. Why not? Me and Mr John Keats. Muddiford's favourite double act. Ha ha ha.' This time we all held on tight, with minimal casualties. 'To be honest, I'm the only poet in the village, so to speak.'

Big Al's attempt at a Welsh lilt was less than ideal and I was quite glad we weren't going to have to endure him regaling us with a comedy routine. Then I remembered Norman's practice runs that afternoon and I was reminded of glass houses and stones and what happened when they made contact. But Leonard had already sprung into action, playing his managerial duties to perfection.

'Ah. OK, right. Mr Big Al the poet. Excellent! Our Norman here is a comedian.' I couldn't miss the overtone of pride in his voice, and it made me want to cry that Norman had someone else in his corner apart from me.

Without waiting for an invitation, Big Al came over and manoeuvred himself into the tiny bit of space left on the bench seat beside Norman, casually stretching a beefcake arm around his shoulder and giving it a squeeze. Norman looked like he was about to liquefy right there and then and disappear into the rancid carpet of the Noble Goat. I remembered there was a huge lump of weeping scab on his shoulder and that squeeze would have hurt like hell, but he didn't look like he was in any hurry to move away. Which was interesting, to say the least.

'A comedian, eh? Well, God knows this place could use a laugh or two. Budge up a bit more, young fella, and let a man get to know his competition. First rule of open mic night. Keep your enemies close. Ha ha ha.'

We obediently shuffled over, and Norman threw me a look that was part confusion, part terror and, oh please let it be true, part delight. I knew he was thinking the same thing as me. Damned if bloody Big Al wasn't just what you'd imagine Jax to be when he was thirty-five. Or possibly fifty-five. It was hard to tell under all that beard.

It turned out there was a local production of *Grease* on in the next village and, according to Big Al, the entire regular patronage of the Noble Goat was there instead of at the pub for open mic night. As was apparently the microphone itself.

'Never mind all that, though. It's past the hour and the show must go on! Come on, Lou. Drumroll, please, lass, ha ha ha!' John o' Groats was razed to the ground but Lou lifted one eyebrow and tapped the bar obligingly with her fingernails.

Notwithstanding the lack of audience, Big Al could obviously see how nervous Norman was, so he declared himself up first. And while I'm no expert on live poetry readings, I don't think anyone could have argued it wasn't a pretty impressive performance. All I can say is that if you ever get the chance to witness a giant beard on legs with a voice like a foghorn rolling off a misty ocean reciting 'When I Have Fears', well, you should take it.

The effect of Big Al's resonant tones colliding into the tenderness of Keats' sonnet was shockingly beautiful and, when he'd finished, the words still hung in the air around the bar. I wanted to reach up and grab a few to stuff them into my bag for later. Norman and Leonard sat open-mouthed, dripping in the aftermath, and even Lou looked like she was wiping a tear away as she pulled Al another pint of Guinness. Nobody dared break the silence, except Big Al himself.

'Righto, then, Norman. There's the old ham out of the way, now for the young blood! Up you come, lad, you're on!' When he said 'up', it was only a figure of speech, as it was really just a corner of the room, but then out of nowhere Lou appeared with a milk crate, which she handed to Big Al with a flick of her head in Norman's direction. Big Al turned it over, placed it on the floor and swung Norman on to it in one swift but gentle movement, almost before any of us knew what was happening.

Seeing my beautiful boy wobbling up there on that plastic crate, nervously picking at a huge scab on his hand, was almost more than I could bear. I felt a pinching pain in my gut and the sensation of something stirring deep within. *Here's your chance, Sadie. Say something helpful.* But of course you already know I didn't. That'd take quite a bit more than I had at that moment and I was frozen behind the folds of a heavy velvet curtain, watching reruns of my father.

'That's the way, Norman, old man! Hurrah!' Leonard pumped his fist into the air and looked like he couldn't have been more excited if it was opening night of the Royal Variety.

Norman was about ten seconds into his first stumbling sentence before Big Al interrupted.

'Hang on, Norman! Look, sorry . . . wait a sec. If you don't mind . . . do you mind? Does anybody mind if I butt in for a second? Norman's mum?'

'Err, no. Go right ahead. And, um, it's Sadie.'

Big Al flashed me an unsettling grin and a thumbs-up. Definitely thirty-five. It seemed nobody else minded either, especially not Norman, who was looking at Big Al like he might be the second coming of Jesus.

'OK, now. See, you've got to create a buzz, Norman, right? The crowd's here to see *you*. You're the man! So you've got to tease them a little. Know what I mean?' Strangely, Big Al sounded like he might just know what he was talking about. I sat up a little straighter.

'You see, it's like a woman, son. You don't give them everything they want all at once, now, do you? Thrill of the chase, boy. Little by little. Slowly, slowly, catchy monkey.'

OK, then. It appeared Big Al had failed to notice that half of this particular crowd actually *were* women, but he ploughed on.

'Introduce yourself, Normie. Give 'em a taste of what you've got and make that crowd want you – no ifs, no buts. You know what I mean?'

He looked over at me and winked, then took a step forward and placed his hands lightly on Norman's shoulders. I could see the outline of a Hulk Hogan-esque quadricep as he gently adjusted Norman's stance on the crate and I wondered just how well he *did* do with the ladies. And whether there was a Mrs Big Al waiting at home with a rolling pin to berate him for drinking the weekly grocery money away. And why on earth I was thinking about that all of a sudden. I decided I might be in need of a distraction of a far more useful kind.

'Come on, Norman, you can do it! You've got this!' My spontaneous vote of encouragement came out quite a bit louder than I'd intended and I felt my face warm up as Big Al turned to look at me with a surprised chuckle.

'Well, will you look at that, lad. It's working already!'

Nobody could ever say that Norman doesn't take direction well, and he was pretty used to it after six years with Jax. He took on board what Big Al said to the letter, although I could only hope he'd forget the rest of the advice before any girls started to take an interest in him.

'Evening, all!' Theatrical throat clear. 'Well, umm . . . if it isn't your, err . . . umm, lucky night tonight!' Norman shot an anxious look over at Big Al, who was nodding enthusiastically as he drained his pint. Which looked like quite a talent in itself. He slammed the empty glass down on the bar and let out a whoop.

'Woohoo! Work it, Normie, that's the way! Just like that! Good lad!'

I glanced over at Leonard, who raised a startled eyebrow, but Lou was already approaching with another pint, so presumably Big Al wasn't deemed a danger to the public. I looked back to Norman, radiant on his milk crate, and I could have watched him for the rest of my life.

'Wait, wait! One more thing.' Big Al brought his voice down to a reasonable level and walked over and placed his hands on Norman's shoulders again. 'Before you launch, take a deep breath in, lad. The deepest breath you've ever taken. That's it. Now hold it . . . hold it . . . right, now let it out. All the way. Then a bit more. OK. Now you're ready for anything. Breath is life, Norman. Never forget it.'

I exhaled and felt a slight retreat behind my scar. *Breath is life.* I realized Norman wasn't the only one following Big Al's instructions. *Go, Norman, go.*

Norman went.

'Umm, ah . . . umm . . . so . . . err, well . . . like I was saying, your luck's never been better because, umm . . . you've got me! Norman Foreman, the . . . ah, umm . . . Little . . . Little Big Man of comedy. Here for your . . . comedy pleasure for . . . err, one night only. And, umm, all you lot have to do is sit back, relax and enjoy the . . . umm . . . ride!'

'Yeeeehaaaa, nailed it, Normie! The crowd goes wild!'

I was a little worried that Big Al's fourth pint in twenty minutes might have pushed him over the edge, but Lou gave me a wink and a slight shake of her head, as if to say 'Don't worry, he's harmless.' At least, I hoped that's what the wink said. It could well have been 'Quick, you call the police while I padlock the Guinness tap and hide the axe.' I had no way of knowing.

So there it was, and even though the crowd at Norman's first solo public debut was record-smashingly small, the show did indeed go on. He delivered the jokes, his parts and Jax's, too. Shovelling through the words like he was open-cut mining. Too fast, too slow, and sometimes skipping ahead before his brain could catch up with his mouth. But pressing on, hoping nobody would notice.

All the way through it, Leonard held on to a handful of fanned-out Post-it notes, shuffling through them, mouthing along. Occasionally looking confused when Norman jumped ahead, doing some more shuffling, and then looking relieved when he found one to match. But as Norman spilled his heart out on an upturned milk crate, I was thinking about something else altogether.

Because about two minutes into his routine, right after the joke about a London black-cab driver on a Boris Bike, I'd felt my bag vibrating. I snuck a look at my phone to see a barely familiar name illuminated in green and I covered up the muffled noise with a sudden round of applause, much to the surprise of the others. The phone let out a final shiver as the voicemail message sign lit up, and the ceasefire in my stomach was over. Dan McLachlan. Back in the game.

23

NORMAN

First rule of comedy: Three is the funniest number.

I don't even know who John Keats is, but I bet he'd be really happy that Big Al recited his poem at the Noble Goat. And I know he should have won the open mic really, but Lou was the judge and she said that I won by a tit's whisker. Which doesn't sound like much, but Big Al said she had him there, so it was official.

The prize was ten pounds and two packets of pork scratchings, which Big Al ate most of anyhow, so I figured that was fair. He also seemed to be saving quite a few in his beard for later, and when I saw that I made a quick note in my head to try to remember to write it down on an actual Post-it note so I could maybe use it in a joke. I wasn't sure how, but I knew that if I thought hard enough and tried to imagine Jax there helping me, I could most probably think of something pretty funny about that.

After we'd finished the pork scratchings Lou said it was closing time, but then she brought us over another tray of drinks and sat down with us at the table. Big Al even gave me a sip of his pint. To celebrate the win he said, but he checked with Mum first. When she said it was OK I felt a little bit bad because everyone thought it was my first time. But it wasn't, and not even Mum knew that I'd actually drunk beer before. A lot of it.

Last year four cans of lager fell out of Jax's stepdad's fridge in the garage and right into the bottom of his school bag. Well, anyhow, that's his story and I'm sticking to it. They sat in his bag all day, but I knew it wouldn't be long before Jax's ideas factory came up with a plan. And I was right because after school Jax goes, let's go over to Mrs Ackerman's cow paddock and drink them. As an experiment to see if lager makes you any funnier. Well, I drank one and Jax drank two and we were supposed to share the last one, but I couldn't drink any more because the paddock was spinning and the cows were going all blurry and Jax couldn't stop laughing at me hiccupping and trying to make up jokes in case lager actually did make you funnier. Then Mrs Sorrenson from the Post Office walked past with her dog and said what did we think we were doing and if we weren't careful she was going to tell our mothers. And then I fell asleep.

When I woke up I was hugging my one empty can and there were three empty cans beside Jax and he looked so green I almost couldn't see him in the cow paddock. Although that could also have been my fuzzy lager eyes, I suppose. Then Jax threw up, which made me throw up, and after that we felt a bit better and did a pinkie swear that we'd never tell anyone about that day if by chance Mrs Sorrenson didn't. Even though it was a bit of a shame, because we were pretty sure we'd thought up some really funny material while we were drunk and we didn't have any Post-its with us. I mean, I suppose we were drunk. I don't really know how you're supposed to feel when you're drunk, but whatever we were felt pretty good until it felt really awful.

We spent the whole next afternoon in my room trying to

remember those jokes we'd found so funny out there in Mrs Ackerman's cow paddock. Jax called it the Lost Lager Sessions and even though he said it was going to be just down to science and persistence, because they had to be in our brains somewhere, we never did remember them. But I'll tell you something. One day I will, because I'm not ever going to stop trying.

When Lou said, OK, it really was closing time now, Leonard said that we'd better be getting back to Toad Hall before Bill locks us out anyhow. Big Al and Mum gave each other their mobile numbers, although Mum didn't seem too keen at first. But I said, please, please, please, and she did, because I really liked Big Al and I think maybe she did too. I felt a little bit guilty that I'd won the open mic by a tit's whisker when really he should have, but he shook my hand and said he was going to be watching my career with interest and that the Edinburgh Fringe better watch out.

Even though I knew we hadn't found anywhere that would give me a place for a show at the Fringe yet, what Big Al said about watching my career with interest made me feel like maybe we actually would. Also, because look at what Leonard had already made happen. We were loads of miles from Penzance, I was staying in my first B&B ever and I'd met my first fellow performer and heard my first John Keats poem as a bonus. And I'd done my first real-life show without Jax.

If you looked at it like that it would look like everything was working out perfectly, wouldn't it? Except that in the car on the way back to Toad Hall, even though I had some leftover bits of pork scratchings in my teeth and ten pounds in my pocket that said different, I knew I still wasn't really any good. I know how I sound and I just don't know how to make myself sound any better. Because that was Jax's job.

*

I don't think people should be allowed to promise you something if they're not really going to be able to give it to you. But it turned out not only was Gloria not in the kitchen making our crispy bacon and the rest of our full English when we got up the next morning, well, she wasn't even there at all. When Bill finally came downstairs, looking like he'd just spent the night parachuting out of a rocket at warp speed with no goggles, he said it was going to be at least twenty minutes before breakfast was ready. He went into the kitchen and started banging some pans around for a bit and then he came back out and said he had to go to the shops for bacon.

I think maybe Mum was waiting until we'd had our full English before she told me about Dan McLachlan ringing back, but then she must have realized it was probably going to take ages so she just blurted it out in the middle of Leonard telling us how long it takes to cook the perfect fried egg. Which is three and a half minutes by the way.

'So, everybody, I got a message back from Dan McLachlan last night. Errr, number one.' When she said it Leonard didn't even care about the fried egg information any more and did one of his fist pump thingys and goes, aha, do tell! But I didn't really know what to say or do. I mean, I sort of wanted to try a fist pump too and I guess if I was ever going to do it that was the time. But I didn't have a proper technique ready and Mum was looking at me a bit funny so I knew I had to come up with something quick or she'd start getting worried she'd done the wrong thing. Which is how she thinks. So I just said the very first thing that came into my head, which was I'm starving.

It's not that I didn't want to hear about what Dan said in his message and when we'd be meeting him and all that. It's just that I really and truly *was* starving, which was quite weird for me, and there was no sign of Bill coming back with our bacon. I guess maybe I was a little bit scared of what Dan McWhatsy might have to say as well. Because the thing is, like I said, I'm not even a hundred per cent sure wanting to find my dad was actually my idea. I'm not saying it was definitely Jax that changed the Five Year Plan on the wall or anything, but you know, one never knows and all that.

Anyway, once everyone had agreed that they were all starving too, Mum asked me if I wanted to listen to the message, and as soon as she said that I knew it wasn't going to be great. Because Mum always says that bad news is better coming straight from the horse's mouth and not second-hand. Which made me think straight away that it was probably going to sound better coming from Dan McThingy himself that he was busy or out of town, or that we'd made a big mistake and he wasn't who we thought he was. Only it was worse than that.

Mum put her phone on speaker and we all leaned forward and, right at the minute when I heard Dan go, 'Hello? Look, hello, ummm . . .' Bill came back and slammed the front door so loud we couldn't hear and Mum had to start the message again. But straight after I did hear it I really wished that instead of Bill coming through that door it had been some robbers who stole Mum's phone and then made us all lie face down on the floor while they burgled Toad Hall. Because Dan McNasty was a lot worse than a whole gang of robbers.

What he said was that he wasn't interested and he didn't want to know anything about me and Mum. Nothing, *nada, nyet.* Which I think is even meaner than if he'd said all those other things like being away or pretending he was someone else. Because by just saying he's not interested what he's really saying is, well, lady, maybe I am your kid's father and maybe I'm not.

Who knows. But whatever. I don't care and I don't want to meet you or your son. Ever. Sorry. I have a very important job and a wife and I already have a family, and actually you can scratch the sorry because he didn't say sorry.

But he did say what did Mum think she was playing at anyhow and yes he remembered her all right. He remembered her quite well, thanks very much. She'd been the reason he'd lost his licence for three months and lost his girlfriend for over a year. But they got back together and now they had three sons and he wasn't interested in this kind of craziness coming into his life. And that if Mum tried to contact him again he'd take measures, whatever that means.

It really made me wonder how many ways he thought he had to say that he wasn't interested. I felt like ringing him back and saying, hey buddy, we got you at I'm not interested. Which were actually his first words after the hello and the stupid long umm.

Before I heard that message my psoriasis had stopped itching for the first time since before Jax left. I know that because I lay there for ages and didn't itch once when I woke up at Toad Hall, thinking about how great the night before had been in the pub with Big Al and Lou and John Keats and winning my first open mic by a tit's whisker. And even though I knew I wasn't really that funny, it hadn't mattered because I'd tried.

But by the end of listening to Dan McFurfeature's message, which was fifty-four seconds long, according to Mum's phone, it felt like my skin was trying to turn itself inside out. Like it woke up all of a sudden and woke up angry. Not that I was surprised. That last doctor Mum took me to, who wasn't really a doctor and wore a dress and burned lots of incense, totally got it all wrong. I definitely *wasn't* in control of my own skin, and I reckon we both knew it.

After the message everyone looked like they were waiting for me to say something, so I did. What I said wasn't really true but I thought to myself, well, if ever there's going to be a time when it's OK to tell a lie it's now. Anyhow, after I said that it was OK, honest, Mum hugged me and said, oh Norman, and Leonard just rubbed my arm and said bugger a few times. So maybe they knew it wasn't true.

Nothing was really any different to a few minutes before I heard that message, when I'd just been Norman who didn't have a dad. I just still didn't have a dad, that's all, is what I told myself. But even when Bill finally brought out the full English and the fried eggs were three-and-a-half-minutes perfect and the bacon was lovely and crispy, how me and Jax like it, all I could think about was Dan McSnotface and how maybe I'd just lost the only chance I'd ever get of having three little brothers.

Leonard said the one good thing about Dan not wanting to see us was that at least we didn't have to hang around Barnstaple another night. I'd already noticed that Leonard's great at finding good stuff about whatever happens, even if it seems really bad at the time. So I thought maybe it would help if I tried to do that too, and so the good thing I found was that I liked the way Leonard said us. Like it wasn't just me and Mum that Dan McPoo wasn't interested in. Like we were all in it together. Which felt nice, because I'd only ever been in it with Mum and Jax before, so having Leonard made it feel like maybe there was three in our us again.

Jax reckons three is the funniest number because the Comic Triple is the first rule of comedy. It's like when you start with a line, then you repeat it in a different way and then on the third time you hit the audience with a twist in the punchline that's the exact opposite of what they're expecting. Which is kind of what Jax did for real, but I don't really want to think about that.

When Mum and I were packing our stuff into the back of the car to leave, Leonard said he had to make a phone call and did we mind? Mum said of course not, and even though we couldn't hear what he was saying because he had his back to us and anyhow Mum always says it's not polite to listen to other people's phone calls, I reckon that maybe and probably definitely he would have been talking to his wife, Iris.

I'll tell you something I know for sure, though, which is that Leonard really and truly understands what it's like to have the Rolls-bloody-Royce of best friends, like me and Jax. Because he told me that's exactly the way he felt about Iris from the minute he first looked into her big baby blues at the Gresham dance hall on the Holloway Road. And he reckons he's never stopped looking since. It made me think that it must be nice to have someone who still wants to be your friend after sixty-two years, which is how long Leonard and his wife have been married. That's nearly two times as long as how old Mum is and five times as long as Jax's whole entire life.

After Leonard finished talking on the phone, when he turned around he looked kind of sad, so I guess he was already missing Iris a bit. But before I could ask him if he was OK Big Al showed up, which was a big surprise to me and Mum, but maybe not to Leonard, because someone must have told him where we were staying. When I saw him come around the corner I got butterflies in my tummy straight away, which reminded me of how I feel when Jax and I are having a really good day. Which was pretty much every day when he was here.

Big Al said he couldn't let us leave without saying goodbye and he gave me a book called *The Big Book of British Comedy Greats*, which I knew he must have bought especially, because it was brand new. So then I had the butterflies feeling *and* I'd got a great new book. Which you'd think would have made me feel pretty good, but instead it made me feel guilty because I'd forgotten to be sad about Jax again, like I did when I was sorting out the Comedy Pot with Leonard. And this whole trip was supposed to be about remembering Jax, not forgetting him.

Then something funny happened and I definitely don't mean in a good Comic Triple punchline kind of way. I was just standing there trying to say thank you to Big Al for the book, but instead my brain just started thinking about Dan McFartfeatures-Poo-Bottom, who didn't care even if he was my dad. And about his three boys who might or might not be my little brothers but now I'd never know. And about how Leonard and Iris had got to be best friends and married for five times as long as Jax got to even be alive. And I started crying. Like a baby. Not at all like a twelve-year-old almost stand-up comedian. And I just couldn't stop, because it looks like the Comic Triple works in reverse too.

It felt like when you turn the tomato sauce bottle upside down and you bang and bang on the end of it and nothing comes out, but then you do one last bang and all the sauce just explodes out of the bottle on to your chips. I reckon Big Al's book was the last big bang on my sauce bottle because it was like I exploded all over the street, all over Toad Hall, all over Leonard's car and, for how bad it felt, maybe all the way from Barnstaple to Swansea.

24

Sadie

If Toad Hall was a blight on the good name of bed and breakfasts (and it was), Eden Rock Guesthouse in Swansea was a shining beacon of righteousness. When we pulled up out the front it seemed like even Leonard's old Austin breathed a sigh of appreciation, although my romanticism about that was short-lived when I noticed a delicate wisp of smoke drifting up from under the bonnet to accompany it. But before I had time to worry if the car had plans to retire in Wales and we'd be catching the train to Edinburgh after all, Norman and Leonard were out of the Austin, hopping around to get the blood back into their legs.

'Holy moly, Mum! Is this it? We're staying here?'

You'd think the kid had never seen an example of fine Georgian architecture by the way he was staring at the building Google Maps had very kindly directed us to. I took in the sweeping views of the Swansea beachfront and turned back to look at the rather grand entrance of the Eden Rock, and for a second it crossed my mind that I might have made a mistake and booked a place that was actually five hundred pounds a night and not the fifty I'd thought it was. On the spot I decided it didn't even matter. I would have paid five thousand just so I could see the look on Norman's face when I said yes.

Because Norman breaking down like that just before we left Barnstaple had terrified me, and although I'd given myself a mental pat on the back for not showing it, not for the first time it made me worry about how easily this thing could go pear-shaped. But I knew there was no way of safeguarding against that completely, short of calling an end to the whole trip. And I wouldn't – couldn't – do that. Not to Norman, and now it looked like probably not to Leonard either, judging by his level of investment. How the hell had I become responsible for two people's happiness all of a sudden? I still wasn't sure I was up to the job of one.

Which, by the way, must have been pretty clear, because when Norman chose the footpath out the front of Toad Hall to lose it for the first time since Jax died, everybody seemed to know what to do except me. Without even hesitating, Big Al had grabbed him in a massive Hulk Hogan hug, squashing the life out of the shuddering sobs that were bursting from his little chest and shocking them just about into submission. Leonard had produced a perfectly ironed handkerchief from his jacket pocket and, even though I'm ashamed to say it was quite possible Norman had never even seen a hanky in his life before, let alone used one, he took it like it was the most precious thing he'd ever been offered. Even Bill got in on the act by shoving a handful of bacon sandwiches into Norman's hands.

'Now, now, there, there. A greasy treat for the journey, boy-o, that'll sort you out.'

But all I could do was stand there. Like I was in one of those TV ads where everything around the person speeds up and they're left standing dead still as the world rushes on around them in super-fast motion. Outside, I was paralysed, but inside, I was falling at a million miles an hour and the only real thing I had to hold on to was the warm, pulsing pain behind the scar on my stomach.

The feeling hadn't subsided much in the four hours it took to drive up through Somerset, Bristol, across the Severn and into Wales. But as I stood in front of the Eden Rock Guesthouse and said yes to my son, it backed off and dulled to an uneasy background hum. Because Norman seemed almost back to normal. Not the old normal, of course, but a passable version of my new, sad son. I'd take anything, though, because anything was better than what I'd seen back there on the footpath in Barnstaple.

Even though we were a day early, the manager of the Eden Rock seemed quite delighted to see us. So much so, in fact, that he upgraded the two rooms I'd booked us to a suite. Which by the way was drop-dead, how-the-hell-did-I-get-this-so-right gorgeous, with huge sash windows, views of the ocean, two bedrooms, a sitting room and even a tiny balcony.

After the manager had left, Norman and Leonard went out to check on the view, and I took a step back and checked out mine. I followed the arc of Leonard's arm, set within a perfect frame of sky and ocean, as he pointed out something far off towards the horizon, while the other rested easily on Norman's shoulder. A sudden strong gust caught the bottom of the white voile curtains and whipped them out the doors. Just for a moment, the two of them were obscured from my view and I got the feeling there was more than one thing shifting in my universe.

Norman couldn't wait to get down to the beach, but as far as I'm concerned, if you've seen one beach, you've seen them all. I mean, how different can a few miles of sand be? Was Welsh sand any better than Cornish? I doubted it and, frankly, all the conversation

I'd been forced to make lately, combined with the worry of Norman's meltdown and keeping this plan on the rails, had taken its toll. So, tucked up on the little balcony with a cup of tea seemed like it might be a pretty good place to be.

I leaned back on the hard wicker chair and closed my eyes, enjoying the feeling of the sea breeze sharpening in my nostrils and what I realized was my first bit of solitude for two days. Had it really been that long? And that short? The screech of seagulls and the dull crash of the waves filled my ears and, just like that, the Swansea breeze picked me up and carried me down to the beach. I ran along the sand, chasing the birds, arms outstretched, shouting and laughing into the spray. I felt something warm and safe and bent into my father's body as he lifted me up high and kissed my salty six-year-old head. *I've got you, Sadie love.*

A car horn sounded and my neck jerked forward on to my chest as I came back with a thud, heart pounding and eyes wide open to the ocean.

'Sadie, my dear, are you alright?'

Leonard was leaning forward from the other chair on the balcony, his hand on my arm, looking anxiously into my face. So much for my alone time.

'I must say you're very pale. You look like you've . . .' I willed him not to say it. Hoped against hope. Just leave it. '. . . seen a ghost.' Ahh. Good shot, old soldier.

I drew my body up straight and looked hard into the sun for as long as I could stand it. I changed the direction of my gaze and, through the black spots shooting around my eyeballs, I could just make out Norman walking slowly along the beach. Head down, hands in pockets. Looking for shells or the perfect rock, or perhaps the meaning of life.

'Hey, Leonard?' Even inside my own head my voice sounded far, far away, and I wondered if he could even hear me.

'Do you think I'm doing the right thing? Looking for Norman's father and taking him to the Fringe and, I mean . . . this trip. You know . . . everything.' I swallowed hard, sending a mouthful of words back down unused.

Leonard rearranged his bones on the chair, smoothing his trousers and straightening each shirt sleeve deliberately. He had the air of someone who hadn't been asked their opinion for a very long time and wasn't about to blow it by rushing in.

'You know, I never got to see my Iris as a mother,' he said finally. 'We tried for such a long time, but in the end we just . . . well, we had to let it go. The idea. She was just too sad after four dear little ones who . . . didn't quite make it. So she never had the chance to know what kind of a mother she might have been. What sort of a child ours would have been.' He turned his old grey head to the sea and the breeze gently lifted a wisp of his hair.

'But you do, Sadie. You know what kind of child you have. Norman is an extraordinary boy. Quite extraordinary. But, my dear, even an old codger like me can see how much he's suffering from the loss of young Jax. As are you.'

The unexpected mention of Jax's name landed a punch right in the tender part of my stomach and I sucked in my breath while the pain passed. *Hold it, hold it, let it out.* Leonard leaned back in his chair and patted his windblown hair back into place.

'I don't know if it's the right thing to do any more than you, Sadie, my dear, and it's really not for me to say. But I do believe it's worth a try. And maybe there's a young man who would benefit from being a father to a boy like your Norman. Perhaps he's out there just waiting to be found. Maybe he needs Norman as much as Norman needs him. One just never knows, my dear.'

As soon as he said it, I knew where I'd heard that before. Jax and Norman often talked about how that one exact phrase could sum up everything you needed to know about the world. The idea that if none of us can ever know what's going to happen next, then wasn't absolutely anything possible? Even two teen-aged, nobody, would-be comedians getting to the Edinburgh Fringe and making the whole world laugh. Because one just never knows. *Oh, Jax.*

But Leonard hadn't finished.

'On the other hand, my dear, you've also got to consider the ramifications of this trip for you. What would finding Norman's father mean for *you*?' I wasn't sure I liked where this was going. Correction. I knew I didn't like where it was going.

'And Sadie, I know I'm old, my dear, but . . . I see things . . . in you. I can see that you want to make Norman's dream come true more than anything else in the world. I see that. But my question is, just what is it you're so scared of?' Bloody hell. Monday evenings in May, Psychology for Beginners? I decided it was entirely possible.

In the ensuing silence, I took a good, long look at Mr Leonard-all-learning-is-good-learning Cobcroft. He was gazing out to sea with a faraway expression, possibly reliving a border clash with ten thousand charging Chinese soldiers, or maybe just creaming butter and sugar to ice a cake.

Then it could have been the way his neatly trimmed eyebrows raised and lowered in time with his breathing, or the kindly glint in his dusty blue eyes as they turned back and locked on to mine, or perhaps it was just the right moment. I don't know. It appeared Leonard had a bit of a knack of making me talk, and this time it was a story I hadn't told to anyone in thirteen years. Not even Norman, the one person in this world I actually trusted. And after all those years of carrying around such a hot stone of truth in the pit of my stomach it rose to the surface with surprising ease.

I told Leonard about the countless Monday, Wednesday or Tuesday nights (oh, but never the big-ticket Fridays or Saturdays) that I'd spent waiting around in pubs and clubs for my father after my mum died. Making a dinner of lemonade and salt-and-vinegar crisps drag out as long as I could while he spilled his guts trying to get a laugh in some seedy venue in Eastbourne or Margate or the outskirts of Brighton.

How on one particularly memorable night, a Thursday as it goes, the manager of the Grand Hotel Eastbourne found a ten-year-old me crouched on the floor in a corner of the back bar, with my fingers in my ears and my eyes screwed so tightly shut I could see the stars and every single planet as sharp as a pin. Silently, desperately, willing the audience to laugh at my dad and apparently breaking all kinds of liquor laws in the process.

Night after night, year after year, the shows continued to go on, as they apparently must. But the spaces in between them got longer and the venues got smaller and emptier as it seemed to me my father got smaller and emptier himself.

'You know, Norman's favourite photo of his grandfather, the one you used on the poster, Leonard, that was actually taken on a night he played a show to two barmaids, a drunken chef and me. And I was asleep under his coat as soon as I'd finished my geography homework.' *Time to go home, love.*

I told Leonard how I saw so much of my father in Norman, the boy he never met. The same hopefulness, the same intelligence, the same kind of sensitive soul that would go out to get dinner and come home with just a dozen eggs and a single head of broccoli because he'd given the rest away to the homeless man who lived under the bridge. But then we'd eat two-minute noodles with egg stirred through and a side of steamed broccoli and, somehow, my father would make it feel like a dégustation at Marco Pierre White's. And he'd joke about how much that guy under the bridge would be enjoying his cold M&S chicken tikka for two washed down with a bottle of ginger beer, probably wishing it was a can of Tennent's Super Lager. *Ah, it's so nice to be nice, Sadie.*

I hesitated there, but then I heard Jax shouting, 'In for a penny, in for a pound, Sadie,' as he convinced me to bet all my matches (and lose) on a pair of sixes in a game of three-hand poker one rainy Sunday afternoon. And so I told Leonard how my father died.

Not a heart attack at all, like I'd told Norman and anyone else who'd asked, but by hanging himself from a beam in the kitchen of the house where we'd lived my entire life. The very beam where he'd painted the words 'World's Best Daughter' in glitter paint for my sixth-birthday party. Bare, bony feet dangling over the table where the three of us had eaten countless breakfasts, lunches and chicken-hotpot dinners before my mum got sick. Where all my little six-year-old friends had eaten cake under the words that declared I was somebody. I was the world's best daughter.

I kept on talking because Leonard didn't tell me to stop. So I told him that my dad hadn't worn socks to kill himself in January and I'd never know why. That the neighbour who'd found him also found a note tucked neatly into the fruit bowl between a banana and an apple that said, *I've already hung around too long.* That even the punchline of his last joke was far from funny, and for some reason that made me even angrier than the fact he was dead.

I told Leonard that note said everything anyone ever needed to know about Robert Foreman's comedy career, and that I was terrified of all that Dad lurking around there inside Norman, having itself a gene-pool party. Because what if history spun back around on its bungee cord and repeated itself?

'What if he . . . Leonard, what if, without Jax, Norman never gets to be as funny as he so desperately wants to be? As he . . . as he thinks he should be.'

That's what I'm scared of, old man. In fact, it terrifies me to the very core of whoever the hell I am now I'm not the world's best daughter. So how do you like them apples? Leonard's breathing was measured and heavy like he was considering his answer carefully again, but it was also somewhat loud and nasal. I snuck a sideways glance at him for the first time since I'd started talking, and it shouldn't have surprised me, but somewhere between the M&S chicken-tikka dinner and my father's bad-joke death, Leonard had dropped off.

As the gentle whistling from his hairy old nostrils followed my story out on the Swansea sea breeze, down on the beach I saw Norman stop, half turn and lift his nose to the wind. For a moment I thought he was going to look in my direction and I raised my arm, but his tousled head bent slowly into his chest and he turned his body down the beach and kept walking.

I dropped my arm back down to my side, but not quickly enough, and I was standing in the street outside my student digs waving my father goodbye, double thumbs-up as he drove away. Back to his first gig in a month after a twelve-hour round-trip drive to Edinburgh in a hired van with me, my bed and six months' worth of teabags and toilet paper. My hilarious leaving-home present from the man who always knew how to make me laugh. *Hold on tight, Sadie. I've got you.* I shook my head, but not quickly enough, and I was at his funeral, red-eyed and furious that my father was dead and I still had two months' worth of toilet paper and teabags to get through. It made me wonder if he'd already known. If I could have known. *What if I'd known?* Down on the beach, the slow-moving speck of Norman kept moving.

I left Leonard dozing and went inside to the suite to retrieve my phone out of my bag. I scrolled through the contacts and there it was, in its handy little alphabetical order. Of course. Leonard's perfect system made perfect sense. T for Tony Simmons, Swansea, last known phone number. When I tried to remember the last time I'd been able to find what I was looking for on the first try, I had to give up on the first try. I was starting to see the benefits of an organized life.

25

I don't know if it was the talk with Leonard or because I was genuinely better at it after the practice run with Dan McLachlan, but calling Tony Simmons wasn't anywhere near as hard as I'd expected. And really, it should have been worse, because he answered on the first ring.

In actual fact, it was the total opposite to what shall forever be known as the Dastardly Dan Debacle (courtesy of Norman, Leonard and a couple of Post-it notes), because Tony Simmons living in Swansea actually sounded quite pleased to hear from me. Which, to be honest, was ever so slightly more disturbing than Dan McLachlan living in Barnstaple never wanting to hear from me again.

'Sadie . . . ? Wow, Sadie Foreman. Wow! Well, of course I remember you – what are you on about? What a blast from the past! What are you . . . ? How did you get my number? And how on earth are you?'

Now, never let it be said that I don't know how to learn a lesson, and this time there was no way I was going to blurt out the real reason I was calling. After getting over the shock of Tony answering, I managed to stutter that I was very well thank you very much and I was currently on a road trip up to Edinburgh with my son. It did head off on a bit of a bumbling tangent when I got to the bit about it making me think about my university days, which in turn had reminded me of him, but I felt like I finished quite strongly.

'And then, well . . . you know how it is, I found you on, err . . . LinkedIn, and as it goes, Swansea was on our itinerary so . . . well, here we are!'

At least part of that was true anyway. According to Leonard, Tony had been far and away the easiest of all the fathers to find, having diligently recorded his squiggly career path all the way from Edinburgh English Literature student to Swansea social worker via a few years of part-time work at William Hill.

When Tony said that of course he'd love to catch up it reminded me that he'd been quite lovely, really, and we probably could have stayed on track for a pretty solid friendship if we hadn't made the mistake of going back to his flat after that long, boozy afternoon in the university bar discussing the Brontë girls. Which then degenerated into a conversation about whether Liam Gallagher was goon or genius. Which then degenerated further into a story that probably doesn't need retelling.

Hearing Tony's voice also reminded me that it wasn't from lack of trying on his part that we weren't in fact friends. He'd tried to call me, quite a few times, after I snuck out through his laundry room while he was asleep so I wouldn't have to see his flatmates. Or him. But after ignoring about ten answer-machine messages and not going back to our shared lecture for a couple of weeks, which turned into forever, it all went quiet and I totally forgot about him. And, I had presumed, vice versa. It took hearing him for the first time in thirteen years to make me realize that I'd actually treated Tony quite shabbily. *It's nice to be nice, Sadie love.*

It didn't seem to be worrying him too much, though, because when I told him where we were staying he suggested we meet up in his favourite café on the seafront nearby. On the off-chance that he'd left 'part-time axe murderer' off his comprehensive LinkedIn profile, I mentioned that as well as myself and Norman I'd be bringing my friend Leonard with me.

'Absolutely, no problem! The more the merrier!'

It didn't seem like anything would be a problem for Tony, and in that case did I mind if he brought along his partner, Kathy, as well, who he was sure would be delighted to meet me. I couldn't decide on the spot whether the prospect of disappointing Tony's girlfriend or them thinking I had a boyfriend in his eighties worried me more, but we made arrangements to meet the next morning. I hung up wondering if Kathy would be so happy to meet me once I'd laid the news of Norman's possible parentage at her pretty Welsh feet.

Tony looked exactly the same as the last time I'd seen him. Actually, that was naked and asleep, so maybe I'm exaggerating slightly, but apart from a few more clothes (and, come to mention it, that looked suspiciously like the same shirt and jeans I'd trampled over so cavalierly on his bedroom floor while making my escape) and the addition of some black-rimmed glasses, he really hadn't changed at all. When I saw him walk into the café, 2007 picked me up and slammed me right back against the wall without even shaking my hand.

Kathy wasn't Welsh, she was from Leeds and she was lovely, if perhaps a little less delighted to meet me than Tony had promised. Not that I blamed her, and she didn't even know the half of it. She was literally the female version of Tony, which did make me wonder about life, the universe and everything just a bit. How the hell had those two lucked out and found each other? Not only did they have identical wavy brown, mid-shoulder-length hair and the same dark brown eyes, they also looked like they chose their outfits from the same pile of clothes off their bedroom floor each morning. Shabby, crumpled and androgynous, because they had better things to do with their time than wash, iron or separate their whites. Which was probably true, because they were both full-time social workers and ran a drop-in centre and soup kitchen in the evenings and on weekends. Of course they did.

In between tea and carrot cake all round, Tony and Kathy chatted away about the down-and-outers of Swansea, and their poetry slam group that had started with one old guy who came for the free biscuits and now had forty-three chocolate-digestive-eating members. And how a committee member from the Cardiff Harbour Festival had got wind of the group and invited them up there to perform. And about Big Joe, who was fifty-six and had never been further than the Swansea seafront in his entire life and was now going to Cardiff to sing for the mayor.

'Imagine that!' said Kathy. When she spoke she said it straight to Tony, like he was finding out this amazing fact for the first time and wasn't the guy she woke up to every morning of her life. Tony responded equally as enthusiastically.

'I know, right? Incredible, Kath.' Then they gave each other a little squeeze, like they'd just shared the most amazing piece of information in the world.

It was just as well Leonard was along for the ride because Norman and I were both as awkward as each other when it came to keeping up even the light end of a conversation. When it became obvious I wasn't going to be too much use, Leonard chimed in and started asking Kathy and Tony some polite questions. Like how long they'd been living in Swansea, which was eight years for Tony, since he'd arrived for his first social-work job, and seven and a half for Kathy, since she'd arrived for a three-month work secondment.

'I met Tony on my first day on the job and, well, that was that. I was a goner!' That look again, a squeeze, and an assurance from Tony that it was in fact he that had been the goner from the moment she walked through the doors.

'Actually, Sadie, we might even have you to thank in a funny kind of way,' he said. 'I'd probably have gone back home and ended up being the Big Joe of Carlisle if it hadn't been for you.'

All eyes went to me. I had no idea what he meant and I must have looked as terrified as I felt because Tony leaned forward and put his hand on my arm in reassurance.

'No, no, it's good, Sadie. You probably don't even remember, but ...' Considering I'd struggle to remember even one good thing about that time in my life, I certainly didn't think I'd be able remember something that was apparently life-changing for Tony. '... Well, it was what you said to me that ... err ... um, one night.'

Tony flashed a slightly embarrassed look around the table and I'm pretty sure at least three of us knew immediately what night he was talking about. Leonard ducked his head and coughed, Kathy looked down at her lap and I suddenly found the back of my spoon extremely interesting. Norman just looked like he was on the edge of his seat, waiting for the punchline.

'You told me that I should look at what people like the Brontës and Liam Gallagher had achieved in their lives. That the world was bigger than one bloody city and if I wanted a life for myself I had to go out and bloody well get one.' To be honest, it didn't sound like me at all, and I wondered if Tony might have had me mixed up with some other girl, some other one-night stand.

'I . . . well, I don't really . . . I mean, maybe I . . .' But Tony was on a roll down memory lane and picking up speed.

'You know, you were different from everyone else I met at university, Sadie. You were so intent on doing things your way and it was like you didn't give a toss what the world and its wife thought about any of it. I was actually a little bit in awe of your fierceness and your . . . your fearlessness. You know?'

OK, now I knew Tony had me confused with someone else and that's why he had been so happy to meet up. Someone fearless and fierce who didn't give a toss about what the world thought. But before I could open my mouth to correct him he barrelled on.

'I had some funny ideas back then, Sadie. You know, postadolescence angst and all that. I think I thought that if . . . well, that some of your brilliance might rub off on me if we . . . you know. But . . . well, to be honest, you probably did me a big favour by cutting me loose.'

OK, then. I saw Kathy staring at me intently, probably searching for even an inkling of brilliance. Without even looking at her, Tony reached for her hand and landed it first go.

'It made me see that we're nothing without the life lessons that make us, Sadie. You didn't seem like you were afraid of anything or anyone, and it made me realize I wasn't even close to being who I wanted to be, so I had to change.'

I could feel the weight of Norman's silence next to me and I wanted to grab him in a hug and send him one of my telepathic messages that don't seem to work any more. *I'm sorry, son. This crazy hippy's got me all mixed up. He's mistaken blind anger and desperation for courage and passion, and maybe he is your dad and maybe he isn't, but we don't need to know. Let's just pack it in and head home.* But Tony was relentless.

'Remember all the chats we had during those boring lectures about the effect that the Thatcher years had on the British social-justice system?' No idea. None.

'Well, that's what I ended up doing my thesis on after I changed courses. Then I got my first social-work job in Swansea and I just never left. So the way I see it, following my heart brought me to Swansea and then Swansea brought me to Kathy. Or brought Kathy to me, really!'

Either way, they looked delighted at the way the universe had conspired and, apparently, I'd had something to do with it. *One never knows.* Indeed. I snuck a glance at Norman and had to do a double take. Damned if he wasn't looking at me and basking in some kind of a glow. Well, hadn't I turned out to be a regular Cilla Black? Surprise, surprise. I wondered what else Tony and I had spoken about that I had no recollection of and decided that, actually, that was probably quite enough ancient history for one day. So once I'd agreed to accept that me being an absolute cow to Tony had led him to the love of his life, I decided the best course of action was to steer away from the subject before some of the less complimentary details started surfacing.

After I made a lame and unsuccessful attempt to divert the conversation to something about the weather in Penzance, Leonard came to my rescue. Again. He started talking to Tony and Kathy about how lovely Swansea was, how the beach was so different to ours in Cornwall, and how we were so glad we decided to stop off here on our way up to Edinburgh. Which then took him nicely into why we were going to Edinburgh in the first place, which then unexpectedly took a side road into what had happened to Jax.

It's bound to be a bit of a conversation stopper, isn't it? The death of an eleven-year-old boy. Only, strangely, it wasn't. I don't know, maybe it was the social-work thing kicking in, but Tony and Kathy seemed to know exactly how much and how little to say. And to my amazement, after a while it was Norman who was talking, not Leonard.

He told them Jax had been the best friend in the whole world, and Tony and Kathy nodded like they knew it to be true.

'He's . . . actually, he's . . .' Norman shot a sideways look at me and underneath the table we reached for each other's hand at exactly the same moment. 'He was the Rolls-blood— the Rolls-Royce of best friends.' I squeezed gently and felt his small fingers link into mine.

With Tony and Kathy listening like it was an address to the nation, Norman told them about Jax and the first rules of comedy and the Five Year Plan to get to the Fringe, which was now a new plan. Norman's Plan. And how Leonard had set up practice runs along the way, which started with the open mic at the Noble Goat where we'd met Big Al and he'd done his first ever stand-up and wasn't that genius?

'We've got another one here in Swansea this afternoon at the Tally something pub, and even though none of the places . . . I mean the ven— venues from the Fringe have got back to us yet about a real show, Leonard reckons there's still loads of time, right, Leonard? Right, Mum?' I wasn't quite sure what to make of Norman's surprisingly firm squeeze of my hand at that very moment, but I nodded and smiled.

I hadn't heard Norman talk that much since, well, it felt like forever, but I suppose it was really just a couple of months. It was like accidentally finding an omnibus rerun of your favourite show on telly, and even he looked slightly surprised at the sound of his own voice. I didn't want it to stop. I held on to that small hand in mine with all that I had.

'So, Leonard, the Swansea open mic thing, it's not at a place called the Taliesin, by any chance, is it?' After the breathless tumbling of Norman's voice Kathy sounded calm and unhurried.

'Yes, yes, that's it! The Taliesin pub.' Leonard seemed delighted that Kathy knew the place, probably because that might mean there would be a slightly larger audience than the Noble Goat. 'Are you familiar with it?'

'Mmm hmm. And the thing . . . the event's called Swansea's Got Talent, right?'

'Yes indeed, that's right!' Leonard clapped his hands together. 'But it's OK. You don't have to be from Swansea, I checked that. You just need to have talent, of which our Norman most certainly—'

I saw a look pass between Kathy and Tony and a faint alarm began to sound in the back of my head, nudging some words over my tongue and cutting Leonard off mid-sentence.

'Kathy? What's the . . . I mean, is there a problem? Is it cancelled or something?'

Norman was also watching Kathy and Tony closely and had gone a slightly paler shade of pasty, which made the lacework of psoriasis around his hairline stand out like raspberry ripple. He'd clearly seen the look as well, and if there was something to be anxious about he wanted in. I felt a slight sweatiness in our joined hands, but I couldn't tell whose it was.

'No, no. It's just that, well . . . um . . .' Kathy cleared her throat and started again. 'Look, I have a friend whose daughter is, err . . . performing in that. It's, ah . . . actually kind of like a talent show, with dancers and singers, and it's quite . . . um, you know . . . well, it actually *is* a talent show. And the Taliesin isn't a pub, it's an arts centre, it's . . . well, I don't mean to . . . but it isn't anything like an open mic at all, really.'

I tried to catch Norman's eye to reassure him, but he wasn't looking at me because he was too busy swivelling his head from Kathy to Tony to Leonard and back again. The urgent telepathic messages I was sending out were getting lost on the table between the leftover carrot cake and teacups, so I gave up and concentrated on worrying about the vision I suddenly had of Norman sandwiched in to perform between Swansea's finest up-and-comers. He let go of my hand, but the sweatiness remained.

Poor Leonard looked absolutely mortified as the penny began to drop. But then Tony, Kathy and the waitress, who'd stopped by to offer an opinion along with a top-up of tea, all started talking at the same time, tripping over each other's words and saying things like, 'Well, comedy might not be singing and dancing but it's definitely a talent. It'll be fine, of course it will be fine and, anyhow, where's the harm? Why shouldn't Norman have a go?' *How long have you got?*

It was a worrying turn of events and no doubt about it. Even the name of the thing suggested the idea that Swansea already *had* talent was a given, and this was just a way of giving a bit of extra kudos to the best of the best. I really wasn't sure how my beautiful boy and his Post-it note jokes would survive. Norman and Jax's plan was never supposed to be about competing, it was always about the comedy. About a couple of mates having the bollocks to get out there and make people laugh for a couple of minutes. This just felt like an ambush.

Clearly used to thinking on her feet, probably from all those years of picking up the spirits of Swansea's disaffected community members, Kathy sprang into action.

'Listen, Norman, I didn't mean to scare you off or anything.

I just didn't want you to think . . . well, anyhow, maybe you could just go along and have a look first and see what you think? Tony and I could come, too, if . . . Tony?' Tony was already nodding enthusiastically so Kathy turned her attention back to Norman.

'You could take a look at the set-up of the place and the other contest— err, entrants, and then, if you decide it's not for you, well, nobody says you have to do it, right? What do you think, Sadie?'

She swung her head around to include me and I thought for a second it might be possible to fall in love with Kathy, just like Tony had. I had the feeling she'd be able to take anything in her stride. Just lift up her Birkenstocks, step right over the hard stuff life threw at her and keep on walking. I nodded mutely and wondered when would be the best time to deliver the news of why we were really here.

I looked over at Norman, his raspberry-ripple rash melting down his forehead and cheek, into his collar and who knows where else underneath his clothes. He opened his mouth to speak, but before he could get anything out there was a soft rustle and a strong waft of Imperial Leather as Leonard, who'd been silent since Kathy's revelation, shifted in his seat and leaned forward over the table.

'I . . . I know it's not what you expected, Norman, and I'm so terribly sorry about my error. I . . . I don't know how I could have got things so mixed up like that . . . really, I don't. But, you know, nothing ventured, nothing gained, as they say. Why not just say you'll do it and damn the torpedoes!'

Now that he had our attention, Leonard sat up straight in his chair, put his shoulders back, cleared his throat and delivered his finale.

'I say, get in there, my boy! This is no time to be a pussy!'

It couldn't have been more unexpected if Charlotte Church herself had popped down to the seafront in her leisurewear to have tea with us.

Everyone was looking at Norman, but his eyes were fixed on a point beyond Leonard, out through the door of the café and way, way past the shoreline of Swansea Beach. When he spoke, his voice sounded infinitely distant and I knew he was out there, swinging his legs over the edge of the horizon, eating cheesy toast with his best mate. Softly, so softly, his voice came back like a used-up echo.

'That's exactly what Jax would have said.'

I glanced over at Leonard, who was sat there looking pretty pleased with himself, and he gave me a slow wink. For someone who was partial to a bit of an afternoon kip during the important parts he was pretty good at keeping up with the movie.

26

Kathy wasn't wrong. When we pulled up in the car park of the Taliesin Arts Centre it looked like a refugee camp for looky-likies. Amongst the sequinned flotsam and jetsam I spotted a teenaged Sia, a pair of pint-sized twin Mariahs, a middle-aged Britney and a guy who may or may not have been the real Rick Astley coming around for another shot. I definitely couldn't see any other nervy-looking twelve-year-old boys in purple velvet jackets masquerading as comedians, so at least Norman had the element of surprise on his side.

Leonard, Norman and I sat silently in the car for a good few minutes, taking in the scene. My mental powers were useless yet again and my telepathic motherly advice just kept bouncing off the windows and reverberating back into my head. Norman heard nothing. He was pressed up against the back door of the car, eyes closed and a fist full of Post-it notes, mouth moving silently and furiously.

Leonard sat forward and very upright in the driver's seat, star-ing intently into the crowd. He might have been checking out the competition, but he could just as easily have been scanning for snipers. Who would know? I could see Kathy and Tony looking kindly and eager, waving from the steps like a pair of benevolent Jesuses giving blessings to a car park full of impostery superstars and I knew I needed to pull myself well and truly together if I was going to be any help at all to Norman.

I felt a bit like I was having an out-of-body experience and the Macarena in my stomach that had been steadily getting worse since we left Barnstaple was hitting a chorus. I was about to deliver my highly under-prepared son up to a packed hall of Welsh vultures who were probably ready to eat him for their supper and not even spit out the bones, and Tony still had no idea he could be a father. Could things get any worse?

We've all been around long enough to know that the answer to that question is always yes.

Just inside the doors, Leonard found the desk to register and I handed over five pounds to a large woman sitting behind a flimsy table that looked like it was about to collapse from the weight of her roast-beefy elbows. She gave Norman a yellow sticker printed with 'contestant' and a handwritten number fourteen on it to stick on the lapel of his jacket.

'Hello, love, it's good to have you here, and all the best of luck. Make sure you show your number to Elvis, the stage manager, and let him know you're there so he can slot you in correctly. Hurry along now, there's a good boy. Quick sticks. No dallying around.'

As we stepped away from the desk I turned around to Norman, hoping I might come up with something brilliant and encouraging to say, but the words jammed in my throat. I realized there had to be at least two hundred people milling around in the foyer waiting for the show to start. Even though most of them looked like the families or support crew of the entrants, judging by the amount of hairspray, water bottles and snack supplies they were carrying, it was still at least 196 more people than Norman had ever performed to on his own.

As we stood in a silent huddle off to the side, Leonard put a hand on Norman's shoulder to give it a reassuring squeeze and I saw my boy wince. I knew even a gentle touch like that would be hurting because, that morning, through a flash of fluffy Eden Rock embossed towel, I'd caught a glimpse of the monster that took over his body at will. Its latest path of destruction had taken it around his torso and off on a jaunty day trip to circumnavigate his neck, but I knew Norman would rather suffer ten times as much than say anything to hurt Leonard's feelings. That kid. My heart ached with love for him, but my gut continued to ache with something else entirely, and for just a moment I wondered if there might be something else brewing that I should be worrying about. I closed my eyes briefly against the thought and took a slow, deep breath in. *Get in line, buddy.*

Unlike the Noble Goat, not only was there a real stage at the Taliesin Arts Centre, it was in a proper auditorium with dozens of rows of seating, high ceilings and massive curtains disappearing up into the roof. When the tinny electronic bell signalled ten minutes to lift-off, Leonard said he would accompany Norman backstage to go over some last-minute practice, and I certainly wasn't going to argue, because judging by Norman's porridge-coloured face as they disappeared behind the performers' door, he was going to need all the help he could get.

Tony and Kathy had managed to snaffle us four seats in the very front row, and in the awkward shuffley dance of 'You first, No, after you, But I insist, Oh well, then, OK . . .' somehow it ended with me sitting down smack bang between the two love-birds. When Leonard returned to join us I saw a barely there twitch of his eyebrows at the final arrangement, but he said nothing and sidled in beside Tony at the end of the row.

The house lights went down and the woman from the registration desk, who I'd rather unkindly begun thinking of as the Fat Controller as a distraction, waddled on to the stage to introduce 'the fifth annual and no doubt the best yet Swansea's Got Talent'. The crowd didn't quite go wild, but the level of applause was enough to buy my heart a one-way ticket to my boots. There were just so many of them.

Kathy leaned closer into me and gave my arm a squeeze. Before I could get over the shock of the contact, I felt her breath on my neck and she bent in to speak over the noise of the clapping.

'Sadie, I hope you didn't mind us butting in and coming along like this. It's just that . . . well, even though it was a bit of a surprise, Tony seemed so happy that you got in touch and . . . well, after you called he told me how much he'd . . . when you . . . well, anyhow, I just think he really wanted me to like you, too. So I thought I'd try, and then, when I met you, well, I didn't even have to try very hard at all, Sadie. I just think it's wonderful what you're doing for Norman. I don't . . . I mean, you really are amazing, what you're doing to make his dream come true. And your Norman is a such a lovely boy.'

Her hand still rested on my arm and all I could do was stare at her chipped navy-blue nail polish and think, Hang on, did she just say I was amazing? And then another voice piped up, trying to drown out the sound of my own questions. *Tell them.*

I imagined myself rising out of my body and hovering over Kathy and Tony like the Cheshire Cat. Clearing a small hairball out of my throat to purr, 'I'm so glad you think I'm amazing and that my son is so lovely, because, guess what?' And I imagined Tony's far bluer than I'd remembered eyes twinkling in delight, and him saying, 'I knew it! I knew we made magic that night.' And I could almost see lovely, serene earth mother Kathy clasping her hands together, cheeks bright, eyes shiny, saying, 'I'm so happy for Norman and Tony that they finally found each other. But I promise I'll never try to replace you, Sadie. Don't worry, nobody could ever be as good a mother as you. You are amazing.'

I was enjoying my reverie so much that I was a bit disoriented when I opened my eyes to see a greasy hipster with a tinny guitar shredding Alex Lloyd's lovely lyrics into a chorus of coleslaw. '*You were amaaaaaazing, we did amaaaaaazing things.*' Frankly, it was amazing my ears didn't start bleeding, and it made me doubt whether Kathy had even said what I thought she'd said in the first place. It could just have easily been the hipster warming up.

After sitting through a rendition of 'I Kissed a Girl' by a four-year-old in head-to-toe red sequins and a teeny-tiny piano protégée being eaten alive by Beethoven's Piano Concerto No. 5, by the time a portly, pushing-seventy Frank Sinatra strolled out to entertain us with the off-key strains of 'Fly Me to the Moon', I had a glimmer of hope that Norman wasn't actually going to be anywhere near the worst of Swansea's best.

Now, I'm willing to admit that I don't know a lot about talent shows, that being my first and all, but I reckon I know enough to realize that scheduling two Frank Sinatra impersonators in a row is never going to be a good idea. I mean, why wouldn't you throw in a Baby Britney or a set of Antandecs to mix it up? Surely that would make more sense. Clearly, though, whoever was in charge *did* think it was a good idea. But less than a minute after the second Frank (who was a couple of decades younger, much svelter and actually not half bad) began his rendition of 'My Way', it became clear it most definitely was not.

To be fair, it seemed OK at first, as Not Half Bad Frank resonantly began to state his case of which he was so certain. All was still going smoothly as he travelled each and every highway, but by the time he began reminiscing about his regrets that were apparently too few to mention, it became impossible to ignore the very slow but very loud booing coming out of the speakers on the side of the stage, accompanied by random single claps as Very Bloody Bad Frank, still in possession of his microphone, made his feelings clear.

'Booooo.' Clap. 'Boooo, booooo.' Clap. 'Boooooooo.' Clap, clap.

Not Half Bad Frank went from confident imposter to flustered amateur as he peered into the darkened wings, unable to quite comprehend what was going so wrong with his act, which had been going so well. After a few stutters he fell completely out of time with his backing tape and his crooning degenerated into a stammering word soup. But he carried on, singing louder and louder to try to drown out his nemesis, whose boos got louder and louder at the same rate.

'And so I faced it all ... umm, ahhh, and I stood ... umm, tall ...'

After a final valiant but excruciating verse, there was no denying Not Half Bad Frank was most certainly doing it his way. In a merciful intervention, the backing music came to an abrupt stop and the poor guy trailed off into silence, miserably twisting his bow tie and melting under a spotlight that nobody thought to move off him. He was broken. I recognized the shape of him from my father's many near-fatalities on many other stages. *Come on, love, let's go home.*

A handful of the kinder audience members began a lacklustre

ripple of applause, then someone appeared from the wings to thrust the next poor bugger out on to the stage. And there he was. My boy. Blinking in the light, holding a huge microphone awkwardly between two red-raw, hopeful hands. Lamb. To. The. Slaughter.

The broken Not Half Bad Frank limped off stage and, at the sight of Norman, Tony and Kathy elbowed me excitedly at the same time from either side. I glanced out of the corner of my left eye at Kathy, then out of the corner of my right eye at Tony, and felt an army gathering its forces behind my scar. *Now or never, Sadie.* And although never was a far more appealing prospect, I told myself that if Norman could get up there on that stage and do what he was about to do, I could at least have the courtesy to do my lousy part. I leaned slowly sideways towards Tony.

'Tony. There's something ... I ... I need to tell you something.' Tony half turned his head and gave me a look as if to say, 'Why would you want to strike up a conversation just as your son is about to have his big moment?' *Wait for it, fella.*

'H— hell— hello. I ... good even— I mean, good afternoon, ladies and gent— gentlemen ...' Race you to the bottom, Norman.

'Tony,' I whispered. 'Remember when you, when we ... well, you know, that night after the Brontë sisters in Edinburgh?' Even from Tony's profile I could tell that he remembered. *I am amaaaaaaazing, we did amaaaaaaazing things.*

'Tony, I ... did you ... look, do you know ... well, have you thought about how old Norman is? He's twelve. Just turned twelve a month ago, actually. The thing is ...' I felt like I was trying to suck a duvet through a straw. 'Look, I'm not saying for sure, I mean ... I don't really know ... but anyhow, there's a chance, maybe a good one, that ... that Norman could be yours.' Then, just in case. 'Your son.'

'Umm, la— ladies and gentlemen, I . . . I'd like to tell you a couple of jokes that I think . . . I hope maybe you might . . . umm, like.' Wild-eyed and pasty-faced, Norman ploughed on. *Go get 'em, you gorgeous kid.*

Suddenly there was a massive shriek of feedback and everyone in the audience threw their hands over their ears at the same time. For a brief but truly magnificent moment, I thought there was about to be a flash mob and Norman would be saved from his ordeal at the last minute while they filmed a resurrection of the old T-Mobile ads. But all that happened was he started waving the microphone closer and then further away from his face, trying to judge the right distance to stop the feedback.

I could see him mouthing words, trying to get through his first joke, something about meerkats and telescopes, and every couple of seconds he looked desperately left and right into the wings, as if he was hoping against hope to see Leonard with a handful of Post-its.

I felt Tony's eyes boring into the side of my head and Kathy's warm body leaning into me on the other side, but I couldn't bear to look at either of them. Because it was out now. Job done. Tony's court. His serve. I caught a movement as he turned his head away from me and up to Norman on the stage, and then back to me again. He put his hand on my arm and squeezed gently, just as Kathy had before. What was it with these two? I wasn't used to being touched by anyone other than Norman, really, and I was finding I didn't quite hate it.

It was a couple of seconds before I realized that Tony's hand on my arm felt a lot firmer than Kathy's had. More like he was pushing down, and quite hard. It didn't have that reassuring feel, like Kathy's, it almost felt as if it was to stop me from saying anything else. No problem there. I looked over at him and 'Don't say anything else' was also what his face was telling me. He shook his head very slightly and leaned down like he was about to whisper in my ear. But then, as they say in the classics, all hell broke loose.

Accompanied by a strangled roar and a couple of triumphant boos, in a flash of black, white and red bow tie the artist currently known as Not Half Bad Frank came skidding across the stage on his bum at about ninety miles an hour, propelled by the force of an unseen but definitely not unheard assailant. His trajectory took him right past Norman and directly towards the edge of the stage and the front row of the audience. Us.

Everything went into slow motion and I felt my jaw actually unhinge and drop open as the Frank became airborne. I had a microsecond of pin-sharp focus and got a brilliant view of the broken capillaries in the whites of his eyes before he face-planted squarely into the laps of me, Kathy and Tony, ricocheting a shiny black brogue off Leonard's cheek on the way through.

There was a lot of yelping and writhing as he desperately tried to regain a shred of dignity and balance, with very little hope of either. But even with all the commotion and at least a third of a full-sized man on my lap, I could still hear Norman's voice. And although I couldn't make out the words, and the voice was definitely shaky, I knew he wasn't finished.

I gave the Frank an almighty shove and felt my hand connect with a spongy body part, maybe a nose, perhaps an eye socket, I'll never know. He went crashing the rest of the way to the floor and Norman was in my sights again.

He'd abandoned the microphone and was staring out beyond the audience to an invisible focus point, just like I'd heard Big Al tell him in his post-performance pep talk. But he was still going. The knights of Armageddon could have marched in with an arsenal of high-powered flamethrowers and they wouldn't have broken his stride. It didn't matter, though, because nobody was listening to my son any more except me.

Bad Frank appeared on the edge of the stage, seemingly intent on finishing the job he'd started, still shouting abuse but hampered considerably by the Fat Controller, who was practically astride him in her determination to hold him back. Tony and Kathy, good in an emergency of course (of *course*), began helping the other dazed and confused Frank to his feet, brushing him off and offering some comforting words. But Not Half Bad Frank was past caring. He'd well and truly conceded defeat, his lovely slicked-back forelock of hair now skewed to a dangerous tilt, making him look less Frank Sinatra and more Frank Spencer.

I'm not sure how long it was before I clocked that Norman had finally stopped. I looked past the mess of people fussing around their respective Franks and there he was. Standing still and now silent on the stage, the sleeves of his velvet jacket hanging way too far past his hands. A slip of a boy trying to hold up a weight that was never meant for him. *I've already hung around too long.*

I've always run at the first sign of trouble, but not Norman. Everything had gone to shit, chaos reigned around him, but he'd dug in and there it was. Job done. As I looked up at my brave, beautiful, much-cleverer-than-me boy and tried to find some meaningful words, from behind my right shoulder came a quavering, joyful shout.

'Bravo, Norman! Bravo, bravo, you bloody little beauty!' I turned around to look at Leonard, and a wink and a smile nearly broke my heart.

I'm fairly sure the grammatically dubious Cosy Tree Café had never had such a good day. Even though the rest of Swansea's

Got Talent was officially cancelled, some kind of show was apparently destined to go on. It looked like nearly the entire audience had migrated across to the Cosy Tree for tea, cake and a reliving of the afternoon's events. Us included. A few mini pop stars and their mothers were bonding over cupcakes, possibly working on forming a supergroup, but generally there seemed to be one thing on everyone's minds, and two distinct camps. Bad Frank's supporters and Not Half Bad Frank's supporters. Everybody had an opinion and they were all determined to voice it. Who'd have thought Swansea history would be made according to the division of Frank Sinatras? You'd have thought it'd be Tom Joneses, if anything.

Our own little supergroup was squeezed into a booth right by the front door of the café and, somehow, I managed to end up between Tony and Kathy again. I know. But something about the way Tony hesitated and stood back when we went to sit down made it feel like it was a bit more on purpose this time.

The two of them held hands across the back of the booth behind me and it actually felt quite nice to be protected by that little force field when Tony told us that he was really sorry, but he definitely wasn't Norman's father. Because he and Kathy had been trying to have a baby for years, and when they finally got tested a few years ago it turned out the problem wasn't Kathy's uncooperative eggs, it was Tony's lazy sperm. More than likely caused by a serious bout of chickenpox when he was eleven. He had virtually zero sperm count, the lowest the specialist had ever seen in someone who wasn't a woman, apparently. Or something like that. I really didn't listen to the details too closely because I was too busy watching my son.

Even though Norman's face was pretty unreadable, when Tony softly dropped his clanger it seemed to me like the empty shoulders of that jacket collapsed just a little more into the space around him. But if I know myself, and I think I'm getting close, it's a safe bet my own face said it all.

It felt like Tony was breaking up with me thirteen years later and he'd brought his lovely girlfriend along to let me down gently. After the way I'd behaved back then I figured it was only fair, though. Break up with me, Tony, I can take it. But I wish you didn't have to break up with Norman.

'Well, now. There you are! I need to see you, young man.'

I was shaken out of my musings by the sight of the Fat Controller, who had suddenly materialized at our booth, looking frazzled, flustered and actually quite a bit less substantial out in the real world.

'I've been looking all over for you!'

Across the table I saw Norman shrink down into his seat and, straight away, Leonard cleared his throat and puffed out a protective chest as if to shield him.

'Of course, the entire show's had to be cancelled for this year, as you know. Due to . . . well, due to my husband's bad behaviour, quite frankly. Pardon the pun, won't you! I should leave the jokes to you, really, shouldn't I, Norman? Ha ha!'

It appeared we all did pardon the pun, or in a few cases maybe didn't get it. And again, while I'm no expert, an organizer being married to one of the contestants definitely seemed like a giant conflict of interest. It seems to me it's just asking for trouble, really, and I rest my case.

'But anyhow, I wanted to find you so I could give you this, Norman.'

She pulled a rolled-up piece of cardboard tied with a blue ribbon out of her tote bag and balanced it delicately across Norman's teacup.

'It's a very special award for being a good sport . . . and you know, for trying. You were a real trooper, love. Well done, and I'm so sorry you didn't get the chance to perform properly. You come back and see us next year, won't you?'

Over the entire population of Swansea's dead bodies, I thought. And only then. This time next year, the closest I'm hoping to be to Swansea is nibbling on a bit of cheesy rarebit for my supper and watching *Gavin and Stacey* reruns. But it looked like Norman might have had other ideas. He'd unrolled the flimsy bit of cardboard on the table and was staring at it, eyes wide. I could see the generic Certificate of Excellence was printed with a sponsor's logo along the top and Norman's name hastily scrawled across it in gold pen.

When he spoke, Norman's voice was soft, but it was full to overflowing with more of everything wonderful than I could muster in a month of Sundays.

'Mum. Mum, look. Do you see it?'

I leaned forward across the table to get a closer look at the upside-down certificate where his finger rested on a line of text.

Swansea's Got Talent. Proudly sponsored by
Hooper and Collins Urban Planning.
Never give up on a good plan.

Bloody hell. I saw it.

27

NORMAN

First rule of comedy: If somebody laughs, it's funny.

Even if I don't ever go back to Swansea again in my entire life, I'll never forget it. And that's not just because I met Kathy and Tony or saw two Frank Sinatras in a dust-up, or even because I got given a certificate of encouragement for a talent show that I didn't even know I was going to be in. Even though all those things were pretty cool, especially the meeting Tony and Kathy part. But the reason I'm never going to forget about my trip to Swansea is because it was the place where I had my first real, proper, couldn't actually help myself laugh since the day before Jax went.

I remember, because two months, four days and seven hours is a long time to wait around for a laugh. Even though some comedians I've seen on late-night TV probably had to wait around for a lot longer than that. I wrote that down on a Post-it because I thought maybe I could use the line in a joke. But it was a bit hard to tell if it was really funny or not without having Jax around to tell me, that's rubbish, Normie. Or that's about as funny as a train wreck, you numpty. Or boom boom, that's comedy gold, you bleedin' genius! Which is all actually pretty helpful.

Anyway, you'd think that after what happened at Swansea's Got Talent I wouldn't have had much to laugh about, wouldn't you? I mean, first of all I totally bombed in the talent show. Actually, first of all I was *in* a talent show, and who would ever have thought that would happen? Then I found out Tony was no way, no how, no sirree Bob my dad. Which if I'm honest did make me a bit sad, because Tony is a really cool guy and I reckon he'd be a pretty cool dad too.

So all up it doesn't sound like a great time, does it? Because you name it and just about everything went wrong. But somehow all the lots of little things going wrong didn't add up to a big disaster like you'd think. In fact, funnily enough, it kind of went the other way and actually all added up to something pretty good. Don't ask me how that happened, but it did. And don't bother asking Mum by the way, because she reckons she's got no idea either.

When I was standing on that stage with a spotlight burning so bright into my eyes that I couldn't see a thing, let alone my mum, while some guy went for a slide across the stage and landed on everyone's laps, well, if someone had told me that half an hour later I'd be sitting in a café called the Cosy Tree proper laughing my head nearly off, no way would I have believed them. Never and not in a million years.

Only it really did all happen just like that. Before the laughing my head off part, though, there was the bit where Tony had to explain about his lazy old sperm and why he couldn't be my dad. We already did sex education last year so I kind of know the general idea of what's supposed to happen with sperms and ovaries and all that. Scientifically, I mean, not the sex stuff. Everyone knows about that.

Even though Kathy and Tony both looked a bit sad when Tony was telling us about the no babies thing, they kept smiling. And they still kept holding hands behind Mum's head in the booth. Mum looked a bit like she was going to cry, though, and I think maybe she was even sadder than me that Tony wasn't going to be my dad.

She didn't say anything straight away, but I knew she would be thinking it was all her fault. Because Mum's like that. Even when something could no way be her fault, like Tony not being my dad, she sometimes blames herself. Which Jax says is called Mother's Guilt, and he knows a lot of stuff like that because he reads a lot. Well, he did.

Anyhow, he read about Mother's Guilt in one of his mum's magazines when he was home sick from school for a week after a really bad asthma attack last year. He was so bored he said he was going to read every single thing in the house and then put it all together to write a comedy skit. He did it too, because he always does what he says. And even though I Think She Prefers Hobnobs to Husbands, which came from reading all the newspapers, flyers, letters, biscuit packets and magazines in the house, maybe wasn't really suitable for an actual audience, boy was it funny to us.

So anyhow, that's kind of the reason I started laughing. Because when the lady from the talent show left after giving me my certificate, Leonard goes, hell's bells, I wonder if she gave her husband an encouragement certificate too. Everyone cracked up, because it was actually pretty funny, but I cracked up because for some weird reason it reminded me of Jax and the She Prefers Hobnobs to Husbands skit.

Also, I think that maybe you have a certain amount of laughing that you're supposed to use up every day or every month or something. And maybe the laughs just store up when you're sad and you get to have them all at once when you stop being sad for the first time. Because once I started laughing after what Leonard said it was pretty hard to stop.

Even though I was totally thinking about Jax, I didn't feel sad like I usually did when I thought about him. Which was always. And because I didn't feel sad I closed my eyes and imagined that he was sitting right there squished into the booth next to me laughing too. Louder than everyone else put together, because that's how it would be. And I know it sounds weird, but I could actually feel him there, because when you sit next to Jax you can feel something coming off him, maybe sort of like electricity. Honest. I swear I heard him buzzing once.

This one time when we were first friends I touched his arm and we both got zapped. We just cracked up when it happened, because it was like when something is bad but it's good at the same time. After that he always used to rub his feet on the carpet when he was coming up behind me and try to zap me when I wasn't expecting it. He got me lots, but I never minded because it was always that bad but good feeling.

When I opened my eyes in the café everyone was still talking and laughing like nothing had happened. Like I hadn't just tried to imagine my dead best friend back to life. But I really, really had, because I'll tell you something else too. I'd already seen him that day.

When I walked out on stage at the talent show I couldn't see a thing in the audience because of the lights, but as soon as I started talking all of a sudden I could see everything right up to the back row of the auditorium. And you'll never guess who was up there, but if you guessed Jax you'd be right.

He was standing on one of the seats holding up a bunch of

cardboard sheets with words painted on them like they do in those old-fashioned music video clips. He kept pulling the cards out of the bunch and holding them up for me to read then dropping them on the ground. And even when the Frank fell off the stage Jax kept on pulling out those cards faster and faster and holding them up for me to say the lines. Which is why I kept on going till the end. Not because I had suddenly got clever or funny or brave. Or because all that practising I did with Leonard had actually worked. I kept going because Jax was helping me.

When I started laughing in the Cosy Tree Café it was like when I started crying in Barnstaple, which got me thinking that maybe the storing up laughing thing was the same for crying. Later, when I went for a wee, I was washing my hands and I looked in the mirror and saw lots and lots of teeny tiny spots of blood coming through my shirt. Because I'd laughed so much remembering about She Prefers Hobnobs to Husbands and getting zapped by Jax that the big bits of scale on my chest had cracked. But even though it hurt and even though I knew all that blood probably wasn't going to come off my one good shirt for the trip I didn't care. Because it was like everything just felt a little bit looser.

28

Sadie

When I'm old and senile and reliving my misspent middle years I think maybe I'll remember our three days in Swansea as the time Norman started to come back. Because even though it was only a brief glimpse, that guy laughing his heart out in the Cosy Tree Café looked very much like the son I used to have.

The next day, while Leonard sat out on the balcony doing whatever it was he did on his laptop, Norman was helping me pack our bags. As I sorted out clothes and shoes and underpants I saw him carefully roll up his certificate from the talent show and wedge it inside a sock at the bottom of his case. He caught me looking and straight away he arranged his face into a smile for my benefit. It didn't quite make it to his eyes, though, turning off down a side street at his cheekbones and slipping off into the neck of his crumpled T-shirt to have a quiet drink alone in a bar.

Oh, because I was definitely jealous I hadn't been the one to make Norman laugh like that at the Cosy Tree. It had been so long since I'd heard that laugh for real I'd sat there watching him, just wanting it to go on and on for ever. But then he stopped and closed his eyes, and he stayed like that for so long it made me wonder if in his head he was standing at a crossroads with tumbleweeds drifting past, deciding which guy he was going to be for ever.

'Hey, Mum?' My son's soft voice brought me back to the now and the sound of distant strangers' laughter drifting up from the Swansea beach. *Come in deeper, Sadie, I've got you.*

'So do you reckon either of the Franks *did* get a certificate too?' Tell me how you could not love this kid.

'Oh, for sure, yeah. I reckon they both got one for joint best and fairest.' There was such a long pause I wondered if he hadn't heard me, because normally he's so polite he laughs at my attempt to make jokes. Just to encourage me, I think. And because he really, really loves me.

'Yeah. Hey, Mum? I've been thinking. The certificate . . . I mean, I know it was only for trying and stuff, and I didn't like really win anything or anything . . . but it's got to count for something, don't you think? So I . . . I was thinking that maybe when we get to Bournemouth, well, maybe . . .'

Norman looked down at his feet and sat down heavily on the bed.

'It's just that, Mum, I'm . . . I'm just not sure if I should do the open mic show in Bournemouth. Like . . . like maybe I could use the time to just practise on my own instead. Or in front of you guys? I mean, maybe that would be even better than an open mic because . . . I . . . I don't know, what do you think?' Ahh, you don't want to know that, Norman.

I'd seen Leonard and Norman hunched over the laptop the night before, checking and double-checking on the Bournemouth open mic details. I knew Leonard felt responsible for the Swansea's Got Talent debacle and he wanted to make sure the next one was exactly what it was supposed to be: a regular, out-of-the-way pub with a lame open mic night. But not quite so out of the way and lame as the Noble Goat, so as to have no punters. It was a fine line and, I guessed, a pretty big ask.

I sat down on the edge of the bed next to Norman and stretched my arm around him. I felt his body relax as he leaned on to my shoulder and, right then, with that small, dear head so close to mine, I wished for the answers to motherhood more than any other time in my life. Any of them. A tip of a cap would do at this stage. I'd been so quick to jump into this plan, be the cool mum, make this crazy dream come true, because I didn't know a real way to take away his pain. But what if everything I was doing was just making things worse? I gently moved Norman's head from my shoulder and knelt on the floor in front of him.

'Norman, listen to me. Of course if you don't want to do the open mic, you don't have to. Of course. We don't have to go to Bournemouth at all. I mean, I don't have to call the next guy if you don't want and . . . we don't even have to go to Edinburgh if you don't want to.' *The show must go on, Sadie.*

'The show doesn't always have to go on, Norman.'

'Mum, no! That's . . . no, that's not it. That's not what I meant at all.' Shit.

'I wouldn't back out now, Mum. I mean, it's . . . it's the Fringe, baby . . . and you know, never give up on a good plan and all that. That was a sign, Mum. I know it was. It's just that . . .'

He paused, and it felt like a thousand years. Like the entire weight of the world was just biding its time and shaping up to fall down and settle on to Norman's scarred little shoulders. I held my breath, waiting for what was coming next. When we find my father I don't care who he is, even if he's just got out of jail for murdering schoolgirls I want to go and live with him? I've decided to double the length of the show just for good measure? I've finally worked out how shit you really are as a mother? His voice, though, when it came, was sweet, shaky and careful. Like I was the one who needed protecting, not him.

'It's just . . . Mum, I . . . it's just that I think I need to work on my material a bit more before Edinburgh. That's all. I . . . I just need to do a bit of work, Mum.' Yeah. Me too, son.

Kathy and Tony showed up at the Eden Rock the next morning to say goodbye, but instead of thinking that maybe it *would* be quite nice to have a farewell and good-luck breakfast, as Kathy put it, it just made me sad that Tony's stupid sperms couldn't have been bothered to swim a little harder. Did they know what they'd missed out on? By the look on Tony's face every time he talked to Norman, I was guessing the answer was that he, at least, did.

Leonard declined the invitation to breakfast, saying he was going to make the most of the free Wi-Fi while he could. He'd definitely been a little bit off since the whole talent-show mess and he seemed distant and even a little bit snappy when I'd asked if he was quite sure he didn't want to come with us.

'Absolutely certain, Sadie. I'm really not hungry and I . . . well, I don't want to risk making any more silly mistakes so I want to double-check the route to . . . to . . .' Leonard stopped mid-sentence and a pained expression flitted across his face as his eyes slid away from mine and landed on some invisible point over my shoulder. I half turned to see what he was looking at, but I couldn't see anything except Kathy, Tony and Norman standing in the doorway, waiting for me. They looked for all the world like a cosy little Swansea family and my next breath wrapped itself around my windpipe and held on way too long. When I managed to look away and turn back to Leonard his faraway gaze hadn't changed. It was a bit disconcerting. All of it.

'Leonard? Are you . . . ?'

He suddenly gave a little shiver and shook his head as if to clear it, looking back at me like he'd just realized I was there.

'What's that? Oh. Yes, sorry, sorry. I . . . well, yes, as I said, I just want to check the route before we set off again. That's all. Really, Sadie, thank you, but please do go on without me.'

I hadn't really seen Leonard anything other than varying degrees of chipper. Perhaps the shine of Norman and me was wearing off and he was wishing he was back home with his lovely Iris. Before I had time to start worrying about it Leonard raised an arm to give a quick wave to the others and turned away.

We left him tapping away at his laptop in the foyer of the Eden Rock and wandered down to the café where we'd met Kathy and Tony two days before. And even though I never thought you'd catch me saying this, the goodbye felt like it was going to be a lot harder than the hello.

Norman chased his toast and jam around the plate and I could tell he was trying very hard not to stare at Kathy and Tony too much, but he was also really concentrating on what they were saying. Kathy talked earnestly about Swansea's homeless problem and how important it was to keep the issues in front of the local politicians, and I wondered what it was like to be so passionate about something that you were willing to stand up and do something about it. *Your fierceness and your fearlessness.*

I looked over at Norman in his stretched and faded T-shirt and his pink, splotchy face, then down at my bitten nails, unravelling jumper and saggy-kneed jeans and wondered if perhaps we weren't just one step away from the homeless folk of Wales ourselves. And that maybe they were actually better off than us, because at least they had Kathy and Tony.

Had that really been me Tony had been talking about, that fierce and fearless girl? A girl who could have a conversation about the Brontë sisters and Liam Gallagher and the bigness and wonderfulness of the world? The same girl who stood in the kitchen where her father killed himself and told kindly people with triangles of ham sandwiches in their hands to fuck right off. The girl who walked out of that house the very next day with just a box full of old DVDs, some photo albums and a purple velvet suit jacket. The girl who had nobody left to disappoint.

I only realized I'd been asked a question when the silence around the table alerted me to the fact that everyone was looking at me. Unless it was about last year's *Come Dine with Me* Champion of Champions, there was no way I was going to be able to fake my way into making them believe I'd been listening, but then, as was quite conveniently becoming something I could rely on, Leonard arrived to my rescue.

A whoosh of wind blew back the hair and scrambled eggs of everyone in the café as Leonard most uncharacteristically flung open the door, laptop in his hands and his glasses balanced wonkily on top of his head. He practically skidded across the greasy café floor in his gleaming Nikes and came to an elegant halt at our table.

Everyone stopped looking expectantly at me and, instead, all expectant glances were directed towards Leonard, whose mouth was wide open and gasping as he tried to catch a breath. The waitress paused at the next table with two cappuccinos in her hands, the guy out the back in the kitchen poised his spatula mid egg flip, and even the traffic outside ground to a halt at a red light. The whole world was looking at Leonard, but Leonard was looking only at Norman.

'Hold on to your hat, Norman old man! You're going to the Fringe, baby!'

29

Of course, I know what you're thinking. That the news a venue had given Little Big Man a slot on its Fringe schedule shouldn't have come as quite such a shock to me. That I should have known there was a reasonable chance it would happen, because, after all, it was one of the crucial points on which Norman's whole plan hung. But now that it had become a reality, all I could think was, holy, holy, holy shit.

In between their excited chattering and congratulating of Norman, Kathy and Tony both gave my arms a squeeze from either side, in tandem of course. Leonard plonked the laptop down on the table and started picking lint out of his jacket pockets with a beatific smile, like he'd known all along. And Norman, well, he just sat there with an expression I couldn't quite read, because, to be honest, I wasn't quite sure I'd ever seen it before.

When everyone calmed down Leonard pulled over a chair from a nearby table, sat down next to Norman and adjusted the screen on his laptop. There was no sign of his previous odd mood and he seemed totally back to his charming self.

'Right then. Listen to this. Oh . . . err, just a moment, I seem to have . . .' There was a delay while he fumbled around with the keys and brought up a few windows on the screen.

'Umm . . . I'm terribly sorry, I . . . oh! Right, here it is.'

He cleared his throat and began reading out loud from an email.

Dear Little Big Man. Thank you very much for requesting to be part of the Edinburgh Festival Fringe event scheduled at the Duke Supper Club downstairs at O'Shaughnessy's Real Ale House.

It seemed they had been impressed by the tenacity of his daily and sometimes twice daily follow-ups (Leonard clearly hadn't made it through three wars and a stint at Pearl's by giving up when the going got tough), so after due consideration and a very last-minute cancellation (and possibly a healthy dose of exasperation, I was willing to bet), they were delighted to offer Little Big Man a fifteen-minute slot at their establishment on the outskirts of Edinburgh. But easily accessible by public transport. Good to know.

'Oh my god, Norman! You did it, you got a venue!'

Kathy was positively beaming as she reached over the table to give Norman's hand an encouraging pat. I knew I needed to say something, too, but when I tried my mouth just did some kind of weird yawning thing as a bunch of words began lining up to commit suicide over my tongue. Jostling around next to the *shit it all*s were a couple of *what the fuck*s and a few token *hell's bells* thrown in for good measure, and it took everything I had to stop them from spewing out all at once in an almighty mess on the café table and be done with it. So I said nothing. But I was thinking plenty.

Even though Norman was so sure he wanted to do all of this, meeting a father was one thing, but what if, when push came to shove, he just couldn't pull off his comedy show without Jax? Or what if he did actually make it through his routine and got laughed at all right, but not in a good way? Leonard may have created Little Big Man to get Norman to the Fringe, but could Norman actually *be* Little Big Man once he got there?

Most of the comedy acts performing at the Fringe would probably have spent years slogging around the clubs paying their dues and hardening their hearts well before they got the balls to front up for something like this. And notwithstanding my pride at his gutsy attempts at the Noble Goat and Swansea's Got Talent, I couldn't help worrying that Norman just wasn't ready for the big time. No matter how small it was. Not even fifteen minutes at the Duke Supper Club on the fringes of the Fringe.

I sucked in my breath as something inside delivered a sharp kick to the back of my scar. It was almost too much for me to bear to think of Norman up there on a stage with only my father's old jacket to protect him. That jacket had seen it all before and, like me, it already knew how things could end. *It doesn't matter, love. Let's go home.*

Tony and Kathy insisted on seeing us off right up to the last goodbye, which was pretty handy because Tony took over the repacking of the car and, for the first time, it looked like Leonard might actually be able to see out the back window. Even though we didn't really have much between the three of us, the boot was tiny and our cases seemed to be getting progressively bulgier as the trip went on and my dedication to folding our clothes waned. Leonard's bag was definitely taking up more room, too, since we'd stopped for petrol at a Tesco garage half an hour outside of

Barnstaple. In the time it had taken me to pay for the petrol and buy a packet of chewing gum and a couple of bottles of water Leonard had managed to purchase an impressive array of spicy-smelling toiletries, a pair of slippers and, surreptitiously, a six-pack of underpants to add to his luggage. Although not surreptitiously enough for Norman not to have noticed.

As we'd walked to the café that morning he said he'd thought of a joke about old men's pants and my third favourite song of all time, Bob Dylan's 'Blowin' in the Wind'.

'Do you think Leonard would mind if I used it, Mum? Should I ask him? It's a pretty funny one. I . . . I think it is, anyway.'

Leonard was a good sport and I was pretty sure it would be fine to talk about his underpants, although that was before I knew they were going to get an airing at the bloody Edinburgh Fringe. Anyhow, Tony took one look at how we'd just chucked everything into the car and took it all back out again. But in a kindly way, not bossy. I had a sudden very unexpected flashback to that night in Edinburgh. It was a hell of a time to remember, but apparently he packed cars like he approached his work with women. Considered, concerned and very neat and tidy with all the ends finished off.

After a bit of jiggling Tony slotted everything back into the boot and, amazingly, it seemed to only take up about half the space it had before. I had room at my feet, Norman didn't have to balance his elbows on the just-in-case box of groceries and, all in all, it looked like it was shaping up to be a far more comfortable trip to Bournemouth than the one from Barnstaple had been.

After promising to call and let Tony and Kathy know how the show went, we drove away. When I turned and leaned out the window to wave at them, their arms were already back around each other. My stomach gave a twang when I realized that there, but for a lazy bunch of sperm and a bad attitude, could have been my life. It could have been me and Tony waving some madwoman and her posse off to Edinburgh. Mine and Norman's lives could have been ordered, neatly laid out, with everything fitting perfectly together like in the car boot. And maybe Kathy would just have been a kindly neighbour. Or my best friend.

But probably not, I decided, because those two were so right together I couldn't imagine they were ever destined to be anyone's interlocking piece but each other's. And as Tony and Kathy blurred into smudges, after all the years of telling myself I didn't need that kind of anchor I found myself quite surprised to have my head out a car window with watery wind-eyes, wondering just how it might feel.

I snuck a look at Norman in the wing mirror. He already had his wad of Post-it notes fanned out in his hands and was mouthing lines out the window. My own reflection loomed large and I met her surprisingly steady gaze. *Your fierceness and your fearlessness.* That girl. Was it possible she really *had* existed?

As we swerved on to the M3 towards the sign that declared Bournemouth to be thataway I focused a little closer on Norman's lips and, while I couldn't be sure, some of those lines looked a little bit like what the fuck, shit it all and hell's bells. If, by some miracle, Tony was right, Norman was going to need every bit of whatever that girl had if he was going to get through this in one piece. And maybe she might make it too.

30

I'd have to say that Adam Linley was the least memorable of all Norman's paternal possibilities. And I think by now you know that's saying something. But I don't just mean the circumstances of our involvement, I mean the actual notion of him as a person. I'd had a vague recollection of lots of greasy blond hair and skin-tight jeans, which might or might not have been removed after a full bottle of vodka had been consumed by two people who might or might not have been him and me. But like I said, beyond that and his crime of nicking my toastie maker, it's all pretty fuzzy.

The only reason I had even been able to recollect his last name is through the stroke of luck that he'd dubbed himself 'The Viscount', after Viscount Linley, Princess Margaret's son. So when I'd begun to trawl the depths of my memory, greased by the wheels of a couple of Hobnobs, the vision of a long-haired guy in a loincloth and a crown had popped into my head for seemingly no reason at all. But then the name Adam Linley followed in fairly quick succession, along with the flashbacks to the aforementioned bad behaviour. When Leonard's line-up had presented me with a picture that looked so suspiciously similar to my cloudy recollection that either Adam had discovered the fountain of youth or he was using a very, very old photo on his Facebook profile, even I couldn't have made a mistake. *Voilà*.

With Tony and his sperm out of the picture, Adam Linley's odds were shortening with every mile we got closer to Bournemouth. The more I thought about it, though, the more I started to think that Leonard and I should probably have been a little more thorough with our task. Maybe added a couple of columns for some details about the potential fathers' lives as they stood now. Because what about the possibility of wives, families, criminal activities or fame and fortune? To name just a few potential problems.

Not that I'd thought they'd all be sitting around waiting for my call or anything, I guess it just hadn't entered my mind any earlier that these guys also had thirteen years of life under their belt since I'd last seen them. To me, they were just names on Leonard's spreadsheet, representing a task I really didn't want to face but was trying my almost best to, because after all it was the least I could do. And, funnily enough, also the most.

With the deep wisdom of hindsight, I decided to approach Adam Linley a little differently than my previous two attempts, with a text rather than a call – even though I generally wasn't that big on texting as a rule, possibly because I didn't have too many people to message. My main text conversations were with Dennis, who usually only texted me when he wanted me to pick him up a coffee on my way back from lunch, and Jax.

I'd tried very hard to ignore the trail of messages that were still attached to Jax's name in my phone. Norman had a mobile that I'd bought him when he'd started catching the bus to school on his own, but more often than not he left it at home, so Jax used to text me to let me know they were OK. *All good, Sadie, at mine* or *at shop,* or *getting fishnchips,* or *me n Normie at beach,*

THE FUNNY THING ABOUT NORMAN FOREMAN

usually accompanied by a photo of them both doing exactly what it said in the message.

In summer the photos featured Jax bare-chested and bronzed like a mini-Tarzan, and Norman hatted, shirted and covered from head to toe so he didn't get sunburn to add to his skin's other woes. In winter it'd be beanies pulled low, jackets zipped high and, once, a chip jauntily stuck up each of Norman's nostrils and one coming out of Jax's ear.

Proof of life, Jax used to call it, so after he died it had been two weeks before I could look at any of those messages. I'd waited until I was sure Norman was asleep so he wouldn't come across me crying over a mobile phone on the sofa. Snotty and hiccuping, cushion corner pushed into my mouth to dull the wracking sobs as I scrolled through endless pictures of Jax, large as life. Large as death.

The messages went back two years, since Jax had managed to convince both his mother and I that two ten-year-old boys absolutely needed mobile phones. They were funny and sassy and some of them might even have been a little too cheeky coming from a kid that age to his best mate's mum. But that was the thing about Jax. No matter how cheeky or rude he was, we forgave him anything, me and Norman. Because he was like that little bit of you that you were always too afraid to let out. The part you push back down your throat and put a hand over your mouth so it doesn't escape by accident. Ah, but sometimes you wished it would.

You can bet Jaxy never put a hand over his own mouth. Not for anything or anyone. He was all the fun and free and naughty parts of life. He *was* life. That kid wasn't afraid of anything and oh, how we loved him for it. Because me and Norman were afraid of almost everything.

*

According to the spreadsheet timetable, I was to contact Adam Linley just before we left Swansea to give him a heads-up on the possible existence of a bombshell in the form of a boy coming his way. I'd managed to conveniently put it off, what with all the excitement of the Duke Supper Club news, but it looked like there were no further distractions to be had. So, with Leonard humming along to a radio jingle for Wetherspoons and Norman mouthing his lines or a cry for help, I clicked on my contacts and headed into the A's.

Just as I tapped on Adam's name the car hit a pothole and my fingers bounced on the keypad. Once the car stopped shuddering, I started to compose a sensitive but compelling text to another man I hadn't seen for thirteen years. That's what I was aiming for anyhow.

Hi Adam. Sadie Foreman here. I'm not sure if you remember me, as it's been a long time and we didn't really know each other that well, but I met you in Edinburgh in 2006 at university. Was there a protocol for the length of this kind of text? Just what depth of background does one offer? Does one say, *Oh and also we shagged, but just the once and if I can barely remember it I guess I can't really expect you to.* I decided it might be best if I went for a more subtle approach.

I discovered that you live in Bournemouth and I'm passing through with my son on our way to the Edinburgh Fringe so I wondered if you'd have time for a quick catch-up. I know it might seem strange, but my son would like to meet you. There is a bit of a possibility that you could be his biological father. OK, not so subtle then. *Please don't worry, he would simply like to meet you, that's all – no strings attached. I understand the sensitivity of the issue and possibly the need for discretion, which I assure you I can guarantee. We don't want anything from you,*

but Norman has recently lost his best friend in tragic circum-
stances and I feel that the opportunity to meet you might settle
some questions and give him some comfort. I appreciate this
will come as a bit of a shock out of the blue like this after so
long, but we are in Bournemouth for just one night so I hope
you will consider meeting us. We'll be at O'Neills on Old
Christchurch Rd at 7 p.m. tonight. I hope to see you there. Bollocks I do and PS: how about you bring my toastie maker? *Many*
thanks and kind regards, Sadie Foreman.

About thirty seconds after I pressed the send button a beep
came back on my phone. At exactly the same time I felt a sharp,
reverberating jolt and my head shot up in time to take in the view
as the little car headed on to the verge with two wheels bumping
noisily along on the grass.

'Jesus! Leonard! Shit! What . . . ?'

I just had time to register a glimpse of a very strange look
on Leonard's face before he swung the steering wheel violently
and heaved us back on to the road, overcorrecting to the wrong
side as an Ocado delivery van came hurtling around the
corner.

Before the scream in my throat was able to even form properly
Leonard let out a startled 'Hell's bells, man!' as he swung the
wheel back the other way and, out of the corner of my eye, I
caught sight of Norman's feet whipping up off the floor and curling beneath him in a semi-foetal position. Within a split second
the van had gone and we were back on the right side of the road,
albeit at a greatly reduced speed and with a very, very shaken-
looking driver at the wheel. Leonard's face was ashen.

'Oh dear, oh dear, dear me. I'm . . . is . . . is everyone OK? I'm
so sorry, I don't know . . . I didn't . . . I . . .'

To be honest, I felt as bad as he looked, but suddenly Norman was leaning forward from the back seat patting our arms reassuringly in tandem and looking from one to the other.

'It's OK, Leonard. Honest. It's OK. We're OK. We're all OK. Aren't we, Mum?' *Are we?*

'Yes, yes of course we are. Perfectly fine, Leonard, it's . . . don't worry about it.' *But what the hell just happened?*

'I . . . I just don't know what happened. One minute I was on the road and the next I . . . I must have lost concentration for just an instant. I . . . it's absolutely unforgiveable. I'm so sorry.'

Norman wriggled even further forward into the front.

'It's not unforgivable, Leonard. Honest! I reckon we would have been a goner if it wasn't for your great driving. We forgive you. Don't we, Mum?' Ah, it's so nice to be nice.

'Of course we do, Leonard. But I do think that maybe it'd be a good idea to pull over at the next stop just to . . . regroup. All of us. What do you think?'

While Leonard had regained some of his composure, thanks to Norman, he looked very relieved when, just a few minutes later, we were able to pull off the motorway at a large roadside services. Norman wandered off to find a loo and Leonard went inside to buy us some much needed tea.

I looked down at the phone in my lap, which was still blinking with the new message that had come through just before our near-death experience. But it had been too quick, surely? Unless Adam Linley really had been waiting around for a text from me for thirteen years and was going to be as happy as Tony had been to see me. Or perhaps it was from his wife, telling me to leave him alone and how dare I. Or maybe he was in the Dan McLachlan camp and the reply was just 'not interested'. Maybe not even prefaced with a sorry.

Part of me wanted to throw the phone back in my bag, put my

head on my lap and just drift off into a coma to try and sleep all this off. After all, my life was proof positive that you could keep that up almost indefinitely if you had nothing else to concentrate on. But I thought that Leonard probably deserved to know how his research was panning out, so I pressed on the message.

Only it wasn't from Adam Linley at all. It was from Al. Of the Big and Barnstaple variety, who'd put his number in my phone and handed it back with a wink to Norman and a 'You know, just in case you want to call me on your way back through.' I'll admit that just for a moment the thought had crossed my mind that there might have been something quite lovely lurking underneath that beard.

> *Hey. I don't think you meant to send this to me, Sadie, because I'm pretty sure I wasn't even in Edinburgh 13 years ago, ha ha. But I kind of wish I had been ;) Think you better resend it to the lucky guy! Hope the trip's going well. Tell Norman to keep up the practice and tell Leonard to drive carefully. Might see you on the way back home. I hope. Al (Big) x*

The thought of typing out that sensitive and compelling message all over again to send to the right person almost did me in, even though hearing back from the wrong person was interestingly pleasant. But then Leonard arrived back with the very strong teas and some handy skills. After making short work of cutting, pasting and resending the message to Adam's number (Get to Know Your iPhone in a Day at the Morrab Library last year), he leaned back in his seat and closed his eyes. To regroup, I sincerely hoped.

He'd loosened his tie and his shirt was open at the neck to reveal a tufty bit of grey hair waving gently in the breeze. With his face relaxed and mouth slightly open, he looked almost like a baby, albeit a very wrinkly one that had just nearly killed us. I wondered how many near-misses Iris had lived through in the Austin, and if, in fact, that was the reason she didn't seem to mind being left at home while he swanned off to Edinburgh with us.

I sat up straighter in my seat to try and ease the pain that had given up coming and going since Swansea and had taken up permanent residence in my stomach. I twisted slightly and it came with me. As I continued to stare at Leonard's oblivious side profile it occurred to me that, actually, he hadn't so much as dropped a mention of Iris's name since we'd left Barnstaple.

31

NORMAN

First rule of comedy: Know how to handle the hecklers.

I don't know what the word is for explaining how I felt when Leonard told us I'd got a place at the Duke Supper Club to do my show for the Fringe. I think it might have to be a brand-new word because it was actually like a whole bunch of feelings coming out like pick 'n' mix. And they were ones you wouldn't think would go together, like strawberry creams and liquorice, but I'm telling you they did.

I was really, really happy because it was the Fringe, baby, and I was actually going to get to do it, but then at the exact same time I was really, really sad because I wasn't going to get to do it with Jax. And I was also really, really scared because Jax wasn't going to be there and now I'm just this one guy on my own without anyone to feed the jokes to and run as fast as I can to keep up with. Hapscaredysad, maybe.

Oh, and proud. I felt proud.

When we got to Bournemouth I knew straight away I wasn't going to be a Bournemouth guy, which is what Jax and me say when we don't really like a place right off the bat. Like for instance we decided we definitely weren't Falmouth guys when we went there on a school trip once. When we had our half hour of free time to walk around on our own, every shop we went into the shopkeepers would look at us like we were going to break something. Or steal something maybe. Even when we weren't touching anything some invisible voice would call out don't touch anything, you boys. For a town that our teacher said relies heavily on tourism to bolster the local economy, I reckon some people in Falmouth need to work on their hospitality skills.

To be fair, Jax probably didn't help things. Every place we went into where there was a sign that said all school bags to be left at the door or the person in charge said don't touch, he walked along with his hands about a millimetre above the snow globes and fridge magnets or whatever was on the shelf. Not touching but almost. Just to annoy them. Mum says Jax doesn't always make it easy for people to like him, which when you think about it is true, and that's an example. But the thing is, all the reasons other people don't like him are pretty much the exact reasons me and Mum do.

Anyhow, no offence to Mum because, like she says, the internet isn't always a clear and accurate representation of reality, but the reason I knew I wasn't going to be a Bournemouth guy was when we saw our Premier Inn hotel. There weren't any signs telling us don't touch or leave our bags outside the door or anything, but it didn't look anything like the one Lenny Henry stays in on the telly. It looked like a toaster from the outside and also felt like one on the inside. Which I wrote down on a Post-it to make a joke out of, but actually it turned out to be not that funny because it was true.

Mum had a bit of an argument with the girl at the desk when we were checking in because of what it cost Leonard to stay in a single room. Mum hardly ever argues with anyone so I got a bit of a surprise when she said, excuse me, but how does it make sense that if we're paying forty-two pounds for a twin room he has to pay forty-five pounds for a single one? Which is right, by the way, and I know you probably think I'm the kind of kid who always thinks his mother's right, but that's just bad maths. Even though my mum really is nearly always right and I am that kind of kid.

So anyhow, that was just another small thing that made me think I wasn't going to be a Bournemouth guy. The biggest one was hiding under my T-shirt. And in my trainers. And under my hat, if I'd had one. And in my pants. You already know what it was, only this time it felt different. I mean, I'm used to being itchy pretty much all of the time and looking like a patchwork quilt made out of leftover scabs most of the time, but ever since we left Swansea something weird had definitely been going on with my skin. And even though I was trying really hard not to think about what my body was up to, that wasn't easy because it kind of felt like I'd drunk a humungous bottle of Coke and all the fizz was trying to escape out through my skin. Everywhere. All over me. And the more I tried to not think about it, the more I couldn't stop thinking about it.

But actually, it was better than trying not to think about the open mic in Bournemouth, which by the way Leonard still thought I should do. When he said, I know it'll be hard, but what could really go wrong Norman old chap, I didn't say anything but I thought, well, actually, lots. Because things go wrong all the time. Like that Dan guy not wanting to see me. Like what happened at Swansea's Got Talent. Like us nearly getting smashed to smithereens by an Ocado van. That's three big things that have gone wrong lately that I can think of straight away.

But then again, Jax reckons that if something's hard then that's what makes it worth doing. Like when you know it's going to hurt or get you in trouble and even if it's the hardest thing you ever thought you could do in the world, even if you know it's all going to go Pete Tong and you're heading to hell in a hand basket, that's when something is most worth doing, he reckons.

Like once when we were nine and Jax was trying to convince me to jump into the empty sea pool at Penzance in winter for no good reason except it'd be fun. That deep end was really deep and I was pretty sure there was a good chance I'd break my neck and die if I did it. And the shallow end was right there and we could have done that easily, but Jax didn't want to. He wanted to jump in the deep end of course. And because Jax did it, I did it too.

I didn't break my neck and die, but I did break my watch and we had to make a written apology to the council for trespassing. Because even though we got out of there before anyone caught us, my library card fell out of my jacket pocket, so when they found it they knew we'd been there. My written apology sounded pretty good, Mum said, and I even found out the names of the right people in the council and everything. But Jax just wrote *I think you all stink* on a piece of paper in really neat writing and drew some stick kids holding their noses standing around a guy in a council uniform. Which got him grounded and no pocket money for a month. So do you see what I mean?

Anyhow, in the end I didn't have to decide whether to go and do the Bournemouth open mic thingy. Because when we got to our room Mum said she was going to have a bit of a sleep so I got out all my Post-it notes to do some practice. But instead of practising I ended up falling asleep too, and I had this weird dream that I was being dive-bombed on the beach by a flock of seagulls throwing chips at me and squawking, he's not a Bournemouth guy! And then when I woke up, I definitely wasn't feeling right.

My skin was even more tingly and itchy than before and my head was kind of fuzzy, which might be why my first thought was, now I know exactly what one of those Coke bottle fizzy sweets feels like. From the inside. Then my next thought was, well maybe I'm still in the dream or I've been abducted by aliens and they've implanted me with something. But then I got up to go to the loo and when I looked in the bathroom mirror I realized it was me who was the alien.

32

Sadie

It had such a short temper, Norman's sly little friend. It had always been like that – the slightest sign of trouble and it'd poke its cranky head above the waterline and get partying. After Jax died I thought it had reached its most magnificent proportions, but this time it had excelled even itself. And while I couldn't identify quite what had changed, there was definitely something about it that was different. Norman's chest, arms and face were a mess of sharp, fleshy peaks, and in some places great slices of raw skin looked to be almost separating from his body. Just below the surface it looked like something was breathing. Eating itself up, spitting itself out on the crisp Premier Inn sheets and smacking its lips as it went.

After a lifetime of going into battle with Norman's psoriasis I'd experimented with every potion, lotion and cream known to man. And even a few known only to animals, courtesy of a well-meaning neighbour with a part-time job at the local vet's. One whole bag of our luggage was filled with a fairly decent selection of them, because it hadn't taken a genius to work out that this trip was just the kind of thing to rile the little bugger up. I had prepared for every eventuality. Or so I thought.

I laid all the creams and lotions out on the faux-timber hotel desk so Norman could see them. It looked like a pharmaceutical police line-up, and we both knew the drill: *identify your perp of choice, son.* As he always did, I could see Norman considering his options carefully before making his selection. His eyes travelled from one bottle and tube to another and another, as the edges of his nostrils turned white from the effort of resisting a scratch.

I knew exactly what he was thinking. If he chose that one, it might offer some quick relief but then it would seep into his eyes and sting like hell and the smell would stay for days. If he chose that other one, it would take longer to work but the relief would also last longer, even if sometimes it had the effect of creating a lump on top of an existing scale.

A few of the many doctors we've been to over the years said there was a possibility he might grow out of it, but there had never even been so much as a hint of that happening. In fact, there've been plenty of times I've been scared it might actually grow out of him. That one day I'd wake up and my son would be gone, replaced by a giant, faceless, victorious scale sitting up in bed demanding its cheese on toast.

Norman often said he didn't mind his psoriasis, because he knew that after a bad bout of pain and itching he always had the next bit to look forward to, when the itch subsided and the tiny bits of pink baby skin started to peek through. At first it looks like just a tiny tear in the scale, but then over a couple of days the vivid fuchsia pales to a soft dusty pink and the new skin takes over. Jax used to say that every piece of Norman's skin that peeled off was getting closer to the real him inside. Jax. Out there breaking hearts since 2007. Still breaking mine.

When Leonard knocked on the door of our room to help Norman run through his lines I could see he was visibly shaken when he took in the situation. It was hard to believe he could endure the front-line action of war yet be so shocked at the state of one small boy's scaly body. After a few minutes of pacing and wringing his hands he pulled a chair up to the bed and resorted to patting the folded-back blanket rather than risk touching Norman's skin and inflicting any more pain on him.

The housekeeper who brought us the half a dozen towels I'd rung through to request took one look at my bare-chested boy and turned pale, stumbling over her words in her haste to leave.

'Extra towels are a pound each and . . . um, no going . . . no taking them off the premises.'

If she'd had any suspicions as to what I was actually going to do with them, which was not take them down to the beach and fill them full of sand but pack them around Norman's body, infusing not only the towels but also the mattress, pillows and probably the walls with the scent of the foulest-smelling ointment of the lot (which he'd finally settled on), she might well have rethought the cost. Because, for me, it was a bargain and the best value we'd had so far at Premier Inn. I considered going on TripAdvisor and giving them a rating. *Psoriasis friendly! Five stars!*

I knelt down beside the bed and laid my head on the pillow next to Norman's. He was scrunched over on his side in the only position that didn't cause pressure on his left hip, where a huge lump had come up the day before Jax's funeral. Over the weeks it had waxed and waned, but this latest development had seen it develop into an open-cut crusty crack the size of the Grand Canyon. I desperately wanted to distract him.

'Hey, Norman, do you know what I think?'

He twisted slightly in the bed, and the shift in position made him wince but I saw the hint of a smile pass over his face and a quiet little voice came back on cue.

'I dunno, Mum. What *do* you think?'

It was a game we'd played a million times before and, just like those other million times, Norman probably knew exactly what I was going to say. But it never stopped him asking anyway. Just for fun. I sat back on my heels and tipped my head slightly to one side so he'd know it was coming. Twelve years evaporated in an instant as I sat on the edge of another bed and marvelled at the brand-new bundle in my arms that would grow into the best person I ever knew. *I've got you.*

'I think, right now, you could be the worst thing I've ever smelled in my entire life.'

And suddenly there it was, my favourite view in the world. That big smile. That beautiful face. My boy. *My father.*

'Good one, Mum.' He closed his eyes, but that smile stayed.

Leonard had wandered over to the desk and was working his way along my little mugs' line-up of creams and potions, picking each one up and turning it to the light to read its ingredients. I had no idea if he knew what any of it meant, but with his wispy grey hair and his glasses tilted up on the end of his nose he looked like the perfect mad scientist. He opened some to take a whiff, or squeeze a bit out and rub between his thumb and forefinger, and every now and again he'd turn to consult Norman.

'What's this? Where do you put this one? How long do you use this for?' When he held up the packet of huge suppositories we'd been given by a well-meaning nurse at Truro hospital, his quizzical one-eyebrow raise made Norman laugh out loud, despite what it cost him. Leonard mimed putting one of the pills in his mouth and Norman shook his head and delicately pointed towards his side-shuffled little bum sticking out beyond the sheet. Leonard's face contorted into a mask of faux shock and terror and they both burst into giggles again. A few seconds later I saw a mass of pin-prick blood spots on the sheet that covered Norman's hip and I hoped the laugh had been worth it.

When Norman closed his eyes to recover from the effort Leonard went back to examining the pharmaceutical stash on the desk.

'Does any of this stuff actually work, Sadie?'

None of it.

'Oh, you know, maybe. Sometimes, some of it. For a while.'

I really don't know how much I've spent over the years on them, but my guess is that I'd be able to buy my very own suite at a Premier Inn for what I'd wasted on all those useless creams. I'd often fantasized that there was a factory somewhere churning out different-coloured stinky salves to keep up with the demands of desperate parents looking for relief for their kids. Red? Blue? Hey, let's try a purple one this week and add the water from an underground spring in the upper Peruvian Andes for good measure.

'It's all full of terrible, terrible chemicals, Sadie.' Leonard clicked his tongue and tut-tutted as he read the back of a tube. 'How on earth can doctors and scientists think that putting all that awful stuff on to poor little human skin could possibly be good for it?'

I'd been asking myself the same question for most of Norman's life but, to me, the risk of *not* trying whatever new miracle cream came on the market far outweighed any other hazards.

'I'm sure you . . . well, please forgive me for asking, Sadie, if it's not appropriate, but have you ever considered alternative medicine for Norman's skin?'

Over the past ten years we'd tried many kinds of alternative treatments, and even a few alternatives to the alternatives. I closed my eyes and tried to remember even one of them that had made the smallest bit of difference. It was an infinite array and I must have zoned out for longer than I'd thought.

'Sorry, sorry, of course you have. I didn't mean to suggest . . .' Leonard looked mortified that he might have offended me. 'The thing is, I went on a lovely little one-day course over in St Ives last October, Sadie. It was . . . well, I can't quite remember what it was called, but this wonderful Chinese chappie showed us the different uses for herbs and flowers and the like for . . . for improving the memory and . . . and other sorts of common ailments. And . . . well, I don't specifically remember anything for skin conditions like Norman's, but . . . I wonder if maybe . . .'

He pulled his iPhone out of his pocket and began tapping away and, after a bit of scrolling up and down, he clicked a few buttons and I saw a Google Map flash up on the screen. *Time to go home?* Not likely.

'Ah yes. Here we are. Perhaps I'll go for a walk. Would . . . is it all right with you if I talk to a Chinese herbalist about Norman's, err . . . predicament?'

While my enthusiasm for new suggestions in terms of a cure for Norman's skin had long ago waned, at this point we really didn't have anything to lose. So, after apologetically taking a few close-up pictures on his phone of Norman's face, arms, legs and torso, Leonard set off to see a man about a boy.

I sat in the armchair watching Norman's chest rise and fall in a fitful sleep and I must have dozed off myself, because I woke with a start and realized nearly two hours had passed. Norman was still asleep in the exact same position he had lain down in and there was no sign of Leonard. Or his alternative Chinese medicine.

After another half-hour passed and he still hadn't returned, I went down the hallway to check his room, just in case he'd come back and decided to take a little nap himself. But after several loud knocks I had to concede he wasn't there and I returned to my armchair vigil. Now with two things to keep me occupied.

Worrying about Norman was one thing, but Leonard was a grown man with a Google Map, I reasoned, and he'd found his way around the jungles of Borneo, for heaven's sake. But I still couldn't shake the uneasy memory of that vague, faraway look I'd seen on his face more than once, and the feeling that maybe he wasn't quite as on the ball as he'd always seemed.

It wasn't until, with a whoosh of relief that genuinely surprised me with its intensity, I finally heard Leonard's soft *knock knock* at the door and I remembered that, any minute now, a certain Adam Linley might be walking into a pub expecting to meet his prodigal son.

33

I had no reason to think that Adam Linley was even going to show up at O'Neill's, as there hadn't been so much as a peep in response to my text. But with Norman out of action and the whole plan unravelling at a rate of knots, I figured the least I could do was keep the rendezvous at seven o'clock, just in case.

By the time Leonard had shown up with a shopping bag full of little newspaper packages tied up with red string and a sheepish exclamation about getting just a tiny bit lost, I had about five minutes to spare to get to the pub. Which was exactly enough because, courtesy of Leonard's planning skills, O'Neill's was literally around the corner.

'I won't be long, Leonard. I'll just wait around for half an hour or so, and if the guy . . . if Adam doesn't show up, I'll come back.'

I kissed Norman's sleeping forehead and left Leonard fussing about with his packages, arranging them on the desk and, I couldn't help noticing, having quite the little chat to himself as he did it.

'Now, mmm, which one did the chappie say was . . . ? Ah, OK,

I think this one first and then . . . no, no . . . this one. That's it . . . I think.' I left him to it.

When I walked into O'Neill's, my plan had been to find a quiet seat in a corner facing the door, on the off-chance that if Adam Linley came through it I'd be able to see him before he saw me. On the even more off-chance that I'd actually recognize him. But that idea went straight out the window, because the place was absolutely jam-packed. Bournemouth was clearly a comedy hotspot and I felt a guilty wave of relief that Norman wasn't going to have to get up in front of that lot.

I managed to fight my way to the bar and crammed myself into a couple of inches of space. I could only see a sliver of the door, but it looked like the best I could hope for. I figured that if I did see Adam Linley come in, I could make a judgement from a distance on whether he'd turned out to be a half-decent person and whether it was at all possible he was Norman's father. If not, I could just slink away into the crowd and tell the others he hadn't shown up.

Since this whole plan started, there had been an irrational part of me that felt like I'd know Norman's father when I saw him. Like some kind of genetic marker would be hovering over the right guy and I'd be able to say without a doubt that our search was over. No paternity test required. *Norman, may I present your father, Prince William of Wales!* I realized the glass of wine I'd been slowly sipping was already starting to go to my head.

'Oi. Are you Sadie?'

There was a split second I thought about denying it, but I realized I probably hadn't changed enough in the past thirteen years to get away with it. My hair was the same, I still fitted into the same size clothes and, for all I could remember, Adam Linley had just recognized me by the same blue M&S T-shirt I'd let him take off me one night. But now clearly he'd seen me before I saw him. Bugger.

I turned in the direction of the voice, but the hefty old guy I'd spotted sitting on a mobility scooter in a corner of the pub when I'd come in had somehow managed to manoeuvre himself through the crowd and had parked himself right next to me. His bulk was all that stood, or sat, between me and Adam Linley's voice, and it was pretty tempting to make a run for it while I still could.

'Geez almighty, mate, get off me!'

The man rammed in next to me at the bar turned and gave the handlebars of the mobility scooter a bit of a shove as it bunny-hopped into him. I moved my head left as I tried not to brush the sweaty arm of the driver, who was leaning out of the scooter in my direction. I stretched my neck around him so I could see Adam, but he half stood up and shifted his body into the same angle as mine. I realized with horror that he was moving in.

'Hey! Piss off, you!'

My voice came out much louder than I'd intended and a handful of people at the bar turned around. And then a terrifying thing happened. A miracle of space cleared around us and I realized that the fat old guy in the scooter was not actually that old at all. He was definitely fat, though. I didn't get that wrong. Then Adam Linley's voice started coming out of his mouth, and before I knew it he'd planted a sweaty kiss on my cheek. Which was a damn sight better than the place it had originally seemed headed for.

'I get that a lot,' said Adam. He sounded quite proud, so I wasn't quite sure if his statement was in reference to being told to piss off or the sudden extra room he commanded around him. Interchangeable, probably.

'You know, I didn't know who the hell you were when you texted, so I wanted to stay on the down low, but I remembered as soon as I saw you. I'd never forget a foxy-looking doll like you. Ha ha. Holy shit, it was a long time ago, but you still look in pretty good shape, don't you? For a woman with a kid.'

I looked around and wondered how much of a head start I'd need to crowd-surf my way out of the pub before a mobility scooter could reach top speed.

One thing that hadn't occurred to me if we did really find Norman's father was that he might be in a worse state than us. I was just a mother trying my best and dragging Norman along through life with me, but the whole assumption of this plan (for me, at least) had been that a father might be able to offer him something else. Something more. *You know, like . . . a guy.*

But as I sat in the corner of the pub with my chair mashed up against Adam Linley's mobility scooter, gripping my wine glass and listening to his interminable ramble that included, among many other self-pitying side notes, how he'd been kicked out of university because of an incident with a stolen exam paper, how he could have been an elite athlete if he hadn't 'popped a fucking gasket' from a hernia that turned gangrenous, and how useless everyone that worked in the DWP was, I realized it was entirely possible I'd assumed wrong.

It turned out the day before the night we'd got together thirteen years ago was actually the last time Adam had ever run around a football field. At any decent speed, anyhow. He'd woken up in my room before dawn with some unreliable memories and the hangover from hell, so after getting himself home (no mention of my toastie maker, I noticed) he'd climbed into his own bed and slept for fourteen hours straight. Naturally, that was the day the selectors from West Ham had come calling, and he'd missed his chance of becoming one of the most famous players in history. Apparently. Although while he was talking I did get a sudden flashback to him pulling a clipping of himself on the front page of the *Edinburgh Evening News* out of his pocket at some stage of our liaison, so I guess it could have been true.

He slowed down and looked a bit thoughtful when he got to that part, and I wondered if he was just now figuring out he might be able to blame me for it. Anyhow, according to Adam, that week turned into the beginning of the end. His coach had been so angry with him that they'd ended up in a huge fight, so he didn't show up to training for the rest of the month either. Then he'd been kicked off the team and then, you know, the hernia and the incident with the stolen exam paper, yada yada yada. With university a bust, he came home to Bournemouth and took a job at a local bakery chain, where his mum had worked her entire adult life. *Aha.*

Persistent complications with his hernia meant even joining the local football team was off the cards, so he'd thrown himself wholeheartedly into his new career. It seems Adam's collaboration with The Crusty Slice turned out to be the most successful thing he'd ever done, working his way up to area manager in twelve months and close on doubling his body weight in eighteen. But his rapid increase in size brought a whole lot of new health issues, and 'fucking Crusty's' ('I gave them two fucking years of my fucking life') had started to object to the amount of time off he needed to go to blood-pressure and obesity clinics. In the end they laid him off with a lousy redundancy package and an excuse that they were downsizing.

'As opposed to what I did myself, clearly. Ha ha ha.'

I resisted the urge to agree with Adam because, despite having almost lost the will to live while listening to his self-directed and -produced *This Is Your Life* episode, just for a microsecond his flash of self-deprecation reminded me of Norman. A nanosecond, maybe. Because occasionally, if he noticed some mouthy kid sizing up the condition of his skin and getting ready to pounce, before they had a chance to come up with a cutting jibe or sneering question, Norman would jump in first.

If he was quick enough to get there, it might be something like, 'I know, I know, I better stay away from the dips at parties. A . . . am . . . amiright?' Or on a good day, 'Come and have a closer look if you like, the doctor said it might not be quite so contagious any more.'

KO'ing their poxy piggin' punchline is what Jax called it. Some nights I'd hear Norman practising potential comebacks, and it damn near broke me, if I'm honest. Because if I ever heard of anyone making fun of him I just wanted to go in all guns blazing, but Jax would always say, 'Nah, Normie's got it covered, Sadie. He can look after himself. He just pounds 'em in the poxy piggin' punchline and they've had it!'

The pride I saw on Norman's face as he basked in Jax's praise was the only thing that saved me sometimes.

Even the start of the open mic and the raucous yelling of the crowd, egging on and heckling the various acts, couldn't distract Adam from his story, but funnily enough, so far he hadn't even mentioned Norman or the possibility that he might be his father. One thing for certain was that there was definitely no tell-tale genetic cloud hovering around him, although to be fair it could have been overpowered by the lingering odour of sweat, lager and something that might have smelled a little bit like wee.

I was trying my best to remind myself that it was nice to be nice, but Adam Linley made it a pretty tough ask. Not for the first time I wished that Jax was still here, because he would have known exactly what to say to Adam to shut down his self-pitying rant. You can bet it wouldn't have been appropriate or even polite, but it would definitely have been right on the money. I blinked slowly and took a deep swig of warm Chardonnay as a smiling, dirty-faced boy filled the space behind my eyes. I managed to get myself into a zone where I could nod and uh huh in synch with the rise and fall of Adam's voice without paying too much attention to what he was saying. But in my head I was trying to work out just how soon I could make my excuses and get back to the Premier Inn, which suddenly seemed like the most desirable place on earth. And right then I'd have handed over a hundred toastie makers if I could have got rid of Adam as easily as I had the last time I'd seen him, because if this drainer was Norman's father, then we were most definitely better off without him.

34

Norman was sleeping when I got back to the hotel room and, as I pushed open the door, Leonard sat up straighter in the armchair and put his finger to his lips to warn me. I tiptoed over to the bed and I could see, even in the low light and half covered by the sheet, that the onslaught on his body had noticeably subsided. Some of the angriness had retreated from the skin on his face and the huge scales on his chest that had looked so rigid just a couple of hours ago now seemed thinner, softer and almost translucent.

The newspaper-wrapped packets were spread out all over the desk and I could see that about five or six of them had been opened. While I couldn't quite put my finger on the smell that hung in the air, something about it reminded me of when the Indian restaurant down the road starts cooking the korma for the evening rush, and I wondered if perhaps Leonard had got so lost he'd had to make a substitution for his Chinese medicines.

'He looks . . . I mean, I think . . . it looks a lot better, right? What did you get for him, Leonard?' Leonard's lips twitched a little and he indicated with his thumb to the bedside table, where the plastic water jug that I'd seen earlier in the fridge was sitting alongside the kettle. In the bottom there looked to be the remnants of a manky compost heap, marinating in a thin golden liquid. I could see Leonard had definitely got good value out of the rest of the formerly white Premier Inn towels, and they lay in a messy pile on the floor, a lovely pale yellow in contrast to the two olive-green-stained ones I'd used on Norman for the ointment.

'You know, you were right, Sadie, this time, it's . . . it's something different.' Leonard's voice was soft so as not to wake Norman, but I could see he was having trouble containing his excitement. 'The Chinese gentleman I went to see saw it as soon as I showed him the photos of Norman.'

'Saw what, Leonard?' I was slightly put out that a complete stranger thought he could give an expert diagnosis on my son's chronic condition from a couple of photos on a phone, but then again, we've had worse.

'Come and look, my dear.' Leonard touched my arm and motioned me a little closer to the bed, pulling back the sheet gently so I could properly see Norman's chest, rising and falling as he breathed.

'Now, really look, Sadie.'

I looked. I really looked. But all I could see was the old familiar enemy Norman had been submitting to for most of his life. Covering his lovely peaches-and-cream skin with its insidious scales and even decorating the spaces in between.

'What, Leonard? What am I looking at? I mean, like I said, it definitely looks a lot better, not as red . . . but all I can see is that bloody psoriasis coming for him, and I just . . .' I'd given up whispering and I saw the rhythm of Norman's breathing change as though he was about to stir.

'Aha! That's just it, Sadie!' Leonard looked like I'd hit the jackpot and he'd supplied me with the winning numbers. He squeezed my arm tightly and did a fist-pump in the air with his other hand.

'That's the very difference. Don't you see?' He paused dramatically and, in his excitement, his whisper came out louder than if he'd spoken normally.

'This time it's *not* coming. It's *going.*'

It took a second or two for me to get my head around what he was saying, but now that I knew what I was looking for I realized Leonard was right. Instead of tripping over themselves on a chaotic rampage across Norman's poor body as they had been before, the scales were now lifting. *Away* from his body.

His skin looked like crazy paving, networked with hairline cracks and deeper crevices, and on top of that, countless flaps of peeling skin of varying thicknesses and size. Norman moved slightly and a flake the size of a twenty-pence piece wafted off his shoulder and on to the sheet. Just like that. Underneath was a triangle of smooth, pink baby skin. *It's a boy, Miss Foreman.* Norman rolled towards the side of the bed, stretching one arm out and opening an eye. When he saw me standing over him he opened the other and was staring bright-eyed at me within seconds. Just like the day he was born. *Hello, you.*

'Mum, Mum. Where's Leonard?' As soon as the words were out, Leonard was beside me, nudging himself into Norman's line of vision.

'Hello there, old chap. Good to see you. Feeling better?' Norman smiled and nodded, taking the tender, wrinkly hand he was offered with both of his own, holding it like a sandwich.

'Yes, I am. I really and truly am. And Leonard, did you tell her? Mum, guess what the Chinese herbalist guy gave Leonard to help me? And it made a difference straight away, didn't it, Leonard? In, like, two minutes! Guess what it was, Mum!'

'Well, I . . .'

'Tell her then, old boy. Don't keep her in suspenders!'

Norman looked from Leonard to me then to the jumble of towels on the floor and back to Leonard again, like they all had the most exciting secret in the world.

'Go on then, Norman, what was it?'

'You'll never believe it!' My son's delight was immeasurable. 'It was just like Iris always says. Cold tea! Cold Chinese tea, Mum!'

That smile.

35

NORMAN

First rule of comedy: Try it, they might like it.

Peter woke with a shock, not knowing where he was until the noise of the giant thrusters of the rocket ship brought him back to reality. He looked out the small porthole window and saw the Earth spiralling below him.

For a few seconds when I woke up I didn't know where I was, because everything looked fuzzy and even when I blinked hard all I could see was snow in front of my eyes. I wondered for a moment if I'd left planet Earth, like Peter from the story Jax made up for my tenth birthday, which was called Leaving Is Believing. But then I saw the Premier Inn pen on the table beside the bed and I remembered that I wasn't in outer space, only Bournemouth.

While I was lying there trying to wake up a bit more I started thinking about if that's what Jax felt like the last time he was awake. Before he wasn't. Like he was in a speeding rocket heading for space and looking back and seeing the Earth spiralling below him. I hope so, because he would have loved that, no matter how scared he was.

Even though I still looked pretty bad I actually felt pretty good when I woke up after our Chinese tea party, which is what Leonard called it. Of course I knew it wasn't really like some miracle cure or anything, because I reckon my psoriasis is always going to come back. What I mean is, and it's not like I've ever said this to Mum or anything, but I know pretty much for sure that it's an actual proper supposed-to-be-there part of me. Like an arm or a leg or an ear. And sometimes I don't even mind.

Anyhow, all I knew for sure was that my outsides hadn't felt that good since before Jax went. Loads of bits of my skin had fallen off while I was asleep and it was all lying around me on the bed, and even though that was kind of gross it was also a bit cool. But the absolute best thing was that nothing seemed to hurt like it did before. Not even the scabs that were still attached to me. And it was weird, but it seemed like maybe my insides felt a little bit better too.

I knew it was going to be one of the good ones as soon as Leonard put that Chinese tea stuff on my skin, because it was like my whole entire body stopped itching straight away and everything just kind of relaxed. I reckon it was probably the best and most amazing thing I've ever used, and it didn't even smell bad. Because by the way that's usually how it works, that the worse the smell is, the better the ointment does its job.

It was also the first time I've ever put something on my skin and then got to drink the rest, and if you smelled some of the other stuff I've used, that would probably make you feel quite happy for me. Jax once said that the one I got Mum to put on me before Leonard's tea smelled like the wee of a thousand Egyptian camels. Which he would know, because he went to Egypt in the school holidays a few years ago with his mum and stepdad and actually got to ride one, which is the coolest thing ever. But even that cream doesn't really work that well, to be honest.

After she woke up, once Mum got over how happy she was that the Chinese tea had actually done something she told me about meeting Adam Linley, who could be my dad. She said she'd found out loads of things about him and that none of them were too good, except then she said he wanted to meet me. Just in case, he reckoned. Mum said it was up to me because she'd already seen quite enough of Adam Linley, thank you very much. But she smiled when she said it so I knew she really did mean that it was up to me and that maybe he wasn't that bad.

I was trying to take some thinking time so I would be able to make the right decision, but all I kept thinking about was how good it felt that the itching had stopped. Usually I itch in at least a few places almost all of the time, and it's really just a matter of how much. So in the end I felt so happy about the absolutely no itching situation I said that I would go and meet Adam.

I decided I didn't really mind if I had to sit and listen to his entire life story like Mum had to, because me and Jax reckon that even the worst episode of *EastEnders* (which is what Mum said Adam's life reminded her of) is still pretty good. And because so what if Adam didn't want to know me and Mum, like Dan McStinky didn't? Who cares? But mainly I decided that I should go and meet him because one never knows and because I reckon Jax would definitely have told me, don't be a pussy, Normie.

Mum texted Adam and told him we'd meet him at a Costa that wasn't too far from our hotel, because of neutral territory and safety in numbers. That last bit is what she said to me, not him, by the way. Plus, she said, we could use the excuse of having to get back to the hotel to pack if we wanted to ditch him, which seemed like a pretty smart idea, considering everything she'd said about him being a bit rude and such a Negative Neville and all that.

Mum told me that when I met Adam I wasn't to take a bit of notice of anything he said, because he was full of himself and he had no filter and she was really sorry she'd put me in the position of him possibly being my dad. She said that, in her defence, she didn't actually remember him being quite that bad when she first met him, but that was a story for another time and she was sorry about that too.

It was probably due to not being itchy for the first time in forever but for some reason I didn't even feel nervous about meeting Adam. While Mum was in the shower I even made up a funny rhyme, which used to mainly be Jax's job, so I was quite surprised when it just popped into my head. When she got out of the bathroom I asked if she wanted to hear it and when I stood up and said, 'Who cares about Adam's bitching, because I ain't itching,' she laughed and laughed. Actually, she laughed so much she started to cry, but then just when I started to get a bit worried I saw that she was also still laughing.

After the laughing and crying Mum hugged me really, really tight, and even though it was pretty sore on the parts where my scabs had fallen off I hugged her back as hard as I could too. And when she went to let go I still kept holding on, which made her hug me back more, and then it started all over again. It was like a never-ending hug, which is the best kind. And it didn't matter that it hurt and that it took up a lot of time and that Mum was crying and that I hadn't had my shower yet so I still stank a little bit like the wee of a thousand Egyptian camels. Because even though neither of us said anything I knew Mum was thinking about Jax at that very moment too.

36

Sadie

As it goes, I would rather have made myself a two-gallon cocktail of every stinking potion I've ever rubbed on Norman's poor little body in the last ten years, stuck an umbrella in it and drunk it through a Marmite-dipped straw than endure another meeting with Adam Linley. But just when I'd been about to wheel out a barrow of lies and make a run for it from the pub, wouldn't you know it, out of the blue he'd said he'd like to meet Norman.

'You know, just in case the kid really is mine. Probably is, too. I was pretty virile back then, if I do say so myself.'

Which he proceeded to do quite loudly, several more times. Throughout the course of our conversation in the pub he'd seemed to swing between totally obnoxious and oddly vulnerable, with not too much in between. It was confusing, to say the least, but either way, despite having softened slightly towards him since our initial sweaty exchange, I really didn't want to have to think about the capabilities of what was (mercifully) hidden in the depths of those enormous pants. I'd tried to distract him with the story of Jax, the other possible fathers, the boys' plan and just why we were on this trip, but he wasn't to be put off.

So now, in lieu of my preferred cocktail, here we were in the back corner of a coffee shop waiting for Adam Linley, drainer extraordinaire, toastie-maker pilferer and possibly the father of my son. Although I sincerely hoped not.

Basking in the aftermath of Leonard's Chinese herbs, Norman looked lovely. There was a dusky pink hue to his face, and even though there were still more scabs than twenty- and fifty-pence-sized patches of new skin showing through, after the detritus he'd left on the sheets that morning the score was definitely evening out. But even though glass houses, pelted stones and all that stuff, I was still nervous at the possibility of what might come out of Adam's mouth when he saw Norman.

The night before, as I'd lain awake for hours with my son next to me shedding skin in his sleep, I'd thought about Adam and all the other mistakes I'd made thirteen years ago and tried to make some kind of sense of it. Which was an interesting experience, because it's not something I'd ever tried to do before. Matter of fact, it was pretty much the exact opposite of anything I'd ever tried to do before.

When I'd arrived in Penzance with a two-week-old baby, a piece of paper with an estate agent's number on it and not much else, I'd closed the door hard on my father's grand finale and everything else that followed in those crazy few months back up in Edinburgh. I just got on with loving Norman, and that was more than enough to concentrate on, I told myself.

But lying in a hotel room halfway between back and beyond, I got to thinking about the stuff I'd left behind that door. The drinking, the blaming, the stupid, careless behaviour, the wilful and deliberate sabotage of the life my father had been so proud I was making. And those tightly packed shelves of anger and resentment for the man who'd been my entire family. The man who made me the world's best daughter then blew the world apart. The man who'd already hung around too long.

I think I might have come close to pushing on that door the day Norman and Jax made their poster for the Five Year Plan. With all the talk of Edinburgh and that old photo of my father that I hadn't seen for years. But I slunk away. Because maybe, just maybe, I was too busy trying to prove I was enough for my son to make up for not being quite enough for my father. And maybe I had never wanted to consider that Norman might actually want a say in it. But now it was looking like I might have to crack that door wide open. Even if behind it was the risk of a booby prize like Adam Linley.

'Sadie! Hey, you there!' Like I hadn't seen him coming, and as if you could miss him in that bloody great lump of a mobility scooter. Adam's navigation left a lot to be desired and, as well as taking out several chairs on the way through the café, there were a couple of small children that had very near misses. At the sound of Adam's voice, I felt Norman involuntarily shrink down in his seat like he was trying to disappear. You and me both, kid. I grabbed his hand under the table and held on tight.

Adam's scooter jerked to a halt at our table, running over my bag in the process and barely missing Norman's legs, which he swung out of the way just in time.

'Hello again, Adam. Lovely to ... mmm. Norman, this is Adam. Adam, Norman.' Norman stuck out his hand and gave him a nervous smile, but Adam barely even looked at him.

'You ordered yet, love?'

For one too-good-to-be-true moment I thought Adam was going to reveal a redeeming feature by offering to buy our drinks. But before I could say, thanks but actually, yes, I already have and in fact here they are now and please don't reverse into the waitress carrying our hot chocolates, Adam shattered my delusion.

'Ah, be a doll and go up and order me a coffee then, would you? Caramel latte, double shot of caramel, three sugars. This thing's a bastard to get up to the counter and those fuckers always try to pretend they can't see me. Excuse my French. Go on now, there's a love. Me and Norman will be OK here.'

There was no offer of any money, but if we could get through this meeting for the cost of a coffee, even with the extra shot, I thought we'd be doing OK. On my way up to the counter I turned to look back over my shoulder. Neither of them had moved. Adam was leaning back in the scooter with his hands behind his head, most definitely now looking at Norman, who was staring downwards, scuffing the floor with his trainers. I knew I needed to get back there quick smart before Adam and his motor mouth ploughed into my son's tender heart at full tilt.

But with four people ahead of me and none of them under seventy it took a good ten minutes to get served. I was sweating at the thought of Norman being back there at the mercy of Adam, but when I finally pushed my way back to the table around a clutch of schoolgirls and a couple of backed-up prams, my son was alive and well and his body, soul and spirit all seemed very much intact.

Norman was out of his seat, leaning casually over the top of the mobility scooter, and it almost looked like he was about to hop on and go for a ride. He and Adam were both engrossed in looking at the screen of an iPad, and when I slid in the other side of the table I steeled myself to what the guy could have exposed him to. Porn? Online gambling? The Cooking Channel? Frankly, it was worse, as it turned out.

When the waitress delivered Adam's drink he began spooning the mountain of cream off the top into his mouth and pushed his iPad over the table to me. I recognized the Facebook page Leonard had set up for Norman, way back when the plan was still just a little old plan on a wall and not a looming reality. The good old days. Judging by the stream of photos and videos, it was clear Leonard had been diligently posting on Little Big Man's page ever since we left Penzance, as promised.

I scrolled past a few old videos of Morecombe and Wise, a couple of stills of *Live at the Apollo*, a few reappearances of the Little Big Man poster and a lot of random pictures of comedians old and new. It looked like Leonard had created an entire world for Little Big Man, and there was no getting around the fact that it was actually pretty impressive. I noticed he'd created something called an Event, in which he'd announced the time and date Norman was due to perform at the Duke, in Edinburgh. I was still reading the details when I realized Adam was talking.

'. . . and so after you told me about Normie's show last night I went and had a look and found this page. Normie tells me some old geezer called Harold is looking after it for you and, OK, it's not bad, but it could be better. Well, anyhow, I don't know if I mentioned it, but I'm pretty big in the online world. Got loads of stuff going viral all over the place. So I shared it out there to my connections and, well, you know, I knew it would happen, but it's a pretty good result, if I do say so myself.'

I didn't have a clue what he was talking about and Norman hadn't had an opportunity to say a word since I'd sat down, so I had no idea what had passed between them, except, obviously, Adam had done something that had something to do with the Facebook page.

'It's Leonard, and anyhow, what is, Adam? What's a good result?'

I really, really didn't want to ask, because he was so clearly gagging to tell me, but I felt the need to at least attempt to fill in the gaps. Adam made a noise that was halfway between a wheeze and a snort, which was as disgusting as it sounds, and he picked up the iPad and pushed it right up to my face. He leaned out of the scooter at a dangerous angle and jabbed a finger into the screen. A blob of cream landed right in the middle of Little Big Man's face and quivered as Adam waved the iPad in front of me.

'Likes, love! Shares. You name it. That bloody thing was only at eleven confirmed people last night. Like I said, now shit's gone viral!'

I squinted at the screen again and focused on the cartoon thumbs-up icon with the number 1,901 beside it, then glanced over at my battle-scarred son, who was looking particularly vulnerable and small next to that great hulking human who better bloody not be his father. *Ah, but it's nice to be nice, Sadie.*

I felt a sudden pang of guilt at being so nasty and it crossed my mind that perhaps it might be a little over the top to hold a grudge primarily based on a toasted sandwich press that, if I'm honest, I'd only ever used twice anyhow. I turned my attention back to the iPad and it took me several more seconds to realize that, large as it was, 1,901 likes wasn't the most disturbing number on the page. Because beside the event *Free at the Edinburgh Fringe – Little Big Man at the Duke* were a couple of other numbers. *Confirmed coming 243. Maybe coming 467.*

I looked over at Norman, and it didn't take telepathy to see he was wondering exactly the same as me. Just what the implications of Little Big Man getting a little too big for his boots were going to be, and whether the Duke Supper Club was going to be good for some extra chairs.

In a way, it was good Adam had hit us with the worst thing early on to distract Norman. Because apart from bragging about his past sporting achievements and his stellar success with women all over again, there were a couple of remarks about Norman's psoriasis, just as I'd feared. The one he laboured the longest was that familiar old chestnut about whether we'd tried calamine lotion as a treatment.

'Always worked a bloody treat for the chafing when I was playing football. You should give it a go. I know what I'm talking about, even if it might not look like it these days.'

He gestured almost apologetically into mid-air and then glanced down to his former football-playing legs, now planted firmly on the rubber footplates of the mobility scooter. My stomach gave that same funny little lurch of recognition.

Pointing out that thigh chafe wasn't really in the ballpark of a debilitating dermatological condition that affected every part of your life was probably useless, so I didn't even try. But Norman was, as ever, incredibly polite and patient when listening to advice. He promised that he'd give the calamine a go one more time. Just in case. And thanks very much, Adam.

When it came to conversation, Adam wasn't big into audience participation. There was a nano-pause when, after he'd drained his caramel latte, he looked quizzically into the glass as if he might have noticed it was skinny milk and only one and a half sugars. But it was a false alarm and it turned out he was just looking for more. Other than that, he barely drew breath as he droned on about his skills on the Web, how his site had over forty thousand views a month, how much money he made from affiliate marketing and his online life-coaching business called Positive Man-Ifestation. At which point I had to bite my tongue. Hard.

As it turned out, Adam didn't leave any room or opportunity for us to even address the question of whether he might or might not be Norman's father. True to his word, he really didn't seem to care either way. There was only one slightly scary moment when, mid-sentence, he stopped and poked Norman in the arm to make sure he had his attention.

'Oi, about this little comedy thing you've got going, Normie. I mean, it doesn't look like it, but it'd be funny if we *were* related, wouldn't it? Because look at you and look at me. Little and Large! You know 'em? I'm the large, by the way, ha ha ha. Talk about chalk and cheese!'

Chalk and cheese were infinitely more alike than that buffoon and my son, but I thought it best not to get caught up in the details, and Norman had looked quite chuffed at Adam's attempt at a joke.

'Anyhow, Normie, if you're half as good as your Facebook page says you are, I might just have to keep an eye on you. I mean, you're going to need a manager and some more social media platforms if you get famous, aren't you? With my connections, you could be huge!'

I managed to pass off my genuine shiver as a cough because, secretly, I'd kind of been hoping never to have to cross Adam Linley's path again, let alone inflict him on Norman on a long-term basis. And anyhow, I told myself, there was no career to manage. It was all smoke and mirrors and fake Facebook pages and disastrous talent nights and out-of-whack routines and unsuitable sperm donors and dead best friends.

I sat there listening to Adam witter on and thought that, so far, absolutely nothing had gone as planned and things were still moving faster than I could run away from them. Norman still didn't have a proper show prepared, and all I'd succeeded in doing was finding one father who didn't want to know, one who did but wasn't, and a third that was Adam Linley.

All of a sudden, I missed Dennis and the car yard and my

boring life where I always knew what was coming next and who was going to get the things off the high shelves. My old life, where I never even had to think about the past, let alone confront the ghosts of it head on in a Costa coffee shop. The life that was totally and very satisfactorily taken up by two beautiful, brilliant boys who were the best friends I'd ever had. Because if Adam was an indication of what was going on in the rest of the world, I wasn't sure I wanted in.

The thing was, though, even while I was busy working myself up about all that stuff, I couldn't help but notice what was happening with Norman. There was a whiff of something different about him, and this time it wasn't anything that had come out of a bottle or a tube. He was chatting away easily to Adam, politely answering his questions and even offering the occasional shy smile. Despite the odd bits of skin dropping off him like fleshy little clover leaves every now and again, there was a kind of glow about him. He was even sitting up straighter than usual, like he was perfectly capable of holding his own against Adam and it was just another day in the office. Not another day on the road to the biggest and scariest event of his life. What the hell had been in that Chinese tea? I got a sharp twang of pain from whatever was down there fighting over the two sides of my scar and wondered if perhaps I shouldn't give it a whirl myself.

Adam insisted on escorting us back to the hotel, despite my best efforts to put him off.

'Honestly, Adam, we're fine . . . aren't we, Norman? It's not that far and, actually, we're . . . um, in a bit of a rush because we . . . umm . . . we've got to . . . you know, our bags and . . .'

But even as I was speaking he and Norman were already on the move through the coffee shop, clearing a path as they went.

I brought up the rear as Norman stepped forward to hold open the door for Adam and his mobility scooter to trundle through, apologizing along the way to a woman who nearly lost her Waitrose shopping under the wheels. It was a strange turn-up for the books, and no mistake. It was almost like . . . was it possible Norman actually liked this guy? As I mulled over that highly unexpected possibility I allowed myself to get caught up in the slipstream of Adam's considerable wake, stepping over the bodies along the way.

When we arrived back at the Premier Inn I could see through the glass frontage that Leonard was already waiting in the foyer, sunken into one of the chairs with our luggage at his feet. There went that excuse. He was turning his iPhone around and around in his hands with a distracted look on his face like he couldn't decide whether or not to make a call.

I stepped into the automatic revolving doors just ahead of Norman, with Adam bringing up the rear. Out of nowhere, I got a heart-dropping vision of a rainy afternoon in Truro, pushing through the same kind of doors at Barclays bank when I had taken Jax and Norman to open their Five Year Plan account. But before I could get to the funny bit where Jax had announced to the teller that yes, Five-Year was his first name and Plan was his last, there was a massive commotion behind me as Adam's scooter wedged itself firmly in the doors, trapping not just him but also three tiny Japanese girls trying to exit the other side.

Leonard's head shot up like he'd never seen a fat man in a mobility scooter wedged in a door before, and Norman immediately tried to double-back to help, but he was already too far out the other side. He began tapping and pointing and making hand gestures through the curved glass while Adam wrenched at the controls on the scooter, causing it to alternately reverse and hop forward.

I saw Leonard take in the scene, from Norman tapping on the glass to Adam swearing his head off to anyone who was listening and me standing back, trying to melt into the floor. I watched as his gaze slowly moved from one to the other and then even more slowly over to me. I think I clocked the exact moment he realized who Adam was, and his eyebrows levitated so high they threatened to disappear into his neatly combed hair. But he didn't say a word. There was really no need.

We made eye contact, and all I could offer was a shrug. I mean, I agreed. I was just as bemused by the idea of Adam being related to Norman as he was. But what could I do? The damage was done, if it was done. Trying to leave the past behind by ignoring it didn't really appear to be working for me any more so my options were wearing pretty thin.

By the time the receptionist, the duty manager and a couple of helpful passers-by had managed to extricate the girls from the revolving-door cavity (freeing them to come inside, but conveniently leaving Adam parked at an awkward angle on the outside), it was clear the Premier Inn Bournemouth wasn't going to win any points on TripAdvisor for being mobility-scooter friendly.

Leonard had sat back watching the action unfold with some delight, and he looked almost disappointed when Adam's moment of freedom arrived, although one of the girls had somehow managed to spike him in the shin with her six-inch heel, so that cheered him up a bit. I was distracted by the three girls giggling and taking photos of Adam through the glass, which I vaguely considered might be in preparation for a potential law suit, so I jumped a bit when there was a very close hiss at my shoulder.

'Err, Sadie, I think it might be time to go now.' Leonard was darting glances around the foyer and making motioning jerks of his head.

'What? Why, what's . . . ?'

Before I could get any further Leonard put his hand very firmly around my elbow and started steering me towards our cases.

'Yes, definitely, Sadie. We need to leave right *now*, my dear.'

I didn't understand what the sudden urgency to leave was at first, but then I saw what he had seen. A housekeeping trolley was parked just outside the lifts, piled high with a veritable mountain of yellow-and-green-stained towels. Even from across the foyer I caught a waft of something unpleasantly pungent and I saw the duty manager stop mid-conversation with a departing guest and frown, raising his nose to sniff the air.

The possible financial ramifications didn't bother me half as much as the potential confrontation when the receptionist and the housemaid started comparing notes, which was looking imminent, so I decided Leonard was right, as usual. It was definitely time to leave.

Leonard and I made eye contact and he raised one bushy eyebrow. I tipped my head and saw the ghost of a smile pass over his face. I felt my own mouth twitch ever so slightly. *Ahh, there she is.* Without another word passing between us we grabbed our cases and walked over to Norman, who was still making signals through the glass to Adam. Leonard took one of his arms, I got hold of a handful of shirt, and we turned him in the direction of the revolving doors.

Amidst the 'Mum, what, what's the rush?' and the 'But I think maybe I should go to the loo first,' we hotfooted through the merry-go-round of madness and out to the world on the other side. Bournemouth wasn't quite Narnia, but it'd have to do.

Fair play to Adam, he didn't even bat an eye as we emerged at an above-average pace and I stammered out something about needing to make just a little bit of a run for it. In fact, he was the model of efficiency.

'Righto, then. Bags on, bags on. Come on, come ON, hurry UP!'

He waved his arms wildly, indicating for us to pile our luggage on to the rack at the back of his scooter and not taking no for an answer. It was quicker to comply than to argue, then I grabbed Norman's hand and set off in the lead at a smart but I hoped not too attention-drawing jog in the direction of where Leonard had parked the car, a couple of blocks away. After a few minutes, a couple of corners and no sign of any hotel staff in pursuit I started to breathe a little easier.

I'd assumed Leonard was right behind us, judging from the 'Jolly good, keep going, lads, left here, that's it' that had been coming from the rear. But when I turned around to check that Adam had not absconded with our belongings, I got what could well go down as one of the biggest shocks of my life. And it was the moment I realized that maybe there was hope for Adam's redemption after all.

Because there, travelling low in a dangerously deep Adam-sized indent on the mobility scooter seat, was Leonard. Arms folded across his chest, imperious expression on his face and the oversized bulk of Adam lumbering along beside him with one hand balanced on the handlebars to steer and the other on Leonard's back, holding him steady.

'Old bastard was slowing us down,' he wheezed.

Amidst Leonard's protestations, I saw Adam give Norman a slow, sweaty wink and a very cheeky grin and, quick as you like, I was transported back thirteen years. Oh, *that* guy. Now I remember.

*

With all the leaving we'd done in the past week, it felt like we were becoming old hands at saying goodbye at the doors of the Austin. As Leonard busied himself checking the boot was packed Tony's way, Norman made sure his shoebox of Post-it notes was within easy access on the back seat and I hovered around, keeping a vague lookout for random housemaids. Adam was back in the warm embrace of his scooter like the miracle of his recent resurrection had never happened.

'So, Normie. Or should I say Little Big Man, eh?' He held out his hand. 'Well, good luck and all that, kid. I don't know if you're funny, but at least you won't be playing to an empty house now. And, by the way, you're welcome, ha ha.'

Norman smiled shyly and stepped forward to put his scaly little paw into Adam's.

'It . . . it was really nice to meet you, Adam, and thanks very much for your help. And I . . . well, even though you didn't get to meet him, I reckon my mate Jax would have really liked you.'

I realized he was dead right. Jax would have absolutely *loved* Adam. He would have given back as good as he'd got and raised the stakes just for fun. And if it turned out Adam was Norman's father, he'd have loved him even more. Because it's nice to be nice, among other things.

Adam looked embarrassed and chuffed at the same time, and even more so when Norman leaned over handlebars of the scooter to give him an awkward hug. That kid. My heart felt like it had turned itself inside out to wear itself for another day and I thought I might drop dead from love for him right there on the pavement in Bournemouth. For Norman, I mean, not Adam. Because, despite that faint glimmer of redemption and the realization that I still had a hell of a lot to learn about judgement from the twelve-year-old boys of this world, I wasn't quite ready to sanctify him yet.

Which turned out to be about right, because the last I saw of him was as he nearly ran over an old lady then let rip with a mouthful like it was her fault and she hadn't just been coming home from Tesco with her squeaky trolley full of shopping, like she'd done every Tuesday for the past thirty years. So he missed us all waving as we drove away, which was also just as well, because Leonard's was less wave and more two strategically raised arthritic fingers as he peered into the wing mirror.

'Young prick,' I heard him mutter. But when I turned to look at his profile, there was no denying the faint smile that lifted the corners of his wrinkly mouth.

As we turned on to the motorway, leaving Bournemouth in our proverbial dust, I crossed my fingers there'd be no fallout from the towels and my credit card after a good wash, but my guess was it was going to be a long time before the smell completely left that room. Even though I was pretty sure it wasn't really the bad odour that had kept me awake most of the night, I still genuinely pitied the next guest. Unless it was Lenny Henry. He deserved it, for false advertising. So that one's for you, Dawn.

37

When we'd plotted our wonky route according to the information in Leonard's spreadsheet and the opportunities for Norman to get his practice in, the plan was to take a couple of days to get from Bournemouth to Edinburgh, with a night at a B&B in Kendal and an appearance at the bi-monthly Tuesday open mic night at the Jolly Anglers. But now that Norman had landed a spot at the Duke, and with the Fringe already in full swing, after a surprisingly quick confirmation that the place I'd booked in Edinburgh could accommodate us a night early, we decided to push through. Of course, there might also have been a little part of me that wanted to put as many miles between Norman and Adam Linley as possible, just in case he decided to come after us with his scooter and a paternity test. Because even though I'd secretly conceded he wasn't quite as bad as my first impressions, I definitely wasn't ready to think beyond that just yet. Or maybe ever.

By arriving in Edinburgh sooner, we'd have two full days and two nights before Norman's show at the Duke, and he'd also be able to check out a few other people's shows to 'get him in the zone', as Leonard put it. I was a bit worried about the possibility of that making him feel worse about his own show, but who knew. At this stage, certainly not me.

What I did know was that the thought of a gaggle of eager Facebook fans trampling down the doors of the Duke to catch Little Big Man's show was tying my stomach in absolute knots, and I made a mental note to get some antacids at the next pit stop.

As the Austin settled in to eat up the four hundred and sixty-odd miles to Edinburgh, Norman huddled in the back seat and began going over his notes for the millionth time. After checking the road ahead for stray Ocado vans first, I quietly relayed the news to Leonard that, thanks to Adam, his humble Little Big Man Facebook event was suddenly threatening nearly three hundred punters in one tiny cellar room in a pub. And I'll tell you right now that a problem shared is not a problem halved at all, because Leonard immediately looked every bit as worried as me. Which of course had the effect of making me even more antsy about it all. The macramé party in my stomach ramped up the fun and invited the neighbours.

When we stopped for a toilet break at a roadside café, as usual I was the first one back to the car. Norman was standing on the forecourt talking to an old lady who'd climbed out of her car with a cat on a leash, and I'd left Leonard having a very civil one-sided conversation with the attendant about how a Mars bar used to be 20 per cent bigger, and where was the justification in increasing the price by 40 per cent and dropping the size? It had looked like it was going to be a bit of a wait, but the attendant must have declared a surrender because Leonard made it back in second place.

We sat in the car in silence, waiting for Norman. Me concentrating on trying not to chew a third antacid too fast or too obviously and Leonard staring out of the windscreen at an invisible point beyond the motorway. He appeared completely lost in his own thoughts, so when he spoke it took me by surprise.

'Sadie, it's all going to be OK, you know.' I swallowed a chalky chunk of antacid whole. 'Somebody once told me that if you have a problem that can be fixed, there is no use in worrying. And if you have a problem that cannot be fixed, then there is no use in worrying.' Leonard laughed softly in the direction of the motorway. 'Smart woman, my Iris.'

I didn't think I was imagining that the slack skin around his jowls appeared to be sagging a little more than usual, but then he turned and looked me directly in the eyes.

'We are all of us stronger than we think, Sadie.'

More often than not, Leonard made a lot of sense and I was usually fairly impressed with the things he had to say. But this time, no matter how well meant his words were, I would have much preferred to hear something along the lines of, 'Iris says if you have a problem heading your way at a hundred miles an hour, run at a hundred and one miles an hour in the other direction.' Which sounds like much better advice to me, and far more what I was used to.

Norman climbed back in the car, bringing a whiff of cat and old-lady lavender with him, and we headed off down the road a great deal slower than a hundred and one miles an hour, and still in the very same direction as our problem. And half a packet of antacids hadn't even touched the sides.

My task at this stage of the journey should have been to start thinking about calling or texting the next possible father. Also, the last possibility. But the thought didn't inspire me with anything other than dread, considering the results to date.

It was nothing personal, though, because, despite the briefness of our brief encounter, my memories of James Knox, who, according to Leonard's research, was probably still kicking around Edinburgh, weren't entirely unpleasant.

Way too cool for me had been my first impression when I'd spotted him setting up with his band in the pub. All crazy spiky hair, tight leather jacket and musical angst, or at least as much as you could have when you've chosen the road to jazz. But after five large vodkas I'd decided to do my worst anyhow – even though, somehow, it cost me a job and probably quite a good bit of my dignity. The next morning he brought me a cup of tea in bed and I told him about my father. It was kind of a funny thing to talk about after a one-night stand, but there you are.

It had been right in the middle of the Fringe, if you're up for that bombshell revelation. And if you believe in fate, or God, or meaningful signposts along a pretty barren road, then you might see the fact that, whoever was responsible, Norman being conceived around the very time of the comedy show he was on the way to perform at thirteen years later presents a pretty good case of synchronicity.

But to tell you the truth, I didn't want to do too much more thinking about any of it, let alone discover that something might Mean Something. The fact is that, despite my grudging but growing realizations about my own motivation for being Norman's one and only parent for so long, while it was all well and good to have a tidy spreadsheet of possibilities, without some kind of DNA testing there was no way we'd really be able to know the truth anyhow. And without pursuing that onus of proof, weren't we really just a bunch of weirdos flailing around the country meeting up with random men? And if you're considering the irony of that, so was I.

Anyhow, in amongst the trifle of my thoughts, I decided that if nobody else mentioned calling James Knox, then I wasn't going to either. It felt like a good decision and, unaccustomed to the effort required in making any of those, I managed to nod off into the sleep of the righteous.

In between dozing I caught snatches of Leonard and Norman's chatter as they ran through jokes. Cutting out a word here, adding a couple more in there and generally working on the delivery.

'The beat and rhythm, old boy. Beat and rhythm.'

Leonard accompanied his words with a volley of helpful slaps on the steering wheel every now and then, but sleepy as I was, I couldn't help hearing that, no matter how many times he fed Norman a line to repeat, the practice seemed to be having little to no effect on my son's off-kilter delivery. It still sounded like something, or someone, was missing.

Somewhere along the road I woke up and realized their voices had stopped and the only sound I could hear was the whirr of the Austin's motor. I looked over at Leonard, hands now firm on the wheel, a look of intense concentration on his face.

'All right, Leonard?'

He half turned his head to me and smiled, and I felt a sudden rush of affection.

'All right, love.' *Come on, Sadie love, let's go home.*

I raised my arms in a stretch and twisted around in my seat. Norman was scrunched up on the far side of the back seat, scraps of paper and Post-it notes spilling off his lap. His head was leaning on the glass of the window and his eyes were wide and unblinking, staring at the blurry passing scenery. I wondered what could possibly be going through his head.

I mean, what *would* a twelve-year-old kid who was about to

get up on a proper stage at one of the world's most famous comedy festivals be thinking? That two days out from the biggest moment in his life his skin was basically peeling off in front of his eyes? That there was a very real chance this one show could destroy every bit of confidence he'd ever had? That, kid or no kid, in a couple of days they might be sweeping him off the floor of the Duke in bits? Of course, I realized there was a strong possibility that could just have been me projecting. But what if it wasn't?

'Leonard! Can you pull over? Please? Now. I mean, as soon as . . .' Startled, Leonard slammed his foot on the brake, causing the Austin to shudder then slow right down.

'What is it, Sadie? Do you need a comfort stop?' He scanned the open paddocks on both sides of the road dubiously.

'No, no. Nothing like that. Just . . . look, can you just pull over as soon as you can? I . . . I need to talk to Norman, that's all. I just need a few minutes.'

As luck would have it, when we rounded the next corner there was a pub a couple of hundred metres up on the left. The Little Creek Arms seemed all but deserted and I had a flashback to the night at the Noble Goat. It had only been five days ago, but it seemed so much longer. And even though now we were only a few hours away from our final destination, suddenly I really didn't feel like I'd come much distance at all.

Norman's little head had popped up when he heard me ask Leonard to slow down, and he leaned forward and touched my arm as we pulled into the car park.

'What's up, Mum?'

I smiled what I hoped was a reassuring smile and patted his hand.

'I just need . . . I . . . I just want to stop for a minute, Norman.'

When we got out Leonard tactfully wandered off away from the car. I saw him take out his phone and squint at the screen, and his face immediately got that same worried expression I now knew hadn't been a coincidence. I made a mental note to try and get to the bottom of it next time I had a chance, but right now I had other fish to fry.

Norman and I walked towards a section of fence overlooking a narrow channel of fast-flowing water. I hazarded a guess that this was the Little Creek of the Little Creek Arms and marvelled at how simple some things in life were and how difficult others could be.

Why couldn't being a good mother be as easy as referring to the Good Mother chapter of a *Manual for Life*? Thumb through a few pages and come up with a solution to the latest problem: *Apply cream X to remove all traces of psoriasis, apply cream Y to remove all traces of sadness. Follow up with a liberal rubbing of cream Z to erase all traces of history and bad judgement and emerge as the best mother in the world.*

But there was no sign of any such manual to hand and, as I looked at my beautiful boy looking slightly worriedly back at me, I marvelled at just how useless my talent for spotting the important parenting moments was, how I could never quite get there when it came to saying or doing the right thing.

Like the time that Mrs bloody stuck-up Sorrenson from the Post Office rang me and told me she'd just seen Jax and Norman drinking cans of beer in somebody's cow paddock. Seen them with her own eyes, she had. I know I should have confronted them about the beer drinking, grounded Norman and banned Jax from coming over for two weeks. But instead I made a crack about how it was lucky she hadn't been looking with someone else's eyes then, or else she might have missed something. You nosey old bag. I was pretty sure that was the reason my electricity bill and two reminders went missing so I didn't even know it was overdue until they cut it off.

When Jax and Norman came home, green around the gills from their beer-drinking experiment, they stood there with the flowers they'd picked for me along the way and waited for their medicine. When I didn't say anything Jax even asked if I'd heard from Mrs Sorrenson lately. No, I said. Not a peep. Because part of me loved the fact that those boys had gone out and sat in some old cow paddock and done some secret beer drinking together. I mean, actually, half their bloody luck.

But this was different, and I knew it. All those other times I hadn't said or done the right thing might be forgiven if I could just say and do the right thing, right here and now, leaning over the fence behind the Little Creek Arms, slightly west of the middle of nowhere. Only the truth of it was that I still didn't know what the right thing was. Because making the choice between protecting Norman from what might happen and mending him from what had already happened felt way beyond my skills.

Norman scuffed the ground with his trainers, silently waiting for me to be the parent.

'Norman, I . . . you . . . you know none of this . . . I mean, we can still . . . if you don't think you . . .' My words were whipped up by the wind, clipping into disjointed syllables. Everything I wanted to say was right there waiting in the wings, but something had hold of my larynx and was strangling the life out it.

Why couldn't we just have a bit more time to work it out? A couple more years for him to get over the loss of the funny one. To grow out of his dream. To change his mind and want to be a teacher or a doctor or even a used-car salesman. Anything other than the person he thought he wanted to be. Because doesn't he know it's hands down the saddest bloody job in the world, spending your life trying to make people laugh? *It doesn't matter, love, let's go home.*

'I . . . look, what I'm trying to say is that you shouldn't feel like . . . I mean, you could wait till next year and we . . . I just think maybe you're not . . . not quite . . . Norman, please don't do it.'

My voice was so quiet by the end I wasn't even sure I'd really said it. I hoped I hadn't, but I already knew I'd done it all wrong anyhow. I should have eased him into it, let him think it was his idea. Told him it would all be OK, that Jax would have understood if he couldn't do it. Played dirty.

But wind or no wind, Norman hadn't missed a thing. He looked down at the hand that he'd placed on the fence next to mine, turning it over to pick at an errant loose scab on his shiny pink palm. He moved the flap of skin back and forth, back and forth, like he was playing a tiny foosball machine, knowing exactly how much pressure it could take before it drew blood or fell off. All those years of practice. There was so much tenderness in him, even for the monster that had tormented him for most of his life.

He bent his body forward and laid his forehead gently on the back of my hand. I felt the smoothness of his new skin and the breath caught in the back of my throat. I could have died happy right there and then with that silky small-boy forehead on my hand, but the moment was gone all too soon.

Norman raised his head and slowly smiled at me and, for a glorious moment, there was my boy again.

'Don't worry about it, Mum.' *Of course* he's going to do it.

'Of course I'm going to do it.' Norman stared out into another universe somewhere over my shoulder. 'Do you remember what

Jax used to say? That when you're scared to do something, even if everything's going to hell in a hand basket you should just think about the worst thing that could possibly happen and then get in there and have a go anyhow? Remember?'

I remembered. I braced myself on the rickety wooden fence, because it felt a bit like the ground was moving towards me.

'And Mum, don't you see?' He turned to face me and a wobbly smile attempted a run at the corners of his mouth. 'The worst thing already happened. Everything already went to hell in a hand basket, so it's all got to be OK from now on, because nothing else could ever, ever be that bad. You don't have to worry about me, Mum, honest.' *Look after Mum.*

I felt the world slow down, shudder and grind to a halt as I looked into my son's eyes and all of a sudden realized with absolute clarity what I'd been way too blinded by my own sadness to notice since Jax had died. Norman was so much braver than I would ever be. I pressed the ball of one hand into my stomach to dull the tingling around the edges of my scar and heard a faraway voice that might have been mine.

'OK, Norman.'

38

The thing about a place as old as Edinburgh is that a decade and spare change doesn't really make much difference. Heading up George Street in the Austin at gone midnight, it felt like I'd just nipped out for a quick thirteen-year trip to the supermarket. Everything looked exactly the same, and here was I, just another speck of historical dust blown back into town by mistake. *Welcome back, you meaningless speck of dust.*

Luckily, in a rare moment of forethought, I'd made sure I'd booked our accommodation in Edinburgh before we did anything else, because, call me genius, but I'd had an inkling that finding a place to stay during the busiest week of the year might be a little difficult. I'd still had virtually zero choice by then, but with the assistance of Leonard's superior googling skills, we'd managed to find an obscure private owners' website offering what I'm pretty sure was the last room in the last place that could conceivably call itself the city.

Discover your home away from home in Edinburgh at the Soft Fudge Guesthouse, the listing had enticed. Righto, then. Don't mind if we do, I'd thought. Sounds delicious. There'd only been one room available to book at the Soft Fudge, but from the photos it looked like, in addition to the double bed, there was an alcove with a very wide upholstered window seat, which Leonard had insisted he'd be more than happy to sleep on.

'Veritable luxury compared to some of the places I had to sleep in the army, my dear. It'll be an adventure!'

I wasn't so convinced anyone really needed an adventure like that and I also wasn't quite sure about having to share quarters that close, but I'd figured that, by that stage, I'd have plenty of other things to worry about and also it didn't seem like there was an alternative. So there we were.

Thanks to Leonard's pre-loaded directions on Google Maps, we navigated our way through the city and over to Leith with surprising ease. But finding the Soft Fudge itself proved a little more tricky, because even having the street name and number isn't all that helpful when the majority of the signs have been bent or graffitied out of recognition. When we turned into what half a street sign dangling from a post declared was *ngton stree*, it looked like as close to a clue as we were going to get. We crawled along (presumably) Kensington Street and pulled up in front of (apparently) number 14. I decided on the spot that if the last week had taught me anything it was a) never to believe what you read on TripAdvisor, and b) never be fooled into thinking that booking-site photos are even in the same neighbourhood as reality. Or in the case of the Soft Fudge Guesthouse, the same planet.

Norman and I leaned sideways in the car to get a closer look at the place, and I could see Leonard's foot hovering over the accelerator. For a moment I considered suggesting he floor it and head up to the castle so we could top and tail it in the Austin instead. But when a car behind us tooted impatiently he drove on a little way and pulled over into the only empty parking space to let it pass. In the end, the Austin made its own decision, elegantly stalling the engine and jerking us all forward to a dramatic stop. Clearly, we had arrived.

I wouldn't have expected to see all lights blazing at that time of the night, but when we unloaded our bags and walked the short distance back to number 14 the place was in total darkness and there was more than a whiff of abandonment about it. I'd been emailed a confirmation with a code to the key safe, but while with any luck there was going to be a lock on our room, we certainly didn't need a key for the front door. It was wide open and looked like it was hanging on by a cobweb. It wouldn't have stood a chance against Jax, but at least it would have been a quick way out of its misery.

Norman retrieved the keys, which, thankfully, were exactly where they were supposed to be, and the three of us stepped into the abyss of the Soft Fudge. According to the handwritten note attached to the keys, we were to head up the stairs to the Caramel Suite. We did as we were told and opened a door to both good and bad news.

The good news was that the room was absolutely huge. The bad news was that it had clearly been decorated by a very literal-minded painter and decorator back in the 1970s, because it was like stepping into a diabetic coma. Every surface was a sickly tan (or, at a stretch, caramel), excluding the ceiling, which was beige, and two ancient red velvet loungers and a matching red velvet bedspread across the double bed. But it was charming in an Addams Family meets Willy Wonka kind of way and at least it looked like we'd all fit.

'Great! There's lots of room, anyway, isn't there?'

I was too tired to try and make it sound very convincing, and I saw Leonard eyeing his window-seat bed with what could easily have been a few second thoughts. Norman, though, looked like he'd been given the keys to Edinburgh Castle itself. He'd managed to open one of the big bay windows and was hanging the top half of his body out, craning his neck to get a better look.

'Wow, Mum! This place is so cool!'

'Oh my God, Norman, be careful! Don't lean so far out!'

Norman obediently slipped down the wall and grinned at me. *Grinned!*

'But Mum, it really is cool.'

For once in my life, I was grateful to have passed on the Foreman family trait of aiming low to avoid disappointment.

Fringe or no Fringe, we were definitely the only guests taking advantage of the Soft Fudge's hospitality on that particular night, and perhaps since 1978. Of the other five doors on the upstairs level (which we discovered after I relented to Norman's request to explore before going to bed), four of them were boarded up. The fifth was open just a crack and, when Norman pushed on it lightly, the slightly wider crack revealed a room stacked so full of furniture that it physically wouldn't open much more than a few inches.

'Hey, Mum?' Norman whispered as we peered into the semi-darkness. 'Remember when you, me and Jax watched that telly show where the old guy hoarded so much they had to take the roof off his house?'

'Mmm. I certainly do, Norman.'

I also remembered that the real reason they'd taken the roof off was because the guy had eaten himself to forty-five stone and had fallen and couldn't get up. A vision of Adam popped unbidden into my head and I shut the door hard and shepherded Norman back to the Caramel Suite.

*

Even with Norman and me occupying the bed and Leonard curled up on the lumpy window seat, the Caramel Suite was big enough not to feel awkward. The regular but indeterminable noises coming from Leonard's creaky old body and the soft banging of the plumbing from inside the walls seemed to soothe Norman, and he fell asleep within minutes. But despite being dog-tired, I lay awake, savouring the presence of his warm, still body next to mine.

A sporadic burst of drunken shouting and the sound of cars going past every now and again even at that early hour of the morning made me realize how quiet our house in Penzance was. Most often, the first sound of my day was the guy across the road starting his delivery van at 5 a.m. If I concentrated hard, I could hear the crash of the waves on the foreshore as the noise of his motor faded away, and there were times I was tempted to get up and go for a walk. But I hadn't walked on the beach for years, even though I knew that the sting of the salty wind on my face would probably feel quite wonderful. The thought of the sand squeezing up between my toes without my father there in his rolled-up trousers and vest seemed impossible. And so it was.

A thin ray of light from the street elbowed its way through the curtains of the Caramel Suite and in the red glow of the digital clock by the bedside table I could see the outline of Norman's face on the pillow. His mouth hung open a little and he looked like he was about to say something. He was sleeping so deeply I was tempted to mark a cross on his forehead for old times' sake, but it probably wouldn't have had the same effect with my manky Vaseline chapstick.

I lay there and looked at his face for a long, long time, examining every part of it from top to bottom, then bottom to top. Left to right, then right to left. I squinted and closed one eye until the two sides of his face became far from symmetrical, then I did the same with the other eye. When he was unmasked and down the rabbit hole of sleep, I knew every inch of that face, committed to memory by the countless hours I'd done just this over the years, marvelling that such a perfect human had anything to do with me. But now I was searching for something else. Perhaps a sign of Tony on the off-chance a stray sperm might have slipped through before abandoning ship? Dan McLachlan, who didn't want to know? God forbid, something of Adam? James Knox, who I wasn't going to call?

I couldn't see any of them. But I found me, I found my father, and in the sliver of street light in the early hours of the morning I caught a fleeting glimpse of my mum. But, somewhat reassuringly, there really wasn't a sign of anybody else, and so I thought, well, maybe that's it. Maybe it's true, after all, and Norman really is totally and only mine. Maybe all those years ago the universe decided that Sadie Foreman had tried enough and cried enough and was done looking in all the wrong places. So here you go, here's someone just for you. You did this. And he's perfect. Well done, love, and that's your lot.

By 4.04 a.m., in a fug of sleeplessness, antacid overload and nagging stomach pain, I came to the conclusion that I'd been absolutely right all along and there really was no need for the search for Norman's other parent to continue. Then, at 4.05 I remembered that it hadn't been my idea to look for him in the first place, it had been Norman's. So there went that.

Somewhere in the longest, noisiest and most sleep-deprived night of my life, I must have dropped off, though, because the next thing I knew I was being shaken none too gently awake. Norman's pink-and-white splotchy face loomed large and in living colour an inch from my nose as the Edinburgh sun jostled through the window behind him.

'Mum, Mum, wake up. Leonard's gone.'

39

Leonard was indeed gone. Although his overnight bag was exactly where he'd placed it the night before, his coat was hung neatly over the back of a chair and his laptop was sitting on the window-seat bed. At Norman's insistence, we searched the house, which was just as empty in the light of day as it had been the previous night, but we couldn't find hide nor wispy grey hair of him. We did find the kitchen, though, so for a moment I had high hopes for a cup of tea, but the chances of finding a stray teabag within a decade of its use-by date didn't look promising.

While we were looking for Leonard, pushing open downstairs-loo doors and calling up through attic hatches, I couldn't help thinking that, despite Norman's obvious agitation, it was a bit early to start worrying seriously.

'You know, Norman, it's not like . . . well, I mean, we don't even know if Leonard has gone missing, as such. Maybe he just got up early and went for a walk to, you know, check out the neighbourhood or something. He'll probably be back in a minute.'

But the thing was, if I'd learned anything about Leonard over the past week, it was that he loved a good sleep-in now he didn't have to be up at the crack of dawn for his cleaning job. He was usually the last to wake up, although, come to think of it, he was always the first waiting by the car ready to go. It was probably all that army training. But anyhow, for him to be up before 7 a.m. now seemed fairly uncharacteristic, as far as I could tell.

After a thorough search of the house revealed nothing and it became very clear I wasn't going to get a cup of tea, we reconvened in the Caramel Suite. For want of a better plan, I thought it would be a good idea to check my phone, just in case Leonard had called or left a message as to his whereabouts while we'd been on our search.

I'd plugged my mobile in the previous night, which I had to do at every opportunity, since it only held its charge for a day, and quite a lot less on the rare occasions I made or received any calls. When I picked it up, it was a couple of seconds before I realized something wasn't quite right.

'Hey, Norman, look at this.'

The phone I had in my hand was definitely not my out-of-date, banged-up Samsung. It was bigger, thinner and much sleeker. A very un-banged-up iPhone. Leonard's iPhone.

Then I remembered the last time I'd seen him with it was just before we'd gone to bed the night before. He'd taken it out of his jacket pocket and looked at it as if he might be going to make a call, thought twice and then placed it down on the table next to mine. I looked at the mobile phone I was holding and it wasn't hard to imagine that, in the dim light of a pre-dawn get-away, to an old man with dicky eyes one phone might look very much like another.

'I think this means that wherever Leonard is, we can safely assume that he has my phone. What do you think?'

'I reckon you're right, Mum. Here, pass it over.'

253

Delighted to have some kind of a clue, Norman swung into action and dialled my number off by heart from Leonard's phone. It rang out, which didn't surprise me one bit, although I decided it probably wasn't the time or place to admit I had a habit of leaving my phone on silent mode. Just in case anyone wanted to speak to me. Deflated, Norman passed the iPhone back and we sat on the edge of the bed for a couple of minutes, just looking at it.

There was a screech of brakes and a sudden shout outside, and Norman leapt up and ran to the window. His head swivelled from side to side as he scanned the street for signs that the kerfuffle had anything to do with Leonard. After a few seconds he turned back and shook his head dejectedly.

'Nothing, Mum. What are we going to do? Where is he?'

He brushed his fringe out of his eyes and a small piece of skin detached itself from his forehead and wafted down to land on the screen of Leonard's iPhone. Norman sat back down heavily on the bed without noticing and the skin bounced off and landed on the duvet, right near my hand. I felt an almost irresistible urge to reach out and put it in my pocket.

He picked up Leonard's phone again and started turning it around in his hands.

'Hey, Mum. Do you think . . . ? I mean, it's kind of an emergency, so do you reckon . . . could we maybe look in Leonard's phone and see if we can phone Iris or something?'

And because I was clueless as to what to do next myself, I agreed that, in these circumstances, it might be OK to nosey through an old man's private property without his permission. Within a few seconds, Norman passed the phone back to me with the trail of Leonard's call-history revealed.

There was a landline number at the top with double digits in brackets beside it indicating the number of recent incoming calls. In fact, it appeared to be the one and only number Leonard had been called from in the last two weeks or so. It had a south-west prefix, so I assumed it had to be his home number, with Iris waiting on the other end.

'Mum, do you think we should call her? Iris? Maybe Leonard mentioned something to her and she'll be able to tell us where he's gone. Just to . . . you know, put our minds at rest.'

Norman's voice was slightly shaky and I could tell he was getting worried about his new old mate. I thought it was doubtful that Iris, several hundred miles away in Penzance, would know where her husband might be at this time of the morning in Edinburgh, but we didn't have anything else. And I had to admit, when I realized how much time had passed, I was definitely starting to worry a little.

I hit return call against the number and put it on speaker, gesturing for Norman to lean in. I figured I'd just wing it with some small talk rather than straight out declare to Iris that her husband had disappeared without even taking his coat, but as I was gathering some thoughts about the weather the number barely even got to ring before a voice answered.

'Good morning. Wheeler Centre Exeter, Emily-Jade speaking, howmayIhelpyou?'

I hadn't expected anything other than a sweet old lady's voice on the other end, so I was a little taken aback.

'Hello . . . umm . . . I . . . I . . .'

Norman was way ahead of me, though, and started making the hang-up sign before Emily-Jade could say anything else. I hit the red button just as a slightly concerned-sounding 'Hello? Hello, can you hear me? This is the Wheeler . . .' came down the line, then dropped the phone back on the bed.

'Well, I think we can safely say that wasn't Iris, can't we?' I was still a little flustered at being put on the spot by Emily-Jade.

'Did she say the Wheeler Centre, Mum? Do you think I should . . . ? We could check . . .'

I nodded yes, and Norman picked up Leonard's phone and started typing into Google search. After a few seconds his forehead wrinkled into a frown and he slowly turned the phone around to face me. On the screen was a slick-looking photo of a grim brick administrational building. There were a few well-dressed OAPs staged in the foreground like mannequins, pushing walkers, chatting to young people, patting dogs and generally looking happy and content. Across the front of the entrance to the building was a large sign.

Fred Wheeler Dementia Care Centre
Secure Residential Unit

Why had Leonard received a total of twenty-seven calls from this place since we left Penzance? New cleaning job, maybe? But why hadn't he mentioned it? As I scrolled through the website, the phone suddenly dimmed and gave a low-battery warning. After trying to plug it into my charger and realizing it didn't fit, Norman opened up Leonard's holdall and did some delicate rummaging with no luck, then sat back on his haunches with a look of concentration on his face.

'I know I saw him with it yesterday, Mum. I remember, because he nearly left it behind at . . . oh, wait! I know!'

He sprang up and went over to where Leonard's coat was hanging on the chair, reached into the inside pocket and, within seconds, he was holding the charger triumphantly in the air, as the rest of the contents of the pocket fluttered to the floor.

I plugged the phone into the wall and Norman began gathering up the folded hanky, two pencils, half a packet of Mentos and a couple of pieces of paper that had dropped out to put back in Leonard's coat. I was engrossed back in the Wheeler Centre website when I looked up and Norman was standing in front of me.

'Mum, look at this,' he said quietly.

One of the pieces of paper that had fallen out of Leonard's pocket was in his hand. He passed it over to me and I immediately saw why it had caught his eye. Printed across the top of the torn-off piece of headed paper were the words *Fred Wheeler Dementia Centre*. There were some handwritten details below the letterhead in neat cursive.

Cobcroft CL1576. New Admissions. Level 2.
Bring signed forms, personal effects, medications.

There was a date and time on the piece of paper, which I quickly calculated was the day before we left on our trip. I stared at the words, trying to work out what exactly I was looking at, and my eyes were drawn back to the phone on my lap. I glanced between the paper and the Wheeler Centre website several times, and as my focus adjusted, the words 'secure' and 'dementia' jumped out of the phone screen and started to do a little tap dance in front of my eyes. There was a second when they seemed to pause for effect, before taking a low, flourishing bow to herald a flurry of dropping pennies.

Because there definitely had been a few times when Leonard seemed a little vague or absent since we'd left Penzance. More than the usual, I mean. Then there was that weird moody thing in Swansea, the near-miss with the Ocado van, the evasiveness about getting lost in Bournemouth when he went to find the Chinese tea. And now, disappearing like this.

Now that I thought about it, maybe there really had been something just a little too keen about how quickly Leonard had decided to join us on the trip. Because if the pennies had dropped into their correct slots, the date on the note and the evidence presented suggested that at this very moment he might actually be supposed to be safely and securely tucked up in the Wheeler Centre with his medications and personal possessions. Had Norman and I just been a lucky coincidence that happened along in the nick of time to aid and abet him in absconding? Were Iris and the police at this very moment monitoring APBs and scouring the country looking for him?

All of a sudden, it felt to me like Leonard's disappearance was shaping up to be a whole lot more serious than we'd thought. Because what if the poor guy had just planned to go out for a walk and then had some kind of funny turn? What if he was out there now on the mean streets of Edinburgh without a clue as to where, or possibly even who, he was? My stomach began tying itself to a couple of vital organs and tightening the knots. *OK, then.*

'Right, Norman, we need to find Leonard. And fast.'

Of course, finding someone fast is all relative to your plan of action, so if you don't have one, well, then you can't expect too much. When ten o'clock came and Norman was still running to the window every two minutes to report back, 'Nope, nothing,' I finally decided more proactive measures were needed.

My big, bold plan was for us to tackle a search of the immediate neighbourhood around the Soft Fudge. Even at that hour, though, there were way too many people around for my liking, and I felt the need to hold on to Norman's arm as tightly as I dared without hurting his skin. As we walked up and down the streets of Leith, we saw plenty of little old men limping along with their poodles, or papers or pints of milk under their arm, but none of them was our little old man.

I was relieved when, after the agreed half-hour we'd allotted ourselves, it was time to retrace our steps back to the Soft Fudge, with the help of Norman's Boy Scout map, which he'd been scribbling along the way. *Left at Chapel, right at Water, left at the Spar then left again.* It's a good thing one of us was sensible. We stopped at a little grocery shop to buy teabags, a carton of milk, some apples and a deadweight of crisps and chocolate, so at least that was one problem solved. I couldn't do much right, but I could make tea and feed my son junk food.

We rounded the last corner on Norman's notes and we were back on Kensington Street. Not that I ever had any doubt. But even though I'd known it was a long shot that we'd just come across Leonard a few streets away, sitting on a park bench waiting for us to find him, my heart felt like it was slipping down my chest with every step. We trudged back up the stairs to the Caramel Suite and I looked at the digital clock by the bed, realizing it was probably at least five hours since he'd left. The old bugger could be anywhere by now.

Norman walked over to the window seat and curled up on it, alternating glances between Leonard's laptop and overnight bag and checking out the window every few seconds. He looked like he was about to cry. Aeons passed as I struggled to think of something reassuring to say, then I saw his gaze fix on a point somewhere outside the window. His jaw slowly dropped, as if he was about to say something, then he closed his mouth again without making a sound. He swallowed deeply before opening it to have another go.

'Mum. He's . . . I just realized something. The car . . . the Austin's gone.'

What with the potential bombshell we'd discovered on Leonard's phone, we'd been too distracted to even think about the car, but Norman was right. I climbed on to the window seat and cricked my neck to get a good look up the road to the spot we'd parked the night before, but unless a cheeky teal 1971 Austin Maxi had morphed into a regular, garden-variety grey Ford Focus overnight, it was definitely and irrefutably gone.

Despite the fact that the neighbourhood looked like it was pretty conducive to grand theft auto, when we looked in the side pocket of Leonard's bag where he usually put the keys, the jury filed in quietly with a unanimous vote. Not only was Leonard missing and possibly demented, he also had wheels. For all we knew, he was doing burnouts down Princes Street that very minute, or was halfway to John o' Groats with the wind in his hair.

'Norman, I don't know about this. I . . . I have to say it isn't great. I mean, if he's out there driving around and he doesn't even . . . well, if he gets lost . . .'

'It's OK, Mum. He'll be all right if he's in the car, I reckon.' Norman suddenly looked a bit brighter. 'He did a refresher defensive city driving course last summer in Truro. And anyhow, he was the British off-road rally champion in 1969. Leonard can drive a car blindfolded, I reckon, even . . . well, even if . . .'

His voice trailed off and I could tell he was considering just what limitations Leonard might be facing if he really was MIA from the Wheeler Centre.

I'm not sure what shocked me more, though, to be honest. The fact that Leonard might really and truly be a former national champion rally driver, or that Norman knew about it. What else had they been talking about while I thought they were shuffling Post-it notes? My bad parenting skills? Why Norman wanted to find his father? Something inside my gut twanged and I sucked in my breath and held it until the pain passed. But even when it did, I prepared for another, because it was pretty clear that the car was a game-changer. How the hell could we expect to find him now? I looked from Norman out to the Ford Focus under the tree and back again.

'Norman, look ... I've been thinking. We ... we might have to call someone if he doesn't show up soon. The Wheeler Centre, or Iris or ... or the police, I mean.'

'Mum, no!' Norman looked stricken, and he grabbed my arm. 'What if he gets into trouble? What if Iris gets mad at him? What if there's ... like a ... a car chase with the police and everything? Mum, what if it's like *Thelma & Louise*?'

The kid was good bringing that up, because there weren't a lot of movies that got to me more than that one and we watched it every year on my birthday. Me, Norman and Jax. My scar gave itself another sharp jab as I got a flashback to last year, the three of us sitting scrunched up on the sofa together under a duvet eating Quavers and shouting at the telly screen.

'Don't do it, don't do it! Just surrender and you'll be OK! Surrenderrrrrrrrrr!'

Hoping against hope that, this time, those wild, crazy, wonderful women would turn around and let the nice policeman help them out so they could all live happily ever after.

'Please, Mum, don't call anyone. Not until we ... please. Not ... not yet anyhow.' Norman's face was right up in mine. Red, pleading and lovely.

'What then, Norman?' I asked, as gently as I could. 'What are we going to do? Just sit here and hope he comes back?'

Never snitch. Nobody likes a snitch, Normie, I once heard Jax saying.

I wasn't convinced of that, though, because I think some people actually do like a snitch. The police, for starters. And maybe the Wheeler Centre. But, of course, I gave in. Because of *Thelma & Louise* and because who wants their kid to think they're a snitch? And we did end up sitting in the room for another hour, drinking tea and hoping Leonard would just come back. I even tried visualizing him zooming up the road, executing a perfect reverse parallel park out the front of the Soft Fudge and bounding out of the Austin in top hat, tails and with a bag of fresh-baked croissants. For all the good it did. In the end, it was Norman who broke the long, tea-sodden silence.

'Mum, I think I've got a plan.' I braced myself. 'We need to find Leonard, right?'

Norman spoke very slowly and clearly, like he'd thought this through and rehearsed exactly what he was going to say in his head. Which of course he probably had. I nodded and maintained the brace position.

'So, we need to start looking. But I mean, like, really looking properly. And if we can't call anyone else . . . yet' – he stopped and made sure I was looking him right in the eyes – 'and we can't . . . well, we have to do it ourselves. Or, that is . . . I mean yourself. You.'

I didn't think I liked where this was going, but I was paying attention.

'Look, Mum, someone's got to stay here in case Leonard comes back, don't you think? So that someone should be me. Because, well . . .' And the kid, bless him, looked like he felt he had to apologize. 'I . . . I still have to practise for the show tomorrow night. I've got tons of stuff to go over and, actually . . . I don't mean to be rude, Mum, but I could do with some time on my own to . . . to try and get it right. Or . . . at least better, anyhow. You know, because . . . because practice makes perfect and all that.'

I still wasn't sure that a few hours' practice was going to be nearly enough to help Little Big Man at this late stage, and it crossed my mind that it would be an ideal opportunity to try to convince him to reconsider again. *Forget it, Norman. Just surrender and it'll all be OK.*

But something stopped me. And maybe it was my mini epiphany at the Little Creek Arms, or perhaps it was just because Norman's was the only plan we had and practice really might make perfect, but for the first time in my life I entertained the thought that running away mightn't always be the only way to save yourself.

'Don't worry, Mum. I'll lock the door and I won't even leave the room. I promise. I've got my phone to call you if I need to. And I've got the crisps and chocolate and I . . . I won't answer the door to anyone. Except if it's Leonard, of course.'

He'd thought of everything. The words were tumbling out now and, even as they landed in a messy heap on the floor, I realized that Norman's plan did make sense.

'If you're out there, you'll have much more of a chance on your own of finding him before anything . . . well, you know . . . just finding him. I know you can find him, Mum. I know it.'

He had me on the ropes.

'Oh, and apples. I've got the apples, too, Mum.' Kapow.

40

There wasn't one bone in my body that was happy about leaving Norman alone, but I knew he was right and that if he stayed in the room he'd be perfectly safe. I could also see that without outside help, aka snitching to the police, getting out and scouring the streets of Edinburgh really was our only option of finding Leonard. And even though there was only a remote to nonexistent chance that I'd succeed, I had to try.

It was eleven o'clock, and Leonard had potentially been on the run for six hours already. That was long enough for him to be halfway up Ben Nevis in first gear if he'd so chosen. Or in Paris, if the 1969 British rally champ had really put his foot down.

I set Norman up on the huge bed in the Caramel Suite, surrounded by Post-it notes and crisps, with the big free-standing mirror angled so he could practise his onstage facial expressions. I made sure his fully charged mobile phone was right beside him and went through the rules. Don't OD on chocolate, do alternate a glass of water and an apple with the crisps, and don't set foot outside this door except to go to the toilet, and even then be quick.

'I mean it, Norman. And no matter what happens, I'll be back by six o'clock at the latest. OK? No ifs, no buts. That's a promise. Whatever you do, just do not go anywhere, not for anything.'

'I'll be fine, Mum, honest. I promise. Don't worry.'

And the thing was, I knew he would be. He was the sensible one in the family, and I should probably have worried more about myself being out there loose on the streets of Edinburgh. Again. I didn't want to think about what would happen if I hadn't found Leonard by six o'clock, because I'd probably have no choice but to call the police then, and who knows what turn things would take. It wouldn't be the first time I'd cooled my heels at a police station in this particular city, although losing an old man with dementia probably had far more serious ramifications than being drunk and disorderly after a Cure concert.

I stepped off the number 10 bus from Leith on to St Andrew Square with the bare bones of a plan. I'd got a free map from the bus driver, with Edinburgh on one side and the whole of Scotland on the other (non-existent god forbid I'd need that), and I decided for once in my life to be methodical and cover the city grid, street by street. The task Norman had set me felt overwhelming and, if I'm honest, I didn't hold out much hope, but I told myself the car was pretty distinctive, so that was in my favour. Come to think of it, so was Leonard. So one never knew.

With random performers and crowds of spectators for Fringe events on virtually every corner, the city was heaving, and it took me a good hour to walk the length of just two streets on the map. My neck began to ache from double-taking on every blue car that caught my eye, and I became quite the expert on old men, learning more with every one I spotted. How they walk, the hunch of their shoulders, the way their heads seem to sink into their necks, and the angle at which they seem to tip forward, as if in constant fascination with their shoes.

I wondered how far forward my dad would have tipped by now, at sixty-seven. How he'd have walked and bent and curved into an old body, and if he'd have found his peace with the blunting of age. And as I rounded a corner and set off down the next street, I wondered for the millionth time why the world's best daughter hadn't been enough to make him want to stay around long enough for me to find out.

By the time I stopped to eat lunch on a bench out the front of the train station, I was tired, hot and all that thinking hadn't been without its consequences. My scar had noticeably warmed up, and underneath my clothes it was starting to feel like it was stretched to its absolute limits. I surreptitiously opened a button and pushed down the waistband of my jeans to see if it looked as bad as it felt. It was a bit of a shock to be reassured that it was still just the neatly zipped-together silvery track I had all but ignored for the past thirty years. On the outside, at least. I could only guess at what was going on inside me because, whatever it was back there, it was definitely getting angrier.

There was a constant stream of people scurrying past and I continued to scan the crowd as I forced myself to swallow bites of my Pret Posh Cheddar. Every now and again, as I'd scuffed around the streets, I'd kept calling my own number from Leonard's phone in the hope that he might eventually answer. As I absently hit the redial button again and put the phone to my ear I nearly choked on the last mouthful of my lunch.

'Hello? Hello? Leonard, is that you?' I could definitely hear a voice and it sounded like his, but it was muffled and tinny and felt like it was coming from very far away.

'Leonard, hello? Can you speak up? It's me, Sadie. Where are you? Are you OK?'

His voice kept cutting in and out, but from the snatches I got he sounded very flustered and upset. Confused, even.

'I . . . oh . . . so terribly sorry. I just wanted . . . well, because, I promised Iris . . . and I thought . . . I just . . . oh, I really don't know . . . but I just thought I would try to . . . so silly of me. And then the phone wouldn't . . . I'm so sorry, Sadie, I . . . rather a mess of things I'm afraid.'

I suddenly remembered that I'd put a pin lock on my phone after I'd come back from the toilet one day at work to find Dennis scrolling through it. 'Just checking you haven't been texting your boyfriends on my time, Sadie, ha ha.'

I realized that if I really had left my phone on silent, not only would poor old Leonard not have known we were trying to call unless he had it in his hand, he also wouldn't have been able to call us back, even if he'd wanted to.

'Leonard, don't worry about all that. But are you all right? And where *are* you?' There were a couple of seconds' silence and I thought we'd been cut off. 'Leonard? Are you . . . ?'

'Well, now . . . not far, really. About an hour out of the city, I think, and . . . I actually found some on the side of the road . . . then, oh dear, the Austin wouldn't start and . . . I tried a little something but . . .'

Leonard's patchy voice trailed off entirely at that point, but I could still hear his raggedy old-man breathing. And all I could think was, this is all my fault. If it wasn't for me opening my big mouth about Norman's plan, right now Leonard would be ensconced safely at the Wheeler Centre, most likely enjoying an online class in Mandarin and drinking hibiscus tea. But instead, he was stuck on the side of the road in the middle of nowhere, probably with no clue as to how to get back. To a place he wasn't even supposed to be. *Come on, Sadie, in for a penny in for a pound!*

'It's OK, Leonard. Don't worry. I . . . I can come and get you. No problem. Don't worry about a thing. But, Leonard, you need to tell me: WHERE ARE YOU?'

There were another few seconds of radio silence, like Leonard was definitely trying very hard to remember where he was. I held my breath. I had absolutely no idea what I was doing, and all I really wanted was for someone to tell *me* not to worry about a thing. That they'd come and get *me*.

'Oh, sorry . . . of course. Well, it's near . . . Quothquan, it's called. Quothquan. I can spell it for you, shall I? Q. U. O . . .'

But even as Leonard was painstakingly spelling out the letters I'd opened up my map, turned it over and begun tracing my finger around the area immediately surrounding Edinburgh.

'Got it!'

Leonard had just hit the final N in his spellathon, and nobody was more shocked than me that I'd actually found it.

'OK, Leonard, here it is, I see it on the map. It's not too far at all, you're right. You wait there, though. Wait there, OK? Don't move. I'll be there as soon as possible. OK?'

I knew now was not the time to be asking him if he was of sound mind, but after reassurance from Leonard that yes he was OK, even though no, he didn't think it was necessary that I come and get him, I managed to extract a promise that he'd wait with the car and not move a muscle until I got there. I hung up and headed into the train station on a fact-finding mission, feeling far less confident than I'd made myself sound on the phone.

But, to my own utter amazement, in under two minutes I was

running back out of the station with a timetable in my hand and the wind at my heels, heading for Princes Street and a bus that was due to leave in six minutes. I wouldn't call myself an athlete by any stretch, but credit where credit's due, because I skidded to a halt at the bus stop opposite M&S just as the 101 to Biggar pulled up. And as I climbed on board and took the closest empty seat I distinctly remember thinking that maybe this was going to be easier than I'd anticipated.

Of course, you know that's never the case.

41

NORMAN

First rule of comedy: Pause for effect.

It's funny, but even though I was pretty worried about Leonard being missing, I really and truly didn't feel scared about Mum going off and leaving me on my own at the Soft Fudge. I wasn't just saying that to make Mum feel OK about it, even though I was doing that too. And when I say it was funny I don't mean in a write it on a Post-it note and use it in my show sort of funny. I mean in the I'm not usually a very brave person so it was interesting sort of funny.

Even though I was all alone, when I was sat on the bed in the Caramel Suite with Big Al's *Big Book of British Comedy Greats* and all my Post-it notes and screwed up bits of paper from the Comedy Pot spread around me, trying to make something good out of it all, out of the blue it just felt like Jaxy was there with me as well. And because there wasn't anybody else around I thought it might be OK if I had a chat to him. And so I did.

I didn't really think Jax could talk back to me or anything, but once I got started it was just like we were back in my bedroom practising jokes or lying around downstairs watching Dave Allen DVDs with Mum bringing us cheesy toast and hot chocolates. So because of how nice that felt I wanted to keep it going, because who wouldn't, and so I decided to tell him everything that had happened since he went.

I talked and talked and talked and talked for ages, and even though it made me a bit sad that Jax couldn't really talk back it also made me smile because actually, if he was there, there's no way I would have been able to get all that out without him interrupting me about a million times. But I wouldn't have minded.

After a while, when I ran out of things to say because I'd told Jax absolutely everything, I thought I'd better get on with practising for the show. Which was what I was actually supposed to be doing. I put on Grandad's jacket, because that's called getting into character, and I know you might think I'm making this up, but as soon as I put on that jacket Jax started talking back to me. Honest.

I could actually hear him going, count it out in your head, Normie. One wait, two wait, three wait. Just like always, when we were trying out a new routine for Mum and I'd start to come in early or miss a mark and come in too late. Jaxy would give me the elbow, but gentle, not so it hurt. Just to remind me. And he'd always be right near my ear when it was my turn, whispering without moving his lips and saying, wait for it, wait for it . . . one, two, three, ready, aim, fire!

By the way, I know I'm not the funny one. Jax is. Was. I'm the straight guy, and that's kind of like Dean Martin or Bud Abbott. The straight guy sets the funny guy up with the joke and then the funny guy comes in and finishes it off and gets the laughs, which is a pretty genius system, I reckon, as long as nothing happens to the guy standing beside you.

But something did happen to the guy that always stands beside me and it was really hard to keep having to remember that I wasn't part of a comedy duo any more. I was supposed to be Little Big Man, one guy with a one-man show for one night only. Even though no way no how am I anywhere near being a man. But Leonard told me I shouldn't think about the whole Little Big Man thing too much, because it was just something he nicked from an old movie to make me look good for the Facebook page. He said all I had to do was just get up there and be Norman Foreman, because that's who I am and I'm the only one who can do it.

But the thing is, all the jokes me and Jax wrote or collected were made for two people and it was pretty hard for me to have to do both parts, no matter how many times I could hear Jax telling me to count it in and wait for it, Normie boy. It just wasn't the same on my own, and when I looked in the mirror to see what I looked like when I was telling a joke all I could see was a little kid in a big jacket with bits of his skin falling off. And an empty space where the funny guy used to stand.

Jax would have been able to do both parts easily, though, and I know that because he actually did do it once. It was when he was trying to help me get my timing right for this really cool comedy sketch we made up about what would happen if the doughnut had been invented square instead of round. And if you want a laugh, you should maybe think about that for a minute. Jax was trying to explain when would be the funniest time for me to come in with my bits and so he kept on jumping from one spot to the other, pretending to be me saying my part and then really being him saying his part. It was so funny when he was putting on a squeaky voice and doing the me bits that I nearly peed and he had to get his puffer out because he lost his breath.

But he never in a million years would have imagined that I'd be the one trying to do *his* part one day. And neither did I.

I knew that if Jax was really there with me in the Caramel Suite there's no way he would have let me give up, though. He'd have made me keep on practising and practising until I got it kind of right. He'd be saying stuff like, pause for effect, Normie! Pauuuussssssssse for eeeeeffect! Jax can stretch out a pause for effect better than anyone, and the longer he stares and says nothing, the funnier it gets. But whenever I pause for effect it just sounds like I've forgotten the next joke. Which is actually true some of the time.

And so, because I knew Jax would want me to, I kept on practising to try and get it right. I put all my Post-it notes in order, with the funniest jokes at the beginning and the end and the unfunniest ones in the middle, and then I tried. I really did. I tried loads and loads of times, because practice makes perfect, Jax says.

First I told every single joke in a different accent, which sounded lame and stupid. Then I tried making weird faces in the mirror when I talked, which just looked weird. Then I tried running from one side of the room to the other while I told jokes, which just puffed me out and then I couldn't talk properly. No matter what I did, all I could hear was a bunch of random jokes floating around the room then landing on to the floor and flopping about like a load of fish out of water. Even the best first and last ones, which are most important. And all the time, I just knew that I wasn't being funny. I was being the opposite of funny. I was being totally unfunny.

Nobody knows this, but I didn't for one minute think I was actually going to get to go to the Fringe on my own. Not really. If Mum hadn't seen the poster that Jax might or might not have changed while I was sleeping, I'm pretty sure I would still have been sitting on my bed back in Penzance staring at the walls and missing him. Instead of sitting on a bed in Edinburgh all by myself trying to do jokes and talking to invisible Jax. And missing him.

When I looked over at the clock beside the bed I didn't need Jax talking in my ear to tell me I had exactly twenty-seven hours and twenty-three minutes before I was going to be up on stage at the Duke, most likely being the opposite of funny. Because maths is one thing I *am* good at.

42

Sadie

As I bounced along on the bus on the next leg of my mission to rescue Leonard I had to admit that the job of ignoring the regular eye-watering jabs to my stomach was becoming quite considerable. I'd managed reasonably well up to that point by telling myself that as soon as Norman's show was over and we were safely back in our lovely boring little lives my very next task would be getting to a doctor. Or a therapist. Whatever it turned out I needed most. Definitely. Absolutely. But now, what with the pain, the unexpected reminiscing about my father, the worry of both Norman and Leonard being on their own, and the regret of never having known how damn beautiful the countryside was just ten minutes out of Edinburgh, my mood wasn't exactly what you'd call upbeat.

So it was never going to take much. When the bus hit a pothole half an hour into the journey my head jerked back with a snap. At first it just made me blink a couple of times, but then it was like the shock had loosened some kind of internal valve and, out of nowhere, my chest started contracting uncontrollably. Before I even knew what was happening I was sobbing into both fists, very much in view of a teenaged Goth girl with a small dog on her lap sitting across the aisle.

The burst water main only lasted about thirty seconds, but it was long enough that I definitely wasn't going to be able to pass it off as a bad case of hiccups. When I'd managed to compose myself the young girl leaned over and patted my hand gently, tilting her head to one side and giving me an enigmatic pencilled-in eyebrow raise. Her dog did exactly the same, and to me it looked like they were saying, 'Tell us, don't tell us, it's up to you.'

But there was something comforting about that small, smooth hand with its bitten-down black fingernails and the motion of the bus trundling through the majestic Scottish countryside that made me think, *well, all right then*. And when she plonked the warm little animal on my lap then slipped into the empty seat next to me, I really couldn't find a reason not to tell a girl and her dog something that had been chewing me up from the inside out for this entire trip. And way before that. I hoped they were ready.

To be honest, I didn't need a therapist (or even a girl and a dog) to tell me I hadn't ever dealt with my father's death. Although several of them have done – thanks for coming and that's seventy-five pounds you'll never see again. But that I'd allowed my son to build a dream, a life, a plan around the premise that he came from comedy royalty was a whole other issue.

'The thing is . . . all of this is my fault. The whole reason Norman even wanted to be a comedian so much is because I . . . I've always . . .' I stopped for a hiccup and blinked hard to stave off another flood. 'I just couldn't bear to tell him the truth about his grandfather . . . my father. He's got no idea that the person he's been trying so hard to live up to his entire life was just a mediocre comedian and big old bloody fraud who chose to top himself rather than go on with the show.' *Damn hiccups.*

I took a deep breath, and the pain in my stomach felt like it might be about to shoot out through my eyeballs, along with the other stuff.

'But I . . . I couldn't . . . I didn't want to take him away from Norman, too, so . . . I mean, I've only ever shown him . . . told him, the good stuff. The things I . . .'

'The things *you* want to remember about your dad. You gave him the story you *wish* you'd had, right?'

Jesus. Ten solid minutes of spilling my guts and it only took Goth girl two seconds to wipe the floor with me. I closed my eyes and leaned back against the seat, because I didn't have to hand over seventy-five pounds to know there was only one place to go from here. What I really wanted to do was crawl back under my Penzance-shaped rock and go back to the way my life used to be. I wanted my teapot, I wanted my Tesco sofa and I wanted my direct access to endless re-runs of *Come Dine with Me.* But it was pretty clear that wasn't an option, so in the end I told a complete stranger my biggest truth, which, coincidentally (although probably not), turned out to include the answer to the very question Leonard had asked me back in Swansea.

Because the truth was that when I looked at Norman I saw the same hopeful, desperate look in his eyes that filled the still frames of my childhood. The snapshots of my father. And what I was so terrified of, thank you very much, Leonard, was that Norman was about to get up on a stage in just over twenty-four hours and embark on a journey that would eventually drive him full tilt into the same wall that broke my dad.

I'd been resolutely staring out the window of the bus for the entire conversation, and in the silence that followed my final revelation I wondered if perhaps Goth girl had peaked early and I'd managed to put another person to sleep with the story of my father's death. The dog had long ago nodded off on my lap and the only noise was the sound of the engine and the soft, springy pings coming from the bus seats. But when I turned to check, she was wide awake and looking back at me, forehead creased in concentration. Her waxy, deadpan face somehow made me feel like her reply was going to be a doozie. A nugget of truth and wisdom and an assurance that maybe everything was going to be OK after all. *It's all right, Sadie love, let's go home.*

I shifted slightly on the seat to rearrange the pain in my stomach and waited.

'Your stop, lady.'

My stop was Cross Street, Biggar, in front of a group of stone-fronted shops and a Post Office which declared on a handwritten sign that it also sold shortbread. It also just happened to be the Goth girl's stop, and she told me I'd need to get the local taxi to take me the rest of the ten-minute drive to Quothquan, unless I fancied a five-mile walk. I didn't. My new friend took me into the Post Office and shortbread shop to introduce me to the postmistress, who said she'd be more than happy to ring for said taxi, the driver of which just happened to be her husband.

After a brief exchange on the phone she confirmed Dicky would be with me just as soon as *Bargain Hunt* finished in five minutes. I wandered outside to wait patiently, because, despite the thought of Leonard twiddling his thumbs on the side of the road trying to remember his own name, who was I to come between someone and their telly?

To be honest, I was also all of a sudden very much in need of a moment to catch my breath, because that bus trip seemed to have loosened more than a couple of tear-duct valves. Deep down in the pit of my guts, the nagging pain that had previously been concentrated around my scar was rapidly morphing into something else altogether as a web of cramps encompassed my entire stomach. I could feel a warm layer of sweat gathering on my back and a very strange sensation, as though searing-hot liquid was seeping in and filling up the spaces between my organs. *Next job. Definitely. Absolutely.* I wondered if the postmistress might by chance serve a side of medical attention with her stamps and shortbread.

I lowered myself carefully down on to the wooden bench outside the Post Office, leaned my head back and closed my eyes, doing my best to make out I was just enjoying a bit of sun on my face. *One, two, three, breathe. It'll pass.* I tried to imagine I was back in Penzance, trundling along in the bus on my way to Pearl's to spend another interminable day at my meaningless job, where the only questions I got were about spare parts and overdue invoices and the only memories I had to face were about where I might have left my pen. *One, two, three, breathe.*

I'd rather hoped that, kind as she'd been, the girl and her dog might have just ambled away out of my life, but they were clearly intent on seeing the job through. When the wave of pain eased off to take another run-up, I opened my eyes and she was crouched on her haunches in front of me, arms wrapped around her knees, eye-line locked and loaded.

'See, the thing is, and don't freak out when I say this, lady, but I've been thinking and I reckon I know what the problem is.'

'Oh?' I sucked my breath in and held it.

'Yeah. The way I see it, the main reason you've got your knickers in such a twist about all of this stuff is that, when it comes down to it, when push comes to shove, you just don't trust your son.'

There's really nothing quite like getting a serving of home truths on the side of a road in an out-of-the-way corner of Scotland. I heartily recommend it. I'm joking. I don't recommend it at all. It's possibly the worst place to hear your home truths, because there is *literally* nowhere to hide. You even have to sit there on a bench outside a Post Office trying to breathe your way through the most pain you've ever felt in your life and wait for a second helping.

'What . . . what do you mean? Of course I trust him. You don't . . .' I knew it was me talking, but I didn't feel like I had any control over the sounds that were coming out of my mouth and my throat felt like it was closing in. 'He's . . . Norman's my son, I . . . I love him. I love him more than anything, I . . .' *Whatcha got, Sadie?* 'Of *course* I do!'

I blinked a couple of times to focus and I could see the girl still crouched at my feet, hands loosely linked over her black tights, waiting for me to finish. I wondered if perhaps I should mention that all three of her heads seemed to be having trouble balancing on her shoulders.

'Well, yeah, of course you *love* him. I didn't say you don't. I said you don't *trust* him. Because if you truly trusted him, you wouldn't be so afraid of all the bad things that *could* happen. Think about it. Why are you so scared of your bairn trying to be a comedian like your dad? Maybe even better than what he was?'

I tried to blink the fuzz out of my brain. Geez, hadn't she been listening?

'Because you don't believe he can do it, that's why. You don't believe it. Now, your boy, well, I'll bet he's scared shitless, too, but he's decided he's going to do it anyway. No matter what.'

A couple of stray minutes slithered by with their heads down as Goth girl's words settled around me, sitting quietly, awaiting the finale. Because, somehow, it just felt like there was one coming.

'You know, Jeff Buckley once said . . .' *Here it comes.* 'Wait, lady, are you OK?'

The girl leaned forward and put her hand on my knee and, just for a moment, I felt rock steady. I looked into her black-smudged eyes and nodded.

'Sock it to me, Jeff.'

'Well, like, I don't think he made it up or anything, but he said a bird sitting in a tree isn't scared of the branch breaking because its trust isn't in the branch, it's in its own wings.'

Now there's a home truth for you.

Here's another. Which may or may not have been related. The excruciating pain in my stomach chose that very moment to reach critical mass. With a huge involuntary spasm, my entire body bent double, causing me to lose my balance and topple sideways on to the bench.

Beyond Goth girl's startled upside-down face, off into the distance on the other side of Cross Street, Biggar, I thought I saw a tiny bluebird with Norman's face perched on the highest branch of a tree. Then the pain got so intense that I wasn't sure of anything except that right there and then could be the moment I died.

43

NORMAN

First rule of comedy: Always have a back-up plan.

I must have been practising for longer than I thought, because when I got up to get a glass of water, due to feeling a bit sick from all the chocolate and crisps I'd eaten, I nearly couldn't believe my eyes when I looked at the time again. It was 5.31 p.m., and the last time I'd looked it had been 2.07 p.m. I couldn't believe how fast time had gone and I wasn't even close to coming up with a whole new routine, which is what me and Jax had decided I needed. Also, Mum wasn't back and, even though she had said six, it was six at the latest. So that only left half an hour before it was going to be later than the latest she'd said.

By the time 6.01 came and there was still no sign of Mum or Leonard, I found out that maybe I wasn't as brave as I'd started to think I was. Then at 6.10 I remembered I had my phone so I could just call Mum. But then at 6.10 and two seconds I realized that I didn't have Leonard's number programmed into my phone, which is probably something me and Mum should have thought of before she left. So the next thing I thought to do was call Mum's phone because of Leonard having it and because her number *is* programmed in. Plus I know it off by heart anyhow. But it just went straight to the message and because I didn't know what else to do and I was starting to get a bit worried I called it again straight away. It went to the message again but at least it was nice to hear Mum's voice.

I tried to stay as brave as I could, but it got harder and harder the later it got and I didn't even have any chocolate left to make me feel better. When it was an hour later than the latest Mum said she'd be back I thought I should try talking to Jax again, but he didn't talk back at all that time. Not even one little hey, loser, which you might not think a person would look forward to hearing but I would have.

I went over to the window for the millionth time, hoping to see Mum and Leonard coming up the street together. Or even separately from different directions. But the only people I could see were a couple of dodgy-looking guys in pulled-up hoodies who looked like they were up to no good. They kept turning around to look up and down the street and then, all of a sudden, one of them stared right up at the window to where I was kneeling on Leonard's window-seat bed. I dropped down straight away, because the last thing I wanted was a couple of gangsters coming after me, and my knee banged into something hard, which turned out to be Leonard's laptop. Which then gave me the idea to try to find his phone number on there somewhere, which I think might have been synchronicity, so maybe Jaxy *was* still talking to me after all.

I sat on the edge of the bed and opened and closed a few folders on the laptop. There was a lot of stuff about candle making and welding and some notes about Photoshop but I couldn't find anything that looked like it might have Leonard's phone number on it. I was about to give up and just go back to worrying when I saw a folder called *Sadie*. When I clicked on that there was another folder inside called *Finding Fathers* and when I clicked on that I found the spreadsheet Leonard had made way back when we first decided to come on the trip.

I opened it up and the list of my maybe dads' names and phone numbers came up. Since the last time I saw it Leonard had added another column called *Miscellaneous Contacts*, and next to where it said *Mr Big Al* was Big Al's phone number. And when I saw all those phone numbers it gave me a bit of an idea for a contingency plan, which was pretty handy because I didn't have anything else.

Mum and Jax are both big on contingency plans. Jax says having a back-up idea in case everything goes wrong is the first rule of comedy, but Mum says it's a pretty good rule for life in general. So, like, if we're going over to Falmouth and me and Jax want to go to the library to look up comedy autobiographies while Mum does shopping, we'll arrange to meet back up at a certain time but we also make a contingency plan. So we'll maybe say we'll all meet at the Co-op at three o'clock, but if anything happens we'll keep going back there every half-hour to check for the others. Stuff like that.

I guess Mum didn't have time to think of a contingency plan that morning. Like, 'If I'm not back by six at the latest, Norman, go to the nearest police station and then alert the media.' Although maybe not that. But I did realize that calling a responsible adult was probably a pretty good back-up plan and that if Mum hadn't been in such a hurry that's probably exactly what she would have said to do. And because you've got to work with what you've got, even though I didn't have any proof that any of them were actually responsible, what I had was a bunch of phone numbers for quite a few adults, so I decided they'd have to do.

I called Tony's number first, because I felt like he'd know what to do in a scary situation like this and also, if he didn't, then Kathy definitely would. I thought that was cool, sort of like a back-up for my contingency plan, except that Tony's phone rang a few times and then nobody answered so it went to his message. It was funny to hear his voice again, because even though I'd thought about him quite a lot since we left Swansea, it already seemed like it was ages ago.

Hearing Tony's voice on his message also made me realize I didn't actually have any idea of what I was going to say to the responsible adults I was calling. Like, hey, everybody's disappeared and I'm all alone and really scared and I've run out of chocolate and there are a couple of suspicious-looking gangster types outside. Oh and also, I'm not very funny and I'm booked in to do a show by myself at the biggest comedy festival in the world tomorrow.

That didn't sound great when I said it in my head, though, so I just left a message for Tony saying, it's me, Norman, and we're in Edinburgh but Leonard has gone missing and I've sort of lost Mum too now and would he mind giving me a call back. And it's me, Norman. I said that twice, because for all I knew Tony and Kathy forgot all about us the minute we left Swansea.

There was no way I was calling Dan McFerretfeatures, and anyway, I was pretty sure what his answer would be, so my next choice on the list was Adam. The way he helped us in Bournemouth sort of already proved he was the type of guy you could rely on when the you-know-what hits the fan, and also there was still a chance he could actually be my dad. Which was pretty weird, although if he was it might explain why I love crisps and cheesy toast so much.

When I called Adam's number it rang and rang about a million times, and I was just about to hang up but then an answer thing came on. Only it wasn't his voice, it was one of those robot ones that tells you to leave a short message and it'll get translated into a text. I waited for the beep and then I talked as slowly and clearly as I could.

'Mum's gone. Need help. From Norman.' I was really hoping it didn't translate to one prawn, green kelp, wrong doorman, otherwise there'd be no hope of Adam helping at all.

My contingency plan wasn't looking great because I'd tried everyone except Big Al, but then I remembered what it felt like when he hugged me on the street outside Toad Hall when I started crying like a baby and how much better it made me feel. And I thought, well, a guy that can do that could probably do anything. So I called.

Howdy. You've called Al, and guess what? I don't want to talk to you. If I wanted to, I'd have answered, wouldn't I? Just kidding, leave your name and number and I'll get back to you as soon as I can. If I want to, that is. Ha ha.

I don't really know if it was because of hearing Big Al's voice or because nobody in the whole world seemed to be answering their phone, or maybe it was because it was 7.43 p.m. and I was feeling pretty scared about being all on my own in the Soft Fudge, but I suddenly got a huge whoosh in my tummy. And even though I tried to stop the crying coming, I couldn't.

Instead of hanging up and trying again later, which maybe would have been a better idea, I left a message on Big Al's phone. And what came out was a pretty big mess, what with all the crying. Like, 'I don't know where anyone is and I can't call Mum and there are some dodgy-looking guys outside and I think they saw me looking and I don't know what to do and I'm all alone and I can't even be funny without Jax. It's Norman.' Which wasn't great. And now I'd cried twice in front of Big Al.

After I hung up from Big Al I sat on the bed sniffing for about ten minutes and even though I didn't feel much better, at least I'd run out of tears. I went to close Leonard's laptop and the spreadsheet with all those names and numbers was still sitting there staring at me.

And isn't it funny how quickly things can change and one never knows? Because when I saw that spreadsheet I realized that, what with Leonard going missing and Mum disappearing and all the crying and being scared, I'd totally forgotten there was one more dad left on the list.

44

First rule of comedy: Jump in the deep end
and just start swimming.

I figured that if I could get over Dan McLachlan not wanting to know me, which I did, and if I could get over Adam *wanting* to know me, which I also did, and I could get over Tony not being my dad, even though I really, really wished he could have been, I would definitely be able to get over whatever the last guy on the list had to throw at me. Plus I'd never heard of anyone called James who was an axe murderer, so that made me feel a little better. Not that I'm an expert or anything, but Jax always said that if he was ever going to do a crime he'd change his name to Allan, because of something called involuntary bias and who ever heard of a criminal called Allan. Mind you, I've never heard of a criminal called Jax either and anyway, I was pretty sure Jax was joking about the becoming a criminal thing. But one never knows.

I decided to write down what I wanted to say to James Knox before I called him, because there was no way I wanted to mess up like I had with Big Al, especially if it turned out I had to leave another message. It was just a few lines on the back of a menu for a Thai restaurant that I found in a drawer and there wasn't anything about him maybe being my dad. Just did he remember his friend Sadie Foreman from a long time ago and she's my mum, and she had his number to look him up when we got to Edinburgh but now there was a little bit of an emergency if he didn't mind helping out. Thank you very much and sorry to bother you. Norman speaking.

But it wasn't another answer machine and James Knox answered on the first ring. He didn't actually say any words at first, but I did hear a lot of *mmmpphh* and *phfffmmmth* and some other weird, echoey noises. After a few seconds of that he did say hello, though. Actually, he said, hello, hello, hello, who's this? So then I said hello back and he said hello again and I was so nervous I totally forgot how to talk.

But the funny thing was that James Knox seemed quite glad I'd called. Not that I could really understand too much of what he said at first, because he was shouty whispering really, really fast in a Scottish accent, but then he stopped for a second to take a breath so I decided to start making my speech from the back of the Thai menu to see what would happen. And what happened was that he stopped talking completely and started listening. So I kept going.

When I mentioned Mum's name he goes, Sadie Fore—? Who . . . ? Oh . . . um . . . Sadie . . . Sadie, well, OK. And then he didn't say anything for a bit, like he might have been thinking. I'd finished my two lines and I didn't want to mess things up, so I kept quiet as well. Then he goes, Sadie Foreman you say, eh? And she's got a kid, eh? It didn't really seem like it was a good time to blurt out that yes she has and actually so might you and it's me.

So I just said yes and I'd sort of lost her and I just happened to find his number and no other responsible adults were answering, so I wondered if he'd mind helping me out. Please. And thank you. It's Norman.

It turned out I'd called at a pretty good time because the reason James had sounded quite happy to hear from me was that he needed my help as much as I needed his. And just so you know, I don't reckon I ever would have dared to do what James asked me to do if I hadn't been so scared. But it was getting really late and there was still no sign of Mum or Leonard, and every time I thought about them my tummy started doing flip flops and not the good kind. So when James said, aye, he'd help me out, and thanks for considering him a responsible adult by the way, but that actually I might have to do him a small favour first, everything about stranger danger just went out the window and I wanted to cry with happiness. Actually, I did cry a bit and it wasn't all for happiness, but I stuck my sleeve in my mouth to make sure he didn't hear.

If I'd been a bit older, I might have thought that what James asked me to do for him was actually quite strange, which is what a few adult type of people pointed out to me later. Including James himself. But the only person I had to ask for advice was Jax. And even though he wasn't really there and so I didn't get a proper answer, I could guess what he would have said. *Jump in! Jump in the deep end, Normie, boy! Come on!* Plus I was pretty sure he would somehow have got a message to me if James was what he called a dodgy geezer.

What James said was that he was a wee bit indisposed and that before he could help with finding Mum he needed me to get him out of a tricky situation involving a tumble dryer and a trip across town. And even though I thought it was probably illegal for a twelve-year-old kid to be out on the streets of Edinburgh alone at night, and even though I was properly scared by then, Jax didn't send me any signs that James was a dodgy geezer so I said yes.

Then I wrote down everything he said about bus numbers and street names and back doors of nightclubs and laundry rooms and calling him if I got lost along the way, because it was just a wee bit difficult for him to call me in his present situation. I listened really, really carefully and wrote everything down, and by the time he finished there was no room left on the back of the Thai menu at all.

Then James goes, so how about it, Norman, reckon you can do it? And I looked at all the stuff I'd written down neatly and in order, and because I had a plan and I knew where I was going so I'd know exactly when I got there, just like Jax says, I honestly really and truly felt like I could. And as soon as I decided that, even though I still had quite a lot of scared inside of me, I also felt really, really proud. Because I'd gone and done it. I'd jumped in the deep end all on my own, feet first, head up, and I was about to start swimming. And I reckon that's just what Jaxy would have done.

I nearly couldn't believe it even came out of my mouth, but what I said was, 'Piece of piss, James!' Which I'd never said before, not even once, but I bet you know who said it a lot. I was beginning to understand James's accent pretty good by then and he shouty whispered down the phone, 'Aye, right then, that's ma boy!'

And I thought, yeah, well. One never knows.

45

First rule of comedy: You've gotta risk it for the biscuit.

I'd never, ever in my whole life broken a promise to Mum, and I'd promised her I wouldn't leave the Soft Fudge under any circumstances. But she'd also promised she'd be back by six o'clock at the latest so I figured, fair dos. Also, it wasn't like I was going off to meet up with a proper stranger or anything. I mean, there was a chance James was my dad so I figured that had to count for something.

He seemed to know a lot about Edinburgh, though, because when I told him we were staying in Leith he said all I had to do was walk up the road and get to any bus stop that said bus number 16 stopped there. And because he was right it was very helpful and so that part was easy. When bus number 16 came I already had my cover story ready, which was that I was on my way home after karate class. It took me ages to decide between that and a late dentist appointment and even then I changed my mind at the last minute. But anyhow, it was nothing like Penzance because the driver didn't even look at me when I got on and pushed my exact change in his little box. It was pretty weird, because if a bus driver had seen a kid on his own after 8 p.m. at home it would have been an interrogation and who's your mother straight up, but this guy just started driving again before I even got to sit down.

There was heaps of stuff to look at on the bus trip, but I had to concentrate on noticing the things James had told me to keep an eye out for so I wouldn't miss the right stop. Like the Tesco Express when the bus was going to turn off Princes Street up Lothian Road, and Usher Hall, which meant I should start getting ready because my stop was next, and then Bread Street, which was my stop. Everything was exactly how I had written it down on the back of the menu, so I almost couldn't believe it, but that part was pretty easy as well.

Even though it was Edinburgh, the being on a bus part wasn't that much different to how I got to school every day, but when I got off the next bit was definitely not like anything I did every day or actually even any day. I made sure I was facing the right way, like James had said, before I started walking left up Grindlay Street until I got to Cornwall Street, which even though I was feeling pretty nervous by then made me laugh on the inside. Because I'd come all the way from the county of Cornwall to end up on a street in Edinburgh called Cornwall. How weird is that?

James had told me the next thing to look out for was a big flashing red and white sign that said Whisky-a-Go-Go. He also said there'd probably be loads of people hanging around and that some of them might be drunk because of the other nightclubs in that street. Maybe not this early, but be careful anyhow, he said. And don't talk to anyone. I made sure I wrote that down so it was part of the list and I wouldn't forget. *Don't talk to anyone. Be careful, Norman.* I didn't and I was.

James was right about the loads of drunk people, but the good thing was that there were so many of them nobody even noticed me when I walked right past the front door of the Whisky-a-Go-Go club and turned left down the alley beside it. And even though my tummy was doing all sorts of scaredy topsy-turvy jumpy stuff, it also felt kind of good too. I felt like a spy or a superhero or something. And I reckon I felt a little bit like Jax too, because it was the sort of stuff he'd do, not me. But when I kept getting that bad but good feeling in my tummy it made me understand a little bit better why Jax always wanted to choose the hard way.

When I got almost to the end of the alley I saw a load of huge metal bins and next to them was a big red door with Emergency Exit on it. I pulled on the metal bar and it opened exactly like James said it would. Before I went in I turned around and looked behind me. Then, because there was nobody there and because I was so topsy turvy and excited I actually couldn't help myself, I did a double fist pump to the empty alleyway. And for a first-timer, I reckon the Norman Foreman technique was pretty good.

There was only one tiny light in the hallway once I got inside and it was so dark it took me quite a few blinks before I could even see my own hands in front of me. Not that it turned out there was too much to see. James had said that even though there shouldn't be anyone in there I should probably try to be really quiet just in case, so I tiptoed past the first green door on the left that said Utilities and then I didn't even need to check my notes to know that the next door on the right called Laundry was the one I was looking for, because I'd pretty much memorized my instructions on the bus. I decided right then and there that if comedy didn't work out the next best thing would definitely be for me to join MI5. I reckon I'm a natural.

46

First rule of comedy: Think funny. Look funny. Be funny.

James looked like a rock star. Not that I've ever been up close to a rock star and even though my first look at him was kind of folded in half and squashed into a massive tumble dryer. That's him by the way, not me. I was the one standing in front of him shaking in my Converses and wondering if I was going to stay alive long enough to ever be able to do another one of those double fist pumps.

Actually, when I looked in the tumble dryer and saw a folded-up rock-star type of person I didn't know for sure if it even was James. Because the first thing he said to me was Dr Livingstone, I presume, and so for a second I thought maybe I had the wrong laundry or even the wrong tumble dryer.

But before I could say, no, it's me, Norman, I spoke to you on the phone remember, he goes, bloody hell, I cannae tell ye how good it is to see ye, Norman, now untie these, lad, and get me out of here. So I thought, well it is pretty dark and maybe he was just confused from being upside down for so long.

James's hands were tied together really tightly with a rolled-up tea towel and he had his phone wedged right in between the knots. It wasn't easy to try and get a good grip with him all higgledy-piggedly in the dryer like that, but he kept really still and said good lad, and ye havnae to worry about hurting me, just go for it. Pull away. So I just went for it and when I took out the phone, after a couple of tries of pulling really hard I got the first knot loose, and then the second one just came undone and the tea towel slipped right off his hands.

When James climbed out of the dryer I knew I was right about the rock-star thing. He was wearing a long black coat, tight black jeans and a skinny silver scarf around his neck. His hair was dead black and stuck out in every direction, and I didn't know if it was because he'd been through a few cycles of the tumble dryer or if he did it like that on purpose. In the end I decided it was probably a bit of both. And when James the rock star stuck out his hand and goes, you're a wee lifesaver, Norman, and no mistake, I was so proud I thought I might pee.

Straight away I realized that getting out of the Whisky-a-Go-Go Gentlemen's Club with James was going to be a whole lot harder than getting in, even though you'd think it'd be just a matter of going out the laundry door, back up the hallway, out into the alley and off to start looking for Mum. But James said that if I didn't mind we needed to take a little detour first.

I know that some paedos and axe murderers only pretend to be good people to get your trust so they can trick you and all that, but I just had a feeling that anyone who looked and sounded as cool as James couldn't be a bad guy. Also when the thought of paedos and axe murderers came into my head I remembered that I'd actually called *him*. So, like, if he was one, he'd have to be the luckiest bad guy in the world, wouldn't he?

Anyhow, it turned out the reason James was in that tumble dryer was because he was having a wee spot of bother with a guy called Slim McGinty the Robbing Bastard. Slim's shonky black-jack dealers at the Whisky-a-Go-Go had been swindling James's dad's pension money out of him every week for three months because he had a liking for cheap whisky, which then made him get a liking for gambling. Which made him lose all reason, James said, which made him gamble his pension money, which meant he couldn't pay his mooring fees because of money troubles, which meant he was in danger of losing his houseboat. Which actually *was* his house and not just some old boat.

Every time James said Slim McGinty's name he shook his head and then he'd say the robbing you-know-what. And he definitely did sound like one, because James had heard from a guy who knew a guy who talked to a guy that worked at the Whisky-a-Go-Go that Slim's dealers were paid to cheat at blackjack. So I reckon it was totally unfair that James's dad had lost all his money to a bunch of cheats, and one never knows, maybe if the dealers hadn't been shonky he could have been a millionaire and looking to upgrade to a yacht instead of wondering how he was going to pay for his moorings after losing all his pension to Slim McGinty. The Robbing Bastard.

Anyhow, James reckoned he just did what any good son would do, which was to come to the gentlemen's club to politely ask Slim for some of his dad's money back. Not even all of it, just the last two hundred pounds that he'd lost the night before. Just the last straw is what he called it. But when James showed up at the club pretending to be a customer and then snuck upstairs to the office to have a wee chat to Slim, he reckons he didnae get a very nice welcome.

Slim didn't just threaten to beat James up for even asking,

when James said he was going to the police if he didn't at least give some of the money back, he called two massive bouncers into his office and they took the keys to James's moped and tied him up and put him in the tumble dryer. Because Slim didn't have time to deal with him due to the fact that he was running late to get to his mum's ninetieth birthday party.

Now can ye imagine that, Norman? he goes. Stick a bloke in a tumble dryer just because you're away to get minced? Nae bloody manners at all. James sounded just like Frankie Boyle and I really wished Jax could have been there to hear him. And then when James said about needing to detour to get the keys to his moped and maybe even his dad's money and was that OK with me, I really, really wished Jax could have been there. To hear me say yes.

James said that a twelve-year-old kid wasn't exactly the regular kind of punter they got at the Whisky-a-Go-Go so it might be best if I wore a disguise just in case anyone asked questions. But even though you'd think a laundry would be a pretty good place to find a disguise because of being full of clothes, everything we pulled out of the dryers looked the same. Out of three giant big tumble dryers the only things in there were a load of black and white checked trousers and a mountain of white jackets. So, James reckoned, kitchen staff it was.

James held up all the trousers against me until he found the smallest ones, which were still about a million times too big for me. But when I put them on over the top of my jeans and turned them up a few times he reckoned I looked the business. I didn't let on they actually felt like they were going to fall down any minute, I just grabbed a handful of material and twisted it up and tucked it into the back of my underpants. Then I put on the smallest of all the white jackets and it was so big that when I saw my reflection in the door of the tumble dryer I looked like a fridge with a couple of black and white checked legs sticking out the bottom. Like someone had been squashed underneath me. But James said, you'll do lad, and I thought, well, maybe I look OK.

He definitely looked a lot more like a proper chef than I did when he put on his outfit, but he said nae bother, and there wasnae any more time to worry about it because it was a fair bet Slim's mum's ninetieth birthday party wasn't going to kick on so time was of the essence. But then he said wait a sec, and rummaged through the dryer again and found a couple of crumpled-up black chef caps and told me to put one on my wee scone. But even when he pulled it down right over my ears to make it fit better it still didn't look as good as the one on his scone. Because with all his hair sticking out every which way his head looked like it was made for a cap to top it off. Mine just looked like it was trying to get away from it. And even if I'd had a Post-it with me so I could write down what might actually happen if your head *did* try to run away from your hat, I wouldn't have been able to. Because time was of the essence and because I was so nervous and excited I felt like I might be about to wee those big old chef's pants right off my legs.

So then James got down on one knee and put his hands on my shoulders and goes, right. This is it, lad. Are ye ready? And even though he had hold of a couple of handfuls of scabs that were in the middle of peeling off, having James hold on to me for a second or two actually felt really, really nice. Like if I stuck with him there was no way anything bad was going to happen, no matter what. Nae bother at all. Then he let go of my shoulders and goes, just remember, Norman, head down, eyes front, walk with a purpose. No guts, no glory, eh? When James said guts it sounded like gootz and I'd never been so scared and happy at the same time in my whole entire life.

James said that the thing about a uniform is that when you're in one people think you belong. So if you do what people are expecting someone who wears that uniform to do, then nobody is going to even look at you twice. At least that was part of what he said when we were sneaking up the back stairs and into the kitchen of the Whisky-a-Go-Go Gentlemen's Club. The rest I couldn't really hear, but I got enough to get that because I was dressed like I worked in a kitchen James wanted me to act like I worked in a kitchen. However that was.

I'd never been in a gentlemen's club before or actually even heard of one, come to think of it, so of course that means I'd never been into any kitchens of any gentlemen's clubs either. But all I know is that place wasn't like any kitchen I'd ever seen before, which wasn't many, but still. It looked like it might be bigger than our entire house, and even though I had my head right down and I was walking as fast as I could I counted at least five massive stoves.

James had hold of the back of my chef's jacket and he was pushing me ahead of him, so I couldn't have stopped walking even if I wanted to, which I definitely didn't. He was whispering stuff into my ear like, steady boyo and steady now lad and don't stop now Norman, ye wee champ, and it was funny because even though it was practically deafening in there with all the yelling and pot banging and dish clattering I could hear him as clear as anything.

We kept walking, and my heart was banging against my chest so hard I could feel the scabs rattling and I was scared it was going to bust me right out of my disguise and rat us out to Slim's bouncers any minute. James's hand was still on my back but then he started pushing me to go a bit faster and I could see he was aiming me at two big white doors with little windows in them. I still didn't know much more about kitchens, because I'd had my head down most of the time, but I did know that looked like a way out.

When I heard someone yell out, oi! you two! really loud, I swear my heart fell right down through my clothes, into my trainers and started squishing around in my socks. Then the voice shouted, didn't I bloody well tell you to get those bloody desserts out to the buffet ten minutes ago and bloody MOOOVE IT! I took a quick sideways look over to where it was coming from, hoping that it wasn't for us and that me and James could just keep walking right out through those doors, because they were only a couple of steps away. But it was for us.

The guy with the voice was dressed exactly the same as me and James, but I tell you what, I know for sure they weren't his uniforms we'd borrowed out of the dryer because he was a real-life ginormous giant. It looked like someone had stood one person on top of another for a joke and just added one angry head on top. That big angry head was eyeballing us down the barrel, and even though James was still holding on to my jacket and pushing, my legs just stopped moving and he ran right into the back of me. I thought right there and then that the piggin' jig was up and that Slim's guys were going to come and put me and James both back in the tumble dryer and I was never going to see my mum again.

But just when I thought the guy's eyes were about to pop right out of his giant head and fall into the frying pan he had in his hand, he swivelled around in the other direction and started yelling even louder at someone else. I didn't get it all, but it was something about julienning someone's bollocks and kicking their arse into a month of Sundays with his bare feet.

All of a sudden James yelled right into my ear, aye, boss, we're on it! Then he pulled me over to a big silver bench full of trays with rows and rows of what looked like thousands of little birds' nests filled with fruit and cream. He let go of me and whispered, quick, grab one, Norman. I didn't think we really had time to be snacking, even though they did look pretty good, but just as I was about to reach for one I saw James picking up a whole tray and I realized that's what he meant. Grab a whole tray, not just one. And all I could think was that those trays looked pretty heavy.

My hat had fallen down a bit over one of my eyes so I had to turn my head right around to see James, and he was just looking back down at me and waiting. He wasn't asking if I could manage it or was it too much or was I OK to balance it or anything. Just, like, grab one, Norman. Waiting for me to pick up one of those huge trays, like it wasn't the biggest and heaviest thing I'd actually ever lifted up in my life. Like I could do it. No question about it. *Come on, you teeny tiny flucker! Just try.* And like a perfect secret agent, I winked (I actually winked!) at him and nodded my head just enough so he could see it and then I grabbed one of those trays with both hands.

And you know what? James was right. Because nobody even looked at us when we walked right out into the middle of the gentlemen's club and put our trays of birds' nests down on a big long table in the corner with all the other food. Nobody looked at us when James got hold of my jacket again and steered me in and out of the rows of tables and chairs full of gentlemen losing their money and eating their dinner. Nobody even looked when we walked straight out another set of doors on the other side, past two cranky-looking guys with black suits and bow ties and then around a corner and up some stairs. Nobody. Any minute I expected to hear someone yelling at us to stop, or freeze or even oi, you, you're just a kid and where do you think you're going? But nobody took any notice of us at all. Can you believe it? I couldn't.

When we got to the top of the stairs James stopped for a second then pointed down the hallway to a door at the very end. Come on lad let's go, home stretch, he goes. So we went, but of course the door was locked because if you were a guy called Slim that ran a club that stole money off gentlemen and you tied up people and put them into tumble dryers, you'd probably have stuff in your office you didn't want anyone to see, wouldn't you?

It seemed like maybe it could be the end of our plan and I started thinking that all that dressing up in a disguise and being brave had ended up being for nothing. Until the thing that happened next. Which was that James looked at me, then he looked at the door, then he looked back at me, then he looked at the top of the door. Then I looked to see what he was looking at, which was a small glass window above the door. Which was half open. And then we looked at each other and James started smiling and even before he said anything I already knew what he was thinking because I was thinking the same. Then he goes, so, are ye game, Norman? Just like that, and ye instead of you in his Scottish accent. Isn't that the coolest?

Well, after what we'd just done I felt like I was pretty much game for anything, so I tried out a bit of a Scottish accent myself and said aye James, piece of piss. I'm not sure if he noticed the accent but he goes, good man, and then straight away started counting one, two, three. I was still trying to get myself ready when he picked me up under the arms and sort of threw me into the air, but without letting go. I missed the ledge of the window thing but James just goes, nae bother, practice run, and was I ready to go again.

The second time I was ready all right, and when James lifted me up in the air I grabbed on to the ledge straight away with both my hands and held on tight. He was still holding on to my legs with both hands, but he squeezed my feet and shouty whispered, ye wee beauty, Norman! Gaun yersel', lad!

I'll tell you something funny. It seems like the more hard stuff you do, the easier it gets to be brave. Because I'm not even joking, it was like from the minute I walked out of the Soft Fudge on my own everything had got easier, even though everything I'd done was actually so much harder than anything I'd ever had to do before. And right at that second, when James was pushing on my feet and I was trying to squeeze through that tiny window, I suddenly thought about Jax pushing me through Mrs Egerton's fence palings with a rose for Mum. And even though I was pretty stuck and the edge of the window frame was digging into all the new skin that was coming through on my chest and it really, really hurt, that's the exact thing that got me through that window. Actually all the way through so quick that I didn't even have time to grab on to anything. It felt like I was flying and for about a hundredth of a second, if you think about it, I really was. Until I landed on Slim's office floor.

I could hear James through the door whispering, holy shite, Norman, are you OK? But I couldn't answer him because I was still thinking about Jax and the fence and I was laughing so hard no words could get out. And because I couldn't answer, James must have got worried because he was pretty loud the second time when he goes, Norman! ARE. YE. OK? I still couldn't stop laughing, so in the end I just got myself up and unlocked the door because that was quicker. When James saw I was OK and just laughing too hard to talk he started laughing too. So then we were both just cracking up and trying to shush each other at the same time.

When we finally stopped laughing James goes, bloody hell, Norman, I thought I shot ye halfway to the castle! Well, I tell ye (see what I did there?), the thought of me flying through the air through the window of Slim the Robbing Bastard's office out the other side and all the way to Edinburgh Castle made me start laughing all over again. James put his hand over my mouth to stop the noise, but then he started up again too, so I put my hand over his mouth and there we were. Just two guys breaking and entering and laughing so hard it felt like we'd never stop. Holding on to each other like we'd known each other our whole lives and not at all like we'd just met in a tumble dryer about twenty minutes ago.

I think maybe James remembered about the same time as me where we were and what we were supposed to be doing, and that actually we really should probably try to be a bit quieter and get on with it. So he said, OK, enough shenanigans, let's get this show on the road, Norman, and first things first, we've got to find my keys. Then he goes, it's not a big bunch, just five or six on a Take That key ring. Now I know I didn't know that much about James after only twenty minutes, but he really didn't seem like the sort of guy who'd like Take That. Robbie Williams solo maybe, but not the band. And if it surprises you that I even know who Take That are, all I can say is that when your mum says, Norman, those boys provided part of the soundtrack to my youth, you sort of want to know what they sound like. Which me and Jax and Mum reckon is pretty good, by the way, but I don't think we'd have them on a key ring.

James said that it was a present from his dad last Christmas and the guy thinks he's hilarious. Knows I cannae stand them, but hey, I did need a key ring and it makes the old bugger laugh every time he sees it, he goes. All the time James was whispering about his Take That key ring he was picking up papers and books and boxes of staples on the desk and putting them down again, looking for his keys. I did a couple of turns around to see if I could think where someone like Slim McGinty would hide some keys, and then probably because I'd just been thinking about Jax he popped into my head again. Because Jax could find anything. Eyes like a hawk, Mum says. He could spot things faster than people even know they're missing them, she reckons. Any time she needed to look for the TV remote or the big serving spoon or something like that she'd say, Jax, have you seen the remote or the big serving spoon or whatever, and straight away in a couple of seconds Jax would have it.

Anyway, as soon as I thought about Jax again that was when I found the keys, so isn't that funny? They were hanging on a hook behind the door with a load of other bunches of keys on little hooks, but as soon as I saw Gary Barlow's smiley face I knew I'd hit the jackpot. And then I thought maybe it was the Jaxpot, and it was the second time I could have done with a Post-it that night. Seeing all those bunches of keys also made me wonder if their owners had been stuck into the tumble dryers as well and if so where they were now.

When I turned around to tell James I'd found the keys he was standing in front of Slim's desk, just staring down into one of the drawers. Then he stuck both his hands in and pulled out two massive wodges of twenty- and fifty-pound notes and I reckon my eyes nearly popped out like that guy in the kitchen. Because I'd never ever seen that much money in my life. It looked like maybe it could be a million pounds, but I guess it was probably a bit less than that or else surely Slim would have taken it to the bank for safekeeping.

James said, holy shite, what I couldnae do with this lot, and then he just stood there with the two handfuls of money, staring at it like he'd gone into some kind of a trance. Just sitting in the top drawer, not even locked, he goes. Deserves to lose it, the right robbin' roaster.

When I shook the Take That keys James came out of his trance and whisper shouted, aye, that's them, you're a wee champ, Norman! But then instead of us getting out of there like I thought would be a very good idea, he just sat down in the chair behind Slim's desk with the money still in his hands and goes, well now, I'd love to take this bunch of cash, but that wouldnae be the right thing tae do, would it, Norman? I didn't know what he wanted me to say. All I knew was that time was of the essence and we needed to get out, and also it looked like James had forgotten he was supposed to be whispering. Plus my head was getting really itchy around my ears where the hat was rubbing and I could feel a pretty big scab was about to fall off so *it* definitely needed to get out. So I kind of nodded and shook my head at the same time at James while also listening out for any noises that might sound like a bouncer coming up the hallway. Which was actually quite a lot to do at one time.

But James wasn't looking at me anyhow. He had the money spread out on the desk in front of him and he was scribbling something on a piece of paper and talking to himself under his breath. Even though I couldn't hear much of what he was saying, I did hear a few words like numbers, pension, times two, no bloody wonder, and lots of other stuff that didn't make any sense to me. I also definitely heard a few robbing bastards in there.

After one last robbing bastard James did a really hard full stop with the pen and started counting out some of the money. He got to seven of the fifties and then stopped and counted one more and said, danger money, right, Norman? I didn't know what was going on really, but I nodded because I thought if I just agreed with him it might hurry things up a bit.

Then he started talking again and quite loudly. So that's three hundred and fifty quid plus our danger money. That's what I'm taking. That's about four weeks of my dad's pension at one seventy-five a pop, added together and divided by two. Fair dos, I reckon, Norman. I wasn't sure if I was supposed to be checking James's adding up, but even though I'm pretty good at maths I didn't even get to the four times a hundred and seventy-five part in my head because he was still talking.

My dad lost the whole lot, right, he goes, but I reckon gambling's a mug's game at the best of times and even if you're not being diddled there's a fair chance you're going to lose. So what I did was split the difference, aye? Fifty–fifty. Rounded it down to what might have happened if the silly old bugger had put the lot through the pokies. Plus, three fifty is exactly what he owes on his moorings so I reckon it's all coming out in the wash. Ye ken, Norman?

I'm telling you now I had no idea what he meant, but we had the keys to his moped and his dad's money and all I knew was I wanted to get as far away from the Whisky-a-Go-Go as fast as possible. Faster even. Before we ended up coming out in the wash and dryer ourselves. James started putting the money back in the drawer and I thought maybe we were finally going, but then he suddenly stopped and looked down into the very back of the drawer and pulled out a thin notebook with a blue cover. He started flicking through it and every time he turned a page he banged the desk with his other hand and let out a few robbing bastards and some other stuff.

I bloody knew it, he goes. This place is totally crooked and it's all in here in black and white. I wanted to say, actually, it was in blue but I wasn't quick enough because he said, right, hang on a wee sec and then we're off. I couldn't believe it was going to be another wee sec before we made our getaway, which meant it was probably actually going to be at least a billion times longer, because that's what adults do.

Not James, though. He stuck the notebook in his jeans, grabbed a thick black felt-tip pen off Slim's desk and wrote something down on the back of a piece of paper. Then he stuck the note right in the middle of the desk where nobody would ever be able to miss it, even if they were almost totally blind. Which I bet Slim probably wasn't. Then he goes, right, adios, amigos. Come on, Norman, we're oot! I don't think I've ever been so glad to be leaving a room, but that didn't stop me from having a quick look at the note before we left:

Slim, I've taken my moped, my dad's money and your cooked-up blackjack book. If you or your goons come after me, it goes straight to the cops. P.S. You really are a total bloody robbing bastard.

Isn't that just the coolest?

James held the office door open so I could go under his arm, and when I went to step out into the hallway he goes, you're pure barry, ye are, Norman. And even though I didn't have a clue who Barry was, by the way James looked at me when he said it I reckon he must have been someone pretty cool. I felt so proud that for a squillionth of a second I thought I was going to cry like a baby all over again, and then I thought, well, how would that look? Not like someone who was pure Barry, that's for sure. I didn't cry. But that was mainly because me and James were too busy running down the hallway towards the fire stairs at a zillion miles an hour with a huge, ugly-looking, most definitely dodgy geezer right behind us shouting, oi! Stop! Get back here, yous!

James reckoned later it was stonking bad luck that bouncer just happened to be going on his dinner break at the exact minute we were getting out of Slim's office or we would probably have made a clean getaway. It was even worse luck that he was one of the goons that had actually put James in the tumble dryer in the first place, so there was no way no how we were going to stop, even if he'd asked nicely. Which he didn't. But he yelled a lot.

He was still yelling at us as we charged out the fire door and into the alley behind the club then up to behind the bins where James's moped was parked. And even though he sounded a lot more puffed out, he was still shouting at us to bloody well stop as James shoved a helmet on my head and picked me up and plonked me right on the back of the bike. Me, Norman Foreman, who can't even ride a pushbike that good, on an actual moped!

Hold on tight, Norman, this could get rough, he goes. And it did too. Because James took off at top speed down the alley right back towards where Slim's goon was standing with his arms out. Still yelling at us to stop. But James didn't stop, no way no how. He just kept right on going until we got to the top of the alley. Even though the moped was bouncing all over the place, I held on tight to James and dared to turn around for a look. The last thing I saw was Slim's goon lying face down in a big pile of black bin bags with his arms in the air and his big old bum poking out a split in his pants for all the world to see.

James took the corner at a million miles an hour and we jumped the gutter and landed on to Lothian Road with a massive skid. It was just like a movie, and that was how I came to make up the first real joke I ever made by myself without Jax, about James and the Giant Screech. And it's a pretty good one too.

47

Sadie

Apparently, some people do die from a small-bowel obstruction, but it turned out I wasn't quite that interesting. I was the type of person who carried the remnants of a dodgy surgery around for thirty-two years without even considering that all that recent pushing and shoving behind my scar might have been something I should sit up and take notice of. The type that puts a steadily worsening pain down to stress, constipation or the past trying to make a break for it. And hoping, as per usual, that if I ignored it, it would disappear. Which, just by the by, sometimes really does work.

There are probably three things worth mentioning about my trip to Wishaw Hospital in the back of Dicky's taxi. The first is that I actually got there in the same number of pieces as I started, because while Dicky's sense of urgency was admirable under the circumstances, collapsed out-of-towner and all that, I do recall thinking the possibility of him killing me before I had a chance to die of my own accord seemed fairly reasonable at the time.

The second thing is that the reason we were even on our way to Wishaw Hospital was because Plan A had gone to porridge due to the fact that the emergency department of the local hospital, which was less than five minutes away, was closed. Don't ask. All I can say is that if you're planning on visiting that part of the world, don't have a medical emergency on the same day as the annual cider-and-scone hospital fundraiser. Unless, of course, you want to run the risk of having to make use of Dicky's services to get you to the next-closest hospital. That's not meant to sound tempting. Refer back to the first point, if you're feeling tempted.

The third thing (which if you believe in fate is exactly what was meant to happen in the giant pre-ordained plan of the universe) is that the fastest route to Wishaw Hospital just happened to be along the same road a dapper old gentleman in his Austin had been on when said vehicle had given up the ghost.

Now, even though it's all a bit of a blur, I wasn't quite so out of it that I don't remember that the overwhelming feeling that enveloped me when I tipped over on that bench and lay there drifting in and out of consciousness while Mrs Dicky and the Goth girl fussed around me was relief. Relief that, finally, here was something that really and truly *was* out of my hands. There was nothing I could do, so I could do nothing. And just for that magnificent blurry crease in time, I could let all my problems become somebody else's. For as long as it lasted, anyhow.

So even when I opened my eyes just in time to see the Austin as we whizzed past, once I'd mustered the strength to convey politely to Dicky that I needed him to stop (Dickyyyyyyyyyy! Bloody stopppppppppp!), and we'd reversed back along the verge to stop in front of a very startled Leonard, I'm a little bit ashamed to say that I decided I was going to make my moment last. Leaving Dicky and Leonard to work it out for themselves, I simply closed my eyes and let the kerfuffle wash over me. Like all the waves that had ever rolled on to the beach in Penzance while I wasn't looking had turned around to roll back home. *Come on in, I've got you, love.*

The pain in my stomach was so bad I was seeing stars in the outer constellations, but for the rest of the journey to the hospital, with my head on a very comfy old lap and the rise and fall of Dicky's voice as he filled Leonard in, for the first time in my adult life I did what Thelma and Louise never could. And while there's not really a chance in hell I would have got around to surrendering any sooner, if I had, it probably wouldn't have taken me and my insides quite so long to get right back to where we all started.

Within five minutes of arriving at the A&E of Wishaw Hospital I realized surrender was actually more of a requirement than a choice. But as it seemed to be working quite well for me anyhow, I allowed myself to drift off to check out the Big Dipper in a compliant haze of pain medication, X-rays, ultrasounds and MRIs.

At one stage I opened my eyes to see an earnest-looking doctor leaning over me so closely I could smell his cheese-and-pickle-sandwich breath. I saw his mouth moving and I heard inflections at the end of a series of noises so I knew he was asking me questions but, in full surrender mode, I just smiled and closed my eyes again. I vaguely remember thinking that Norman hadn't asked for cheese on toast once since we left home, and that any medical person worth their salt would be able to look at my scar and make some assumptions about what had gone on down there without any input from me. Because I was having a break. Or maybe a breakdown. At that point, it didn't seem to matter which.

After several laps of the hospital, up and down in lifts, along corridors, in and out of windowless rooms, lifted off and put back on the trolley bed like an unwanted dessert, I arrived at the end of the road. I don't mean the real end, because I'm pretty sure Leonard wouldn't be the first choice to man the Pearly Gates, bearing in mind the Wheeler Centre secure unit and all that, but it looked like the end of my hospital Grand Prix at least. So when I saw the worried look on Leonard's face as he hovered behind the two nurses fussing around my drug drip I grudgingly decided that, while surrender had been a lovely place to visit and I'd definitely be back, perhaps the holiday was over.

'Well ... the decor's not great, but it's an improvement on Toad Hall, eh?'

My voice sounded weak and croaky and the attempt at humour was lame even by my standards, but Leonard grabbed my hand and brought it up to his face with a chuckle.

'Indeed it is, my dear!'

Thankfully, my audience was easily pleased. I could only hope Norman was going to get that lucky. And with that thought I was catapulted well and truly back from my stargazing.

'Shit, Leonard. Where's ... what happened? When did ... how long have I been here? What's ... what's the time? Norman ...'

I wasn't even sure myself what I was trying to ask, but I knew I needed to catch up. I struggled to raise myself in the bed and Leonard placed a very firm but gentle hand on my shoulder to push me back down.

'Not to worry, Sadie. Just you lie back and relax. You're going to be OK. You've got, um ...'

He reached over to the end of the bed and unhooked a chart, pushing his glasses back on his nose so he could make out the notes.

'Now let me just check to make sure I've got this right. Ah yes, an obstruction in, um . . . your small bowel. Probably caused by the old surgery on your tummy.'

I was pretty sure that I'd never told Leonard anything about my unusual start to life during our early-morning tea sessions, but he didn't seem at all curious and just continued scanning the notes.

'I've spoken to the doctor, Sadie, which was rather a . . . well, anyhow, he did eventually disclose some information after I . . . well, let's just say it might be best if you called me Uncle Lenny when he does his next rounds.' He leaned forward and gave me a wink and squeezed my hand. 'Anyhow, he's deciding whether you need to have new surgery to fix the issue, but he thinks for now they can probably manage it with the antibiotics and pain drugs, and it can possibly, maybe, perhaps wait until we . . . until you get back to Penzance.'

Don't get me wrong, I was glad my number hadn't been up on that bench in Biggar, but at that very moment I didn't care if they'd decided to serve up my obstructed small bowel for staff lunches, like my father had suggested when I was born. I just needed to know that Norman was OK.

'Leonard! Look, whatever, but will you please tell me what the time is?'

I could hear the hysterical edge to my voice, but I didn't have the strength to check it.

'What about Norman? He's on his own. Have you phoned him? Is he . . . we need to see if he's OK!'

'It's five o'clock, but it's . . . it's all right, Sadie. I . . . I haven't quite managed to telephone Norman because, well, as you know, I mistakenly took your phone and the battery has now unfortunately died. I did take the liberty of going in your handbag to retrieve my own phone, but then I realized I don't have young

Norman's telephone number programmed in anyhow. A rather unfortunate oversight, to be honest. But I thought when you awoke you might possibly know it from memory? I could . . .' Leonard's voice trailed off as he saw the look on my face. As if. 'No, no, of course. I . . . I'm quite sure he's fine and safe, though, and it . . . it won't even be dark for hours. I'm sure . . .'

He looked like he'd suddenly realized he'd waded in way too deep without a hand to hold, but I had no time for mercy.

'Five o'clock! And he doesn't even know where we are? We've got to get back to Edinburgh. I told Norman six at the latest, and it's going to take us at least . . .'

I struggled to an upright position, trying to fight the over-whelming rush of nausea and dizziness that hit me like a concrete wall. I managed to swing one leg off the bed, but the other got tangled up in the IV drip on its way through.

'Shit, shit, shit! Leonard . . . help me just . . . I . . . oh SHIT!'

'Now, now, my dear. You must stop. Just calm yourself for a moment. Steady as you go.'

Even as Leonard was speaking he was gently manoeuvring me back on to the bed, untangling the sheet and the IV. He placed a cool hand on my forehead. *Oh, surrender, how I miss you.*

'It's all right, Sadie. I promise you. Shush now. It's OK. I have a plan.'

I had a strong urge to shout that I'd had more than enough of plans, thank you very much. Plans are what got us into this bloody trip in the first place. But the struggle to get out of bed had taken its toll and I didn't quite have it in me. Luckily, though, as plans went, dementia or not, Leonard's seemed OK.

It turned out Dicky was a bit of a champ in times of crisis, despite his rather dubious driving skills. He'd called up his brother, who was not only the best mechanic in Biggar, he'd also had quite a bit of experience with vintage cars. So Dicky and Mickey (I swear) had very kindly towed the Austin back to Mickey's garage. The good news was that it had only taken Mickey ten minutes to diagnose an electrical malfunction; the bad news was that he'd had to order a part from Edinburgh that wasn't going to arrive until the next morning.

Coincidentally, as Leonard had tried telling me earlier, the Austin and I had very similar prognoses. While the immediate emergency was over, thanks to antibiotics and a dangerously enjoyable level of painkillers, the doctor insisted that I stayed in hospital at least overnight for observation while they assessed whether I needed surgery.

Leonard had been waiting for me to come round, and then his plan was to catch the next bus back to Edinburgh, so he'd be back at the Soft Fudge by six, or at least very soon after. Then, in the morning, all things being well with my release, he and Norman would come back on the bus and we'd all drive back to Edinburgh as soon as the car was ready, arriving in plenty of time for Norman's show.

Like I said, it was a good plan. On the surface. I hated the idea of not being with Norman on the night before his big show, but more than that there was the issue of Leonard's own mental health and his suitability as a guardian, no matter how temporary. I had to admit that he was showing absolutely no signs of anything amiss and his take-charge attitude was as impressive as ever. But I did notice that he totally fobbed me off when I tried to get any kind of explanation as to why he'd disappeared at dawn from the Soft Fudge.

'Don't worry about it now, Sadie, we can talk about all that later. I promise. Right now, it's just important for me to get back there to Norman, look after him and make sure he's ready for tomorrow. You're not to worry about a thing, my dear. This time, you just take care of yourself and I'll take care of Norman. Trust me.'

Even in my much-reduced state I knew my body was very clearly telling me I needed to stay put in the hospital for the time being. And even if he was going a bit dotty, I had seen the way Leonard had taken Norman under his wing on this trip so I had no doubt he would indeed take the very best of care. And what choice did I have? But as for being ready, I still wasn't sure Norman was ever going to be ready for what could be coming his way. *You just don't trust your son.*

Goth girl's accusation hung in the air and amused itself by throwing rocks at me. Why *didn't* I trust Norman to get up on stage and still be OK, when it appeared everybody else did? Leonard, Kathy, Tony, Big Al, even bloody Adam – none of them seemed in the least bit doubtful about sending my beautiful, heartbroken, unprepared son out there to try his luck in front of an audience. Why was I?

As I drifted in and out on the gentle tides of pethidine I got to thinking about chances and what seemed to happen when you took them. After all the years you didn't. I washed up on a beach and felt the warmth of two kind hands held tight behind my head and heard the resonant, lingering voice of a beardy poet. With eyes wide open to the sky, I saw the wrinkly wink of a kind-hearted old man and the true and beautiful smile of the boy I thought would never smile again. *Come on, Sadie! In for a penny, in for a pound!*

So maybe Goth girl was right and what mattered wasn't whether Norman was going to put every pause in its right place and get every joke perfect but that he got up there at all. Because maybe nobody ever got anywhere good without taking a chance, and maybe one never knows.

But as hard as I tried, and as many pethidine waves as I rode, I still couldn't think about Norman standing up on a stage in my father's moth-eaten jacket without seeing the emptiness around him. All that space that Jax used to fill with his laughter, his noise, his badness, his goodness and his funniness. And the space that my father could have – *should* have – filled in his life. *Come on, love. Let's go home.* In my life.

48

NORMAN

First rule of comedy: Find your groove and stay in it.

The first night I ever did a break and enter and got to escape on the back of a moped with a guy that might be my dad was also the first night I ever met a man called Lucy who lived on a houseboat. Lucy is short for Lucien and he's James's dad, who just happens to be nearly as cool as James.

After we escaped from the Whisky-a-Go-Go on the moped and we were sure nobody was following us, James got us back to the Soft Fudge without even getting lost. Which was good because, number one, I was hoping that Mum and Leonard would be back there waiting for me, and number two, it meant I didn't have to worry about James being a kidnapper or a paedo any more. Not that I was really, but it was good to be absolutely sure.

But even better than that was the actual ride back, because James rode that moped fast. And I mean *really* fast. We went down side streets and back alleys and took loads of squiggly turns, which actually did make me wonder if maybe he really *was* kidnapping me. But I decided I didn't even mind because it was so much fun. Every time we'd turn a corner James yelled out something like, hold on tight yersel', Normie lad, and I'd close my eyes, squeeze my arms around his tummy a bit tighter and imagine that I was Jax riding on his moped to Venus.

When we got back to the Soft Fudge, straight away I knew nobody was there, though, because when I looked up to the window of the Caramel Suite there were no lights on. I knew Mum would have been waiting up and worrying about me if she was there, which made me very glad that I'd called James when I did instead of still being on my own worrying about her and wondering if she'd found Leonard.

James said we should go up anyhow just to check, but that there was no way he was going to leave me on my own in that neighbourhood in a place that didn't even have a lock on the front door. Which was fine by me. When we got upstairs I got the key from where I'd put it under the mat outside the room and everything inside looked exactly the same as when I'd left. Which was good, because it meant the drug dealers hadn't broken in to steal our stuff and Leonard's laptop, but bad because it meant that Mum was definitely still not back.

When I went to get my phone out of my pocket to try to call her I realized that somewhere between putting on my chef's disguise, flying in through Slim's office window and being on a high-speed, back-of-a-moped ride around Edinburgh it must have dropped out. So then James said that there was nothing else for it and I would have to come with him to his dad's place, but we'd leave a note with his phone number so the minute Mum came back she'd know I was safe and she could call me.

It seemed like a good plan, and even though I was really worried about Mum, I knew she must have a very good reason for not getting back by six at the latest. Because she'd never break a promise on purpose and I know for a fact she never has. And I also knew that if she'd found Leonard, which I reckon she would have, he would definitely be looking after her and she'd be looking after him, because they're both responsible adults.

There were loads of responsible adults on Lucy's houseboat because Wednesdays are when his best mates Beano and Gray come around for a pie, a pint and a piece of their mind. Which James said was just an excuse to get blathered and talk shite, but he winked at me when he said it so I could tell he was only joking.

Lucy's houseboat was pretty small to be a whole house, but it was the coolest place I've ever seen and when we squeezed down the tiny stairs straight away all the guys started going hey and oi and shouting out, what are you doing here, James? James gave his dad a hug hello and then he asked if there was room for a little one, which was me. Lucy said, aye, it was about time they had some new blood in the group, and so even before James told them who I was or why I was there or anything, Beano jumped up and Gray budged down and they gave me a spot in between them. There was hardly even any room for me to move my arms, but the guys smelled like Guinness and chicken pie and it felt pretty nice sitting there.

Lucy cut me off a gigantic bit of his famous home-made pie and Gray poured me two fingers of Guinness into a half-pint glass and said, git that intae ye, lad, without even asking me if I wanted it. Like I was just one of the guys. And you know what's funny? It didn't feel like I was sitting on a boat that was really a house with a bunch of strangers in a strange city and I'd lost my mum and Jax was dead. It felt more like I'd dropped over to a friend's place for dinner after breaking into a gentlemen's club and rescuing a guy from a tumble dryer and getting his dad's mooring money back, and that was just a totally normal day, thanks very much.

And because it didn't feel weird at all and it was actually really nice being with a lot of responsible adults it made me stop worrying about Mum a bit. And maybe because I was still feeling all fizzy inside from rescuing James and escaping from Slim's goon and the ride on the back of the moped and everything, suddenly my mouth just started talking on its own. I'm not even kidding. It was like when Jax has to let something out of his ideas factory and he just blurts it all out in one big long sentence without taking a breath, and then he has to stop and rummage through his backpack or his pocket for a puff on his inhaler because he talked so much he ran out of air.

In between mouthfuls of pie and tiny sips of Guinness so I could make it last, and remembering to keep on taking lots of breaths in between so I wouldn't run out of air, I told the guys about everything. I mean, not my entire life since I was born, but quite a lot and loads about Jax. I told them how me and Jax were the Rolls-bloody-Royce of best friends and how we made a really cool Five Year Plan. And that Jax and Norman's Five Year Plan turned into Norman's Plan because now Jax is gone and he's most probably not coming back. And about Grandad Foreman, who used to be an almost famous comedian, and my mum, who's the best mum in the world because she's helping me get to the Fringe and meet my dad. Even though I know she's just as scared as me about both those things. Maybe even more.

Gray gave me another two fingers of Guinness to wash down my pie and James said, steady on, old-timer, but he winked again so I knew it was OK. And then Lucy goes, come on, lad, don't keep your crowd waiting, go on wi' yer story, so then I told them all about Leonard and his Austin and Little Big Man and why you needed a Facebook page for marketing purposes. And then about Toad Hall and the bush in the middle of the path and Bill's full English brekkie and the invisible Gloria. And about the Noble Goat and how it looked like the dog was driving the milk float, and Lou behind the bar and Big Al reciting a John Keats poem like wow, and me still winning by a tit's whisker.

And you know what's cool? I had to keep stopping because the guys were all laughing so loud they couldn't hear me. Like really and truly proper laughing. Like my story was the funniest thing they'd ever heard. When I got to the bit about the two Franks having a dust-up at Swansea's Got Talent and Leonard asking if the fat lady's husband got an encouragement certificate, Beano slapped the table so hard his glass bounced off and fell into his lap and gave him a trouserful of Guinness. Which made them all laugh even harder, and then Gray nudged me and goes, och, Norman, I haven't seen the old geezer laugh that hard since old Robbie Jones finally bought a round back in '87.

Every time I stopped talking one of them yelled at me to keep on going. So I kept on talking about how I turned into an alien for a night at the Premier Inn in Bournemouth and about meeting Adam. Then about having to make a run for it because of ruining all the towels and Leonard getting to have a go on Adam's mobility scooter. And about Leonard making Little Big Man look so good on Facebook that I actually got a spot at the Fringe for one night only at the Duke.

Then because they kept on saying, gaun yersel, Norman, I told them how when we got to Edinburgh the Soft Fudge turned out to be a weird old empty house in a seedy neighbourhood, but it did have clean sheets. And that we woke up and Leonard had nicked off in the Austin and Mum went out to look for him and she didn't get back by six o'clock at the latest like she promised. Then I said about the dodgy geezers outside the window and how it gave me the idea to call a responsible adult, but that Big Al and Kathy and Tony and even Adam didn't answer their phones and so I called James, who used to know my mum a long time ago.

I looked over at James, and he was frowning a bit, like he was trying to remember something, but then he gave me a nod and a wink, so I told them how I caught the bus to rescue him from the tumble dryer in the Whisky-a-Go-Go, and how we pretended to be chefs and broke into Slim's office and found a load of money and the blue cooked book. Then, after the part about escaping on the moped and seeing Slim's goon with his bum in the bins, I folded my arms and sat back and said, that's it, folks.

Well, I thought old Beano and Gray and Lucy were about ready to wee themselves, they'd laughed so much. Maybe it was partly because of the six empty Guinness bottles sitting in the sink, but I was almost sure it was also because it actually made a pretty funny story when you heard it all together like that.

When everyone stopped laughing Gray slapped the table and said I sure knew how to have an adventure. Which made me think, wow, I can't believe I've actually had a real-life adventure. Then Beano said, aye, and I sure did know how to tell a story, and I just thought, wow full stop. Then they started talking about the good old days when comedians were properly funny and didn't just swear and tell dirty jokes, like they do today. And then that's when the best thing of all happened, because Lucy said that the way I told my story, he could see a lot of those old-style comedians in me. And that I reminded him of a slow-burn type of funny guy like Dave Allen. Dave Allen! Can you believe it?

I was thinking to myself that I wish I knew exactly what about me reminded Lucy of Dave Allen as I could do with some more of it when Beano says, oh yeah, and you know why, don't you? Well, I didn't and I said so, and Beano goes, it's because you're a natural born *rack-on-terr*, lad. Which wasn't much of a help to me, because I didn't know what that meant, but before I could ask if he might please be able to explain James said, enough with the big words, Beano, like you said, Norman can tell a bloody good story.

Then Lucy piped up and said that not everybody knows it but being a stand-up comedian is one of the hardest jobs in the world. Because basically you're getting up there in front of a crowd of people and saying you're the funniest guy in the room. So you better have the chops to back it up or they'll eat you for dinner. But then he said there are the slow-burn ones like me and Dave Allen (which I still can't believe I'm saying) that can reel in the laughs by holding a microscope up to life. An observational monologue is what Lucy said it was called, and when he said that everybody else went quiet and kind of thoughtful. And so did I.

So maybe I figured it out by myself and maybe I didn't, but when Lucy said that I suddenly realized I'd been doing everything wrong. Because even though Jax was gone, I was acting like he was still there. I was still shooting the jokes out into space like the funniest guy in the room was still there to catch them and finish the job. Like I was still the straight man part of a pretty cool comedy duo instead of the guy that's got to reel in the laughs all by himself.

And then just as I was getting a little bit excited about working out that I was probably never going to get anywhere by trying to be like Jax and maybe everywhere by trying to be a bit more like Dave Allen, I noticed James leaning back in his seat with his hands behind his head and looking at me a bit funny. And then he goes, hey, Norman, just why *did* your mother want to look me up when she got to Edinburgh?

And even though I'd only known James for one super-fun-fantastic-cool night, I could tell by the look on his rock-star face that the piggin' jig was up. Again.

49

First rule of comedy: It's fun when you're funny.

It's funny, but it wasn't even hard to tell James that he was the last guy on Leonard's Finding Fathers spreadsheet. When I came clean about it, he totally didn't seem to mind and he just smiled and said, well, what dae ye ken? quite a few times. But what was properly funny in the comedy way was that when I said that James could maybe be my dad Beano let out a big, long woohoo, and then he slapped James on the back so hard that he knocked another full glass of Guinness into his own lap all over again.

After everybody finished cracking up at that, which took a while, James said that it was almost midnight and we should probably try and get a bit of shut-eye so we could be up early in the morning to get back to the Soft Fudge and find Mum. And then I swear, not even one second after he said it his phone rang. He started going, aye, mmm hmm, aye, aye, is that right? OK, nae bother. Then he looked over at me and goes, Norman, it's for you. And I tell you what, after the night I'd just had I wasn't even that surprised.

The only person I would have been happier to hear from at that moment was Mum, but Leonard was almost as good. Straight up he told me that Mum had found him, which I knew she would. But that even though she had tried her hardest to get back to the Soft Fudge by six at the latest like she'd promised, the universe had conspired against her.

When he explained exactly what he meant and that Mum was in hospital, it was scary at first, but then he said I wasn't to be worried because he promised everything was going to be OK, especially Mum. And I knew it was true because Leonard wouldn't lie to me about that, not even if it did turn out that he'd actually told us a pretty big fat lie so he could come on the trip.

It turned out the universe had also conspired against Leonard when he tried to come back to look after me, because there was a lorry rollover on the road and the bus he was on was held up for more than two hours. Then when he finally did get back to Edinburgh the traffic was so bad because of the Fringe it took him almost another whole hour on the number 16 bus to get back to the Soft Fudge. When I said I thought I was the one with bad timing, Leonard laughed so much I wondered if being funny was like being brave and the more you did it, the better you got.

He kept saying how sorry he was for going off in the car and worrying me and Mum and then not being able to get back to look after me in time because Mum had to stay the night in hospital. But I was just thinking how I couldn't wait to see him so I could tell him that he didn't have anything to be sorry for. Because if he hadn't gone off like that I wouldn't have had the absolute, definite, without-a-doubt best night of my life. Which is what I decided it was.

Of course, I was pretty sad that I'd gone and had the best night of my life without Jax, but I also felt quite a lot proud of myself. Because if you'd asked me even two days ago I would have said for sure that I couldn't have done any of that stuff, like going out at night in a city on my own and being chased by a bouncer and ending up on a houseboat drinking Guinness with a bunch of guys, one who might be my grandad, by the way. And being funny. No way no how. But I did. I did all of that on my own and I reckon Jaxy would have been proud of me too.

I don't think anyone could have stopped Leonard from getting in a taxi and coming straight over to Lucy's houseboat in the middle of the night, even if they tried. He said, don't go anywhere, Norman, and I'll be there in a jiffy. And promise me you won't move. Which I did and he was. And when he arrived it was like when me and James got there all over again, with Lucy and the guys trying to give him Guinness and reheated chicken pie and all talking over the top of each other and making room at the table for him.

But before he sat down Leonard put his hand up to shush everyone and goes, one moment, please, friends, and Norman, could you please stand up? And when I did he put both arms around me and gave me a massive big hug, which he said was from my mum but also from him. And even though I reckon I left the tops of about a hundred scabs on that window ledge in Slim's office, and even though Leonard hugged me really, really hard because it was from two people, it didn't even hurt.

Then Leonard said he wanted to hear all about why I was wearing a chef's outfit and it looked like maybe I would have as much of a story to tell Mum as she had to tell me. So I told him how I'd gone from practising my show in the Caramel Suite and being really scared on my own to having an amazing adventure with James and finding out I was a bit like Dave Allen. And then Beano and Gray and Lucy all started talking again and lots more Guinness got drunk, but not by me and Leonard. Because Leonard wanted to keep a clear head and I had a show the next day. Plus after that day in Mrs Ackerman's cow paddock I reckon two finger-fulls at a time is enough until I'm at least eighteen.

Lucy said because it was late we should all just kip on the boat and he'd do us a full English in the morning, and Leonard said it seemed like a good way to finish an adventure and that it was fine by him. So we did. And kipping the night on a houseboat with Leonard and James and the guys was the coolest thing ever.

Even though it was nearly two o'clock in the morning by the time Lucy had finally said it was time to stop blethering and get ye all to bed or what'll pass as one, I woke up earlier than everyone else. When I opened my eyes I knew where I was straight away, though. Because the first person I saw was James, stretched out on one of the bench seats with a tea towel rolled up under his head and his legs sticking way out past the edge. Then the second person I saw was Leonard, curled up on his side on the other seat with his two hands under his head like he was saying a prayer and nothing sticking out off the edge anywhere.

Beano and Gray were top and tailing it at the bottom of the stairs and I could hear Lucy snoring in his little bedroom up the end of the boat. It didn't look like any of them were going to be getting up any time soon, but I was wide awake, so I wrapped my blanket around me and carefully stepped over Beano and Gray and went up on to the deck.

It was totally quiet up there and it kind of felt like the

houseboat was floating out in space. Even though it was still pretty dark the sun was starting to come up behind the trees on the other side of the canal, and I thought how weird it was to only find out what a place looked like when you'd already been there a whole night. It felt like nobody else in the whole world was awake except for me, and for all I know maybe it was true.

I should have been really tired, but I wasn't. I actually felt like I'd just had the best sleep of my life and everything inside my head and my tummy felt kind of different. Like maybe all that stuff that happened to me on the best night of my life had actually made me into a different person. Like one who breaks into nightclubs and dresses in disguise and goes on high-speed rides on the back of a moped. One who hangs out with a bunch of guys on a houseboat and stays up all night blethering. The kind of person like Little Big Man who's actually going to be brave enough to get up in front of a bunch of strangers and try to make them laugh, by telling them a story about a Five Year Plan that turned into a real-life adventure.

But I knew I hadn't woken up an entirely different person really, because even while I was thinking about all that amazing stuff, when I was sat on the deck of the houseboat with maybe nobody in the world awake except for me, the thing I most wanted was to see my mum.

50

Sadie

If I were to say what I'd like to, which was that a miracle occurred at Wishaw Hospital that night and I didn't need the surgery, it wouldn't be entirely true. Because it turned out my very unfashionable obstruction was definitely not going to go away on its own. So there went that theory, once and for all.

'I trust you understand how seriously you need to take your situation, Mrs, er, um . . .' The doctor I'd mistaken for an intern was so young and frail he was practically buckling under the weight of my medical chart. I thought he might blow away in the breeze. 'Um . . . Foreman. Yes, Mrs Foreman.' I was surprised he could read at his age. 'I've seen people come very close to death from an obstruction not even half as bad as yours, you know.'

I was very tempted to say, 'Have you? Have you really? Where was that then, kindergarten?' I didn't, though, because blaming the poor little guy for a hatchet job some absent-minded surgeon did on me more than three decades ago was probably a bit unfair, considering he probably wasn't even born back then.

'I do, I do take it seriously,' I said. 'But it can wait a couple of weeks or so, right? The nurse said if . . .'

'Mrs Foreman. It's really not advisable to delay these things for too long. It's quite a simple operation and . . .'

'Miss. It's Miss Foreman. Mrs Foreman's already dead, and I get it. Of course. Not advisable. Understood. On the record. But possible, right? I mean, I'm not likely to drop dead in the next couple of days now it's under control, if I understand the situation correctly?'

'Well, no. It's not very likely you'd . . . err . . . be rendered deceased in the foreseeable future, but I strongly . . . umm, recommend you . . . err, well . . .'

I almost felt sorry for him. The chance to get in there and clear out my pipes might have been his first big break, for all I knew. He'd probably been planning his little anaesthetized archaeological dig all night. But I had someone else's big break to get to, thanks very much.

'Great! Wonderful! It's a plan, then!'

So, after a bit more blustering about it being very much against his better judgement the doctor reluctantly signed my escape warrant. Whether that was due to the compelling case I'd put forward or he just wanted to get rid of me so he didn't have to listen to me misuse the word 'stat' at every opportunity just for fun wasn't clear. But I didn't care. There was no way I was spending one more minute than I had to lying in that Scottish hospital away from Norman. Getting Junior's grudging blessing was merely the skin around my haggis.

In the end, though, despite winning the battle I had no intention of losing, what with all the temperature taking, poking and prodding and promising to see my GP as soon as I got back to Penzance, it was eleven o'clock before I got the sign-off from the hospital. And then it was another half an hour before Leonard arrived, without Norman, because he was apparently getting in some last-minute practice back at the Soft Fudge.

I don't know if it was Goth girl's pep talk, the drugs I'd been necking for the past eighteen hours, or the gentle reassurance of Leonard's presence, but I felt strangely calm about the whole situation. Everything just felt ... taken care of. When Dicky arrived at the hospital to deliver us to the Austin, I wished my doctor good luck with the rest of his career, Uncle Lenny took my arm like he was walking me into the Oscars and we departed Wishaw Hospital, I sincerely hoped for ever.

There was a small hitch when we got to Mickey's garage in Biggar, when the car wasn't quite as ready as it should have been, but instead of getting worked up about it I simply told myself Norman was perfectly safe back at the Soft Fudge and we still had plenty of time to get back to Edinburgh before his show. Then I lay down across the only two chairs in the oily garage waiting room and took a little nap, if you don't mind. Probably the drugs, then.

When we finally got on the road a little over three hours later, the Zen I'd been emanating was definitely more than a little reduced. But within a few minutes of waving goodbye to Dicky and Mickey I realized that Leonard probably really *had* been the 1969 British off-road rally champion. Because when speed mattered, Leonard stepped up.

I looked over at him leaning into the curves of the narrow road and he suddenly looked about twenty years younger. The steering wheel rested effortlessly in the wrinkled hands I'd seen fumbling ineptly with door handles and mobile phone buttons, and it felt like the car was hovering a few inches above the bumpy bitumen. As I sat back, relaxed and enjoyed the ride, I thought to myself, well, one just never knows, eh? And it turned out there was quite a bit more of that to come.

Back at the hospital, I'd broached the topic of Leonard's early-morning jaunt again, and again he'd dodged my questions, but with a promise to tell me everything on the trip back to Edinburgh. So now that we were well and truly on the road, even though the drugs were definitely wearing off, I decided the best way forward was straight through. Which was uncharacteristic, to say the least.

'All right, Leonard, no more beating around the bush. What were you doing going off like that yesterday morning? Did you . . . I mean . . . well, I'm sorry, but I have to know. Are you on the run from the Wheeler Centre?'

I braced myself. Literally. I held on to both sides of the seat, fully expecting Leonard to veer off the road with the shock of being found out and head off *Dukes of Hazzard* style across an expanse of Scottish cow pasture. But the wheels stayed steady and he gave it to me with both barrels to the heart.

Leonard's story was bit like walking into a movie for the ending without having seen all the best bits. And, of course, I'd got it all wrong. The first year into her ninth decade of life, it wasn't him but Iris who had developed full-blown dementia. And after two years of soul-destroying decline, two months previously she'd virtually stopped recognizing him, except for a few lucid moments once or twice a week.

In measured tones that seemed to follow the shape of the road Leonard told me that even though he'd tried his best, he'd eventually found it impossible to manage Iris on his own. The early-morning cleaning job at Pearl's had been a distraction to help him fill the hours when the carers came in, so he didn't have to watch as strangers tended to the body he'd promised to protect and worship since he'd dropped to one youthful, unwrinkled knee and proposed to her some sixty-odd years before.

In recent months Iris had rarely left her bed, except to

occasionally fling the covers and her nightie off without warning and stand at the window staring at some invisible point in the ocean. On those days Leonard would wrap his arms around her from behind, put his head on her shoulder and gently hold her to him. Most of the time she'd step away or arrange her frame into such a shape that her bones slipped through his fingers, but every now and then he'd feel her relax into the well-worn nook of his arms and, for a few precious moments, the girl with the hibiscus hair was back.

'It's all I live for, Sadie. Those rare little spaces in her mind that she's saved just for us.'

His gnarly hands gripped the steering wheel tighter and as we came up to a bend in the road I found myself leaning into it with him.

'Until I met you and Norman, that is.'

Hell's bells, old-timer, way to break my heart.

After the latest of Iris's all-too-frequent falls out of bed, which had resulted in a broken arm, Leonard had finally conceded defeat and accepted he could no longer keep her safe in their home. She'd been given a place at the Wheeler Centre and the doctors had advised him to refrain from visiting for the first few weeks to allow her to settle into a new routine.

'So when you told me about Norman and his plan, well, it seemed like the perfect distraction. And oh, how marvellous it has been, my dear. But then ... when we got to Edinburgh, I ... I couldn't sleep and ... well, I just started thinking about how it was all nearly over and that I'd have to go back home soon. And ... and Iris wouldn't be there in her kitchen or her garden ... not ever again. And I've spoken to the nurses in the centre regularly, of course, and they say she's doing well, but ... well, I must admit, my dear, the thought of ... of ... well, I just got myself a little upset over it all, if the truth be told.'

It seemed that window-seat bed had been just about as uncomfortable as it looked and, wide awake and worked up, rather than attempt the impossible task of trying to get back to sleep for a couple more hours, Leonard had come up with his own little early-morning plan.

'I would never have wanted to worry you, Sadie, but I thought I'd be back before . . . I didn't even take my coat. The thing is, I remembered . . . well, being in Scotland reminded me about the heather. Iris just loved it. She said it always brought her luck, ever since her grandfather used to send her a dried sprig in the post every year for her birthday as a little girl. She even had it in her wedding bouquet. So I thought . . . it grows wild everywhere here, and if maybe I could just go for a little drive until I found Iris some heather, I might . . . it might bring her some luck for the next stage of her journey. At the Wheeler Centre and . . . and all points beyond.'

We rounded a corner and a long straight section of road stretched out in front of us. Leonard glanced in the rear-view mirror, sat up a little straighter in his seat and put his foot down. A sudden gust of wind slipped through the half-open window and my hair whipped around my face. I closed my eyes and imagined Leonard driving along this road in the direction of the sun, surrounded by all that beauty as dawn and his heart broke. He cleared his throat and gave a small cough.

'I know I'm just a silly old man, Sadie, but I just thought maybe it . . . well, one just never knows, does one?'

I realized, and not for the first time in my life, that I knew exactly nothing. But the flash of purple peeking from the crumpled, aromatic Tesco bag on the back seat of the Austin made me wonder if, quite possibly, that old guy might have known everything.

51

It was nearly 4.30 p.m. by the time Leonard and I swept into Edinburgh in the Austin. And yes, I said swept. All medication aside, I wasn't kidding when I said Leonard drove well under pressure. I was almost sad when we got to the outskirts of the city, although not so much when I realized Norman's show was scheduled to start in just over an hour. I had a moment of mild panic at the thought of how fine we'd be cutting it to get back to the Soft Fudge to pick up Norman and then to the Duke. But of course Leonard had it all in hand.

'If I may make a suggestion, Sadie, I think we should go straight to the venue. I didn't say before, but Norman is getting a lift to . . . that is, there are arrangements in place . . . to get him to the show, and we really don't have time to go back to the accommodation. I think it's best.'

It made me wonder just how big this show at the Duke had got, if they were sending a car for Norman, but Leonard reassured me there was nothing to worry about. And he was right about the timing. So even though I'd be attending the most important event of my son's life in two-day-old clothes, with hospital-bed head and dog's breath, I was alive, I was showing up and, for the first time in Norman's life, it felt like I was actually ready for the job.

Without taking his eyes off the road, Leonard reached into his top pocket and took out his phone with our route to Ground Zero, aka the Duke Supper Club at O'Shaughnessy's Real Ale House, already programmed in to Google Maps, and held it out to me.

'Would you mind holding this, my dear? And perhaps . . . navigating a little?'

As I took the phone from Leonard's old-gentleman hands, in the blink of an eye it was a different car, a different venue, a different gentle man. *Get the A–Z out, Sadie love, you're in charge!* And it was the strangest thing, but for the first time in more than thirteen years I could picture my father's smile. And it didn't hurt a bit.

'No problem at all, Leonard.'

Without a single false turn along the way, Leonard and I pulled into a parking spot almost directly across the road from O'Shaughnessy's. My breath caught in my throat when I saw the crowd of people on the pavement outside the pub, but before I had time to start worrying Leonard had materialized around my side of the car to help me out.

'Easy there, Sadie. Careful, my girl, steady as she goes.'

I had a second to wonder why on earth someone hadn't said that to me years ago, before Leonard took my arm gently to guide me across the road. I looked to the left to check for traffic and saw a moped veer off and tuck in neatly behind a parked car. A tall, scruffy-looking guy with no helmet and crazy, wind-mussed hair stepped off the bike, then turned to help his passenger remove his helmet. The kid had the same windblown look and, although he was slight, I could see the shape that hinted at the man he'd be soon enough. Confident stance, chin out, shoulders trying to hold up the best bits of an oversized jacket. The sudden noise of a car horn made them both turn their heads in our direction and my heart imploded in my chest as the boy-man dropped his helmet on to the road and ran straight into my arms.

With my chin resting on Norman's shoulder and squeezing his body as tight as I dared, it took me all of about five seconds to work out exactly who Mr Moped was. The how and why of him being there with Norman was infinitely less clear, but somehow it didn't seem important. I'd find out later, or I wouldn't. It didn't matter. Now that Norman and I had arrived here, all that mattered was right in front of me. This place. This moment. This boy.

The second Norman and I stepped back from each other he started talking at a hundred overexcited miles an hour. A collection of unfamiliar names fell from his lips and mingled with abandon into disjointed sentences about disguises and tumble dryers and houseboats and Dave Allen. I felt the words ducking and diving and swirling around me, but all I could do was stand there and stare at my son.

The serious, softly rounded face I loved so much was the same, but there was a set to it that was entirely different. Every part of him was animated and the smile that hadn't left his face since he'd seen me was so brilliant it made me feel giddy. Even though I couldn't put my finger on just what it was that had changed about Norman, I knew for certain he wasn't the same boy that had left Penzance.

It was a few seconds before I became aware that Norman's

chattering had trailed off and he was staring over my shoulder, open-mouthed, at the gathering crowd outside the side door leading down to the Duke Supper Club. To my absolute surprise, fully formed sentences began to slide eloquently out of me.

'Don't worry about it, Norman. It's OK. I . . . I know it looks like a lot of people, but once they're inside sitting down it won't look so bad, I promise. You'll be fine. You're going to be amazing.'

Good god. Here it was. Twelve years late but, finally, the good-mother gene had kicked in. I could feel some more good advice bubbling up, trying to get over my tongue, but before I had a chance to find out what it was Norman started waving his arms above his head and pointing across the road.

'No, Mum, look! That's . . . it's Kathy and Tony . . . they're here! And Adam! Oh my god . . . MUM! Look! There's Big Al! They CAME! They actually came!'

As Norman's words started to sink in, my eyes focused on the sea of faces milling around across the road. And sure enough, I couldn't have missed Adam, busy running into people in his mobility scooter, looking like he was even getting a few apologies. Then I saw Kathy and Tony standing slightly to the side of the crowd, deep in a conversation where nobody else existed. And over there, a brown-haired, bearded giant towering over the rest of the heads, staring off into the middle distance like he might be reciting poetry in his head. Big Al. Larger than life. Safe as a house. Lovelier than a sonnet.

I shook my head to change the unexpected direction in which my thoughts had drifted, but my new-found articulation appeared to have lost its way already.

'H— how did they . . . I mean, what . . . when did . . . ?'

'I think, I mean I guess I know . . . well, I called them, Mum.'

Norman's face was close to mine and I could almost see my reflection in his pink, shiny and almost totally scale-free forehead.

'When you and Leonard didn't come back by six at the latest I was so . . . well, I was pretty scared, Mum. So I thought I should make a contingency plan, which was to call a responsible adult and, well . . . they are, I think. But then none of them answered their phones and I had to leave messages and then . . . then I remembered the last name on the list, which was James . . . so I called him and then, well, that's a really, really long story, Mum. I can't wait to tell you, but . . .'

He tipped his head to the left so he could see around me to the crowd across the road.

'I reckon we should . . . come on, Mum, let's go and say hello before the show. Mum, come ON!'

He'd already grabbed my hand and was dragging me across the road, turning his head every couple of steps to check on me but heading full tilt for them. All I could do was follow. And so I did.

We pushed through the crowd, and there they were. Kathy, Tony, Adam and Big Al, now anchored by Leonard, who was busy making introductions and being charming. I hesitated, and I felt Norman's hand slip out of mine as he moved forward into the little circle. Then everyone was talking over the top of each other, trying to get Norman's attention, touching him lightly, a squeeze here, a gentle hair ruffle there.

I took a step backwards, almost losing my footing, and as I tried to right myself I lost sight of Norman. Then I felt the pressure of a gentle, steadying arm on my shoulder and a soft, deep voice in the back of my head. *I've got you, Sadie love.*

I ducked my head and peered through the shoulders and backs

of heads of the people who were no longer strangers to Norman and me, and I could see him again. He was laughing. His head angled back, looking up at Big Al like he was the best thing since Jax. His hand resting on the back of Adam's mobility scooter like it was the only place in the world that hand wanted to be. Leaning ever so slightly to the left into the nook of Leonard's creaky shoulder like he'd been there his entire life. And past Norman, past Kathy and Tony's smiling faces, on the outskirts of the crowd, I caught my second sight of James. Leaning against the wall of the pub, smoking. Watching Norman, too. Over a boy, our eyes met and James raised one eyebrow and smiled a long, slow and steady smile that didn't quit.

Right then and not an instant before was the moment I realized I'd always been wrong. It wasn't the final awful curtain call of a desperately unhappy man dangling from the kitchen rafters, it wasn't the insidious skin disease that waged its relentless war year after year, and it certainly wasn't forty-three series of *Come Dine with Me* that had chiselled out the shape of mine and Norman's world. It was a potty-mouthed, magnificently bad boy who'd had to cram an entire life into just twelve years. It was the hopeful heart of a lousy comedian but a very good man who made it all the way to the top, at least to his appreciative audience of the world's best daughter. And it was two kids' crazy, impossible and totally brilliant plan that took us all the way to the end by making us go right back to the beginning.

I looked back at Norman, who was now listening intently to something Tony was saying, and I knew with absolute clarity that he'd become all he was not just in spite of me but because of me, too. Whatever happened up there on that stage in the next half an hour didn't even matter, because he was going to make it. And we were going to make it.

I felt a twinge as the me-parts that never quite fitted eased into a strangely comfortable place and the warmth of a body moved into the space beside me. Leonard took my hand in his wrinkly old paw and stepped forward, pulling me gently into the circle of our friends. And I let him.

52

NORMAN

First rule of comedy: Always give it everything you've got.

I know it isn't possible to make time go backwards, but if I could, the one thing in the world I'd do is reverse the hands of that big old clock that runs the universe to the night before Jax died, and I'd jam something in good and hard. Then I'd go over to his house just after he went to bed and I'd get his backpack from down near the front door where his mum always yelled at him for dropping it. Then I'd look inside and get out the Boots bag with the brand-new inhaler in it and put it right next to him where he could see it. Maybe on his pillow. Maybe even in his hand. And then I'd tell him that he's the coolest kid that ever walked this and I'll bet any other planet.

But I know that I won't ever be able to make time go backwards, because that's just physics. So instead I just have to do the one thing that I can do.

'Now, folks, next up we've got a young fellow who's come all the way from sunny Cornwall to perform for us here at the Duke for

the Fringe. Ladies and gentlemen, would you be so kind as to put your beers down and your hands together so you can give it up for Little Big Man, in his brand-new show, Sausages and Gravitas. For one night only, Mr Norrrrrman Forrrreman!'

I straighten my back the way Leonard showed me to, by pretending someone has a big, long string on the top of my head and is pulling it up really tight. Then I close my eyes and start to take in my best breath, just like Big Al taught me. Slowly, in through my nose without stopping, until I can feel the new air in the back of my throat, down to my chest, into my tummy, through my legs and right to the very end of my toes. *Breath is life, Norman.*

In between the spots in the back of my eyelids I can see Jax standing right in front of me. He leans forward so his nose is nearly touching mine and I feel a little whoosh of air when he blinks. The biggest breath I've ever taken is swirling around inside me and just when I think there's no more room I take one more huge gulp of air, and I feel the last piece of scale on my chest split wide open. Jax winks at me and then he's gone. I open my eyes and look out to where a microphone, a spotlight and my mum are waiting for me.

I exhale in one giant whoosh and step out into the light. And now I'm breathing for two.

53

Notes for the Fringe 2021
Sausages and Gravitas: A Second Helping

So. Family. (Pause for effect, Jaxy style, and for everyone to think about what might be coming.) There's a part in my favourite book this year that says you can choose your friends but you sure can't choose your family. And yeah, I know a few of you would probably say your home life might look a whole lot different if you could. Am I right? (Pause for laughter and agreement, hopefully.)

But actually, I did. Well, some of them anyhow. For a very long time my family was only me and my mum. No granny or grandpa, no uncles or aunties, no cousins. Not even a dog. I guess the closest we came to adding a few was the Summer of the Sea Monkeys. (Pause for laughter, although don't bet on it. Note: find out how many people actually know about sea monkeys apart from me, Mum and Jax.)

And you know what? It was enough. It's not like me and Mum set out to look for people to join our family on purpose. Except for my dad, of course. Although knowing who he was a little sooner might have helped me make a better choice when I picked a footy team to follow. (Pause for laughter.) As it was, the only advice I had to go on was second-hand from my mum, passed on from my grandad. (Pause for audience to wonder who my team is.) West Bromwich. I know. What can I say? I wish he was still alive so I could get an explanation. (Make eye contact with audience member, pause for more laughter. Hopefully.)

So. Family. (Long pause, look at the audience. Not sure what for. Note: study Jack Dee YouTube clips for more tips on Jaxy's pause for effect rule.) The funny thing is, you might be surprised who you'd choose if they were put in front of you, and then your family might end up looking totally different to anything you've ever imagined. And I speak from experience. (Pause for a little bit of laughter.) Because the family I chose looks like the worst episode of Come Dine with Me *you've ever seen. (Pause for big laughter. Hopefully.) Worse than the celebrity special even. (Pause for even bigger laughter, with any luck.)*

But seriously. Families. (That's the rule of three covered. Pause for everyone to think about their own family. Although how would I know if they were? Correction: pause and hope for the best.) Some of you might have heard about my family because of that story in the papers about what happened up here this time last year. (Pause for some people to maybe clock who I am.) Oh, yeahhhhhhh. I'm THAT guy. But I swear, only about half of what they said was true. I mean, they were right about us cracking one of the biggest gambling scams in Edinburgh once we handed over that notebook to the police. (Jack Dee pause.) But there's no way James and I stopped for a mojito on the way through the club. It was a mocktail, come on – I'm a kid! (Pause for laughter. Surely!)

Actually, what happened that night is pretty much the only reason I'm here tonight, so it turned out to be the reason I've had the best year of my life. In fact, I reckon you'd say it's been a Helluva Year. And that's a whole other story.

End of notes.

As you can see, I haven't really got much down on paper yet for my next show, but Big Al reckons I've got enough material in my head to do a residency in Vegas. He says all I need to do is get it from my brain and out through my mouth without taking too many deviations, which gave me a few ideas. The Vegas part, not the deviations.

But I don't reckon that'll happen until I'm at least eighteen, and maybe by then I'll have made enough money to pay for Mum and Big Al to come with me. That's if Mum ever agrees to be Big Al's girlfriend, which Al says she bloody well will if he has anything to do with it. Mum always just says, we'll see, and I reckon we will see, because slowly, slowly, catchy monkey and all that.

I'm already invited back to the Duke for next year's Fringe, though, because the manager said it was the best night they'd ever had. And even though the jig was up the minute I got on stage that I wasn't actually eighteen in a licensed venue, he said he'd think about turning a blind eye again because he had a soft spot for me and he believes in something called nurturing the arts. Mum reckons it's his bar takings he's interested in nurturing, but that's OK by me.

What's even more OK by me is that Jax's mum and stepdad might come next year, and it was actually their idea. I haven't seen them much, because Mum reckons we have to tread lightly

350

around their feelings and seeing me without Jax makes them too sad. But she's gone around there a couple of times for coffee, and last time she took one of her really excellent almond and only-slightly-out-of-date lemon curd cakes. So I reckon by next year and a few more cakes they'll be able to come and watch my show and think of Jax without feeling like a big hairy yin is eating its way out of their tummies. I'm still always going to tread lightly around their feelings, though, because I know exactly how they feel.

But anyhow, before then I could get run over by a bus, or lose an eye in a freak accident with a piece of cutlery. Or God might come good on one of my deals and Jax could be back in Penzance, looking after his armless, legless, no-eyed, very happy best mate. Or I could even finally get abducted by aliens. I mean, probably not, because nothing like that ever happens down here, but if these last few months proved anything, it's that one never knows. And that James is probably my dad.

Actually, it was a DNA test that proved that. And the funniest thing is that it wasn't even me or Mum or James that wanted that test in the end. It was Adam. Can you believe it? He said that as someone with a vested interest he wanted to be absolutely sure where everyone stood. Mum said over her effing dead body was she going to risk him having any kind of vested interest in me, so me, James and Adam did the test. Adam even came down from Bournemouth on the train for the opening of the results, which we decided to do in the pub because it had easy access for his mobility scooter and because that's where James is staying until he finds a proper flat.

The DNA test said that it was a 99.8 per cent probability James was my dad, which is pretty probable but still not guaranteed. I thought Adam would have been happy he was off the hook except for that 0.2 per cent, but he didn't seem to be at all really. When Mum opened the envelope and read out the results he stopped talking for about five minutes, which is a LOT for him. Except he did say bollocks quite a few times and that he must have something in his eye.

But even though I really, really like James, and it's pretty cool that he's moved all the way from Scotland so I get to see him nearly every day, and it's kind of nice to have another guy to shoot the breeze with, and even though we know that there's a 99.8 per cent chance that he actually is my dad, I'd never say it, but I know that really and truly I just belong to mum. And that even if she finally says yes to a date with Big Al before he turns seventy-five, like he's hoping, she'll really and truly always just belong to me.

Oh, and by the way, I've added another first rule of comedy to Jaxy's book. I don't think he'd mind. I mean, I'm not saying I made it up or anything, but I figured after last summer if I hadn't learned something from what I'd observed, then what kind of observational comedian would I be?

See, when I started thinking about everyone I know, like Tony and Kathy and their baby that hasn't shown up yet, and Adam and his football career that never got to happen, and Leonard with his wife who doesn't remember him any more, and Jax's mum and stepdad, who lost their boy, and Mum who finally told me what really happened to Grandad, I realized they've all got one thing in common. Which is that even though bad things happened to them they all still kept on going.

So I reckon that's the last First Rule of Comedy. Never give up. Because no matter if everything goes to hell in a hand basket and you lose your father, your footy career, your baby, your memory, your son, your breath or your best friend, you've just got to keep on going.

And even though I really do know he's gone forever, I'll never forget how lucky I was to know a guy as cool and as crazy and as wonderful as Jax. A guy who taught me that one really and truly best friend is a hundred times better than a whole bunch who just aren't quite sure. And that one honestly never knows what's coming next.

THE END

Signed, Norman Foreman.
Teenage Super Flucking Comedy Genius

Acknowledgements

I feel like the luckiest person in the world because it's my great good fortune to find myself surrounded by the kindest, most supportive book-loving people I could ever hope to meet.

My deepest thanks go to my beautiful agent Sue Armstrong at C&W Agency for your friendship, sage advice, and for taking Norman into your heart and finding him a perfect place in the world.

Everlasting thanks to my amazing editor Molly Crawford, for your support, wise words and encouragement, and the entire team at Transworld, for welcoming me so warmly and making me feel like part of a very special family. Big sunny Aussie thanks to Bev Cousins, Lou Ryan and the Penguin Random House team in Sydney and Melbourne, for believing so fiercely in my book and making sure Norman made it even further than Edinburgh!

Thank you to my early readers, Iris, Jane, Sue, Josie, Dee and Jo, and extra-special thanks to Leanne, for not only reading various versions but nagging me all the way to the finish line and being there to cheer me when I made it!

ACKNOWLEDGEMENTS

To my fabulous Curtis Brown Creative writing friends, Alex Clare, Elin Daniels, Grace Coleman, Catherine Bennetto, Moyette Gibbons, Alice Clark-Platts, Heidi Perks and Dawn Goodwin – you ladies continue to inspire me with your talent and tenacity. To Anna Davis and everyone at Curtis Brown Creative, thank you for the push I needed, the support I wanted and the courage I discovered.

Finally, to my family, Beverly, Tristan, Sidra, Oliver, Bec and Hamish, and my lovely and much-appreciated friends who've encouraged me along the way. Thank you all – I hope the wait has been worth it.

Julietta Henderson grew up in North Queensland, Australia, and developed her passion for the written word producing 'magazines' for school friends and neighbours with her sister. She has worked her way through jobs as diverse as bicycle tour guide in Tuscany, nanny in the Italian Alps and breakfast waitress in the wilds of Scotland. Like many Australians, her love affair with Europe began when she came to London on a working holiday and stayed for more than a decade. Now a full-time writer, Julietta divides her life between Melbourne, the UK and wherever she can find winter.